THE
STARDUST
THIEF

5/23 ①
7/23 dc

THE
STARDUST
THIEF

THE SANDSEA TRILOGY:
BOOK ONE

CHELSEA
ABDULLAH

orbitbooks.net

Cover design by Lisa Marie Pompilio
Cover illustration by Mike Heath | Magnus Creative
Cover copyright © 2022 by Hachette Book Group, Inc.
Map by Tim Paul

Orbit
Hachette Book Group
1290 Avenue of the Americas
New York, NY 10104
orbitbooks.net

First Edition: May 2022
Simultaneously published in Great Britain by Orbit

Orbit is an imprint of Hachette Book Group.
The Orbit name and logo are trademarks of Little, Brown Book Group Limited.

The publisher is not responsible for websites (or their content) that are not owned by the publisher.

The Hachette Speakers Bureau provides a wide range of authors for speaking events. To find out more, go to www.hachettespeakersbureau.com or call (866) 376-6591.

Library of Congress Cataloging-in-Publication Data
Names: Abdullah, Chelsea, author.
Title: The stardust thief / Chelsea Abdullah.
Description: First edition. | New York, NY : Orbit, 2022. | Series: The Sandsea Trilogy ; Book 1
Identifiers: LCCN 2021045600 | ISBN 9780316368766 (hardcover) | ISBN 9780316368964 (ebook) | ISBN 9780316375481 (ebook other)
Subjects: LCGFT: Fantasy fiction.
Classification: LCC PS3601.B429 S73 2022 | DDC 813/.6—dc23/eng/20211220
LC record available at https://lccn.loc.gov/2021045600

ISBNs: 9780316368766 (hardcover), 9780316368964 (ebook)

Printed in Canada

MRQ

10 9 8 7 6 5 4 3 2 1

For my mother, who fostered my love of words and writing.
My father, who taught me the power of remembered tales.
And my sister, who always asked for one more story.
This one's for you.

Map by Tim Paul

THE
STARDUST
THIEF

The Tale of the Jinn

Neither here nor there, but long ago…

Our world belonged to the jinn, those doomed creatures who roam our desert like lost spirits. Unlike us humans, who were created from the earth, the gods crafted the jinn from an ancient flame that allowed them to live for hundreds of years and gave them the power to use magic. This is why some jinn can change shape and others can breathe fire or travel the world in the blink of an eye.

For a time, the jinn did as the gods commanded: they loved and nurtured the world they were given, and there was peace. But while most jinn were grateful to the gods, there were seven jinn kings who were dissatisfied with their meager magic, and they expressed their discontent by destroying the land. They created winds so wild they blew the water from lakes and oceans, and flames so hot they burned away fields of grass, leaving behind nothing but sand.

When the gods saw the havoc the kings had wreaked, they decided to punish them. They gave them what they desired most—they made their magic more powerful, but at the cost of it being uncontrollable. The magic was so strong it burned holes in the sand, sinking the jinn cities and causing the jinn to vanish from this world.

In the wake of their disappearance, the gods created us

humans. Magicless and mortal we may be, but we are the gods' faithful servants.

There are some who believe we must use our faith to restore life to this barren world. They say the only reason we have any nature left is because there are hunters who capture escaped jinn and sacrifice them to the gods. They claim that a jinn's silver blood is filled with life—that it can turn sand to water and make trees and flowers bloom.

But our faith need not be so twisted.

Remember, Layla, not all jinn are evil.

—◈—

Loulie had buried many things since her mother last told her that story.

Her name. Her past. Her parents.

But the story, she had never forgotten.

1

LOULIE

When Loulie al-Nazari was told by the One-Eyed Merchant to meet on a small and humble dhow, she expected, quite reasonably, a small and humble dhow. But the dhow was not small, and it was not humble. It was, in fact, quite the opposite.

The *Aysham* was a behemoth of a ship, with full sails, a spacious deck, an impressive assortment of rooms, and a lofty crow's nest. It was, by any measure, a very nice ship. Had she been here as a passenger, she would have enjoyed exploring it.

But Loulie was not here as a passenger. She was here as the Midnight Merchant, an esteemed magic seller, and she had come to meet with a client who was keeping her waiting long past their scheduled meeting time. *I will call for you the first hour of moonrise*, his message had said. Only, the hour had come and gone, and Loulie was still waiting for him on deck, dressed in the star-patterned merchant's robe that made her stick out like a sore thumb.

She turned her back on the gawking, well-dressed passengers and focused on the horizon. There were no familiar constellations in the sky, and the night was dark and gloomy, which hardly helped her mood. For what was probably the dozenth time that hour, she sighed.

"I wish you were in your lizard shape," she said to the man standing beside her.

He angled his head to look at her. Though his stony expression barely shifted, Loulie perceived a very slight height difference between his brows. He was most certainly raising one at her. "And what good would that do us in this situation?"

"You could sneak belowdecks and find our client's room. You're useless in your man shape."

The umber-skinned man said nothing, but his silence was easy to decipher. Loulie had known him for nine years—long enough to understand all his mannerisms and magics. She was no longer surprised by his shapeshifting or by the fire that danced in his eyes when he grew emotional. Right now, he was quiet because he knew she would not like what he had to say.

"We're offering the man magic," Loulie said. "The least he can do is be on time for a meeting *he* proposed."

"Don't think too hard on it. What will be will be."

"Sage advice, oh mighty jinn," she mumbled beneath her breath.

Qadir's lips twitched into a brief smile. He enjoyed toying with her—he was the only one who got away with it.

Loulie was considering breaking into the ship's interior when she heard approaching footsteps and turned to see a man in a white thobe.

"Midnight Merchant." He bowed. "I have been sent by Rasul al-Jasheen to bring you to the designated meeting place."

She and Qadir exchanged a look. His deadpan expression said, *I told you not to worry.*

"It's about time." She gestured to Qadir. "This man is my bodyguard. He shall accompany me."

The messenger nodded before leading them through crowds of colorfully dressed nobles to an obscure back door on the other side of the ship. He rapped on the door in a specific fashion until it was opened by a burly man, who guided them down a dimly lit corridor. At the end of the hallway, the man rapped on a different door in a different pattern. There was the sound of a lock and a key, then the messenger opened the door and beckoned them inside.

Loulie looked at Qadir. *After you,* his silence said. She smiled before ducking inside.

The first thing she noticed upon her entry was that there were mercenaries—three of them, each positioned in a different corner of the small room. Unlike the nobles on deck wearing brilliant robes, these men were dressed mostly in weapons.

Her mind filled with images of bloodshed and murder. Of her mother, waving frantically at an empty jar, telling her to hide. Of her father, lying in a pool of his own blood.

She took a deep, steadying breath and looked to the center of the room, where a merchant dressed in hues of green sat on a cushion behind a low-rising table. True to his title, Rasul al-Jasheen had only one muddy-brown eye. The other was a glossy white orb half-hidden beneath layers of scarred skin. He had a nose that looked as if it had been broken and reset many times, and a forehead that was at once impressive and unfortunate in size. He was vaguely familiar, and Loulie wondered if maybe she'd passed his stall in some souk before.

The merchant's lips parted to reveal a shining smile composed of gold, bronze, and white teeth. "Midnight Merchant. What a pleasure to see you in the flesh. I apologize for the late summons. I was entertaining important guests." His eyes roved over her.

She imagined what he was seeing: a short, seemingly fragile woman dressed in layers of blue velvet shawls dusted with soft white. Stardust, she called the pattern. Appropriate, for it had belonged to her tribe. The Najima tribe. The Night Dwellers.

As was usual, the merchant stared at her half-covered face longer than at her robes. Most of the men in this business tried to intimidate her by looking right into her eyes.

It never worked.

"Please." He gestured to the cushion on the other side of the table. "Have a seat."

She glanced over her shoulder at Qadir, who had not budged from his spot by the door. Though the merchant had not acknowledged him, the mercenaries eyed him warily. Qadir showed no sign of being perturbed. But then, he rarely did.

Loulie sat.

The merchant offered his hand. "Rasul al-Jasheen. It is an honor."

She clasped it. "Loulie al-Nazari." She pulled her hand away quickly, wary of the way his eyes lingered on her iron rings.

"I must confess, I was not expecting you to be so . . . young."

Ah yes. Because twenty is so young.

She smiled at him pleasantly. "You are exactly as I expected. One eye and all."

Silence. Then, remarkably, the merchant started laughing. "That is where I get my title, yes. As you can imagine, it is also the reason I called you here tonight. I assume you have the magic I requested?" Loulie nodded. Rasul cleared his throat. "Well, let's see it, then."

She reached into her pocket and withdrew a coin. The merchant watched skeptically as she vanished it between her fingers. From his side of the table, he could not see the face on either side: a jinn warrior on one and a human sultan on the other. Every time the coin reappeared, it sported a different face.

Human, jinn, human, jinn.

"Must I remind you of our deal?" She held up the coin between pinched fingers.

Rasul frowned. "I already paid you in advance."

"You paid in advance *once*. Now you must pay the other half."

"I will not pay for a magic I have yet to see with my own eyes."

Loulie did her best to ignore the stares of the armed men around her. *Nothing can happen to me. Not while Qadir is here.*

She shrugged, feigning nonchalance as she reached into her merchant's bag. The bag of infinite space, Qadir called it, for it had a seemingly endless bottom. "If seeing is believing . . ." She withdrew a vial. It was a small thing, no bigger than one of her fingers. The minute the One-Eyed Merchant beheld the sparkling liquid inside, he tried to snatch it from her hand.

She tucked it away, into her sleeve. "I'll take the other half of my payment now."

"That could be water, for all I know!"

"And? If it is water, steal your gold back." She gestured to the human weapons lining the room. "That is why they're here, isn't it? To make sure this exchange goes as planned?"

The merchant pressed his lips together and snapped his fingers. One of the men set a pouch in Rasul's hands, which he offered to Loulie. She scanned the coins inside and, just to make sure she wasn't being scammed, flipped the two-faced coin. It came down on the human side. *Truth.*

She offered him the vial. "Your requested magic: the Elixir of Revival."

The merchant snatched it from her, and Loulie smiled beneath her scarf as he fumbled with the stopper. He was so excited, his hands were shaking.

If only he realized how easy this magic was to find.

Her eyes slid to Qadir. Though his expression was stony as always, she imagined a smug smile on his lips. She recalled the words he'd spoken the day she shared Rasul's request with him: *One jinn's blood is a human man's medicine.*

There was a reason humans called it the Elixir of Revival.

That reason became apparent as the One-Eyed Merchant blinked the silvery contents of the vial into his eye. Loulie watched as sparkling tears streamed down his cheek, making his skin glow. But while this effect was temporary, something more permanent was happening to the merchant's blind eye.

Darkness bloomed in the center of his iris like an inkblot spreading on a scroll. With every blink it spread, growing wider and wider until the blackness lightened to a dark brown.

Medicine indeed.

Soon it was not just the so-called elixir that fell from his eyes, but real tears. Even the mercenaries were unable to mask their shock as Rasul fixed both of his eyes on them.

"Praise be to the gods," he whispered.

Loulie grinned. "Worth the price?"

"Such a miracle is priceless." Rasul rubbed at his tearstained face, carefully avoiding the newly revived eye. "A thousand blessings upon you, Loulie al-Nazari."

Loulie dipped her head. "And a thousand upon you. May I offer a piece of advice?" Rasul paused to look at her. "I suggest you come up with a new title. One-Eyed is a little melodramatic."

The merchant burst out laughing. Loulie found, much to her surprise, that she was laughing with him. Once Rasul had finished heaping praises upon her and insisted on treating her to a stupendous feast later that evening, she left.

She and Qadir shared a look as they walked back down the corridor. The jinn lifted his hand to showcase the healing scab from a self-inflicted wound he'd made mere days ago.

She mouthed the words *Shukran, oh holy, priceless miracle.*

Qadir shrugged. He looked like he was trying not to smile.

~‹‹‹~

Mama and Baba are dead. *The words kept cycling through her mind. Every time Layla buried them, they resurfaced, a reality she could not escape.*

Had the jinn not been dragging her through the desert, she would have succumbed to the weight of her sorrow days ago. But even when her body grew heavy with fatigue, he pressed forward. At first, she despised him for this—even feared him.

But the fear eventually faded. First into reluctance, then defeat. Why did it matter where the jinn was taking her? He'd told her that the compass her father had given her would lead them to a city, but she did not care about the city.

She did not care about anything.

Many sunrises later, she collapsed. She wanted to cry, but her chest was too heavy and her eyes too dry. The jinn waited patiently. When she did not rise, he picked her up and set her atop his shoulders. She was forced to hold on to him as he scaled a cliff.

That night, after the jinn had started a fire with nothing but a snap of his fingers, he took a coin from his pocket and set it on his palm.

"Watch." He curled his fingers over the coin. When he next uncurled them, his palm was empty. Layla was intrigued despite herself. When she asked if it was magic, the jinn clenched and unclenched his fingers, and the coin was again on his palm.

"A trick," he said.

Layla looked closely at the coin. It appeared to be a foreign currency, with the face of a human sultan on one side and a jinn wreathed in fire on the other. "There are two lands in this world," Qadir said. "Human and jinn. And so there are two sides to this coin."

He made the coin vanish and reappear between his fingers, moving so quickly she could not track the movement. "This may be a trick, but the coin itself is magic. It will tell you the real or moral truth of any situation."

He set the coin down on Layla's palm. "See for yourself. Flip it, and if it comes up on the human side, the answer is yes. If it comes up on the other, the answer is no."

Layla would not have believed it was truly magic had the coin been given to her a few days ago. But things had changed. She was no longer so naive.

"My family is dead," she whispered as she flipped the coin.

It came up on the human side.

She breathed out and tried again. "A jinn saved my life."

Human.

Tears sprang to her eyes as the coin continued to come up on the human side, confirming her new reality. Truth. Truth. Truth.

"I am alone." Her shoulders shook with sobs as she threw the coin into the air. It bounced off her knee and rolled away, back to the jinn. For a few moments, Qadir said nothing. Then he silently reached for her hand and set the coin on her palm.

Jinn.

He curled her fingers around it. "Not alone," he said. "Not anymore."

—⟨∞⟩—

Loulie was lost in her memories and absently making the two-faced coin vanish between her fingers when she returned to the *Aysham*'s deck the next morning. The crowds from the previous night had dispersed, and the sailors paid her no mind as she wandered past them in her plain brown robes. She had traded the scarves obscuring her

face for a light shawl, which she wrapped loosely around her head
and shoulders to better feel the sun on her cheeks. It was a relief, as
always, to doff her merchant apparel and bask in anonymity the day
after a sale.

Also a relief: the familiar, hazy shape of Madinne in the distance.
Loulie smiled at the sight of the city. "Qadir, do you see that?"

The jinn, now in his lizard form and humming softly in her ear,
shifted on her shoulder. He made a sound of confirmation.

She drew closer to the ship's railings. Even through an orange veil
of sand, the sun was bright enough she could make out the tiers of
the great desert city of Madinne. At the top was the sultan's palace,
made up of beautiful white domed towers and minarets that reached
for the sun. It was surrounded on all sides by colorful buildings—
stone and wooden constructions both domed and flat, tall and squat.
And somewhere in the midst of those buildings, nestled in a nexus
of crooked, winding alleyways, was home. Their home.

"I wonder how Dahlia is doing." Qadir's voice, made much softer
by his smaller form, was directly in her ear.

"However she's doing, she'll be much better when we drop by
with our rent."

Qadir made a clicking sound—she still wasn't sure whether he
did it with his teeth or tongue—and said, "Yes, because our rent is
equivalent to all the coin in our bag."

"I won't give her *all* of our earnings."

"That last exchange was for my blood, you know."

Loulie suppressed a smile as she looked over her shoulder at the
sailors. Though the men were far from graceful, she could not help
but think they resembled dancers in the easy way they went about
their docking preparations.

"Would you like me to keep your blood money, then?"

Qadir hissed. "I do not need your human gold."

"Ah, what a shame. And here I thought you'd enjoy spending
it on wine or women. You know the dealers won't take your commemorative coins." She glanced at the two-faced coin between her
fingers.

"Loulie?"

"Mm?" She slid the coin into her pocket.

"I overhear talk of the sultan."

Suppressing a groan, Loulie turned and surveyed the deck. Other than the sailors, she spotted a few scattered groups of people. She walked between them, keeping her expression blank as she eavesdropped. As little interest as she had in the sultan, she could not afford to ignore the gossip. Not when she, a criminal, always tried to avoid his men.

But while she caught two sailors trading profanity-laden opinions, heard a couple confessing forbidden love to one another, and was audience to a strange riddle game, she overheard nothing about the sultan.

She had just given up hope when she spotted Rasul al-Jasheen speaking with a man wearing the uniform of the sultan's guard. Loulie quickly glanced away and slowed her pace as she approached them.

"The sultan's councillors are beside themselves," the guard was saying.

Rasul snorted. "Why does he not send the high prince to search for the relic?"

The guard glanced in her direction. Loulie grabbed hold of a passing sailor and asked him in her most pleasant voice if he knew where they were docking. The sailor responded, but she was not listening. Not to him, anyway.

"Could such a treasure really exist?" Rasul said.

"The rumors are that the sultan's late wife brought up the artifact in one of her stories."

She thanked the sailor and angled her head to catch Rasul's response.

"Poor man. Does he truly believe Lady Shafia's stories were true?"

The guard shrugged. "They had power enough to stop the killings, so perhaps." There was a mournful pause. All desert dwellers knew of the sultan's wife killings, just as all knew of Shafia, who had stopped them with her stories. She was as much a legend as the tales she'd told.

"His Majesty believes there is something in one of her stories that will help him claim a victory over the jinn."

"Against the jinn? They are like flies; surely you cannot kill them all." Rasul's voice died down to a murmur. By the time the wind brought the conversation back to her ears, they were speaking about something else.

"But tell me about this miracle!" the guard said. "I hear the Midnight Merchant herself delivered the elixir to you? Do you have any idea how she obtained it?"

"None. But I suppose it wouldn't be much of a miracle if we knew the how of it." Rasul laughed. "Regardless, I bless the gods for my good luck. I did not think she would so readily accept my request."

Qadir sighed in her ear. "Why do humans thank the gods for things they do not do?"

"Because they are fools that believe in fate," Loulie said bitterly. If these gods existed, they had not batted their lashes when her family was murdered.

She glanced over her shoulder at the looming city. They were close enough now that she could make out people on the docks waving at the ship. She turned and made her way toward the bow for a better view. Behind her, the guard was still talking.

"What a shame she disappeared! I would have liked to see this legendary merchant."

Rasul sighed. "She had a sharp tongue, to be sure, but what a rare gem she was. Had she not disappeared last night, I would have convinced her to have dinner with me in Madinne. Can you imagine it? Having the Midnight Merchant on your arm?"

Loulie thought again of how relieved she was to have slipped out of her merchant's clothing and rubbed the kohl from her eyes this morning. For if the formerly one-eyed merchant had invited her to dinner with the intention of flaunting her, she would have punched him.

"So." Qadir spoke in her ear. "The sultan is looking for a relic. Do you think we can find the magic before he sends his hounds to track it?"

Loulie paused at the ship's bow and stared wordlessly up at the city. She stretched out her arms, allowing the wind to push and pull at her sleeves. Qadir had the sense to stop talking. Later, they would speak of relics and gold and magic. But for now, all of it disappeared from her mind. The world folded into a single, simple truth.

She was home.

2

MAZEN

When Mazen bin Malik was told by his most trusted servant that his older brother would return home the first hour of sunset, he expected, quite reasonably, for his older brother to return the first hour of sunset.

Omar never returned from his hunts in the morning, and it was common for him to spend his afternoons with his thieves. This was why, when Omar threw open the doors to Mazen's bedroom, Mazen was already halfway out the window. As Omar stepped inside, it occurred to Mazen that not accounting for his brother's early return had been a severe oversight.

He tried to picture this scene through Omar's eyes: he, the sultan's youngest son, dressed as a commoner and sneaking out the window of his bedroom in broad daylight. The last time he'd been caught like this, he'd been a child pretending to be an adventurer. He didn't suppose that excuse would be as endearing now, coming from a man of twenty-two years.

Mazen cleared his throat. "Salaam, Omar."

One of Omar's brows inched up far enough to wrinkle his forehead. "Salaam, Mazen."

"How was your hunt?"

"I found both marks." Omar gestured to his clothing: an

embroidered tunic tucked into sirwal trousers held up by a knife-notched belt. The silver jinn blood staining his clothes looked more like twinkling stardust than gore.

"You sparkle like the moon, brother of mine." Mazen tried a smile.

"While I appreciate your flattery, I am more interested in the truth." Omar closed the doors behind him. "Perhaps it would be easier to talk inside?"

"But it's so stuffy inside—"

"Does Father know you're sneaking out?"

Mazen froze. No, his father most certainly did *not* know. If he caught wind of this—of any of Mazen's clandestine excursions—he would lock Mazen in his room forever. Being trapped in the palace was bad, but being trapped in his room? Mazen would die.

He forced himself to laugh. "I wasn't sneaking out! I was just getting some fresh air."

"By hanging precariously out a window."

"Not at all. This curtain is surprisingly sturdy."

"You must sneak out often, mm?" Omar approached, hands clasped behind his back.

Mazen glimpsed the knives at his belt and swallowed. The small child in him who still feared his brother worried that Omar might grab one of those knives and slit the curtain.

"So what is it? Are you going out to see a woman?" Omar paused at the windowsill and leaned forward, his smile inches from Mazen's face. "Are you going sightseeing? Plotting something nefarious?"

"Nothing of the sort!" Mazen gripped his makeshift rope-curtain tighter. "It's just—I heard rumors that Old Rhuba was returning to Madinne today."

Omar looked at him blankly. "You're sneaking out to listen to an old man tell stories?"

"He's from the White Dunes, Omar. *The White Dunes.* You know what they say about the sand there. That it's made from the ashes of ghouls who—"

"Fine." Omar drew away with a sigh. "Leave. Go listen to old men wag their tongues."

Mazen blinked. "You won't tell Father?"

"It will be our secret." Omar smiled. "For a price, of course." Before Mazen could protest, Omar held up a hand and said, "You have no choice in the matter. Either you pay me for my silence or I walk out the door and tell the sultan."

Mazen almost forgot how to breathe. A price, a price from Omar. He could not imagine what his brother might blackmail him into, but he would make a dozen deals with Omar before telling the sultan the truth: that he, despite his father's orders, was leaving the palace without guards. That he, a prince, was walking straight into supposedly jinn-infested streets unprotected.

"Remember, Mazen. A favor for a favor. You owe me, akhi." Omar flashed one last smile before stepping out of the room and closing the doors behind him.

The ominous smile remained etched in Mazen's mind as he snuck through the palace courtyard. He tried to distract himself by focusing on the wonders of the garden, but their majesty was dulled by his worry. The stone pathways lined with white roses suddenly seemed colorless and mundane, and the exquisite fountain made up of dancing glass figures didn't so much as glint in the sunlight. Even the garden topiaries, shaped like the fantastical creatures from his mother's stories, seemed to lack their usual splendor.

Mazen passed all these sights like a ghost in his plain tunic and trousers, following the winding garden paths past streams filled with colorful fish and through empty pavilions that sported intricately patterned ceilings. Cushioned benches lay undisturbed beneath the arched roofs and would remain so until later in the day, when the sultan's councillors took a reprieve from discussing politics to trade gossip. The thought made Mazen tense. He had purposefully planned this outing so he would not be missed by anyone at court. He was confident in his preparations—he only hoped Omar kept his word and did not tell their father.

Dread weighed his footsteps until he arrived at the servants' entrance, at which point he perked up. The man guarding the silver gate was the one he'd been expecting, and he was able to pay his way past. He tried not to think about how anxious the guard looked when he let him through or how quickly he pocketed the coins Mazen gave him.

We all have our needs. I need to escape, and he needs gold for his soon-to-be-born child. It was, he thought, an honorable exchange.

The elevated portion of Madinne that housed the palace and noble quarter was but a small oasis on the plain that formed the city, so it was a simple thing to reach the commoners' souk in the lower quarter. The fields of green fell away to barren dust, the wide cobblestone streets narrowed into paved dirt pathways, and shops were replaced with rickety but charming stalls sporting crudely painted signs. The peace and quiet gave way to the melodic sounds of lutes and drums, and the air filled with smells: musk and sweat, oil and bakhoor, and a tantalizing mixture of spices that made his mouth water.

Merchants marked their shops with bright colors to stand out in the market. Mazen's search for Old Rhuba's golden tarp took him down paths littered with all manner of stalls. But it was the artists' goods that caught his attention. He eyed ceramic bowls, shatranj boards, glazed zodiac plates—and then he stopped, eyes snagging on a small but intricate rug that had a series of geometric patterns repeating across its surface. He recognized this design. He had a carpet with nearly the exact same shapes on the floor of his bedroom.

He looked up and caught the eyes of the merchant behind the stall, a middle-aged woman garbed in red-orange layers. A scrawny young man sat on a stool behind her, watching the souk with glazed, bored eyes. Her son, Mazen assumed, there for security purposes.

"Salaam, ya sayyid." The merchant spoke in a soft voice, barely audible above the noise.

"Salaam," Mazen said automatically. He sidestepped a pair of stumbling, singing musicians and planted himself on the other side of the stall. He gestured to the pattern that had caught his eye. "Your rugs are beautiful."

The weaver's eyes crinkled in a smile. "Shukran. Though I cannot take credit for the one you're eyeing right now. That is my daughter's handiwork. I only supervised her." She reached out to brush her fingers against the tassels. "It was woven from the finest camel hair over many weeks, as we were traveling with our sister tribe through the cliffs overlooking Ghiban."

Tribe. The word sparked a misplaced longing in Mazen. Though his family was descended from wanderers, they had not been nomads for a long time—not on his father's side, at least. He wondered what it was like, to be able to call the entire desert your home.

He smiled. "The gods have blessed your daughter with natural talent. This rug reminds me of a carpet I was gifted years ago. It has a similar texture and design. Blue diamonds on white, with a crescent moon at the center. I was told it was woven by a master."

"Ah, that is my pattern." The weaver chuckled. "How flattering, to be called a master."

Mazen reflected her smile back at her. "It is an honor to meet you in person."

"You're quite the charmer, aren't you?"

"I speak the truth, nothing less." He glanced at the rug again, one of many stunning designs draped across wooden display blocks. Had he been able to sneak a carpet back without anyone noticing, he might have done it. But these excursions were not shopping trips.

"You wouldn't happen to know a storyteller named Old Rhuba, would you?"

The weaver's eyes twinkled. "The better question is who here does *not* know him. I have not seen him today, but you cannot miss his golden tarp." She raised a brow. "If it is stories you seek, these carpets tell tales of their own."

"Ah, tales I do not have the coin for." The lie was so outrageous it made him cringe.

"What, you're not even going to *try* to haggle?"

"To pay anything less than the full price would be an insult, surely."

"You're lucky you have a gilded tongue." The weaver dismissed him with a laugh and a wave of her hand. "Come back when you can praise me with gold rather than words."

Mazen gave his promise with a nod and a smile before resuming his search for Old Rhuba. When he inquired further, he found out the ship Old Rhuba was on, the *Aysham*, had not yet docked. There was nothing he could do but wait, so he made business for himself at a nearby chai shop. He chose a seat at the edge of the establishment, one with a good view of the incoming ships, and ordered himself a coffee with cardamom.

While he waited, he entertained himself by making up stories about passersby. The man dressed in multicolored layers was running from his performance troupe, and the men speaking in conspiratorial whispers were illegal intoxicant dealers. The child holding tight to her father's hand and smiling brightly was a foreigner seeing Madinne's souk for the first time.

His coffee had just been delivered when he caught wind of a conversation from the table beside his, where five men sat hunched over their drinks, gossiping like old women.

"They say the high prince brought a jinn back with him."

"What, for some ceremonial killing?"

Mazen stole a glance at the man speaking and immediately turned away. He recognized him; he was an off-duty palace guard. *Relax!* he thought. *He won't recognize you.*

This was a hopeful if not entirely rational thought. The only reason the populace didn't recognize him on these outings was because he never wore his royal ornaments. He took off the three earrings that marked him as the sultan's third-born son and removed his mother's scarf. He also took off all his gold and silver.

But though everything that marked him a prince was gone, he couldn't hide his features. Not his wavy black hair nor his golden eyes. Thus, he was still very much Mazen, baggy beige clothes and all. He didn't suppose the ghutra on his head would help much if they saw his eyes.

Relax. There's no need to draw attention to yourself.

He sipped his coffee.

And promptly choked on it. The guards stopped mumbling to stare at his back.

Today is a cursed day.

One guard approached Mazen to ask if he was okay. Mazen tried to laugh and failed. "Fine," he managed. "I'm fine. Thank you for your concern."

His heart trembled with panic. *Turn around, turn around.*

Thankfully, the man returned to his conversation. "There've been more jinn in the city recently."

"More? I thought the high prince's security measures were meant to keep them out."

Mazen gripped his cup. Walking into Madinne was a death sentence for jinn—what reason did they have for invading?

"Who needs complicated security measures?" One man waved a dismissive hand. "They ought to have public killings. Bleed the creatures out, then pick the flowers from their blood and give them to the audience. That will scare them away."

Mazen thought of the terrible silver blood on his brother's clothing. He wondered where Omar had killed his marks and what sort of life had sprung from their blood. Had they begged his heartless brother to spare their lives? Or had they fought futilely until the end? Mazen did not like to imagine them pleading. Did not like to think of their lives being cut short with bloodshed.

It was amazing—horrifyingly amazing—that the silver blood spilled in that violent struggle could provoke nature into existence.

Unlike human blood, which only ever signified loss. Pain. Absence.

Unbidden, Mazen recalled the last time he'd seen his mother. It had been ten years ago; he'd been only twelve years old. He remembered she had been sleeping. Or so he'd believed. He'd gone to deliver a message from his father—and found her lying limp on her bed, staring blankly at the ceiling with a crimson stain on her chest.

Mazen breathed out slowly as he forced the memory away. Every once in a while, it resurfaced with a vengeance. A jinn had killed his mother—it was the reason his father forbade him from leaving the palace without guards.

He lifted his head, desperately seeking a distraction. He did not have to look far; only feet away a woman stood frozen in the crowd, smiling at him. She was tall and fine-boned, with generous curves and long legs accentuated by the thin layers of silk and gossamer she wore.

Desire flared in the pit of Mazen's stomach as he took in her radiant appearance. As he looked into her hypnotizing eyes, which shifted color in the light, fading from coffee black to amber.

Vaguely, he recognized that the lascivious shudder running through him was unnatural, but the more present part of him did not intend to think about it.

The woman fluttered her lashes, turned, and walked away.

Some strange tension hung in the air like a taut string.

And snapped.

Mazen stood, a slow smile stretching his lips as he followed the goddess into the chaos of the souk. Because what else could she be?

He had never felt such a deep concupiscence take hold of him. Of course he had to follow her. He had to ... had to ...

Make her mine.

3

LOULIE

"What say you, talking lizard—would you prefer sugared almonds or roasted pistachios?"

No one could hear Loulie whispering to the jinn lizard beneath her head scarf, and no one heard his response: an exasperated sigh.

Qadir had been in a sullen mood since they docked in Madinne an hour ago, suggesting at every opportunity they return to Dahlia's. Loulie had ignored him. Why rush back to the tavern when they had coin to spend?

"Roasted pistachios it is." She approached the stall with two bronze coins. The owner, a kindly old man who smelled of sesame, was happy to trade her for a bag of nuts.

"What a wonderful thing it is to see you again, Layla. Arrived on the *Aysham*, did you?"

Layla. Over the years, her birth name had become an alias, one she offered to people she didn't trust to keep her identity as the Midnight Merchant a secret. She preferred it that way—a buried identity, a buried past.

"That I did." She popped a pistachio into her mouth and sighed. As always, they were perfection. The only thing that would have made them better was the shells, and that was just because she enjoyed cracking them open to annoy Qadir.

"Any news from around the souk?"

The old man beckoned her forward. "Don't tell anyone I told you this, but..."

She let him speak, nodding occasionally to show she was listening. The stall owner liked to gossip, and she was happy to indulge him. Sometimes he unknowingly gave her leads on potential customers or filled her in on governmental rumors. Qadir especially was interested in the latter; he cared more for politics than she did.

Eventually, though, even Qadir grew bored. "Can we go home? We should—" His words collapsed into a sharp inhale. "Loulie, to your right."

At first, she saw nothing out of the ordinary. Stall owners waved their hands and beckoned to crowds. City folk strolled through the cramped thoroughfare garbed in everything from black veils to colorful silk robes.

But then she caught sight of the woman fading in and out of the hordes like a mirage. Tall and radiant, with impossibly sculpted features that betrayed no imperfection. Loulie was awestruck by her beauty.

Qadir hissed in her ear, and she hurriedly rubbed at the iron rings on her fingers. Slowly, Loulie's mind cleared. It occurred to her that despite the woman's otherworldly perfection, no one so much as glanced in her direction. She may as well have been a wraith. Even now, Loulie had to consciously focus to keep her in sight. Had Qadir not alerted her to the woman's presence, Loulie's gaze would have slid off her like water.

A jinn?

No sooner had she come to the realization than she saw a human man in plain beige attire trailing behind the jinn. He had an odd smile on his face that did not reach his glazed eyes.

"What could possibly bring a jinn to Madinne?" Qadir inched closer to her ear.

"I don't know," she murmured. "But I would like to find out."

She politely broke up her conversation with the merchant, then followed the jinn and the smiling man from a distance. "You think the human's a hunter?" She withdrew the two-faced coin and flipped it. It came down on the jinn side. *No.*

"Strange. I have only known jinn to follow humans into cities for revenge," Qadir said. Loulie picked up her pace. Qadir hissed in her ear, "What are you doing?"

"Following them."

The two-faced coin had never lied to her, which meant the jinn had enthralled this man for other reasons. She returned the coin to her pocket and took out her compass. "Lead me to the jinn," she whispered. The enchanted arrow obeyed, pointing her toward the vanishing jinn.

"This is unwise," Qadir said.

"When has that ever stopped me?"

Qadir sighed. "One day, your curiosity is going to get you killed."

But Loulie had stopped listening. Her focus was on the compass, the magic that had never led her astray. The magic that, many years ago, had saved her life.

—◈—

"How does it work?" Layla asked as she tilted the compass.

She had been traveling with the jinn through the desert for a week now, and she noticed the way he commanded the compass to lead them to shelter and quarry.

"It provides me with direction. When I am looking for something, it helps me locate it." Qadir looked at the compass with a fond smile on his face.

Layla tilted it left and right, but the red arrow always swished back to her. Temperamental, her father had called it. But he had not understood its magic when he gave it to her, just as he hadn't anticipated that Qadir, its true owner, would return for it.

And that, in doing so, he would save her life.

Qadir moved closer to their dying fire. He waved his hand over the faintly burning embers, and they flared back to life. Other than the fire, there was little else in the camp save for their weather-beaten tent and Qadir's bag of infinite space.

The jinn rolled his shoulders. "The compass is mine. It insisted I accompany you, and so it is with you I shall stay until it points me in some other direction."

"Why would it do such a thing?"

He looked at her for a long moment. "I was lost in your human desert and could not return home. That is why, when I tracked the compass to you, it saw fit to guide me down a different path." His dark eyes bored into her. "Your path."

Layla swallowed a lump in her throat. "Why can't you return home?"

He shook his head. "Because I am no longer welcome there. But it does not matter; the compass has never led me astray." He said the words with a bold certainty, but his eyes . . .

Even awash in firelight, there were haunted shadows in them.

—⁂—

Loulie passed through a network of alleys before she saw the jinn again. She was guiding the man into an abandoned building of worship, a humble clay structure with latticed windows and faded crescent and star patterns running up the walls. The large metal doors leading into the building were open, barely revealing a chamber draped in unnatural darkness.

"What is your plan?" Qadir's voice was a whisper.

"I'm going to talk to her. But just in case . . ." Loulie reached into the bag for her weapon of choice: a curved dagger with a hilt of black obsidian. A qaf—the first letter in Qadir's name—was painted in gold on the backside. It was the only mark of his ownership.

"What do you hope to gain from threatening a jinn?"

"A man's life, mayhap."

The knife was a final resort. She avoided violence when possible, and the last thing she needed was for the jinn to realize the blade was a relic: a tool enchanted with jinn magic. She knew from experience that flashing relics in front of jinn was foolish. Asking-to-die foolish.

She entered the building. The spacious room inside was dark and empty, the worship alcoves carved into the walls covered in dust and cobwebs. The ceiling, despite depicting sunny skies, was gloomy and gray. What little light came through the windows was muted and dusty. It was as if the room had been sucked dry of its color.

The jinn stood at its center, arms crossed. Loulie stared at her. At her hair, which was a river of living darkness that cascaded down her shoulders and faded to smoke at her back. The human man stood beside her with the strange smile still plastered to his face.

"Human girl," the jinn said flatly. "Leave. I have no business with you." Her gaze landed on Loulie's hands. Belatedly, Loulie realized the jinn could see her rings. She clasped her hands behind her back, but too late. "You dare approach me with those rings?" the jinn hissed.

Loulie suppressed a groan. The rings were a common protection against jinn possession. Naturally, the iron also invoked their wrath. Though she was skeptical of their efficiency, Qadir insisted she wear them. *Superstitions that do not kill you may save you*, he often chided.

"The rings are for avoiding unfortunate misunderstandings like this one," Loulie said carefully. "And I only came to warn you against harming a human on city grounds."

Her eyes flitted to the shadows on the walls, which stretched toward her like spilled ink. She fought a shudder as the jinn's soft voice filled the quiet space. "Do you know how many of my people this man has killed?" She prodded his chest with a finger. "He is mine to do with as I please."

The jinn stepped back and flicked her wrist. The darkness on the walls grew limbs and pushed Loulie unceremoniously out the doors and into the light. Loulie blinked. She glanced behind her at the receding darkness.

She hesitated for one heartbeat. Two. Three.

"*Loulie.*" Qadir dug his claws into her shoulder in warning. She ignored him and chased the shadows back inside. The doors slammed shut, trapping her in darkness. She heard movement behind her but, when she turned, saw nothing.

"I have never seen a human so willing to die." The jinn's voice came from everywhere and nowhere.

Loulie readied her blade. Steadied her shaking hands. "The man is not a hunter."

No response. She clutched the dagger tighter, waiting for something to strike at her. But the moment never came. Instead, she began to feel a subtle burning in her lungs.

Smoke.

Loulie stabbed desperately at the air in front of her, behind her. There was no resistance. Pressure swelled in her lungs until she couldn't breathe. Until she was on her knees, gasping for air. The blade slid through her fingers and clattered to the ground. If it made a sound, Loulie couldn't hear it. There was nothing but that pressure, building, building, building—

"Struggle all you like, foolish girl. You cannot strike down shadows."

Loulie was vaguely aware of Qadir crawling off her shoulder. Then the world fell away, and only pain remained. Loulie's bones cracked. Her ears popped. Her vision clouded, and in the agonizing haze she saw snippets of her own blood-drenched memories.

Pools of crimson on the desert sand. Corpses. Men in black wielding swords.

Her mother and father, dead. Her tribe, destroyed.

"Ah…" The jinn's voice echoed through the barren room.

The pain eased until Loulie was aware of every burning inch of her body. Her head felt as if it were full of cotton as she looked up and saw ruby-red eyes staring at her from the dark. "You are a victim of the men in black?" The darkness rippled, and Loulie had the impression the jinn was reaching for her. Her assailant's voice softened with hesitation. "You—"

The word pitched into a shriek as sunlight burst through the room. The shadow writhed and screamed until it was nothing but darkness bleeding into the tile cracks. Slowly, Loulie turned toward the doors, where a man stood haloed in sunlight.

Dark spots danced behind her eyelids as the world slowly refilled with color.

She managed one blessed intake of air before collapsing.

4

MAZEN

Mazen had no idea how long he'd been transfixed by this lovely creature, but he found he did not care. He'd already decided he wanted nothing more than to bask in her glory for the rest of his days. No desire but to taste her red lips.

But—

To run his hands over the smooth skin of her hips, her stomach...

But—

To push his hands through her hair, press his lips to her neck...

But—

His inner voice was as persistent as an alarm. It made it impossible to focus on the goddess. And there was another disturbance too, something that kept distracting her from him. Mazen was considering investigating the darkening room, when the goddess looked at him and said, "He is mine to do with as I please," and he again stopped thinking.

She reached out and trailed a finger down his cheek. A helpless shudder racked his body at her touch. "Oh, sweet human." Her voice was honeyed as nectar. "Sweet, conniving human—how many of us have you killed?"

The goddess moved closer until their bodies were flush. Mazen's heart lurched as he felt the warm press of her skin against his own. Somewhere in the depths of his mind, he screamed.

"You thought you could escape," the goddess whispered in his ear. "But I know your blood. I would chase you to the ends of the world if that were what it took."

He blinked. Black and red danced before his eyes. Behind the muted colors he saw a leering smile that faded in and out of the dark. His goddess was nothing but a phantom, her lips a bloody smile.

"I'm going to take my time with you, lest your suffering be over too quickly." She pressed her lips to his. And breathed into him. Out of him? He was vaguely aware of his lungs collapsing, his body convulsing.

Mazen tried to push her away, but there was nothing to push. The woman was a silhouette of smoke. He tried to step back, but his feet wouldn't move and his throat was on fire and oh gods, he was going to die—

Abruptly, he could breathe. He tried to speak, but nothing left his air-starved lungs. Awareness flared inside him like a flame, but it was short lived.

"I have never seen a human so willing to die." The demon's words wound around him like silk, and his mind dimmed as she stepped away.

Somewhere in the dark, he heard someone choking. He was trying to puzzle this out when he felt something travel up his body, moving so quickly he didn't have the time to brush it off. He felt a prick of pain in his shoulder. A gruff voice in his ear. "Find the doors," it said. Then both the voice and the pain disappeared.

Mazen blinked slowly as he tried to compose his surroundings. He ventured one shaky step forward, squinting into the dark. It was then that he saw a tiny flaming object traveling across the room. Only, that was impossible, wasn't it? Fire engulfed everything in its path; it could never be so self-contained.

Mazen stumbled after it anyway. It was a brief chase, the light burning out when he crashed into a wall. He reached out—and felt cold metal beneath his hands. The doors. He pushed on them without a thought. With a sigh, the doors opened and light poured into the room, eating away at the darkness, which was . . . screaming?

A shudder climbed Mazen's spine as he whirled to face the enchantress. He blinked in confusion at the sight of her bleeding into the tiles. He'd followed her through sunny streets, enamored of the way the light reflected in her beautiful eyes. But now she was no longer a woman but a shadow, and the sunlight ate away at her form until there was nothing left.

Where she had been standing, there was now a stranger in plain brown robes.

Mazen stared, wondering if they were an illusion.

The person looked at him beneath the shadow of their shawl. Then they collapsed.

Mazen inched forward, eyeing the shadows bleeding into the ground. He had just reached the stranger when they suddenly surged upright. The shawl on their head tumbled loose, revealing a nest of wild brown curls. It was a woman. A woman with remarkable brown eyes tinted the color of rust. He flinched back.

She scowled. "Well, salaam to you too," she said in a raspy voice.

He swallowed. "My apologies." His words came out soft, quavering. He cleared his throat to steady it. "I didn't know if you were an illusion. If you were…" He gestured around them, but the shadows had already been replaced with patches of sunlight.

The stranger glanced around the room with narrowed eyes, as if looking for something. The demon, perhaps.

Mazen realized his hands were trembling and shoved them into his pockets. "We should leave," he said. A wink of silver caught his eyes and he paused, noticing the blade in the woman's hands. She tucked it into the bag lying beside her before he could get a good look at it.

"You removed yourself from the trance." She rose and dusted off her clothing. The movement was slow, pronounced, as if it required great effort.

He hesitated. "Yes?"

"You sound uncertain."

Mazen thought about the mysterious voice in his ear and the strange fire that had led him to the doors. Had that been a hallucination? It was, he decided, better to not mention it.

"I think it was you," he said instead. He'd heard a struggle in the darkness, after all. Who else could it have been but her? "You distracted the demon and gave me an opening."

"I was a *distraction*?" She grumbled beneath her breath. "Is she gone, then? Dead?"

"She, ah, faded into the tiles."

Silence ensued as they both stared suspiciously at the floor.

He cleared his throat. "But tell me, why were you here in the first place"—he hesitated, realizing he didn't know her name—"desert flower?" It was the first thing his scrambled mind came up with. He regretted it immediately.

The woman started toward him with an outward glare. Mazen flinched, thinking she might slap him, but she simply brushed past him on her way to the exit.

"I saw people enter this abandoned place and was curious enough to investigate." She turned at the doorway to face him. "I saw a shadow with red eyes..." She waved her hand, and Mazen saw rings gleam on her fingers. "And you, standing still as a date tree."

Outside, the city was draped in the reds and golds of sunset. Mazen savored the heat of the desert air on his skin and the crunch of the sand beneath his feet as he exited. He sighed as a gentle breeze tousled his hair. The trembling in his hands eased somewhat.

He turned to the stranger. "My thanks for saving me, uh..."

"Layla." She dipped her head, looked at him expectantly.

He paused, realizing he'd yet to offer his name. "Yousef." It was the first false name he could think up. "A thousand blessings upon you, Layla. Had you not come to investigate, I would have lost my soul to the Sandsea." He crossed his arms as he glanced at the abandoned building. "Do you think she was a jinn?"

"Hard to think she could be anything else." She raised a brow. "Are you a hunter, Yousef?"

The blatant question took him off guard. A hunter? Him? Even just the thought made his knees weak. "No! I'm not a murderer."

Murderer. The realization hit like a bolt of lightning. There were many killers in this city—hunters and thieves who killed jinn for coin and sport—but there was only one murderer he was well acquainted with. He recalled the sight of his brother covered in silver blood. His brother, returned earlier than expected.

You thought you could escape, the jinn had said. *But I know your blood. I would chase you to the ends of the world if that were what it took.*

Layla was grinning. "I didn't think you were a murderer. You'd have been a lot more competent if you were."

Mazen frowned. "I was *possessed.*"

Layla just laughed, as if he'd said something funny. She turned and walked away.

Mazen trailed after her. "Wait! Is there any way I can thank you? Can I escort you back home or...ah." He paused, remembering why he'd come to the city in the first place.

Layla turned. "Ah?"

"I was on my way to see someone in the souk when this all happened. A storyteller named Rhuba." He glanced up at the sky, at the sun dipping below the buildings. He needed to return to the palace soon to meet with one of his father's guests; he did not have time to get lost wandering the souk. But the thought of sitting before the sultan and keeping all of this a secret...

"Come on." Layla resumed walking.

"Where are you going?"

"To Old Rhuba's." She cast a look over her shoulder. "Try to keep up, Yousef."

Mazen hesitated. He was exhausted, and all he wanted was to forget this whole day had happened. But he was reluctant to part ways with Layla. She had saved his life. Even better, she didn't know who he was, which meant he had the opportunity to speak to her without his reputation coloring her opinion of him. Who knew when he would get such a chance again?

Perhaps he could still salvage this day.

Mazen chased after her.

The souk was quieter upon his return, sleepy with the coming of twilight. Though the merchants and crowds remained, they moved more languidly, less like ceaseless surf crashing against the shore and more like gentle, lapping waves. Many marketgoers had taken their business to the food shops in the center of the souk, where piquant aromas of spiced meats and fried dough hung in the air.

Mazen tried and failed to ignore his stomach's grumbling as he trailed behind Layla. The appetizing smells made him remember that he had not eaten since iftar and that the morning meal had consisted of nothing but olives and hummus. He was doing his best to *not* think about how empty his stomach was when, without warning, Layla pulled him toward a stall stacked high with pans of apricot leather.

The thick paste had been rolled into varying sizes. One of the men behind the stall was stacking these rolls and delivering them to customers while the other carefully cut the leather sheets into more edible strips. Layla pushed her way through the long line to the front, where she waved down the seller. Mazen marveled at the familiar way they bantered, leaning close and speaking in low voices as if exchanging illicit gossip. At the end of the conversation, Layla came away with a single roll of apricot leather, which she handed to Mazen.

"It's no meal, but it should at least stop the grumbling for a bit." When Mazen gave her a curious look, she looked away and said, "I delivered a message for the stall owner. He owed me a favor for it. I decided to take it in the form of dessert."

Mazen smiled. "You didn't have to waste that favor on me. Shukran."

Layla simply shrugged and resumed walking. Mazen hurried after her. "So, you are a messenger, then?" He tore off a piece of the leather and bit into it. It was startlingly sweet, and pleasant to chew.

Layla nodded as they veered into a souk alley. "That's right. And you? Which quarter do you work in?" The question seemed nonchalant, but Mazen had spoken with enough crafty nobles to recognize a quest for information.

A story began to unfold in his head. A story for Yousef. "I work as a scribe for a high-ranking nobleman." He smiled sheepishly. "I'm afraid I cannot offer more details about the correspondences. That information is confidential."

Layla angled her head. "And what is a scribe doing in the souk, looking for a storyteller?"

Mazen stuffed another piece of the dessert into his mouth, swallowed, and said, "Is it so strange for a man to seek out entertainment beyond his occupation?"

Or freedom beyond the walls of his home? He bit down on the words.

Layla's lips quirked. "Of course not. I've just never known a grown man to seek out a storyteller in his free time."

Mazen laughed. "And until I met you, I'd never made the acquaintance of someone who would jump headfirst into a dark building to investigate a stranger."

At first, Mazen thought it was a trick of the light, but no, Layla actually did blush at his words. When she next spoke, it was in a mumble. "You're lucky I *did* investigate."

"I am. I will forever be grateful for it."

"Careful, Yousef." She grinned. "Forever is a long time to be beholden to someone."

She stopped suddenly and gestured ahead. Mazen ate the last of the leather as he took in the sight before them. Finally, they had arrived at Old Rhuba's golden-tarped stall, which was open for business. The space was humble and austere, nothing but a simple rug stretched beneath an eye-catching cloth canopy. Old Rhuba sat cross-legged on the carpet with an elaborate cane resting across his knees. Mazen had met the storyteller only once before, but he immediately recognized that there were new carvings on the instrument. The observation filled him with awe, as he knew each mark constituted a new story Old Rhuba had added to his repertoire of tales.

Though the cane was remarkable, the storyteller was even more so; he was the only merchant in the souk with such unique eyes:

one the shade of oak and the other the hue of golden sand. His face was like crinkled parchment, and he had an impressive silver-white beard that bunched at his lap. Though it was impossible to see his lips beneath the beard, Mazen could tell he was smiling by the wrinkles at the edges of his eyes.

"Why, if it isn't Layla! And I have seen your face before, ya sayyid, but I am afraid you never offered your name."

Mazen was surprised—and pleased—he'd been remembered. He couldn't help his smile. "Yousef. It is a pleasure to see you again."

"Likewise, Yousef." The old man turned his attention to Layla. "And you, Layla. Would you deliver a message to Dahlia for me? Tell her I accept her invitation to perform tomorrow evening."

Layla smiled. Not the crooked grin she'd flashed earlier, but a bright smile that made her eyes sparkle. "Of course. It's always an honor to have you with us."

Mazen blinked. "Will you be telling a special story?"

"Indeed! I have spent the past months gathering tales from the Bedouin tribes of the eastern plains. Tomorrow will be the first time I share them. These are tales from Dhahab."

Mazen gasped. Tales from Dhahab! It was a rare treat to hear about the jinn cities. They were said to be filled with magic and mystical beasts no one had seen for hundreds of years.

Old Rhuba chuckled. "You are an appreciator of such stories, Yousef?"

"Yes," Mazen admitted with a sheepish smile. "I was hoping to hear you tell them earlier today. But then something, ah, came up."

"You speak as if there is a specific time for stories." Old Rhuba's eyes twinkled with mirth. "Please, sit awhile and listen to an old man prattle on about legends."

Mazen needed no further convincing. He ducked into the storyteller's tent while Layla stood outside at the entrance. Old Rhuba began by asking questions. Did Mazen know anything about the ghouls of the White Dunes? What about the Queen of Dunes, the powerful jinn said to command them?

With each question, Old Rhuba's voice grew louder and clearer, until he'd drawn quite a crowd to his space. Marketgoers both old and young all gathered around him, and once he'd quieted everyone, he began: "Desert folk, allow me to enlighten you! I shall tell you the story of the bone ghouls and their keeper, the Queen of Dunes. Neither here nor there, but long ago..."

Mazen was at the mercy of the story the moment it started. It was like being in the middle of a storm. He was barely able to catch his breath as he was buffeted by words. Time got away from him, and when the story eventually ended, stars glinted in the sky and the souk's thoroughfares were lined with lit lanterns. Mazen came back to himself abruptly. Old Rhuba had made him forget about the jinn, his brother, *and* tonight's meeting. He had to leave now.

After ascertaining the location of tomorrow's performance from the storyteller, he stepped out of the stall and found Layla at the crowd's outskirts.

"Tired, Yousef?" She cocked a brow. "You've had a long day."

Mazen shook his head. "I just realized what time it is. I have a curfew, you see."

Layla looked skeptical. "Ah."

"Will I see you tomorrow at Dahlia's tavern?" He'd already decided he would do whatever was necessary to attend. He would feign sickness and pay off as many guards as needed.

Layla simply shrugged. "Perhaps."

He was a little disheartened by the noncommittal answer, but he had no time to convince her to be there. Not while the sun, undeterred by his indecisiveness, continued its descent. "Perhaps, then." He smiled. "It would be an honor to speak with you once more."

He thanked her one last time before hurrying back to his gilded cage.

5

LOULIE

The minute Yousef left, Loulie tailed him. *A grown man with a curfew? More likely a man with secrets.* Even if he was not a hunter, there was something suspicious about Yousef, and she intended to find out what it was. She did not believe his nebulous backstory, and she refused to let him remain a mystery after she had rescued him.

"Do not forget it was I who saved him," Qadir said.

Loulie suppressed a sigh. Qadir had already explained this to her. While she'd been suffocating beneath the jinn's magic, Qadir had pulled Yousef from his trance and led him to the doors and to the sunlight that had—temporarily—vanquished the jinn. He'd returned to Loulie's shoulder before they exited the place of worship.

"You couldn't have helped me yourself?" she'd asked him earlier, at Old Rhuba's stall.

"And reveal myself to another jinn? Never."

"I could have died."

"And it would have been your own damn fault for ignoring me."

And so here they were, chasing after Yousef in the hopes of discovering why the jinn had mistaken him for a hunter in the first place. Loulie's gold was on family ties.

Eventually, the dirt paths of the commoners' quarters gave way to paved cobblestone streets, and the ramshackle houses became small box-shaped manors with impressive gilded doorways and beautiful latticed windows. The more extravagant homes had multiple floors and fenced-off gardens. One especially lavish dwelling even had two balconies.

Loulie shifted her attention away from the ostentatious buildings and back to Yousef, who was seamlessly ducking into the alleyways between them.

Definitely a man of secrets.

She had just followed him around the corner of a particularly narrow alley when she saw a man leaning against one of the walls and stopped. The moment he looked up, her heart jumped into her throat.

Omar bin Malik, the sultan's eldest son, regarded her with a dazzling smile.

When he moved, he seemed to glimmer; Loulie saw silver rings on his fingers and a belt of daggers at his waist. Even his earring, a crescent that curved around his earlobe, seemed to glint menacingly beneath the moonlight.

Loulie was not taken in by his smile. Though Omar bin Malik had a reputation for being charismatic, he was also, above all else, a hunter. And not just any hunter, but the King of the Forty Thieves— the most prestigious band of jinn killers in the desert.

She surveyed him warily, taking in features she'd only ever observed from a distance. Olive skin, almond-colored eyes, hair cut close to his neck, and a stunning smile that somehow did not reach his eyes.

She briefly considered feigning naivete, then decided on humility. She fell to her knees. "High Prince!"

The prince chuckled. "In the flesh."

"It is an honor, sayyidi." She tried not to tremble as he approached. Here was one of the most feared hunters in the desert, and sitting on her shoulder was a jinn he would kill in a heartbeat just to add to his tally. Qadir, thankfully, had scrambled down her neck and out of sight.

"I suppose it must be." She could make out the dirt on his boots as he stopped in front of her. "Please, rise. You'll get your robes dirty."

She stood with as much pride as she could muster. The high prince was still smiling at her, but his brows were raised just enough to make it into a look of condescension. He reached into one of his pockets and withdrew a few copper coins. "Here," he said. "For your trouble."

She blinked. He thought she was a *beggar*?

"Oh, no, sayyidi, I'm—"

"I insist." He jiggled the coins in his palm and waited, still with that arrogant smile on his face, for her to take them. Was it better to look right at him or away?

The best and worst thing would be to punch him, she thought with irritation.

She settled on looking through him and tried not to flinch when their fingers brushed. Afterward, he drew his hand away and said, "Return home. It is getting late, and dangerous things stalk the streets at night."

She bristled at what was clearly a command but forced herself to nod and turn away. The prince called after her. "Be wary of shadows. That is where jinn roam."

Loulie turned, but the high prince was already walking away, hands tucked into his pockets. She did not know how long she stood there, waiting for his shadow to disappear, but it occurred to her afterward that she'd lost Yousef.

She could use the compass to pick up his trail again, but—no, there would be time later.

"Let's go home," she muttered to the air.

"Yes," Qadir said softly. "Let's."

Exhaustion settled on Loulie's shoulders like a heavy blanket as she made her way back to Dahlia's tavern.

— ∾ —

Stars had overtaken the night sky by the time they returned. Loulie popped a pistachio into her mouth as she tried and failed to focus on the constellations. After the run-in with the jinn, it had been difficult to turn her mind away from the memory of her family's death. Somehow, the shadow jinn had seen the killers in her mind and recognized them.

She frowned at the sky. *She must have run into them before Qadir killed them.*

Qadir made a sound in his throat that might have been a cough but sounded like a wheeze. "Remember to go into the tavern through the back door this time."

Loulie sighed. "Yes, yes." She diverted her attention to the tavern, an unspectacular two-story building with a slanted, dilapidated roof. Lanterns hung from the low scaffolding, illuminating dusty glass windows. Loulie could just barely make out the drunken crowds hooting and trilling inside. It was the beginning of the Cold Season, which meant Dahlia had just received a new shipment of wine— and *that* was always cause for celebration. Loulie had no doubt the revelers were drinking themselves into a stupor.

"Do not make the same mistake as last time." Loulie flicked his tail but Qadir continued, undeterred. "'No one will notice a girl plain as me,' you said. And then I had to bite a man."

She was glad Qadir was not in his man shape; he would have teased her for the flush in her cheeks.

The jinn had already crawled into their bag and retrieved the key they needed when they reached the back door. Loulie unlocked it and passed through a storage room packed with wine barrels to the staircase at the back of the building. Inside, the boisterous voices grew louder until she could make out verses of poetry. Though she herself preferred to deal in coin rather than words, she enjoyed listening to the impromptu poetry contests at the tavern. Tonight, however, she was too exhausted to make an appearance. She would converse with Dahlia tomorrow.

She made her way through the upstairs corridor to her apartments, which were in the state she'd left them in. There in the center of the room was the low-rising table where she and Qadir tested their relics and ate their meals together, and there was the divan by the window, where Loulie liked to lounge in the sun. To the right: a series of tome-filled shelves that contained everything from maps to stories to philosophical musings. Her walls were home to a collection of tapestries featuring desert landscapes, and an assortment of rugs, most of which had been purchased from the Bedouin tribes selling out of Madinne's market, lay scattered on the floor.

It was small, familiar, and comfortable. A good place to rest between ventures.

As Loulie set down the bag of infinite space by the table, her eyes went to the single item on display that belonged to Qadir. It was tucked into a corner, barely noticeable from the door, but there was the shamshir she had purchased for him years ago, mounted on the wall beside the shelves. It was a simple but elegant thing, a steel blade with an ivory grip that had a single red gem on its guard. Qadir rarely wore the blade, preferring a bow when he had to rely on a weapon and couldn't use magic, but Loulie had never regretted gifting it to him.

It had been the first thing she'd ever purchased for the jinn with her own means. She would always remember his delighted surprise, as well as the uncharacteristically fullmouthed grin that had been on his face when he accepted the blade from her. Those smiles of his were rare, and Loulie felt accomplished when she was able to coax them out of him. Never mind that the blade was mostly used as décor now. Qadir treasured it in his own way, and that was enough.

Loulie closed the door, made her way into the room, and threw herself on the divan by the window. "Home. Finally." She sighed as she stretched out on the pillows.

"We could have been back sooner, but you insisted on chasing a man around the souk."

She looked up and saw Qadir looming over her in his human form. As always, he looked unimpressed. "Last I recall, there was a vengeful jinn involved," she said.

Qadir frowned. "What you did today was dangerous."

"Yes, I know. You've told me a thousand and one times."

"What did you gain by intervening?"

"*I* gained nothing, but a man got to keep his life. Though…" She sat up and brushed her curls out of her eyes. "I told you earlier that the shadow jinn said something strange."

Qadir seated himself on a cushion beside their table. "About the cutthroats in black? It means nothing. Perhaps killers favor the color."

Loulie glanced out the window. At this time of night, the streets were filled with drunken men—many coming from Dahlia's tavern. She could hear them downstairs thumping tables and singing loudly, badly.

She swallowed. "Perhaps." She could not shake the feeling that the jinn had been on the cusp of revealing important information. Loulie had watched her tribe's murderers die, but no matter how much distance she put between herself and the past, the memories would always be there.

"They are dead, Loulie." Qadir had been in the middle of organizing their relics; now he stopped to look at her. "I made sure of it."

His confidence eased the tension in her heart, even if she was still wary. She nodded, then joined him at the table to help sort their inventory. Most of the relics in their bag were unspectacular: an hourglass filled with endless sand; a dusty mirror that offered a reflection of the person one loved most; and a string of beads that, when rubbed together, created a gentle sound that lulled one to sleep.

But there were other, more useful relics too. Loulie's personal favorite was an orb cushioned between two luminous wings. It glowed when touched and became steadily brighter when she pressed her palm to it. She and Qadir used it to light their way through the desert.

Now she sat sullenly staring at the shadows it cast upon the walls, thinking of everything that had happened today. She considered Prince Omar. If he was so competent a hunter, why had he not captured the shadow jinn before she came to Madinne? Why had he not captured *any* of the jinn supposedly infesting the city?

"Princes," Loulie grumbled.

Qadir raised a brow. "I hear Prince Mazen and Prince Hakim are not so terrible."

"How would anyone know? Neither of them ever leaves the palace." Loulie folded her arms on the table and set her chin atop them. "Do you think Omar knows the shadow jinn is in Madinne?" She couldn't stop thinking of his comment about the shadows.

Qadir shrugged. "I hope for her sake he does not."

Loulie watched as Qadir cleaned the relics with a rag. She thought about asking him how and why he was able to live in a world where jinn were persecuted for simply existing, but hesitated. She had asked many times and received the same cryptic answer. *I am but a single jinn,* he would say. *I cannot change your land's prejudices.*

It was an infuriating answer because it *wasn't* an answer. But she had long ago learned that Qadir was not like her. While she frequently stuck her nose into others' business, Qadir never involved himself unless it was necessary. It was strange, how they could both be so distant from people yet have such different ways of coexisting with them.

"Hmm," Qadir said. "You are suspiciously quiet."

Loulie blew a loose curl out of her eyes. "I'm thinking."

"About?"

"About you."

Qadir frowned. "Now I'm even more concerned."

"You should stop that. The worrying, I mean. It's going to give your ageless skin wrinkles."

The edges of Qadir's lips curled ever so slightly. "I have aged more in the nine years I have known you than in the hundreds I lived before our meeting."

Loulie grabbed a cushion off the floor and threw it at him. She grumbled when he caught it and set it on his lap. "How old are you, anyway?"

The half smile was still on his lips. "Ancient."

"It's no wonder you're so cynical. You should take more naps; they might improve your temperament." She gestured to the closed door on her right, behind which lay their sleeping chambers. There were two beds inside, though Qadir's was rarely occupied. "What is it you are so fond of telling me? That even exasperating people become tolerable after a good night's rest?"

Qadir snorted. "If you truly wanted to make my life easier, you wouldn't leap so carelessly into danger." He set one relic aside and picked up another: the string of sleep-inducing relic beads. "I do not need sleep. You, on the other hand, have been chasing trouble all day."

Trouble that I would very much like to get to the root of.

When she'd first come to Madinne, Loulie had paid for her accommodations by delivering messages and tracking rumors for Dahlia. The tavernkeeper had taught her that knowledge was power. Blackmail, favors, connections—all of it sprang from a web of constantly shifting rumors. Not understanding the web increased one's risk of becoming ensnared in it.

Loulie had taken that lesson to heart. It was why she always made it a priority to seek out gossip and why she still delivered and received messages for Dahlia when she was in Madinne. She hadn't become so successful by ignoring suspicious people and occurrences.

This thought spiraled in her mind like an eddy until it mellowed to nothingness. Until she felt her eyelids drooping.

Qadir dimmed the orb with a touch of his hand. "You should get some rest. A tired merchant is easy to fool in the souk." He was running the relic beads through his fingers.

"That's why I have you as a bodyguard, fearsome old man." She smiled as she closed her eyes, and when darkness came, she let it take her.

6

MAZEN

"A jinn!" Mazen threw open the door to his brother's room. "There's a jinn in the city!"

Save for a single lantern, there was no light in Hakim's room. Mazen paused in the doorway. After the incident with the jinn, he was not eager to step into a dark room. But this was not the abandoned place of worship. This was Hakim's room—a cozy if somewhat claustrophobic prison filled with towering stacks of tomes and maps. They surrounded even Hakim's bed, making it impossible to spot from the doorway.

"Hakim?" He looked beseechingly at his brother's back.

Hakim remained hunched over the scrolls and mapmaking instruments on his desk. "What's this about a jinn? Is this from one of your stories, Mazen?"

"If only. No, I'm talking about a real jinn, Hakim."

"Mm." Hakim continued working on whatever he was working on.

Mazen blinked. *Maybe I was not clear?*

He drew closer until he could see what his brother was drawing: an intricate map of the desert that featured cities and oases so detailed they seemed to breathe off the parchment. It was stunningly beautiful, and for a few moments, Mazen let himself get lost in the landscapes he'd only ever visited in stories. The places he'd dreamed of traveling to since he was a child. He watched his brother work, and he forgot why he'd come.

And then, abruptly, he remembered.

"Hakim, the jinn was real. It ensnared me with magic! It was a woman, you see, and she put me under some kind of spell with her beauty."

"That's nice, Mazen."

"She took me into an abandoned building and nearly suffocated me to death!"

"I must say, this story lacks the suspense of your usual tales."

"It's not a story!" Mazen gripped his brother's shoulder. "This is the truth, Hakim."

Hakim carefully set down his paintbrush and looked up. In this lighting, he could have passed as the sultan's son, even with his hazel eyes. "You seem in one piece to me," he said.

"Thanks to a random passerby."

Hakim regarded him quietly for a few moments, brows scrunched. Then, slowly, he laid his hand over Mazen's. "Peace, Mazen. I believe you." His eyes flitted to the hourglass on his desk. "We must meet with the sultan's guest soon, but we have time for you to tell me more of the story."

Mazen was more than happy to oblige. After he had finished, Hakim eyed Mazen's hands and said, "You aren't wearing the rings."

Mazen glanced down at his bare fingers. "Why would I walk around in disguise with the royal rings? The guards would come running if I so much as raised my hand."

Hakim sighed. "Melodramatic as always." He raised his own hand, revealing five elaborately designed iron rings nearly identical to the ones the sultan had gifted Mazen. "We have these rings for a reason. Wear gloves if you must, but don't put yourself in danger for the sake of making a disguise more convincing."

Mazen had nothing to say to that. Hakim was right; a disguise was not armor if it had such exploitable weaknesses.

"I am glad you are safe." Hakim leaned forward in his chair.

"I know you do not wish to tell Omar about this, but have you considered—"

"Omar knows."

Hakim pinched the bridge of his nose. "Ah."

"He caught me sneaking out and said he would keep it a secret so long as I did him a favor." Mazen could only pray Omar honored their deal.

Hakim looked like he was on the verge of scolding Mazen when he paused, glancing at the depleted sand in the hourglass. He stood. "We must go meet with the sultan." He eyed Mazen's baggy attire. "You might want to change into something more appropriate. Go, quickly. I will tell the sultan you were helping me with the map."

Mazen sighed with relief. "Bless you, Hakim."

Hakim simply smiled as he waved him outside. "Yalla, you don't have all night."

Knowing that his father did indeed despise tardiness, Mazen hurried to his rooms to prepare. The servants inside said nothing upon his return—they never did, when he paid them to keep his secrets—and left the chamber without comment when he dismissed them.

Without them, the space felt enormous. Mazen had spent years trying to fill it, but to little avail. Because he was, on occasion, obligated to entertain esteemed guests here, his father had forced him to dispose of anything "too personal." So Mazen kept his most treasured possessions out of sight. The two mother-of-pearl chests on either side of his canopied bed contained city maps Hakim had drawn for him over the years, and he had stored the commemorative coins he'd stolen from the treasury in an extravagant wooden cupboard by the window. The only sentimental collection he had on display was the dozens of miniature clay creatures he and his mother had purchased in the souk when he was a child. The collection was showcased in the alcove where he entertained his guests, on the shelves surrounding the perimeter.

And then there was the blue-and-white carpet beneath his feet—the one that was nearly identical to the rug in the souk. He'd told the weaver it was a gift when, in truth, he had taken it from his mother's rooms knowing it was one of her favorite possessions. He could still remember the way her eyes had lit up when the sultan gave it to her. Before she'd married him, she had been a wanderer; no doubt the carpet had reminded her of her own tribe and travels.

Mazen had never met the family on his mother's side, had never even seen another city outside of Madinne, but he was plagued by that same wanderlust.

He sighed as he threw off his nondescript robe and donned a rich-red tunic and sirwal trousers. He pinned his mother's red-gold scarf—the only heirloom he possessed from her tribe—around his neck and slipped his ten rings onto his fingers. Last came the three royal earrings: a small crescent, a star, and a sun.

Once he was prepared, he left his room and hurried through the open-air corridors until he came to the diwan, which was marked by gargantuan doors painted with extravagant depictions of Madinne's city life: marketgoers bartering with merchants, pearl divers riding sambuks across the waves, soldiers striding through fields made green by jinn blood. The images vanished from view as guards opened the doors.

The sultan's diwan was intimidating in its grandiosity. The walls sparkled with mosaic images that featured Madinne's first sultan slaying jinn and befriending fantastical creatures. Elaborately painted lanterns hung above the art, illuminating the rest of the interior—the spacious mezzanines; the impressive half stage; and in the heart of the room, the dining area.

Only four people sat at the low-rising table, though asha'a had been served for at least six. At the head of the table, dressed in the finest cloaks and jewels, was the sultan. Today he wore an expensive silk shawl around his head, with a band of gold wrapped around his forehead like a circlet. His hair was a smoky gray beneath the fabric.

Sitting to his right was Omar, whose definition of dressing down was to remove *some* of the knives from his person. On the sultan's left was his guest, a middle-aged man dressed in vibrant green. He looked vaguely familiar, though Mazen could not remember when and where he had seen him. Hakim sat at the guest's left, clutching a scroll. His discomfort was clear in the tenseness of his shoulders; he looked less at home than the stranger.

But then, Hakim had always been an outsider. A prince in title but not in blood. He was a living reminder of the infidelity of the sultan's second wife—a fact he was made aware of constantly. Mazen forced the gloomy thought away as he sat and greeted the guest.

"Mazen," his father said as he made himself comfortable. "This is Rasul al-Jasheen, one of the merchants I do business with. You recognize him?"

Mazen smiled. "Ya sayyid, you must forgive me. Your appearance is familiar in the way a dream is. Has something about you changed?"

The merchant grinned. "Only in the face, sayyidi."

The memory clicked. The single eye, the beautiful robes, the mouth filled with colorful teeth—yes, Mazen knew this man. He received generous compensation from the sultan for presenting his rare trinkets to him first.

"You have..." Mazen tapped his right eye.

The merchant laughed. "Yes, I am one-eyed no longer. A miracle, wouldn't you say?"

The sultan cleared his throat. "You were about to tell us of this miracle when my son arrived, Rasul."

"Ah yes! Allow me to enlighten you, my sultan."

And so he told them of the elixir delivered to him by the elusive Midnight Merchant. Mazen was fascinated. He'd heard tales of the merchant and her adventures but had never gotten an account from someone who'd *met* her. He couldn't help but be envious.

"I know the look in your eyes, sayyidi." Rasul grinned at the sultan. "You want to find this Midnight Merchant, don't you? I hope you do not plan on throwing her into the Bowels."

Mazen shuddered. The Bowels—aptly named because they were prisons erected in holes that ran deep beneath the city—were inescapable. Anyone foolish enough to land themselves inside never saw the sun again.

"While she *is* engaged in many illegal dealings, no. I have a more useful purpose for her." The sultan gestured at Hakim, who unrolled his scroll, revealing his map of the desert.

Rasul stared at it intensely, as if assessing its monetary value. The sultan seemed unimpressed; he never complimented Hakim on his skills. He simply expected him to employ them on demand. The sultan ran his finger over the carefully drawn oases, past the cities of Dhyme and Ghiban, and to an ocean of sparkling sand labeled *Western Sandsea*. Mazen's eyes widened when he saw the word printed in the center of the Sandsea: *Dhahab*. The lost jinn city of legend.

"If the Midnight Merchant is so adept at tracking and collecting magic, then perhaps she can find what others cannot—a priceless relic from the city of Dhahab."

Mazen paled. He knew the relic his father spoke of. The sultan had already sent dozens of men to find it. All had failed. No one ventured into the Sandsea and survived.

He would be sending the merchant to her death. He wanted to object, but to question the sultan would undermine his authority, so Mazen struggled quietly with his distress.

The room was tense after the sultan's proclamation, their meal eaten in near silence. Mazen was relieved when his father dismissed them early, saying he wanted to speak to Rasul alone. Outside the diwan, Hakim followed his guard escorts back to his room while Omar veered in the direction of the courtyard. Mazen trailed him.

And yet despite his resolve to apprehend his brother, he still somehow lost him.

When Mazen turned the bend into the rose garden, Omar had vanished. Mazen was baffled, but nonetheless determined. He rushed down the pathways between the flowers, following them through an orchard filled with various fruit-bearing trees, until he reached the sparring pavilion, a large wooden platform surrounded on all sides by tree-shaped columns.

At first, he saw nothing. But then he backtracked and realized there *were* people standing by the platform. A cloaked woman and, in front of her, Omar. Mazen mentally chided himself for his near-sightedness as he approached.

The two were in the middle of a conversation when Omar abruptly turned toward him, lips curved. "Why, if it isn't my adventurous little brother."

It was an effort to return Omar's smile. "Salaam, Omar. Who's your friend?" He glanced at his brother's female companion, whose face was hidden beneath her hood. Mazen could make out dark brown eyes, fierce eyebrows, and an aquiline nose.

"This is Aisha bint Louas," Omar said. "She is one of my best thieves."

Mazen blanched. This woman, a hunter? One of Omar's forty thieves? Mazen had seen the thieves in passing but never spoken to them. In fact, he tried to avoid them at all costs. Most of the time, this was easily accomplished. The thieves did not participate in court life; they were simply here to report to Omar.

Mazen had definitely never seen this woman before. He would have remembered her piercing stare. He put a hand to his chest and bowed. "It is a pleasure."

Aisha raised a brow. "Is it?"

Mazen blinked, at a loss for how to respond.

Omar just laughed. "Aisha is also my most honest thief. She can cut a man down with her words just as easily as with her knives." He waved a hand. "You are dismissed, Aisha."

Aisha bobbed her head and walked off. When she was gone, Omar leaned against a pavilion column and smirked. "Do not take offense, Mazen. Aisha dislikes most men."

"But not you?"

Omar shrugged. "It hardly matters whether she likes me. She is an excellent hunter and obeys my orders without hesitation. That is all that matters. But..." He cocked a brow. "You are not here to speak about Aisha. What do you want?"

Mazen took a deep, stilted breath. "I want to know why you returned early today."

"Has your memory failed you? I told you I found all my marks.

I have no reason to remain in the desert after my job is done." He grinned. "I am sure you had a much more interesting day than I. You told me you were going to the souk to find a storyteller, but that is not the whole truth, is it? There was a woman."

Mazen stared at him. "What?"

"You must have left quite the impression for her to stalk you through the streets."

Mazen was beginning to feel faint. "What are you talking about?"

"A woman followed you into the noble quarter. I thought you'd broken her heart, the way she was chasing you."

Layla. Or—the shadow jinn? Mazen shook off his fear before it grew roots. He focused on Omar's words. What they implied. "You were following me," he said. "Because you were tracking a jinn, weren't you?"

Omar didn't even bat an eyelash. "A valiant pastime, yes?"

Mazen could hear the thud of his heartbeat in his ears. "You knew there was a jinn in the city when I left the palace. You could have told me it was out for your blood. For *our* blood."

Omar shrugged. "I may have forgotten to mention it."

Mazen's fear burned away, replaced with an anger that shot through his veins like ice. He moved without thinking, grabbing the collar of his brother's tunic and shoving him into the column. "This is no laughing matter, you ass. I could have died!"

His hand quivered as he looked into his brother's eyes. Even now, they sparkled with amusement. Mazen wanted to punch him.

"On the contrary, I find it quite entertaining." Omar set his hand atop Mazen's. Mazen flinched at the coldness of his fingers. "Seeing you angry is always a good time, akhi. But, as always, you are concerned about the wrong things. Let me worry about the jinn. *You* should worry about Father finding out what happened. Imagine what he would do if he realized that you had not only left the palace but were attacked in doing so."

Omar pried Mazen's fingers from his tunic. "You think he would give you a second chance? No, he will do to you what he has done to

Hakim. He will make you a prisoner in this place. There would be no escape, not even with guards."

Mazen stepped away. Omar's gaze had become thoughtful, as if he could read all the insecurities in Mazen's heart. "Remember, akhi, which of us has the upper hand."

Omar smiled pleasantly, tucked his hands into his pockets, and walked away. Mazen watched him go, mute. No argument could save him from this predicament. It would not matter if he proved Omar's incompetence as a hunter to his father. Ultimately, Omar would be scolded, and Mazen would be trapped.

It was a long time before he swallowed his dread and returned to his room.

7

AISHA

When Aisha bint Louas was given an order by her king, she obeyed.

There were fights worth picking, and then there were fights with Omar bin Malik: one-sided battles fought with gilded words and patronizing smiles. It was a battlefield Aisha avoided at all costs. She was a thief, not a politician. Her victories were claimed with blades—shamshirs lined with the silver blood of her victims.

Still, that didn't mean she was always *happy* about acquiescing.

She'd been irritated when Omar asked to meet her in the courtyard after his dinner, and now, with his message beating through her head, she was even more annoyed. Her unexpected encounter with the youngest prince had only soured her mood further. She'd been looking forward to spending the night curled up in her favorite window alcove, with only her knives and whetstone for company. Yet here she was, delivering a message to one of the sultan's most infuriating soldiers instead.

She dragged her feet through corridors glowing with moonlight and up stairwells illuminated by dusty lamplight until she came to the qaid's room in the soldiers' halls, unmarked except for an evil-eye charm hanging on the door. She knocked: four quick taps followed by two louder raps. The door flew open to reveal a bulky middle-aged man in a turban.

The qaid scowled when he saw her. "Thief."

"*Thief* is not my name." She crossed her arms. "Can you say 'Aisha'?"

The qaid ignored her, stepping aside and gesturing her into the room. Aisha walked past him, eyes flicking from the weapons lining the walls to the scrolls strewn across his desk. It certainly looked like a room belonging to the sultan's military leader.

"What do you want, bint Louas?" He eyed her warily as he closed the door.

"I have a message for you from Prince Omar." She paused to relish the fear in his eyes before continuing. "My king brought your concerns to the sultan. Fortunately, His Majesty dismissed them. So, as per his original proposition, Prince Omar will be sending some of my comrades to fill the gaps in your security by the end of the month."

For a few moments the qaid simply gaped at her, lips flapping uselessly as he tried to form a fruitless argument. But then he clamped his jaw shut and stepped toward her, eyes flashing. "Why does the prince not deliver this message to me himself?"

Because he's a royal pain in the ass.

"Ask him yourself. I wasn't sent here to answer your questions."

She moved toward the door—and managed only a single step before the qaid blocked her way. "Tell your prince there are no holes in my security. My men are more than capable of protecting this city. We do not want your help. We do not *need* it."

Aisha could have laughed in his face. All these fools ever did was throw people in the Bowels and cringe at silver blood. Even the sultan knew his men were incompetent; gods knew they'd been unable to protect his late wife.

Aisha wasn't conceited enough to call herself a hero, but at least *she* had never let any of her targets escape. Not since she'd picked up a blade and promised to kill them all, anyway.

"His Majesty seems to think otherwise. Perhaps it was all your pleading. A competent leader wouldn't need to build his case with words; his actions would speak for him." She briskly sidestepped the qaid and headed for the door. The man was visibly shaking with rage, and when he turned toward her, it was with a speed that made her tense.

But the qaid's only riposte was his words, which he hurled at her like throwing knives. "Do not think this scheme will give you power over us, bint Louas." He glared at her. "You all are killers; no one could ever mistake you for soldiers."

Aisha looked at him for a long moment. And then she snorted and turned away.

What did he think soldiers were, if not glorified murderers?

She didn't bother with a response as she ducked outside. A cool breeze nipped at her clothing as she shut the door, ruffling her cloak and tugging at her hood. For a few moments, the world stilled, and Aisha let herself savor the tranquility of the night. It was not lost on her that this type of quiet was rare in this place, but she did not mind it. The silence was somnolent rather than tense and reminded her of the refreshing calm that rolled in after a storm. Even the weather was pleasant: not yet frigid, but cold enough to comfortably don extra layers of clothing.

She was still savoring the peace when a blur of motion caught her eye and she looked up to see a messenger, marked as such by his satchel. The man lowered his gaze as he approached, and Aisha noticed his shoulders tense as he brushed past her. It was not until he was on the stairwell that he visibly relaxed. Aisha watched him disappear without comment. She was accustomed to this type of encounter; those who knew her kept their guard up. She supposed it was for the better, as she preferred avoiding conversation with spineless fools when possible.

Still, she pictured what it might be like to wander these halls as a visitor rather than a thief—to be catered to rather than avoided.

She let the musing evaporate as she started back the way she'd come, heading down the stairwell and back to the ground floor. As she strode down the corridor in the direction of the thieves' hideout, she was aware of every flicker of light and motion. She didn't miss the servants who shrank away from her or the soldiers who glared at her with open hostility. And she did not miss the footsteps trailing hers—the tread that was as familiar to her as her own breathing.

She didn't so much as flinch when Omar fell into step beside her, appearing from gods knew where. He did that sometimes—appeared suddenly from the shadows like some wraith. It irked her that she couldn't always hear him.

"I'm not delivering any more godsdamned messages for you," Aisha muttered.

Omar clucked his tongue. "I take it the qaid didn't receive the news well?"

"Working under him is going to be hell."

Omar flashed a pleasant smile at her. Even in the darkness, it was dazzling. "Then it's a good thing you won't be one of the people I assign to his security force."

Aisha turned away with a grumble. "I'd stab you in the throat if you tried to shove me into that uniform. Is this infiltration really necessary?"

Omar chuckled. "It's not an infiltration if everyone but the qaid consents to it. You know as well as I the failings of Madinne's security. My own brother was assaulted by a jinn in the souk today, you know."

A jinn you *ought to have killed*, she thought, but didn't voice the opinion. Omar's tortuous games had never appealed to her. She preferred to kill her targets on sight, with as little struggle as possible. There was little point in playing with something that wound up dead.

"Your idiot brother walked into the souk of his own accord."

Another laugh from Omar. "You don't find his little ventures courageous?"

"I find them *foolish*."

They were walking through the orchard now, down a path that shot past trees heavy with apples and oranges. Dimly lit lanterns hung from some of the branches, coating the ground in a hazy light that made the grass shimmer. It looked, Aisha thought, like it was covered in dew.

She plucked a golden apple from a branch in passing and tossed it absently between her palms. "What do you want from me, sayyidi?"

Omar blinked at her with faux innocence. "What, can I not simply enjoy your company?"

"Don't flatter me. *You* do not enjoy someone else's company without an ulterior motive." She bit into the apple, wrinkled her nose at the tartness. When Omar flexed his fingers at her, she was more than happy to toss it to him.

"How foolish of me." The prince held the apple up. Its color was dulled in the moonlight. "I should know better than to attempt casual conversation with you." He bit into it, putting the conversation on hold.

They walked the rest of the way to their hideout in companionable silence, following the path to the outer palace wall and then to an unassuming tower that stood sentinel at its southeast corner. The building was a shadow amongst the pale minarets, an ominous-looking place that leaned so heavily against the wall, it looked in danger of crumbling over it.

Ostentatious locations make for the best hiding places, Omar had once told her when she asked why he'd situated their base here. He claimed it was easier to keep secrets from nobles who consciously avoided them than from the curious commoners who hero-worshipped them.

Aisha didn't care about any of that. There was a door on this side of the palace wall they could use to slip covertly out into the city, and that was all that mattered. The less time she had to spend walking through this gold-plated trap, the happier she was.

She turned to Omar expectantly. The prince was twirling the apple core by its stem, lips upturned slightly. "You want to know why I'm following you? Guilt."

Aisha frowned at him, unimpressed.

"Don't give me that look. I wanted to apologize for dismissing you so abruptly earlier. My brother has a bad habit of asking questions he won't understand the answers to. I thought it better to avoid this conversation with him."

"You wanted to avoid the qaid too. That's why you sent me to speak with him."

"*I'm* expected to be pleasant at court. You, on the other hand..." He smirked. "I appreciate you using that needle-sharp honesty for the greater good."

I did it because you ordered *me to, you bastard.*

But she found her lips quirking despite the thought. She liked the prince—enough that she didn't mind taking orders from him, occasional frustrating fights aside. He was straightforward and honest and didn't waste time on words he didn't mean.

"Shukran, Aisha." Omar considered her with a tilt of his head. "I promise I won't hand you over to the qaid. That hardheaded security fool doesn't deserve you."

"No, he doesn't." She huffed out a sigh. "Now, am I free to go?"

"Of course. I just wanted to thank you." He paused to look up at the tower, and Aisha followed his gaze to one of the windows above: her window, hidden behind a gossamer curtain that fluttered softly in the breeze.

"And, I suppose, I wanted to warn you."

She snapped back to attention at the words. Omar was looking at her again, all traces of his smile gone. "The jinn who attacked my brother still skulks through the shadows. Be careful that it does not ambush you. And if you do see the jinn, leave it be. It's *my* mark."

Aisha bristled. She knew she had a tendency to steal kills, but why should it matter who destroyed creatures condemned by the gods? Creatures who would tear down an entire village, who would ruthlessly slaughter children and carve their victory into their victims' flesh...

She dug her nails into her palms hard enough to root herself in the present. The scars hidden beneath her cloak itched at the memory.

"Fine," she said brusquely.

The reluctant admission seemed to be enough for Omar. He was smiling again when he excused himself for the night. Once he was gone, Aisha sighed and got to work on the overcomplicated door locks. Eventually, the bolts gave, and she was about to enter the tower when she heard the sound of crunching grass and froze. She glanced over her shoulder, fingers hovering over one of the knives on her belt.

But though she could have sworn she'd heard footsteps, there was nothing behind her but tree-shaped shadows swaying in the breeze.

Aisha watched the darkness for a long time just to be sure no one was there. Then, disgruntled with herself for being so jumpy, she stepped into the tower.

The last thing she heard before she slammed the door shut was the ominous susurration of the wind, which sounded uncomfortably like laughter.

8

LOULIE

"So." Dahlia bint Adnan lowered her pipe and exhaled a cloud of shisha into the air. It hung like blue mist above her and Loulie's heads. "You met Rasul al-Jasheen." The tavernkeeper's amber eyes shone like coins in the dimness. "How did you like him?"

"He was ugly as sin."

Dahlia smirked. "Not that I don't agree, but that doesn't answer my question."

"He was okay, for a merchant." Loulie glanced at the door to her room for what was probably the dozenth time that hour. While she didn't mind filling Dahlia in on her adventures, the second hour of moonrise was nearly upon them, and she was becoming impatient.

Qadir had left some time ago to gather gossip from around the souk, promising he would keep an ear out for rumors of assassins in black. She'd assumed he would be back in time for their visit to the Night Market, but hours had gone by and though she was in her merchant robes and ready to depart, Qadir was still not here.

"You seem agitated," Dahlia said with a click of her tongue. "Let me guess: Qadir?"

Loulie scowled. "He's late."

"Isn't he always? You ought to find a timelier bodyguard." She grinned. "Or better yet, a husband to distract you from your business. Someone Qadir will not scare away."

Loulie did not smoke shisha, but in that moment, she wanted nothing more than to steal the pipe from Dahlia's hands and blow smoke in her face. They'd had this conversation many times. Loulie always gave Dahlia the same answer.

"I would rather marry a dust-covered relic than a man," they said in unison.

Loulie flushed. Dahlia grinned. "Yes, yes, I know. If only you had better suitors, eh? Maybe if you dismissed your bodyguard when you met with them..."

"Never. I'd much rather leave the rejections to him."

They shared a laugh at this, and the tension in Loulie's shoulders eased. For the briefest of moments, she was tempted to tell Dahlia the truth—that there *was* a man in Dhyme she had feelings for, against her better judgment. But Ahmed's name was a knot in her throat. She had managed to avoid thinking about him for the past few weeks; the last thing she needed was for Dahlia to ask pointed questions about their relationship.

Thankfully, she was spared the turmoil of untangling her complicated feelings for him when the door opened and Qadir entered. He dipped his head. "Dahlia."

Dahlia smiled fondly. "Brute."

"You're late." Loulie held back a sigh of relief as she stood. The bag of infinite space hung off one of her shoulders, and she had draped a glittering shawl over her head and lined her eyes with kohl. Now she pulled the shawl around her face, concealing everything but her eyes.

"But now I am here," he said. "Shall we go?"

"We shall." She wafted smoke away as she strode toward the door.

Dahlia rose from her cushion on the floor. "Are you sure you don't want to stay for Old Rhuba's stories?" She crossed her bulky arms. "He's missed you, you know. You make a very good shill in the audience."

Loulie thought of Yousef, the starry-eyed man with a passion for stories. "I believe there will be a man here who would be more than happy to steal that honor." She was actually a little regretful she couldn't stay to talk with him. It would have been much easier to pry his secrets from him face-to-face.

Dahlia raised a brow. "Is he handsome, this man?"

"I was too distracted by his horrendously baggy clothing to notice, I'm afraid."

Dahlia sighed. "You only ever have eyes for shiny things, don't you?"

"Because I can trade shiny things for gold."

As she turned and walked away, Dahlia called after her. "If you see him again, give Rasul my greetings. He may be ugly, but he has some of the most desirable goods on the market."

It clicked in Loulie's mind then: why Rasul had looked so familiar. He, like her, was a merchant of the Night Market. She'd probably passed his stall many times without realizing.

She and Qadir returned to the wine cellar, where they opened and entered a trapdoor hidden between casks of wine that led into Madinne's underground tunnels. Years ago, Dahlia's father, Adnan, had built these tunnels with a group of like-minded criminals. He'd constructed what was now the Night Market, an underground souk where precious, illegal goods were sold away from the watchful gaze of the sultan. After her father's passing, Dahlia had taken over the business.

Loulie withdrew the glowing orb from her bag and used it to light their way through the tunnels. Some led out of the city and had been used by fleeing criminals. But she did not know those paths; she knew only the way to the underground market.

Turns later, Qadir started humming. He did that sometimes to fill the silence. When he was in a particularly good mood, he sang. It was always the same song about a king who traveled the world looking for his lost love. She'd heard it enough to know the lyrics by heart.

The stars, they burn the night
And guide the sheikh's way.

Go to her, go to her, they say,
The star of your eye.
Go to her, go to her,
The compass of your heart . . .

Loulie coughed. "What news from the souk?"

Qadir stopped humming. "Mostly, it was the same rumors about the increase in jinn attacks. I overheard many ridiculous stories about jinn spiriting people away to the Sandsea."

"The jinn hunters do love to embellish their propaganda, don't they?"

Qadir grunted. "It seems to be in their nature."

They turned another corner. Not too far away, Loulie saw the bright red lanterns that marked the tunnel leading into the Night Market. "Any mention of killers in black?"

Qadir shook his head. Loulie stifled a groan. If only she had been able to speak with the shadow jinn longer. She wondered, vaguely, if there was a way to summon her.

"There was one more thing." Qadir's voice cut through the din of her thoughts. "You remember the relic Rasul mentioned on the *Aysham*? I was able to gather that the sultan is searching for some priceless treasure, but none of the rumors specified what it was."

"We couldn't just command the compass to lead us to 'that thing the sultan wants'?"

A faint smile touched Qadir's lips. "I'm afraid not. We need to know what it is."

"And yet the compass manages to guide you to something as vague as 'your destiny'?"

His smile widened as he strode ahead of her. "Only because I have a special connection to it. I know the jinn who enchanted it."

Loulie scowled at his back. She did not see the correlation, but she would let it pass. Qadir was made up of small secrets—they both were. So long as his secrets didn't harm her, she was content to let him keep them.

She followed after him, and it was not long before the tunnel opened into a spacious cavern lit by multicolored lanterns. Beneath the lights was a cluttered landscape of canopied stalls. Though it was small in comparison to the Madinne souk, the goods hawked here in the Night Market were a hundred times more valuable. Here, merchants set up stalls in gemstone-lined alcoves and advertised rare artisan products beneath painted signs written in elaborate cursive. Intricately designed plush rugs, beautiful blades created from brass and bone and glass, ceramics crafted by famous western artists—it was an impressive assortment of imported goods, to be sure, but nothing near as precious as what she brought to the market.

Loulie knew this. It was why she smiled like a crook every time she visited.

But no one could see that smirk beneath her scarf as she wound her way through the cramped thoroughfares, edging her way past rowdy customers who gave her a wide berth when they noticed Qadir. Though she was the one with the reputation, everyone in the underground souk knew of her so-called mysterious bodyguard. Though rumors still circulated about Qadir, Loulie was glad they had died down in recent years. It had been a profoundly uncomfortable experience to listen to customers guess at their relationship to her face.

Qadir had put an end to the initial speculation when an especially brazen customer had approached their stall to ask how much coin Qadir had offered Loulie for her bridal price. The jinn had looked him dead in the eye and said, *My* employer *is not a commodity to be bought.*

Qadir was many things—business partner, guardian, friend— but husband would never be one of them. Even just the thought made Loulie shudder. Qadir wasn't family, not exactly, but he was something like it. She cast a look over her shoulder and grinned when she saw him glaring warily at the crowds. His frown deepened when he saw her staring. "What are you smiling at?"

"Nothing. I'm just grateful for your glower, which strikes fear into the hearts of men."

Qadir's expression softened. "Oh? Your *smile* strikes fear into the hearts of men."

"Ah, but not so much fear they hesitate to open their wallets." She waved a finger at him. "That's the important thing."

Qadir's only response was a long-suffering sigh. He trailed quietly behind her as she turned into another alley of shops. She made her way to an empty stall wedged between two others. Behind one stood a young man selling bundles of expensive shisha; his visage was foggy behind the smoke he blew out in large rings. The other was managed by an old man who sold rare, foreign coins that had been stacked in neat columns behind glass cases.

The young man lowered his pipe and gaped at her, eyes wide enough to catch flies. "Midnight Merchant," he said in awe.

The old man cackled. "What did I do to deserve you setting up shop next to me, Loulie al-Nazari?"

"Well, salaam to you too, sadiqi." Loulie grinned as she began to set up her stall.

The young man looked between them, confused.

The old merchant shook his head. "Get close enough to a star and it burns you, boy."

"You exaggerate." With some assistance from Qadir, Loulie mounted their treasures on the shelves. "I only burn those who get in the way of good business." She smirked as she set the magic orb down on the counter and tapped it with her hand.

"Magic," the young man whispered as it brightened beneath her touch.

It was not long before marketgoers gathered to eye the merchandise. Earlier, Dahlia had said Rasul had some of the most sought-after merchandise in the market. Loulie didn't know what he sold, but she knew *her* goods were superior. The relics she gathered were extremely rare; a traveler would be extraordinarily lucky to come across *one* in their lifetime.

But she had a compass that could lead her to anything—including stray magic.

And she was the only one who dared ignore the sultan's relic-selling ban, which meant her bravery was rewarded. With coin.

At some point, Qadir stepped away from the merchandise to

stand behind her and look intimidating. His stare was both focused and all-encompassing; no one ever dared purloin a relic beneath his watchful gaze.

Finally, when all the objects were placed, Loulie announced the opening of her business. The crowds flocked to her stall like hungry pigeons, prodding and testing the magic with greedy hands. The young merchant watched from his stall with a mixture of awe and envy.

Loulie raised her hands and wiggled her fingers at him. "Magic," she whispered.

9

MAZEN

The night after the run-in with the jinn, the sultan hosted an impromptu feast to which he invited various court politicians. The palace diwan was decorated in rich reds and golds and made ready for fifty guests. The best dancers and musicians were called to perform, and delicacies from all over the sultanate were prepared. It was an extravagant celebration. All the guests were clearly enjoying themselves.

Except for Mazen, who was miserable.

He'd promised to be at Dahlia bint Adnan's tavern tonight, and yet here he was, mingling with people wearing fake smiles. It was an effort to keep his own false smile affixed when, on the inside, he was screaming.

Gatherings in the diwan were always a grand affair, but tonight's celebration was even more of a show. Because no royal gathering was complete without gifts, some of the invited politicians had decided to compete with each other by bringing expensive offerings. The sultan, naturally, had displayed them to show his appreciation. The cluster of flower-shaped lanterns hanging above Mazen's head was new, as were the gem-embedded brocade curtains framing the windows. An enormous glass plaque featuring spiraling golden lines—the guest had claimed it was a depiction of the royal courtyard—hung behind

the half stage, and small but intricate tapestries with the sultan's legacy written on them had been hung on the walls.

Even just gazing upon the lavish gifts made Mazen tired. He
glanced sullenly down at his plate, which was piled high with lamb
and fattoush and tabbouleh. He had barely touched his food; he was
too busy mulling over the engagement he was missing. Restless, he
looked past the crowds gathered at the low-rising table and to the
windows. The courtyard seemed to glow, the white roses sparkling
beneath the moonlight. *Like jinn blood*, he thought dully. But of
course the courtyard would sparkle like jinn blood; it had sprung
from it.

He turned away, nauseated. How many jinn had been bled out
on that once-barren soil so that they could live this life of luxury?
Though Mazen did not have any memories of his father's victims,
he was still overwhelmed with guilt when he took part in indulgent
celebrations like this. It was hard not to think of all the lives lost in
that garden. Of the jinn that had been slaughtered by his brother,
and of the women his father had killed.

Murderers, both of them. *And family*, he reminded himself dutifully, with a heavy heart.

He realized Hakim was staring at him from the other side of
the table, brows lowered. *Are you all right?* the look said. Mazen
responded with what he hoped was a reassuring smile. Hakim did
not look convinced. But before he could voice his concerns, he was
pulled into conversation by one of the sultan's councillors, a kindly
man who always complimented Hakim on his maps. He was one of
the only court officials who treated Hakim with respect.

Only a few spaces down, the head of the council—the sultan's
ancient-looking wazir—sat watching the conversation with blatant
displeasure. Mazen did not like the man, but then, he did not like
many of the councillors. He was glad his interactions with them
were mostly limited to these gatherings.

He was uninterested in eavesdropping on Hakim's conversation and was relieved when a distraction presented itself. The lanterns above them dimmed, and he turned his attention to a pair of

performers mounting the stage with flaming swords. Golden coins and trinkets hung from their silk clothing, winking like stars as they ascended the darkened stairs. They were a captivating sight, and yet—Mazen found his eyes wandering, unbidden, to the jagged shadows they cast.

His stomach knotted with nerves. *You are safe. The jinn would never come here.*

He had tried to reassure himself of this last night as well, but to no avail. He'd barely slept for fear that the shadows in his room would choke him when he closed his eyes.

"Why the long face, akhi? I thought you enjoyed decadent celebrations." Mazen startled as Omar slid onto the recently vacated cushion beside him. "Could you perhaps have had other plans?" He leaned forward. "Maybe you were thinking of going to a certain tavern to see a certain storyteller?"

Mazen's mouth went dry. He had not brought up his plans to anyone, not even Hakim. So Omar could not have known unless...

"How long were you spying on me?"

"I have better things to do with my time than spy on you. You simply underestimate the skill of the ears I have in the souk." Omar paused to watch the female performer twirl a flaming sword above her head. "Honestly, it is a good thing you're not at the tavern tonight. Father has already set his plan in action, after all."

Mazen stopped mindlessly poking at his fattoush and looked up. "Plan?"

"His plan to find the Midnight Merchant." When Mazen simply stared at him, Omar smiled and said, "The sultan has learned from an invaluable source that there is a secret entrance to the illegal underground market in Dahlia bint Adnan's tavern. The Midnight Merchant will be there."

A secret entrance? Did Old Rhuba know about this? Did Layla? These were questions he couldn't ask Omar, *wouldn't* ask Omar. "What does Father plan on doing?" he asked instead.

Omar raised a brow. "Worried for your woman, are you?"

"She's not *my* woman—" Too late, Mazen realized his mistake.

Omar chuckled. "Ah, so you did go out to see her?"

"I didn't..." The stage, wrapped in so many shadows, began to blur. Mazen felt his eyelids droop, his shoulders slouch. He reached for the threads of his consciousness, only for them to snap beneath his fingers. The present faded. There was just darkness. Ruby-red eyes. A soft, lulling voice. *I would chase you to the ends of the world if that were what it took.*

"You look a little flushed, akhi." Omar's voice was strangely distant. "Have you had too much wine?"

Mazen gripped the edge of the table. He was vaguely aware of how warm his fingers—his iron rings—were. The world became a haze of muted color.

"Could it be that you're angry at me? What have I done to deserve your ire?"

Mazen did not *want* to be terrified of his brother. But how could he not be? His brother was a cold-blooded murderer. He had killed jinn and *killed her lover. He was a monster and she wanted nothing more than to gouge out his eyes and...* Mazen blinked.

His mind was... foggy.

"Ah, I know why you are mad. You are frustrated by your incompetence." Omar was looking right at him, expression solemn. Mazen was overcome with the sudden, violent urge to attack him. "You're a coward," Omar continued. "You are too scared to speak your mind, so you hide in shadows. You bottle up your anger and let it consume you."

Mazen glanced at Omar's shadow. It was a good shadow, he thought. Much better than its owner. He glanced at his own shadow, which inexplicably had eyes—slits of pale moonlight.

Omar was still talking. "So, what will you do?"

Mazen thought of his father and his curfews, of Layla and the shadow jinn and *of the hunter stabbing her beloved, over and over and over again. When he was done, he turned to her and said, "I never knew jinn were such cowards." He laughed as she struggled against the iron chains he had used to bind her. Tears clouded her eyes as she looked at the vibrant green space where her husband's body had been.*

I will find you, hunter, *she thought.* Even if it takes me years. Even if I have to cross the whole damned world. *She had never been so certain of anything in her life.*

"Ah," Omar said. His voice sounded as if it were coming from the depths of the ocean. "I had my suspicions, but it seems you really *were* hiding in my brother's shadow."

Distantly, Mazen was aware of his legs shifting, his heart pounding, his head throbbing. But he observed these things from a distance. His body was numb, all senses dulled except for his sight. And then even his vision blurred, and all he saw was Omar. Omar, looking at him with murder in his eyes. Omar, gripping a knife he'd slid out from his sleeve.

Mazen smiled a smile that was not his. "I promised I would find you, murderer."

Everything that happened next was a shade darker than his worst nightmare. His vision expanded until he was looking at the whole diwan. He had not one eye, but many, all of them hidden in the darkness around him. His ringed fingers were suddenly cold, but every other part of his body was unbearably hot, as if fire ran through his veins. Someone was saying his name—"Mazen, Mazen, Mazen"— but he did not respond. Could not respond. He lifted a heavy hand.

And called the shadows to him.

They sighed and hissed as they stretched toward him, blotting out moonlight, devouring flame, and cackling with pleasure as the humans began to scream.

Mazen turned to Omar and smiled. *I have won*, he thought. *Even a heartless hunter would not attack his own brother.*

Mazen flicked his wrist, and the nearest shadow shoved Omar to his knees, grabbed his knife, and held it to his throat. Even then, the hunter had the audacity to laugh. "You would go so far as to possess my brother for revenge, jinn? You truly are a coward."

Mazen's rage was a tangible thing. It made even his shadows quiver with fear.

"A coward that will have her revenge," he said softly. "Goodbye, hunter."

He snapped his fingers, and the shadows lunged.

10

LOULIE

"I'll pay you fifty gold coins for it."

The young man who had been eyeing the eternal hourglass finally stepped in front of Loulie's stall. In his hand he held a bag of coins. Presumably fifty of them.

Loulie made a show of eyeing the bag, then the hourglass. The man stared at her, ignoring the murmurs of the crowd. Loulie counted down in her head, waiting.

Sure enough, another man, this one significantly more marked by time, stepped in and raised a bag of coins that was, presumably, heavier. "Sixty," he said.

And so it starts. Loulie was glad for her shawl, for it hid her devious smile.

She loved bartering, but more than that, she loved watching customers argue amongst themselves. It was even more amusing when they fought over useless magic like the hourglass. When she and Qadir had first found the relic in a den of ghouls, she had thought it might reverse time or perhaps slow it down.

"No," Qadir had said in response to her speculation. "It just endlessly refills."

"We battled our way through a horde of ghouls for this? It's worthless!"

Qadir had just raised his brows and said, "You should know by now that magic will sell simply because it is magic."

He was right. The bid was finalized at 120 coins.

The hourglass was the last thing she sold that night. Now that she'd met her personal quota, she was eager to see if she could catch one of Old Rhuba's stories. If she was lucky, Yousef would be there.

"You're smiling," Qadir said warily.

She finished packing up the last of the relics and hefted the bag of infinite space over her shoulder. "Aren't *you* excited to hear the stories about Dhahab?"

Qadir snorted. "Hardly. You humans make up the most ridiculous tall tales."

"What do you expect us to do? It's not as if any of us have been there." Loulie kept her eyes out for Rasul as they walked through the souk. She was curious about his merchandise. "And," she added pointedly, "*you* won't tell me anything about it."

Qadir shrugged. "I am no storyteller."

She rolled her eyes. "Kalam farigh. You don't need to be a storyteller to tell me about your home." Dhahab was another one of Qadir's many secrets. He never went into any detail about it; it had taken him long enough to tell her he was *from* the great jinn city.

"You want to know more about Dhahab? It has sand and sun and jinn."

Loulie smiled; she couldn't help it. "Oh, I feel so enlightened."

"As you should be." Qadir looked dangerously close to a smile himself.

They turned down a bend in the pathway and came into the heart of the souk, where the most experienced merchants sold their goods. Loulie knew most of these people by name and had bartered with them before, offering magic for tools. This was where she had acquired Qadir's shamshir, trading a relic—a glass filled with fire that sparked to life at a single touch—for the blade.

She eyed the smith's shop in passing, noting the array of swords and knives hanging on the mounted wooden boards. The dagger Qadir had given *her* was not nearly as ornate as any of the weapons on that display, but she could not imagine replacing it. Her hand went to a hidden pocket in her robe, where she could feel the shape of the enchanted blade.

Small but lethal, she thought. And then she remembered her encounter with the shadow jinn and grimaced. The next time she was in a fight, she would make sure she did not lose.

The two of them had still not found Rasul as they approached the outskirts, but Loulie was unconcerned. There would be more opportunities to find him before they left for the desert. For tonight, she was done with the souk.

She was approaching the entrance when she heard the shouts. The same call, rising and rising in a panicked crescendo that made her vision darken with fear.

"Rat!" they cried. "Rat in the souk!"

Someone had revealed the location of the market to the sultan's guard.

The alarm went up at once, crashing through the market like a tidal wave. From there, the pandemonium swelled. Loulie heard the hiss of metal and the fleeing footsteps of merchants and customers. They came in droves, pushing her in too many directions at once. Someone stepped on her foot—hard—and she nearly toppled. Qadir grabbed her before she hit the ground.

"We need to move." His voice was soft but firm, an anchor in the chaos.

Loulie sharpened her fear into a plan. There were many entrances to the souk. If these were the sultan's men, they had likely come from an entrance closer to the noble quarter. "We leave the way we came," she said.

Qadir nodded. He took the lead so as to shield her against the surging crowds, which grew more frantic by the moment. Loulie spotted one of the sultan's men amidst the chaos, struggling to capture a woman in dark blue robes. He'd just grabbed her arm when a man rushed him from behind and knocked him to the ground. "Get off my wife!"

The woman screamed as her husband grappled with the guard. And then—

The glimmer of a sword. A splash of crimson. The husband fell, gripping his injured arm. The guard regained his footing, holding a sword dripping with the man's blood. He turned and caught her gaze. His eyes widened, but before he could say anything, Qadir rammed an elbow into his head and knocked him unconscious.

Loulie stumbled back. *They're looking for me.* She knew it with certainty then. Knew it was the reason they had tried to capture the woman in blue.

"They have the area secured." Qadir pointed, and Loulie followed his gesture to the entrance they had come from. Guards had already congregated, blocking the way out. "What's your plan, Loulie?"

She pressed a fist to her forehead. *Think. You've gotten out of scuffles with ghouls! With jinn! Think!* But with jinn and ghouls, she could solve her problems with a blade. In this situation, there were repercussions for assault.

A call rose from the center of the souk, not far from where they stood. "Midnight Merchant, the sultan summons you!" The voice had the deep, booming quality of thunder. "Step forward, or we shall burn this place and everyone in it to the ground!"

Everyone was looking at her now. An older man lurched forward to grab her, but Qadir shoved him back before he could touch her. He looked at her expectantly, urgently. She knew that if she commanded him to find a way out, he would. He would burn a path if it was necessary. But then what? She could not run for long. This was the sultan's city.

She squeezed her eyes shut. The people around her knew the dangers of the illegal market. She had no reason to give herself up for any of them. And yet . . .

I will not let anyone die for me.

"Loulie?" This close, Qadir's eyes shimmered gold, as if a fire had ignited in them.

She tapped the knife hidden in her pocket. "Find me."

Qadir hesitated. When he glanced at the bag on her shoulder, she shook her head and mouthed the word *Insurance.* She was not the Midnight Merchant without her relics, after all.

The two of them looked at each other for a long moment before the threat came again. Slowly, Qadir retreated into the crowds. Loulie took a deep breath and continued forward. The crowds parted without a command.

The sultan's guards stood at the center of the souk in a half circle with Dahlia bint Adnan in the middle. Despite the fact that her shawl was in tatters and her long black hair was in disarray, she still looked every inch the proud tavernkeeper. She appeared just as surprised to see Loulie as Loulie was to see her.

For a few moments, the two stared at each other. Then, quietly, Dahlia pressed her lips together and stepped aside. Loulie approached the guards, hands raised.

"You wanted to see me?"

It was an effort to keep herself from fighting back as they pulled the bag of infinite space off her shoulder and shackled her hands behind her back. The raid leader, the man with the booming voice, watched the proceedings stoically.

Loulie glared at him. "So this is how the sultan treats those he summons?"

He laughed. "I can assure you he has nothing but the utmost respect for you, Midnight Merchant. If he did not, you and all your criminal friends would already be burned to cinders." He turned and barked orders at his men. When the way was cleared, the guards led Loulie back through the crowds and up toward the moonlit world.

She cast one final look back at Dahlia. The tavernkeeper put a hand to her chest and bowed. *Good luck*, she mouthed. Loulie held tight to those words, useless as they were.

—※—

Blessedly, the souk aboveground was empty, the lanterns snuffed out, which meant there were barely any citizens around to witness her public humiliation. Every once in a while, shutters snapped open and people peered through their windows at her. When they did, Loulie made sure they saw her with her head held high. She was the only woman in a sea of men, and she did not intend to look frail or pathetic. Never mind that she *felt* frail and pathetic.

They led her through the streets to the sultan's palace, which, at this time of night, glowed with a wraithlike quality, the red roses winding up the walls resembling bloody wounds. The courtyard inside was just as beautiful and terrible. Loulie felt ill as she gazed upon the unnatural white roses and the trees heavy with fruit, knowing they had been born of jinn blood. Everywhere she looked she saw excessive finery: sconces shaped like sunflowers, a fountain of twirling glass dancers, a garden hedged in by towering topiaries.

She was filled with disgust. *How many jinn were killed to make this immortal garden?*

They led her to a set of elaborate double doors, where a dozen soldiers crowded the corridor, yelling at each other while a bearded man in a turban—no doubt the qaid—barked orders. "What are you, cowards? We do not need the prince's thieves. Get in there!"

"The jinn will kill us before we even raise our swords!"

"What of Prince Mazen!"

Loulie stared at the doors, perplexed. *A jinn? No...*

The raid leader strode ahead and demanded an explanation. Apparently, Prince Mazen had been possessed by a jinn and was wreaking havoc in the diwan. None of the guests could escape, and every soldier who entered had yet to return.

Loulie's mind whirled with speculation. Was it the shadow jinn? Was the hunter the jinn had been searching for here? Was it *Omar*?

She cleared her throat. "Excuse me."

The qaid and the raid leader paused to look at her. "Midnight Merchant," the qaid said coolly. He glanced at the soldier beside her, at the bag of infinite space he carried. The moment he reached for it, Loulie instinctively stepped in front of him.

"Keep your hands off my bag. If you use my relics without paying for them"—she glowered at him—"you will be cursed to a slow and painful death."

The qaid unceremoniously shoved her out of the way.

Loulie whirled to face him as the guards grabbed her from

behind. "Try it, why don't you? I'm the only one who knows how to use the magic in that bag. I alone can use those relics to save your sultan and his sons."

She cringed when the qaid gave her a hard look. She was a damned fool! The sultan had nearly burned down a market to capture her, and now she was going to help him? But—Madinne would collapse without him. And Madinne was still home.

Besides, this would force the sultan into her debt.

The qaid relented, but the guards kept their weapons out and in sight as they unbound her hands. She reached into her bag to withdraw the orb, which she would need to navigate the darkness, then slid Qadir's knife from her pocket and headed for the doors. The night had gone deadly quiet, and the only sound was the tapping of her pointed slippers on the floor.

At the doors, she faltered, wondering if she could do this without Qadir. Last time, she had nearly suffocated to death. She shook the thought from her head.

This time, things will be different. This time, I'm ready.

She gripped her knife and stepped into the dark.

11

LOULIE

The first thing Loulie saw when she entered the diwan was…nothing. The darkness was so complete it swallowed even the swaths of moonlight that ought to have illuminated the chamber. She was seized by the sudden urge to flee, even if it meant rushing back into the arms of her captors. She wasn't a hero. She was simply a merchant with a knife and a glowing orb. What chance did she stand against a jinn who wielded shadows as a weapon?

But the doors slammed shut before she could retreat. She had just a few moments to panic before some invisible weight pushed down on her shoulders and forced her to the ground. Then her panic gave way to desperation, and she reacted on instinct, pressing her hands to the orb until it was bright enough to bring to light the invisible force.

She saw shadows. Strange, limb-like things that withdrew with a shriek when the light touched them. She stumbled to her feet as they shrank back, revealing the room that had been hidden moments before. Men and women squinted against the light and stared at her as if in a trance. The closer she drew to them, the more aware of their surroundings they seemed to become, until their eyes lit up with fear.

"Look out!" a man cried, and Loulie barely managed to turn in time to face the shadow shooting toward her. The moment it reached the light, it shivered and retreated. All around her, the darkness rippled and whispered.

When she turned toward the man who had warned her, she saw nothing. The darkness had again engulfed everything and everyone.

"Jinn!" Loulie held the orb up. The darkness barely pulled back. "Where are you, jinn?"

A laugh echoed behind her. A man's laugh. "You did not learn your lesson the first time, human girl?" He stepped into the darkness. Though Loulie had never seen him in person, she knew immediately that it had to be Prince Mazen, for he was dressed in fine, rich clothing.

He shifted on his feet, and the shadows beneath him slowly stretched toward her, bleeding into the light. She stepped back. Once, twice, until she was walking backward, trying to put as much distance between herself and the possessed prince as possible. "Have you come again to 'convince' me?" The prince held out his arms, and the shadows surged forward, nipping at her heels. "You have no power here."

She took another step back. Another and another—until she felt the cold press of the wall against her back. Prince Mazen drew close enough for her to make out his features. She saw his eyes—and stopped. She knew those eyes. The last time she'd seen them, they had been filled with innocent wonder.

"Yousef?"

The prince stopped in front of her. She thought she saw something pass over his face—fear or regret—before he smiled and said, "Yousef no more."

"He's not the one you want," Loulie said with forced calm. Her hand was shaking, and it made the light quiver on the walls. "I told you before: he's not a hunter."

"No," the jinn wearing the prince's skin said. "He is not. He is, in fact, inconsequential."

Inconsequential. The word was a strike of flint against her dark memories.

Loulie remembered her father, starry-eyed and full of laughter. Her mother, with her sly smiles and warm hugs. She remembered a knife against her throat, a man with a serpentine smile. *You are all inconsequential*, he had said.

Loulie breathed out softly. She forced herself to look into the prince's eyes. "No life is inconsequential." She didn't know whom she was speaking to anymore. She only hoped that whoever it was would see the truth in her words.

"Oh?" the prince said dryly.

A strange thing happened then. The darkness in the room abated, giving way to a dusky gray. Loulie heard the shouts of an audience that had moments ago been trapped in the dark. She saw the prince quiver like a leaf in the wind, then collapse to his knees with a gasp.

His shadow rose up from the ground. It sharpened itself into a blade.

The world suddenly seemed too fast, and she, too slow. She cried out a warning, but the prince's movements were sluggish. He looked up. Recognition flashed through his eyes.

And then the shadow stabbed him through the chest, and his eyes went wide with pain.

He collapsed silently to the ground as the shadow pulled back. Crimson pooled on the floor beneath him, and it seemed to Loulie that it was the only color in the room.

"I told you." The jinn's voice was everywhere and nowhere. "He is inconsequential."

Loulie could feel the jinn watching her from the shadows, but she could not stop staring at the prince, willing him to move.

He did not.

Loulie heard screaming, but the sound seemed to come from a great distance. She did not realize the source of it until the sultan rushed to his son's side and collapsed to his knees. He yelled Mazen's name as he took his limp body into his arms.

Loulie could only stare on numbly. *Is this... my fault?*

The jinn lunged at her from the shadows as an angry stream of smoke. She filled Loulie's sight, appearing before her as a crimson-eyed wraith. Loulie swept the blade through the smoky shape, but her knife hissed through empty air.

"You are too softhearted for your own good," the jinn said softly. "How will you seek revenge on the assassins in black with such a fragile heart?"

Loulie swung the blade wildly through the air. With every motion, she became aware of a familiar burning sensation in her lungs. She did not care. She kept slicing and screaming until her body was shaking with fatigue. Memories of blood and stars and corpses flashed before her eyes. *I am not fragile*, she thought. *I am not fragile. I am not fragile.*

But the shadows were persistent. They grabbed her arms and legs and threw her to the ground. There was a loud crack, and the light from the orb blinked and died. The room went a nightmare pitch black. Loulie scratched at the ground. Grasped her knife with numb fingers. She wouldn't die here; she *refused* to die here—

GET UP. A deep voice, familiar as her own heartbeat, thudded through her mind.

Loulie gasped and opened her eyes. She saw Qadir's knife lying beside her, blazing with blue fire. Red eyes blinked at her from the blade's surface.

I found you, Qadir said.

The flames on the blade snapped gently at her fingers, urging her into action. Loulie drew slowly to her feet. She spared a glance at the orb, which lay shattered on the floor, then faced the jinn, who stared at her with wide eyes.

"Impossible." The jinn stepped back. "That blade—how did you get that blade?"

Move, Qadir said, and though he was not in the room with her, his magic—his *presence*—gave her the confidence to act. Loulie tore at the darkness until she cleared a path, and then she fell on the shadow jinn with her blade.

The jinn caught her strike against a wall of solidified shadow. Loulie gritted her teeth against the shock of the impact. She tightened her grip on the knife and threw her weight into the stab. The fire coating the blade's edge flared, and the obstacle peeled away like burning parchment.

But the jinn had already fled.

Behind you, Qadir snapped.

Loulie whirled just in time to catch the edge of a razor-sharp darkness against her knife. The jinn's glowing eyes flashed with surprise. It was enough of an opening for Loulie to change her deflection into a parry and throw her opponent off balance. The jinn withdrew, breathing heavily. She wasn't a warrior, Loulie realized. Just a puppeteer trying to command wild magic.

Good. The fire on her blade cackled, as if with amusement. *That makes two of us.*

They fought—fire against shadows, dark barriers against flaming dagger—until the flaming knife charred away the jinn's magic bit by bit and the room's color returned. The shadow jinn fell back, her body flickering in and out like a dying flame.

But though she was fading, Loulie could tell she was not wounded. The fire could make her disappear, but it could not kill her. The jinn, reduced to nothing but a faint shape in the moonlight, began to disappear into the walls. It was exactly like what had happened in the place of worship. Loulie hesitated. The blade grew warm in her hands.

But before she could decide whether to pursue, she was distracted by a wink of silver in the dark. A sharp, glimmering object that shot past her head and caught the jinn in the chest. She released an agonized, bloodcurdling scream that made the air tremble.

Loulie spun to search for the attacker. She froze when she saw Omar bin Malik striding out of the gloom. He flashed a smile as he brushed past her toward the vanishing jinn, who had solidified into a beautiful woman with rivers of darkness streaming down her back. Blood dribbled down her lips when she coughed. "You..." She gasped when Omar pulled out the knife. "Impossible." The jinn staggered away. "You—I *killed* you!"

Omar's grin was a feral flash of teeth. "You, kill the King of the Forty Thieves? What a conceited notion."

Loulie glanced at him. At the strange black knife. *He made her tangible. But how?*

The shadow jinn attempted to flee, but she was too slow.

Omar stabbed her. Again and again and again. Until her screams faded and died.

Loulie turned away and closed her eyes. She knew, even without looking, that the jinn's body would crumble to dust and her blood would seep into the tiles and coax nature into being where there had been none before.

"Get out!" Her eyes shot open at the sultan's command. "All of you, *out*!"

Both guests and guards fled the room, stumbling toward the doors as if they'd just woken from a dream. Loulie remained. Now that everyone had left, she could see the sultan again. He and a young man with hazel eyes leaned over a bloodied Prince Mazen.

The fire in her blade disappeared as she ventured a step forward.

"Omar!" The sultan didn't even see her. "What are you doing, boy? The blood!"

Prince Omar turned stiffly toward the dead jinn. Loulie watched as he sliced off one of his sleeves and soaked it in jinn blood. Understanding flared within her as he crouched beside Prince Mazen and squeezed the fabric over his brother's fatal wound. When Prince Mazen began to struggle, the sultan and the hazel-eyed man held him down. This process was repeated until the prince's wound was sealed and he lay limp on the floor. Unconscious, but not dead.

The Elixir of Revival, the masses called it. *The miracle of jinn blood*, Loulie thought. Her stomach twisted with revulsion. And relief.

The sultan pressed his forehead to his son's. The hazel-eyed man—Hakim, the bastard prince, Loulie realized—clasped his shaking hands together in prayer. But Omar was not looking at Mazen or the rest of his family. He was looking at *her*. He never looked away, not even when he called the qaid to remove her from the room. Outside, she reflected that it was not his gaze that had been disarming, but the anger darkening his eyes.

12

MAZEN

Mazen dreamed he was being stabbed to death by his brother. He was in the palace diwan, and the room was empty of people save for Omar, who stalked toward him with a black knife. Mazen held up his hands. He begged. He screamed. But there was no compassion in Omar's eyes, just a terrible, all-encompassing hatred. He stabbed Mazen in the throat. In the chest. Again and again and again and...

Mazen woke in a panic, heart tight and body trembling. The minute he opened his eyes, sunlight assaulted his senses. He shrank back with a groan. There was a voice and footsteps and then hands leaning him back against his pillows.

"Shh, sayyidi. You are safe."

It was a voice Mazen recognized. *Karima?* Sure enough, when he looked up, his personal servant stood over him. Her thick brown hair was tied into a bun, and there was a wan smile on her face. "Welcome back to the world of the living, sayyidi."

Mazen balked at the tears in her brown eyes. "Karima, why are you crying?"

"Because you are alive."

Alive? He glanced down at his uncovered chest and froze when he saw the huge gash marring the skin above his heart. "Karima." His voice was faint. "When did that get there?"

Even when Karima filled him in on what had happened, he could not piece together the memory of the incident. He remembered wanting revenge on his brother for a reason he could no longer recall. He remembered darkness and pain. He remembered the Midnight Merchant standing in a doorway and holding up what looked like a bloated star. And he remembered a word—*inconsequential*—and the sensation of falling into his own body.

How could he *not* remember almost dying? According to Karima, the only ones who'd been there to witness his revival were the sultan, his brothers, and—

"The Midnight Merchant." He sat up abruptly. A sharp ache shot through his chest, making his vision go spotty. Mazen exhaled through clenched teeth as his room became a blur of colors. Karima tutted and tried to get him to lie back down, but he waved her away. "What has the sultan done with the merchant?"

He could still remember the spark of recognition when he'd seen her face in the darkness. Loulie al-Nazari and Layla, the girl from the souk, were one and the same.

Karima shook her head. "The news is that the sultan plans to speak with her over ghada'a. Do not worry, sayyidi; I will deliver the news of your recovery immediately."

"No." The Midnight Merchant had saved him—twice—and now the sultan was going to send her to her death? He would not allow it. Standing was an ordeal, but he forced himself to his feet. Sweat beaded his forehead, and he was breathing hard with exertion, but it was a small price to pay for movement.

Slowly, painstakingly, he made his way over to his closets. "Sayyidi!" Karima set a steadying hand on his shoulder. "I do not understand. Why would you want to see the Midnight Merchant now? You can barely stand! If the sultan finds out I let you leave your rooms—"

"I'll tell him I pushed past you like a rogue camel."

"But your wounds—"

"Already sealed. Why, I didn't even need stitches!" Pain flickered through his chest when he laughed, and he had to take a deep breath to collect himself. Karima bit her lip. Then, after a few moments' hesitation, she began to assist him. She helped him pull a tunic over his head and carefully pin his mother's shawl, and once he was presentable, she walked him to the doors and the guards outside. When the men protested Mazen's leaving, Mazen stood as tall as he could manage under the crippling pain and said, "I am going to see my father, even if I have to crawl my way to his diwan."

The men relented, though they insisted on helping him down the stairs and through the corridors. Everywhere Mazen went, servants stared at him in shock and offered flustered greetings. The corridors had never seemed so long, the sun so bright. But then, at last, they were at the diwan doors. The guards outside eyed him warily.

"Sayyidi," one of them said. "The diwan is changed. Please, watch your footing."

Mazen did not understand his meaning until he stepped inside. He nearly stopped breathing when he saw the plethora of green before him: sage-green leaves and chartreuse pathways of grass and emerald shafts of light that burst through the canopies of trees. Mazen stared at it all in wonder as he navigated his way through the vibrant underbrush. Surrounded by the hum of insects and the twittering banter of birds, he found it impossible to conceive of this place as the diwan. But then he saw the tile buried beneath the grass and the mosaicked walls hidden behind the vines and trees.

If he'd had any doubts about what had transpired last night, they would have vanished then. Here was proof that a jinn had died in this room.

He made his way into the diwan slowly, carefully stepping over roots and shrubs. Eventually, the forest thinned, and he was able to make out people sitting on a rug. There sat his father in an uncharacteristically plain beige thobe and ghutra and, beside him, Omar, wearing simple attire and a belt of daggers. Hakim sat on the sultan's other side, dressed almost entirely in white—the color of prayer. And sitting with her back to him, dressed in dark blue shawls dusted white, was the Midnight Merchant.

His father saw him first. He paused midconversation, visibly paling at the sight of him. "Mazen?" The others turned to look at him, equally stunned. Hakim was the first to rise. He rushed toward Mazen and clapped a gentle hand on his shoulder.

"Akhi, are you okay?" He began to lead Mazen to where the others were gathered. "You should not be out of bed! You..." Hakim stopped, swallowed.

"Almost died?" Mazen's laughter came out a wheeze. "I *do* feel a little like a ghoul."

"Mazen." The sultan's voice was soft. "What are you doing here?"

"You know me, yuba. It has never been in my nature to sit around doing nothing. How could I sit in my stuffy room when you all are enjoying such a pleasant chat in this beautiful forest?" He smiled and tried to bow, but the movement sent pain shooting through his limbs, and it was all he could do to keep himself from collapsing.

"For the love of the gods, *sit*. You do not bow to me when you are injured, child." His father's voice was strained, filled with an emotion that startled Mazen. The last time his father had so openly worn his sentiments on his sleeve, Mazen's mother had just died.

Slowly, gracelessly, Mazen lowered himself to the ground and crossed his legs.

"How are you feeling?" His father's ashy brows were scrunched together. "You've barely had time to recover; you should not be here."

"I am well enough to sit and listen to you speak. Besides." He turned to the Midnight Merchant, whose expression was unreadable. Even though half her face was covered, he recognized her eyes—they reminded him of smothered fire. "I had to thank you in person, Midnight Merchant."

The Midnight Merchant tilted her head slightly. In acknowledgment, perhaps. "I simply did what any able-bodied citizen of Madinne would do." She paused, eyes narrowed. At first, he thought she was remembering him from the souk, that she might mention their perilous first meeting. His heart seized with fear, but she only said, "I am glad for your miraculous recovery."

"Miraculous indeed." Omar's voice was soft but lethal. Mazen felt an inexplicable fear take hold of him as he glanced at his brother.

Omar was not looking at him, though; he was looking at the Midnight Merchant. "But I'm sure you've witnessed the power of jinn blood before, al-Nazari. You sold a vial of it to Rasul al-Jasheen, no?"

Mazen instinctively put a hand to his wound. He felt an awful, sinking weight in his chest at the thought of the shadow jinn's blood being used to knit his body back together.

The Midnight Merchant scoffed. "Rasul—he was the rat?"

The sultan smiled thinly. "Even merchants sworn to secrecy can be bought with the right amount of gold." He leaned forward, hands steepled in his lap. "So tell me, Loulie al-Nazari, what is your price?"

Mazen inhaled sharply. Even Omar raised a brow. The sultan had not extended this generosity to any other person he'd sent on his quest. But then, those men had gone willingly—for glory or out of fear, Mazen was not sure.

"I am not for sale," the merchant said coldly. Mazen flinched at her boldness.

The sultan was unmoved. "A shame. I had hoped to buy your services."

"Do you normally preface your sale transactions by threatening to burn down a souk?"

Omar coughed sharply into his hand to hide a smile. Mazen did not share his amusement. He glanced at his father, whose expression had somehow become even stonier.

"I do if the person I am dealing with is a criminal." He tilted his chin slightly so that Mazen had the impression he was, despite his close proximity, looking down at the merchant. "It is necessary, sometimes, to instill a healthy dose of fear in such people. To remind them that destroying their life would be a simple thing."

A frigid silence followed. Mazen did not realize he'd been holding his breath until the merchant broke the quiet with a sigh. "You want me to search for a relic," she said.

"So you have heard of my venture." He raised a brow. "And what say you? I saw your bag of relics; I know you have some way of locating them. Most travelers would be lucky to come across one relic in their lifetime, but you sell them as if they are sesame dates. If anyone can find the relic I am seeking, it is you."

The Midnight Merchant did not respond, only stared coolly at the sultan as if sizing him up. Though Layla had carried herself with the same pride, there had been a lightheartedness to her. The woman before him now may as well have been made of stone.

At last, she spoke. "The question is not what I gain from this endeavor, but what I will lose if I do not accept."

The sultan smiled. A crooked smile that so reminded Mazen of Omar that it made his heart twist. "Smart woman. You are a citizen of Madinne, and you will do as I command, or openly defy me. And you know what happens to those who defy me."

The air in the diwan became tense.

His father had always had a penchant for violence. He had softened after marrying Mazen's mother, but he was still the man who'd started the jinn hunts after her death and, before her arrival, killed a dozen of his wives without batting an eyelash. Before he'd handed the responsibility over to Omar, he'd been the first murderous King of the Forty Thieves, leading his own companions on jinn-hunting quests. Yes, his father was adept at the art of punishment.

Mazen could never—would never—deny that truth, even when he tried to forget it.

Being stripped of one's titles and exiled to the desert would be the mildest sentence the sultan offered. At worst, he would seek vengeance, and no one could run from him then. He had men all over the desert; there was nowhere to hide.

The sultan spread his hands. "I am generous, however, and wish to pay you. Name a price. Any price. I can make you rich beyond your wildest dreams, al-Nazari."

"Yuba...," Mazen said softly. The sultan's harsh grimace faded when he glanced at him. Mazen cleared his throat and said, "What if this relic *is* impossible to find?"

The sultan scoffed. " 'Impossible' is an excuse offered by failures. No, the relic exists, and I will find it." He looked at Loulie. "*You* will find it."

"And?" She clenched her hands in her lap. "What is this impossible relic I am being forced to find?"

On the sultan's command, Hakim took out a map—the same one he had shown Rasul—and handed it to the sultan. His father unrolled it, found the Western Sandsea, and tapped the sunken jinn city of Dhahab. The merchant inhaled sharply.

"Long ago, the first sultan buried an ancient relic in the Western Sandsea. It is the most powerful relic in the world, for it contains a living, breathing jinn bound to the service of the one who finds it. There is a story passed down in our family, a legend that describes how the relic was created and where it was buried. It is a secret of the royal family, but I will share it with you now in the hope that it will convince you of the truth."

His father had told this story many times now, but never the way Mazen's mother had. She had been a storyteller. *Mazen* was a storyteller, and it always made him anxious to hear his father tell his version with only the barest details.

"Yuba," he said softly. "Please, let me tell the tale."

His father paused. The Midnight Merchant raised her brows. Mazen cringed at the looks on their faces. "The story is in the details, and I know all of them." An impromptu plan was forming in his mind. If he could not openly dissent, then maybe he could convince his father the same way his mother once had.

The sultan agreed, but only once Mazen refreshed himself with food and drink. After eating from a platter of nuts and drinking a glass of water, Mazen straightened, clasped his hands, and spoke in a voice that rose above the sound of the whistling leaves and the chattering birds.

"Father, brothers, Midnight Merchant, allow me to share with you an ancient tale."

The Tale of Amir and the Lamp

Neither here nor there, but long ago...

There once lived a Bedouin sheikh named Amir, who was known for his golden heart and cunning mind. He had a younger brother, a valiant warrior named Ghazi, who was strong of heart and body. Many peaceful years passed under their leadership until one year, there came a Storm Season unlike any other. The winds were so fierce they tore down the tribe's tents, the sun so hot it dried up water and blistered the people's skin.

Journeying had never been so difficult, and the brothers were at a loss for how to provide for their people. Then one day, the tribe chanced upon an ocean of shifting sand and knew they could go no farther, for they had reached the dreaded Sandsea. It was then, staring at that endless expanse of sinking sand, that Amir had an idea.

At moonrise he called his brother to him and said, "Beneath this ever-shifting sand is the world of jinn. Tales have been told of jinn who claw their way out and come to this world for revenge." He patted the small satchel he had brought with him. "It is here that I shall wait to meet with one of those fearsome jinn."

Ghazi, who was perplexed by his brother's plan, said, "What do you hope to gain from speaking with a jinn? It would sooner tear you apart than talk with you!"

Amir only smiled. "The jinn are powerful, but I have the mind to outsmart them. If we are to survive this season, we will have need of their magic."

And so Amir described his plan. He showed Ghazi the items in the satchel—a pair of iron shackles and a simple oil lamp—and told Ghazi he would need three weeks. In the end, Ghazi agreed to lead the tribe through the desert to the Golden Dunes, where they would meet. So it was that the two brothers parted: Ghazi to the dunes and Amir to the edge of the Sandsea, where he waited for days with nothing but a cloak to keep him from burning in the sun.

By the time a jinn emerged, the sheikh was starved and thin. Still, he forced himself to bow as the creature approached. The jinn was seven feet tall with eyes of burning fire and skin like golden sand. Its face morphed with every step—a jackal's one moment and an eagle's the next. It was a thing of such terrible majesty it would have made the bravest of men run for the dunes.

The jinn stopped before Amir with a laugh. "Ho! What is this scrap of a human I see before me? It would be a simple thing to crush you beneath my boot."

Amir responded in a voice made raspy by lack of water. "Oh mighty jinn, I have no reason to beg for my life. The sun has baked my body and weakened my eyes, and I am approaching death's door. But alas, I mourn the life I lived as a hunter. I was well known in the desert. If you gave me a bow and arrow, no creature stood a chance against me."

The jinn thought about this. It debated the merits of killing the man or of forcing him to be its servant. Ultimately, it decided a slave was more useful than a corpse, so it snapped its fingers and conjured a bow and a quiver of arrows for Amir.

"Prove your worth, then," the jinn said. "Become my hunter and I will spare your life. Fail me and I will devour you."

Amir consented, and he and the jinn ventured forth. Amir hunted for the jinn every day, and though he was not as strong as his brother, he had spectacular aim—he had not been lying when he said he could fell most creatures. This was how the jinn came to be reluctantly impressed by its human servant and how, over time, it came to trust him.

"Tell me, oh mighty jinn," Amir said one day. "Why is it that you do not hunt? Surely your eyes are better and your aim truer than mine."

The jinn responded, "We jinn are as mighty as gods! Hunting with tools is beneath us. Why complete tasks even a human can do?"

"And tell me, mighty jinn, what things can you do that a human cannot?"

The jinn laughed and said, "I can perform any feat, no matter how impossible, for I am one of the seven jinn kings, and the power of the world is at my fingertips."

Amir was thoughtful. "Can you make the world move?"

The jinn clapped its hands, and the ground trembled and cracked beneath its feet.

"Can you make the sky scream?"

The jinn whistled, and the wind sliced through the sky and tore the clouds asunder.

"Can you make the clouds cry?"

The jinn sighed, and the clouds above them let loose a torrent of rain.

"You truly are a god, mighty jinn!" Amir exclaimed, and he bowed before it. As the weeks passed, Amir challenged the jinn to other tasks. One day, he said, "I have heard tales that your kind is crippled by iron. Is this true? Can you withstand its burn?" The jinn hesitated, but its pride outweighed its fear, so it told Amir that it could indeed endure the burn of iron. Amir took the shackles from his satchel and dared the jinn to travel with them on its wrists.

The smug jinn allowed this. Immediately after the iron was set on its arms, its legs became heavy as lead and its senses clouded. Yet because it was a proud creature, it only gritted its teeth and said, "You see? I am a king and cannot be defeated by iron."

So the two continued on their travels, and now it was Amir who led the way, for the jinn could barely stand. "Mighty jinn," Amir said one day. "I am useless without your magic. Will you not take off the shackles so you can create fires for us and halt the desert winds?" But the jinn refused to doff the cuffs, thinking that to do so would be a weakness. Instead, it asked Amir if he had any other items in his satchel, and when Amir gave it the oil lamp, the jinn drew runes upon it with its blood, enchanting it. It blew fire into the lamp and told Amir he could capture anything within it—be it fire or wind or water—and command it to obey him with these words: *You are bound to me and you will serve me.*

Over the next few days, Amir tested the limitations of the lamp—he trapped wind and sand and even stars in it. The bottomless lamp fit all manner of things. By the time Amir and the jinn arrived at the Golden Dunes, Amir knew it would work for his plan.

That night, he approached the jinn with the lamp in his hands. The jinn, thinking he meant to release their captive fire, sighed with relief. Instead, Amir held the lamp out and said, "Hear me, mighty jinn. With this lamp I bind you by your own magic. From this day forth you will be my servant as I have been yours, and you will do everything I ask of you." The jinn lurched to its feet and rushed at Amir with fire in its eyes, but Amir was unafraid. *"You are bound to me and you will serve me,"* he said, and the jinn was forced to kneel before him.

The jinn cursed and hissed, but it could not resist when Amir commanded it to follow. Together, they made for the sheikh's camp. Amir's return was celebrated by his tribe, who had feared him dead. He commanded the jinn to procure a grand feast, and the starving tribe ate and drank enough food for three men each. Afterward, when their appetites were sated and everyone was sleeping, Ghazi approached Amir and pointed to the lamp, where the jinn now slumbered.

"Amir, your wit and cunning have indeed brought us great prosperity, but what do you plan to do with the jinn? To abuse its power would be unwise."

Amir shook his head. "Nonsense. I served the jinn for many weeks; now I am forcing it to do the same. Come tomorrow, you will know my plans."

The next day, Amir had the jinn king construct walls to protect the tribe from the fierce winds. Then he ordered it to create a town, one that grew as more and more Bedouin came seeking shelter. The jinn did the work of a hundred men in mere weeks—never before had such a prosperous city been created in so short a time. When the creature was done, Amir commanded it to build a palace so he could watch over his tribe from on high.

The jinn reluctantly constructed a palace from the purest white marble and built minarets so the sheikh could see everything in the desert. When it was done, the palace was the most remarkable building in the land, too grand for even a sheikh, so the people named Amir sultan and begged him to be their ruler. They dubbed the desert metropolis Madinne, and it became a place for trade to flourish. Amir went on to take a wife and have many children, and it was in this way that Madinne's royal bloodline was established.

While Amir ruled from Madinne's golden throne, the jinn plotted behind his back. Ghazi's fears had been correct: a man with too much power was blinded by it. One day, Amir gave the lamp to his wife and told her she could command the jinn while he was away.

Amir did not realize his mistake until he returned from his hunt and found his wife dead. He had forgotten to tell her to be clear in her instructions, and so when she had ordered the jinn to procure a feast, it had poisoned the food. Amir was racked with grief. He locked the jinn in the lamp and gave it to his brother, whom he had made qaid of his military.

"You were right, Ghazi," Amir said with tears in his eyes. "I relied on power, and it destroyed me. We must bury the lamp to keep this tragedy from happening again."

And so saying, he bade his brother to bury the lamp so that none could ever find it. Ghazi rode hard and fast, and when he came to the Sandsea, he threw the lamp into the sinking sand and stayed long enough to watch it vanish.

After mourning his wife, Amir resolved never again to rely on magic, for it had made him greedy. He ruled Madinne until his son took over and then his grandson and so on and so forth. Hundreds of years have passed since Ghazi threw the lamp into the Sandsea. But while humans eventually succumb to death, the jinn are near immortal, and legends say that the mighty jinn king still lies buried in the Sandsea. They say that any who possess the lamp will find the world at their fingertips. But beware, gentle friends, for they also say that death will ghost the footsteps of any who lust after its forbidden power...

13

LOULIE

Mazen bin Malik was a good storyteller. His face was like quicksand, his expression alternating between exuberance and solemnity with envious fluidity. If she'd had any doubts that this was Yousef, they were gone now. The prince was just as starry-eyed when he told stories as when he listened to them.

Loulie did not realize how invested in the tale she was until it ended. For a time, she had felt like a child listening to tales around a campfire. But this was no hearth, and the fantastical legend was not a harmless story. Possibly, it would send her to her death.

She glared at the sultan. "You would have me believe this legendary lamp exists?"

The sultan looked at Hakim, who began unrolling a series of dusty, ancient-looking scrolls. The papyrus was stained, the words scrawled on the scrolls faded with age. Loulie saw slanted letters and dates, and a signature: an alif, followed by a meem, a ya, and a ra. *Amir*.

The sultan gestured toward the documents. "These are the papers that founded our kingdom. In them, Amir writes of the jinn he enslaved. He writes of the items the jinn enchanted for him, and the lamp's burial. And he writes, most importantly, of ways to enter the Sandsea. There are paths, al-Nazari: caves that lead beneath the sand and roads hidden between the waves."

"If others have failed to locate your lamp, what makes you think *I* can find it?" The longer Loulie stared at the scrolls, the tighter her lungs became. She had stood in front of the Sandsea before but never ventured into it. It was a land of no return. Even Qadir, who had traveled up through it once, would not approach it again.

"They were not collectors of ancient relics," the sultan said. "But *you* are."

"Why me?" Loulie insisted. "Why not your son, Prince Omar?" She glanced at the eldest prince and frowned. She had not forgotten their last encounter—the way anger had clouded his eyes when the sultan leaned over Mazen. It had occurred to her that the sultan never asked Omar if *he* was unharmed.

"My son is a hunter, not a tracker." He paused, and the silence had an ominous weight, a foreboding that surrounded them like smoke. Loulie wanted to wave it away, to wave *all* this away like she would a bad dream.

"Omar." The sultan turned to his son, and Omar dipped his head in acknowledgment. "You will accompany the merchant to make sure she does not run from her responsibility."

"What?" She and the prince spoke at the same time.

"I hear you employ a bodyguard, al-Nazari. Think of my son as additional security."

Omar shifted, frowned. "But, yuba, my thieves—"

"I will take over your plans for them." The sultan spoke in a cold voice that brooked no disagreement. A muscle feathered in Omar's face as he clenched his jaw. But Loulie would not be cowed. It was bad enough she was being blackmailed, and now she was being forced to journey with the King of the Forty Thieves? With a *jinn killer*?

"I do not need another bodyguard."

The sultan shook his head. "This is not up for negotiation."

"You do not trust me?"

The sultan scoffed. "Trust a conniving merchant woman? I think not." He leaned forward. "Do not forget, al-Nazari: you are a criminal. I could throw you in the Bowels. I could take away your freedom and put a noose around your neck."

Loulie was trembling. With fear. With anger. Because she knew the sultan did not lie. She had not yet been born when he'd killed his wives in cold blood, but she'd heard the tales. And she'd seen him sentence people to imprisonment in the Bowels for lesser crimes.

She had never felt so helpless.

The sultan leaned back, a faint smirk on his lips. "A word of warning: do not think you can steal the lamp. The jinn is *my* ancestor's prisoner. You will not be able to use its magic."

Cocky bastard. She bit down on her tongue before it shaped the words.

"Yuba," Mazen cut in weakly. "Amir threw the lamp into the Sandsea because its power blinded him. I do not think it wise to—"

"Silence, boy." The words had the force of a slap, and the prince went mute beside her. "It is not power that corrupts, but intent," the sultan continued. "And my intentions are pure as they come."

"Oh?" Loulie forced herself to look up, right into the sultan's eyes. What could a murderer possibly want with a jinn servant?

"The jinn have been a plague on our land for years. The hunts are inefficient. The jinn still exist, and we cannot dig them out from the Sandsea, no. But we must eliminate them. I will not let them steal my family from me." His eyes flickered to Mazen, who glanced away, face ashen. "With this magic, I will have the power to end them."

Oh. Loulie clenched her hands in her lap, willing them to stop shaking.

"Defeat magic with magic," Hakim said softly. "A jinn against jinn."

Loulie was having trouble breathing. *Qadir*, she thought. *He would kill Qadir.*

"Not just a jinn, but one of the seven kings," the sultan affirmed. He leveled his stoic gaze on Loulie. "Do you see, al-Nazari? This is a just quest."

It will lead to a massacre.

"What will it be?" The sultan's dark eyes bored into her. "Will you find the relic and become a hero? Or will you flee like a criminal and perish in the desert, with no one there to mourn you?"

Loulie had avoided politics to escape this exact scenario: being a pawn in someone else's game. She was a wanderer, not a mercenary. Yet here she sat, at the edge of a precipice with danger on either side. And for the first time in her life, she was forced to cave.

"I accept your request." She looked down, ashamed. "I will find your lamp."

She did not see the look of triumph on the sultan's face; she did not want to. The sultan insisted she remain at the palace. He would need to discuss specifics with her over the following days and would help her prepare for her journey.

Loulie was barely listening. She thought about Prince Omar, who would be shadowing her like a vulture, and Qadir, who would have no choice but to remain in his human form while they traveled. She thought of their trek through the desert, and of the cities and oases they would need to pass through. But mostly, she thought of the Sandsea and of the relic inside. The relic *she* was somehow meant to collect.

By the time she was dismissed, the forest seemed hostile. Everywhere Loulie looked, she saw silver blood gleaming on the leaves and glittering like dew on the grass and windows.

Behind her, the sultan and his sons had started speaking about something else.

"Did you find the thing I told you to look for?"

"I have searched the whole diwan, my sultan," Omar said. "It is not here."

"You are certain?"

A beat of silence. "Yes."

Loulie walked out without absorbing the words. She had no time for the present, not when the future was much more likely to get her—and Qadir—killed.

She forced air into her lungs. *I will not let that happen.* She lifted her head as she exited the room. *I am Loulie al-Nazari, the Midnight Merchant, and I am the master of my own fate.*

14

MAZEN

Before the incident with the shadow jinn, Mazen had never been afraid of the dark. Now he could not fall asleep without burning a kerosene lamp. It did not fully banish his fear—how could it when the very existence of light caused shadows to form?—but the light was a welcome sight when he woke from his nightmares. They were always the same: Omar stalked toward him in the diwan, knife raised.

Sometimes, when Mazen was being stabbed, he remembered things—silver blood on the lips of a dead man; assassins in black riding through the desert; Omar, smiling, with silver blood on his cheeks.

He always awoke in a cold sweat, blankets thrown off as he struggled to breathe. *You are here*, he would remind himself. *You are you.* But though the words comforted him when he was awake, they did not fend off the nightmares.

Sometimes Mazen would glance at the walls and see the jinn's white-eyed shadow grinning at him. *Inconsequential*, it murmured. And then when he blinked, the shadow would be gone. He could only pray his sleep-addled mind was playing tricks on him.

By the third day of the merchant's stay, Mazen was exhausted. He felt weary and wrung out, a feeling exacerbated by the pain from his wound. He was grateful, at least, that the sting had abated to a dull throb. Still, it took a great effort to force himself up for the morning meal. He'd been trying to make the sultan see reason for days, and he was not going to stop now.

He was groggy-eyed but determined as he carefully changed and exited his room. He was passing through the garden when he paused, noticing the Midnight Merchant crouched down in a bed of white roses. She was glaring at the sun as if it had personally offended her.

Mazen thought she was beautiful.

You really should stop thinking that about a criminal, his inner voice chided.

But he couldn't help it. Here was the Midnight Merchant, the most elusive legend in Madinne! A story brought to life. And she had saved him twice. The fact only endeared her to him more. The merchant, unfortunately, did not share the sentiment.

The minute she saw him, her frown deepened. "Sayyidi."

"Midnight Merchant. Will you be joining us for the morning meal?"

She tilted her chin. "No."

He wasn't surprised; the sultan had forced her to attend many events in the two days she'd been here. She had clearly hated every moment of her stay.

Mazen tried a smile. "Ah." An awkward silence ensued. The merchant turned away first. He cleared his throat. "Nice day, isn't it?"

"Hardly. It's impossible to enjoy the day when you're busy dreading the future."

Mazen swallowed. "I'm sorry." The apology tumbled from his lips before he could think it. "About the quest, my father, the shadow jinn..."

The merchant looked up, a peculiar expression on her face. "Why are you sorry about the jinn?"

Because my brother left her alive and she hurt you. Me. Both of us.

When he didn't respond, the merchant changed the subject. "So, am I to call you Prince Mazen, then? Or...?" Her brows lifted.

"Mazen. Yousef is another identity for another time." He shuffled on his feet, considering—then he tried a question. "But you knew it wasn't my real name, didn't you? It was why you followed me."

The only evidence of the merchant's surprise was a slow, careful blink. "A jinn made it her prerogative to hunt you down. I knew you were more than a simple scribe." The words hung between them, a silent accusation.

But then, he had not been the only one lying. "And you?" he said. "What should I call you?" *Loulie or Layla?*

The merchant's lips quirked. "Loulie. Layla is another identity for another time."

She turned away, leaving Mazen to stare in wonder at her back. He hesitated. Would she flee if he asked more questions? She obviously wasn't keen on speaking to the sultan, but maybe she would talk to him?

Cautiously, he stepped into the rose bed and crouched down beside her. "The stories they tell about you—the tales of Loulie al-Nazari, the Midnight Merchant—are they true?"

The merchant shrugged. "It depends on what they say. I haven't, for instance, single-handedly defeated a group of notorious robbers with magic. *But* I did once set a hideout on fire and let the robbers fight over the rescued spoils until they defeated themselves." There was humor dancing in her eyes. "And what about you, Prince?"

She shifted so that her rust-brown eyes bored right into him. "They tell many stories of your brother, but you are a mystery. You are the son of a storyteller, and a storyteller yourself, yet there are no tales about you."

The words were a simple observation, but they fell on his shoulders like a physical weight. "Yes. There are not many stories to tell of a prince locked in a palace."

"You can't leave?"

"Not without a retinue." He laughed weakly. "Every outing would be a procession."

"And so you become Yousef." She was still looking at him, brow furrowed. Mazen realized there was no judgment in her voice; she spoke matter-of-factly.

"Truth be told, I was just an anonymous man in the souk before I met you. You were the first to wonder about my identity." A sad smile curved his lips. "Though I doubt I'll be able to do it again any-time soon, it was nice to live a fictional life for a time."

Loulie didn't respond, not immediately, but when she did her words were a cold mumble. "I understand what you mean. A reputation can be a nuisance. Apparently, it can even be used to blackmail a person into going on a perilous quest."

Mazen flinched. He knew her bitter words were not directed at him, but that did not make him feel any less responsible for his father's cruelty. He was struggling to come up with a response when someone clamped a hand on his shoulder, startling him. He turned to see Omar looming behind them, surveying the scene with a lazy smile. "Salaam, Mazen." He looked at Loulie. "Midnight Merchant." His voice was cool.

Loulie's expression went rigid. "High Prince."

"It is, as always, a pleasure. I hope you do not mind me stealing my brother away."

Mazen frowned. What now? He was certainly not late for the morning meal.

"Not at all." The merchant rose from the bed of flowers and dusted off her robes. She looked out of place in the sunshine: a patch of night in a field of bright flowers. Yet she carried herself with the confidence of someone who belonged. No, with the confidence of someone who deserved *better* than this place, this quest.

With a sigh, Mazen begrudgingly let Omar steer him away. They had not gotten far when the merchant called out to them. "I'm curious, High Prince. Your black knives—where did you get them? They made even an incorporeal jinn solid."

Mazen thought of the black knife in his dream and flinched. He hadn't considered it before, but his brother's knives *were* strange, weren't they?

"They are the same as your blade. A weapon enchanted by jinn." Omar smiled over his shoulder. His lady-killing smile, Mazen and Hakim called it, though Loulie did not look impressed. "Do not worry; I will use them to protect you if the need arises."

The merchant just rolled her eyes. She turned and walked away without another word, her dark robes flaring behind her. Mazen wished he could join her. She wasn't free, exactly, not anymore, but she had been before his father found her. Free to roam the desert and live as she wished, without the weight of a kingdom on her shoulders.

"Such a pleasant personality she has," Omar said. He gestured for Mazen to follow.

She has a better personality than you, at least, Mazen thought.

He followed Omar through one of the open-air corridors, up a stairwell, and to a simple wooden door. He knew even before entering that it was a storage room, for a piece of parchment listing the inventory inside was pinned to the door. Before Mazen could ask what they were doing there, Omar pulled him inside.

The room was full of cleaning supplies and shoddy, dusty furniture. Two servants sat at a table, playing shatranj. They looked up at Omar's entrance and hurriedly vacated the area on his command. Once they left, Omar slid into one of the chairs and smiled. "This will do perfectly for some peace and quiet."

"Is there a reason we're having this conversation here?"

"I needed a room, and this was the closest one not filled with your spying servants."

Mazen crept to the window ledge and positioned himself on the sill. *Just in case I need to call for someone to rescue me*, he thought. But the corridor outside was empty at this time of day. Knowing Omar, he had planned for even this.

"You remember the favor you promised me, Mazen?" Omar's eyes glittered as he reached into the satchel at his belt and withdrew some golden object. "I have found a way for you to repay me." He tossed the object to him.

Mazen leaned forward barely in time to catch it before it dropped to the floor. He stared at the thing in his hands. It was a golden bangle: a gaudy thing with glittering jewels. "A gift? You shouldn't have, Omar." He tried a smile, hoping it would mask his confusion.

"Oh, but I have." Omar reached into the satchel again and withdrew—the same bangle.

Mazen eyed the replica warily. "I thought you found jewelry distasteful."

Omar snorted. "Not so much distasteful as inconvenient." He slid one of his blades from his belt and held it out to Mazen. "Feed one of the gems on the bracelet your blood." Instinctively, Mazen flinched away. Omar just waved the knife at him. "I assure you there's a good reason."

"Well then, enlighten me. I'm not going to *cut* myself for some unknown reason."

Omar set the knife down on the table with a sigh. "Fine. You want an explanation?" He held out the second bangle. "Put this on."

"But I—"

"Just do it, Mazen."

He caught the bangle when Omar tossed it to him. After a beat of hesitation, he clasped it onto his left wrist. The sensation that followed was one of the strangest he'd experienced: he felt unbalanced and dizzy, as if the center of him had shifted. His body felt too cold, too big. He had the inexplicable urge to scrub at his skin until it flaked off. He blinked, and his vision sharpened, the details of the room becoming more vivid.

"What just happened?" He froze at the sound of his voice. Because it wasn't his voice. The timbre was too low, the words too heavy on his tongue.

"Omar, what—" Mazen stopped abruptly. He'd caught sight of his appearance in a mirror wedged into a corner of the room. He looked away. Then back again. The image remained unchanged.

Omar bin Malik stared back at him, eyes wide with shock.

Mazen touched his face—now his brother's face—and gasped. He said nothing at first, just stared with dawning comprehension at his changed reflection. Then the panic came, sharp and wild, and he pried the bangle from his wrist and threw it on the cushions.

When he again looked in the mirror, he was back in his own body. He brushed his hands over his face with a groan. Omar had the audacity to chuckle.

"Your melodramatic responses never fail to amuse."

Mazen looked up sharply. "What *was* that? Magic? Are these a pair of relics?" He remembered the Midnight Merchant's bag of relics. "Did you steal these from the merchant?"

Omar clicked his tongue. "I only steal things I cannot get through other means. The merchant is not the only one who collects magical items."

Mazen knew this. His father had a small collection of relics that had been "donated" to him by the hunters and nomads who roamed the desert. He paid good gold for them, of course, but the real reason anyone surrendered relics to him was because they feared him finding out they possessed them. It was not a common problem; relics were rare, after all.

Omar continued speaking slowly, calmly, as if to a child. "These bracelets are special. You remember the lamp the jinn king enchanted for Amir? These were also created by that jinn. They are as ancient as Amir's scrolls."

Mazen picked up one of the bangles and ran his fingers over the gemstones in awe. "Passed down through the family?"

"For hundreds of years. They've been in the treasury gathering dust, so I doubt they'll be missed." He leaned forward. "As you can see, I've already fed my blood to one of them. In order to pull off our illusion, you must offer your blood to the other."

Mazen's stomach knotted. "Illusion?"

Omar smiled. "We are going to switch places, Mazen."

The bangle fell from his hands. "But Father wants *you* to accompany the merchant—"

"And that is exactly the problem. I am preparing for an important operation with my thieves, and I cannot miss it." He rested his elbows on his knees, leaned forward. "I thought you would be excited about this. Have you not always wanted to go galivanting around the desert? Now you can."

Mazen bit back a self-mocking laugh. As a child, he'd always craved adventure—the kind in his mother's stories, which featured heroes and magic and fantastical creatures. But that had been then, and this was now. "Not this kind of adventure."

Omar frowned. "I have kept your secrets, akhi, and I have saved your life. You owe me this. Or…" His eyes flashed. "Would you like me to explain to the sultan how the jinn came to possess your shadow?"

Mazen's heart beat in his throat. *It was you who brought the shadow jinn back. You who provoked her!* He held his tongue. He knew he could not afford to say the words, knew that the sultan's disappointment in Omar would be second to his anger at Mazen.

But Omar's request—it was impossible.

"I don't know how to use a blade. I could never pretend to be you."

Omar stabbed his knife into the table and smiled when Mazen recoiled. "Never fear. I will send Aisha, my best thief, with you. She and my other thieves will know your true identity. If there is any fighting to be done, leave it to her."

Mazen faintly remembered the hooded woman he'd seen with Omar in the courtyard. How was it that that meeting had been less than a week ago?

"What say you, Mazen?" Omar tilted his head.

Mazen let out a single, strained "ha" that was half a cry for help, half a laugh.

Before his mother's death, he'd thought the world outside Madinne a magical place. His mother had made it seem full of life and light and endless possibilities. And then she had been killed by one of the creatures in her stories, and the magic had disappeared.

And yet…

Death in a free land is better than life in a gilded cage.

He had told Loulie al-Nazari he enjoyed stepping into a life where he could be someone other than himself. Someone other than the overprotected son of a legendary storyteller.

This was his chance to leave Madinne. His single, dangerous chance.

It would not be the first time he had pretended to be someone other than himself.

"Fine." Mazen lifted his head and met his brother's eyes. "I will go on your adventure."

15

LOULIE

"Do you really need another drink?" Dahlia bint Adnan held the wine bottle a safe distance from Loulie, who sat at the tavern counter, shaking a precariously tipped cup at her.

"No." Loulie frowned. "But I want one anyway."

Dahlia sighed as she set the bottle back on the liquor shelf behind her. "Any more wine and you'll fall off your horse tomorrow during the procession. You don't want that, do you? You may not care what the sultan thinks of you now, but you certainly will tomorrow."

Loulie scowled. "Let him think what he wants. I'm sick of letting him parade me around. *Look* at me, Dahlia!" She grasped the collar of the horrendously shimmering dara'a she was wearing. "Imagine my embarrassment at being forced to wear this tonight. And worse! Being forced to wear it while hanging off of Prince Omar's arm."

Prince Omar had been all cocky smiles as he led her around the diwan earlier that evening, introducing her to guests she'd never wanted to meet. The nobles had gaped at her like she was some treasure on display, cooing over her dress and waggling their brows at her.

Loulie hated them, all of them.

It had been a small relief to escape the nobles tonight, to have been given *permission* by the sultan to spend the last night before her terrible journey here in Dahlia's tavern.

"Listen to yourself. You hardly sound like the Midnight Merchant."

Loulie laughed. A hollow, bitter sound. "The Midnight Merchant you know is gone. I may as well be a celebrity now." She focused intensely on the inside of her empty cup; it was the only way to keep her frustrated tears at bay.

What was she doing confiding in Dahlia? She'd never broken down in front of the woman, never let her see any of her insecurities. Dahlia may have been a generous landlord and a shrewd confidante, but Loulie took great pains to hide the more sentimental parts of her personal life from her. The less vulnerable she was with someone, the easier it was to leave them behind.

That was why, even with Ahmed, she'd—

Loulie cut the thought off with a growl. *Damn that man for sneaking into my thoughts as soon as I let my guard down.* She ignored Dahlia's raised brow and turned her mind to more productive musings. She wondered, not for the first time, where Qadir was. Though he'd assisted her in the diwan, he'd been missing since their separation at the Night Market three days ago.

"A person's reputation is determined by how they interact with others," Dahlia said as she set another bottle down on the shelf behind her. She was cleaning them with a rag, as was her habit when she couldn't sleep. Normally, all the tables would be occupied at this time, and the tavern would be full of customers sharing wine and snacks. But after the incident at the souk, all of Dahlia's patrons had vanished. It was likely they'd decided to lie low after the purge.

"The Midnight Merchant does not converse with uppity *nobles*." Loulie slammed her cup on the table. Then she did it a few more times, because it made her feel better.

Dahlia groaned. "Oh for gods' sake..."

It was at that moment that the tavern's front door opened and a man stepped inside. Loulie whirled, half expecting one of the sultan's guards. But it was not a soldier.

It was Qadir, standing before them in all his unimpressed glory. He raised a brow. "Who is this sorry drunk?"

Dahlia smirked. "I don't know, but I have half a mind to throw her out."

Loulie straightened. Too fast. The world blurred, and she had to steady herself against the counter before she could focus on Qadir. "Where have you been?"

He sighed as he slid onto the stool beside hers. "A hearty salaam to you too." His gaze grew frosty when he saw the gown she was wearing.

"A present from the sultan," she said. "I'm sure the customers will love it; they won't be able to tear their eyes away."

"Which is exactly why I should burn it," Qadir said.

Dahlia just snorted. The tavernkeeper had no idea Qadir really *could* burn the dress with just a snap of his fingers. She slid one last bottle onto the shelf before turning to them with her hands on her hips. "I'll leave you two to catch up. Burn out the lanterns when you're done."

Qadir dipped his head. "Tesbaheen ala khair."

Dahlia responded only with a yawn before heading upstairs, leaving Loulie and Qadir alone. Loulie felt the urge to throw her arms around his neck and cry into his shoulder. She waited for it to pass before she repeated, "Where have you been?"

"Watching from a distance. I know about the quest."

Loulie thought about the rooms she'd wandered into, and of the lanterns that lit those rooms. Qadir could watch her from those fires if he chose to; fire magic was his affinity, after all. Short of shape-shifting into a lizard, there was no other magic he could perform.

"And what do you think?" She mindlessly spun the cup between her hands. "About the legend and the lamp?" She looked up. "About what comes afterward?"

Qadir stole the cup before she could twirl it across the wood again. "I think it is useless to worry about a future not set in stone. As for the lamp—have you tried asking the compass where it is?"

Loulie set her chin on the table with a sigh. "It exists. I asked the coin *and* the compass."

"Then it can be obtained."

"And you have no qualms about handing an imprisoned jinn to the sultan?" She paused. "Do *you* know anything about this lamp?"

"Me?" Qadir shrugged. "Nothing. I was not in the human world that long ago. But if your sultan's story contains even an inkling of truth, it is likely the jinn he is looking for is an ifrit." His lips quirked at her puzzlement. "Ifrit are what we call the seven jinn kings in our land. It is a title bestowed upon beings of fire who are powerful enough to use various magic affinities."

Ifrit. The word was raw with power, more ominous by far than *jinn king.*

"Why didn't you tell me about the ifrit before?"

He shrugged. "We have never run into one, and no one in your land uses the word. *Jinn kings* may be an inaccurate title, but it does not merit a history lesson."

It was true that all the jinn they'd come across specialized in only one type of magic. Opponents like the shadow jinn who could manipulate the world through a single element. Jinn were rare, and the so-called jinn kings were legend. It was no wonder Qadir hadn't brought up the term before.

"Fair enough." She sighed. "So, say we find this all-powerful ifrit. Do we simply hand it over to the sultan?"

"Who says we have to hand anything over?" Qadir angled his head toward the nearest lantern. The flame inside flickered and died, and the other lanterns dimmed shortly after. Qadir's eyes danced with a playful fire that made his irises flash gold and red. "Think of the sultan as a customer to be scammed."

I think it is useless to worry about a future not set in stone. Maybe Qadir had a point. She had not become so successful by overthinking.

"You're recommending I leap before I think? How irresponsible of you."

Qadir set his hand on the table. "I live to be a bad influence."

Loulie set her hand atop his, savoring the warmth of his touch. It occurred to her that she was becoming drowsy and that this was only because Qadir had returned and was sitting beside her. It was difficult to let her guard down when he was absent. She had spent the last three nights worrying what would become of him on this quest.

As he always did, Qadir read the concern on her face. "I never thought I'd see the fearless Midnight Merchant look so defeated before the journey even began."

"The ifrit in the lamp isn't the only jinn in danger." She gave him a pointed look.

"You ought to have more faith in me. I haven't lived this long just to be bested by an arrogant human." He cocked a brow. "And I have never known *you* to concede victory to someone either."

Loulie bristled. Qadir was right; she may have been a citizen of Madinne, but she was no one's servant. She refused to let the sultan destroy the life she had worked so hard to make.

"You're right; the Midnight Merchant would never yield to some conceited noble. Not even the sultan." She laced her fingers through Qadir's, suddenly feeling resolute. "He'll regret threatening us."

Qadir smiled. "They always do, in the end."

16

AISHA

It was a suspiciously tranquil night.

Usually, on evenings like this when the sultan had guests, the courtyard was scattered with loud and annoyingly curious nobles. Tonight, however, the area was empty, and Aisha did not hesitate to pull open her curtain. She seated herself in her window alcove, and with only the moon and stars as her audience, she put a brush to her arm and began to paint.

Most travelers had pre-journey rituals. They prayed; they kissed their loved ones. Aisha had not been able to do either of those things for a long time. So instead, she drew.

She painted henna designs atop her scars and allowed herself the brief luxury of rumination. She let herself remember the softness of her mother's henna brush as she drew petals on her skin. Recalled her sisters' scolding when she didn't wait long enough for the henna to dry and accidentally smudged the ink while cooking or cleaning or digging in the fields.

I look forward to the day you learn patience, her mother had often teased her. *You will be a force to be reckoned with then.*

Now, as Aisha inked the tattoos across her skin, she was patient. Careful. She imagined each stroke of the brush was a memory unfurling across her skin. A thread, snapped and repurposed to create a new tapestry. One filled with determination rather than grief. She raised her arm to the moonlight and observed the painted sleeve of jagged leaves and flowers.

Her mother had been right. Patience was a hard but necessary lesson. Obtaining revenge was not a sprint; it was a journey. Aisha sighed as she lowered her arm to her lap.

An hour elapsed in peace. And then, as she was putting the finishing touches on her last tattoo, a knock came at her door. Aisha tensed, then relaxed when she heard Samar's voice. "Permission to come in, Princess?"

The title—one of the thief's many irritating nicknames for her—made her groan. "Call me *Princess* again and I'll stab out your eye." She reached for the featherlight shawl resting on her pillows and, carefully avoiding the fresh henna paste on her arms, draped it over her shoulders. "What do you want?"

The entrance burst open, and a rosy-cheeked man stumbled inside.

In a heartbeat, Aisha had grabbed the newly sharpened shamshir off her wall and was approaching with the blade pointed at his chest. The man looked up and stared at her owlishly.

Aisha stared at him in shock. "Prince Mazen?"

The bumbling prince was dressed in a blue-black robe that looked sizes too big for him. His golden eyes were unfocused, and he blinked at her slowly, as if coming out of a daze. Behind him, Samar inched into the room. Aisha shot him a look, but the thief just shrugged. If this was some kind of prank, she was going to kill him.

"O-oh," the prince said softly. "I'm sorry. I didn't realize..." He glanced around the room, and Aisha flinched as his gaze fell on her bare-bones surroundings. There was hardly anything to take in—the place was as impersonal as an inn room, with nothing but a bed, a simple table, and a chest for her clothing. The only individual touch was the sheets of henna patterns hanging on the wall. But that didn't matter. This was still *her* room. However the prince had come to be here, she refused to let him stay.

"Get out."

The prince's eyes widened as she stepped toward him. "I'm sorry." He fiddled nervously with a piece of jewelry on his wrist. "Please, let me explain..."

Aisha was feet away from him when she stopped, noticing his bracelet—the jewel-studded bangle Omar had shown her days ago, when he'd come to her with his bizarre request to accompany his brother on a journey. Her eyes settled again on the prince's face. His lips were curled in an all-too-familiar smirk that did *not* belong to Prince Mazen.

With an exaggerated bow, he unclasped the bangle from his arm, and between one blink and the next, he was suddenly Omar. The robe was no longer ill fitting, and his eyes were bright with amusement. "What do you think? I make a convincing Prince Mazen, no?"

Aisha returned his smile with a scowl. She had not been expecting Omar until after midnight, when his dinner was over. And she definitely hadn't been expecting him in disguise.

She shoved him in the shoulder. "I *should* have stabbed out your eye."

Samar laughed from the doorway. The big man leaned against the wall and crossed his arms over his black tunic. "If it makes you feel any better, he put on the act for all of us. *Most* of us were fooled." His dark eyes crinkled with his teasing smile. "Present company excluded. I thought it'd be worth losing an eye to see your reaction."

Aisha pointed at the door. "I'll throw you out the window if you don't leave right now."

Samar fluttered his lashes at her. "Touchy as always." He was reaching for the door when she noticed something on his arm—a jagged gash so colorless it looked like a crack in his skin.

"What in nine hells did you do to yourself?"

When Samar only blinked at her in confusion, the prince shook his head and said, "The fool got cut up by a jinn on his way back from a hunt yesterday."

Samar set a hand on the wound. "Ah, right. I killed the beast, but not before it injured me. It wasn't my most heroic moment." He smiled sheepishly. "I was actually about to rebandage it when the prince showed up with...that face. He's been a terrible distraction."

Aisha looked skeptically at the wound. "You didn't mend the cut with jinn blood before it scabbed?"

Samar sighed. "I'd rather not have that vile stuff in my veins. But good thing I have thick skin, sah? Helpful for our occupation." He cast a look over his shoulder as he exited the room. "Omar told me you agreed to go on his little mission. Good luck out there, little thief. We'll sing your praises when you return."

He tipped his head in salute before shutting the door behind him. Aisha scoffed as she placed her shamshir back on the wall beside its twin. "Sing my praises for what? I won't be doing anything but keeping a pathetic prince safe." She returned to her window alcove, where her henna brushes and jar still lay. She set them aside as Omar sank onto the pillows across from her.

He arched a brow. "You underestimate the importance of your task. Besides, you *did* threaten to stab me in the throat if I recruited you into the qaid's army. I thought sending you out with my brother would be a more pleasant alternative for both of us."

"You thought correctly." She rested her drying arms on her knees and turned her gaze to the view outside her window. From her tilted tower room, she could see the whole city—even the distant lights of the lower quarter. It was strange to think she had been living on those streets nine years ago. That it had been where she tried to pick Omar's pockets. He could have hanged her for the offense. Instead, he had named her the first of his forty thieves.

"I take it your dinner went well?"

Omar shrugged. "If by 'well' you mean exasperating, then yes."

"Is that not the usual experience?"

"It's different for my brother. The nobles like to flatter him, thinking it'll get them closer to the sultan. But me? The snobs are too scared to do more than kiss my boots."

Aisha caught a glimmer out of the corner of her eye: not the bangle, but a shard of silver Omar was idly turning over in his hands.

She recognized his crescent earring immediately. "You forgot to give that to your brother? Isn't it an important part of his disguise?"

Omar stiffened, curled his fingers over the crescent. "My likeness is more than convincing. He does not need the earring." There was a forlornness in his gaze when he spoke, a vulnerability that made Aisha uncomfortable.

She forgot sometimes that his earring was the only thing he had left of his mother. That while she at least had memories of those she'd lost, the prince would never be able to recall the mother who had died bringing him into the world.

"No," she said after a few moments. "I don't suppose anyone outside of Madinne would think to look for it." Her eyes fell on the bangle. "*That* thing, on the other hand, is impossible to miss. Are you certain no one will notice it?"

She didn't miss the way his shoulders sagged at the change in subject. He reached up to click the earring into his earlobe. "Let them notice. My brother wears flashy trinkets all the time; what's one more? Although..." He looked at her, and there was a silent question in his eyes.

"No," she said simply. "*I'm* not the one in disguise. I don't need any relics."

"It's easier to kill jinn with their own magic, you know."

"I'll kill them with a blade or not at all." The thought of using relics—of using *jinn* magic—made her stomach churn. Self-righteous politics be damned. She wasn't killing jinn for any gods. She was killing them for revenge. And she would cut off her own hands before she won that revenge with the twisted magic that had ruined her life in the first place.

"Stubborn as always." He surveyed her quietly. Aisha recognized the blank look on his face; it was the expression he wore when he was sizing someone up.

She crossed her arms. "Having second thoughts about staying behind?"

"Never." He smiled. "I can trust you to see this through to the end?"

"Of course."

"You promise not to die?"

She scoffed. "A thief steals lives. They do not have their life stolen from them."

"Well said." Omar tucked the bangle into one of the pockets of his robe and stood. "I'm afraid I must excuse myself. I have to help my brother pack before you all depart tomorrow." He paused. "Mazen owes me his secrecy, but you'll help him keep character, I hope?"

"I'll try my best, but no promises." She rested her head against the window with a sigh. "I see why your father keeps him locked inside. He's an easy target."

"Which is why I'm depending on you to protect him." He grinned. "I owe you, Aisha."

Aisha flapped a dismissive hand. She had never cared about earning or trading favors.

Omar put a hand to his chest and bowed. "Until the morrow."

After he'd departed, Aisha glanced down at the patchwork of scars on her arms. At the flowers she had tattooed across them like armor. She did not believe in mourning the past. But the present—that was something she could change for the better with her blade.

The city was the prince's arena. Hers had always been the desert.

And she was looking forward to returning to it.

17

MAZEN

Mazen's adventure had yet to begin, but he was already tired of it. Walking through the halls in his brother's body and flashing his condescending smile at others was taking its toll. He hated the way the servants looked at him with fear in their eyes. Gods, even the *nobles* were nervously talkative around him.

But no response was worse than the Midnight Merchant's. While the others averted their gazes, she glared right at him. Mazen knew she hated him. He couldn't fault her—not after his father had ordered him to shadow her last night. Mazen blamed Omar; his brother had thought it wise to test their disguises, so Omar had gone to last night's celebration as Mazen and Mazen had gone as his brother. He hated that he had been so convincing.

Mazen sighed into his coffee. The sultan looked up from his cup. "You haven't stopped sighing since we sat down. What are you thinking about, Mazen?"

Some of the tension eased from his shoulders at the sound of his name. This afternoon, he would become Omar, King of the Forty Thieves and high prince of Madinne. But right now, seated before his father in the diwan, he was, blessedly, himself.

"The usual." Mazen blew on his coffee. "Jinn, shadows, nightmares."

The sultan set down his cup. It was the same one he always used—a small porcelain cup decorated with multicolored roses. It was the same pattern Mazen's mother had used; she and the sultan had shared a set. "The jinn is dead and, if the gods are just, burning in hell."

Mazen nearly choked on his drink. It didn't matter that the shadow jinn had nearly killed him—he still felt pity for her. It was a weakness, he knew, one he had no right to. And yet he could not stop thinking of the rage and pain that had clouded her mind.

The sultan shook his head. "This will never happen again. Once I have the lamp, I will destroy the jinn. All of them." When Mazen said nothing, the sultan leaned forward, bushy brows drawn together. "Why are you against this search? The Midnight Merchant is a *criminal*. I am giving her a chance to redeem herself."

"Not all jinn are evil, yuba. Mother used to say that in her stories—you remember?"

Mazen knew he'd said the wrong thing when the sultan's expression went icy. "Has your memory grown so patchy you do not remember she was *killed* by one of those jinn?"

"But she believed—"

"Your mother, gods bless her soul, was softhearted." His eyes sparked with some emotion Mazen could not place. "I'll be damned if I let the jinn take you because you inherited her sentimentality. Remember, Mazen, the desert is no place for bleeding hearts."

Mazen's mother had once said the opposite: that in their country, a soft heart was more valuable because the desert dried out a person's emotions. But he did not say this to his father.

The sultan drew back with a sigh. "I hope you understand I just want what's best for you." His gaze was thoughtful as he refilled his cup from the dallah. "That is why I have decided to have you trained in swordplay." He didn't even look up when Mazen cringed. "It will give you something to fill your days with. Until Omar returns, I want you to remain in the palace. It is safer here."

Mazen set down his cup before it fell from his hands. His mother had not believed in responding to violence with violence. It was the reason he'd never been trained to use a weapon. The reason the sultan had stepped down as the King of the Forty Thieves. But that had been *before* her death. Mazen ought to have known it would only be a matter of time before his father put a blade in his hands.

If only he knew it was Omar who was going to wield that blade. It was almost humorous. While he would have to pretend to be adept at using a sword, Omar would have to play at being incompetent. It seemed they would both have their work cut out for them.

His father smiled. Not a crooked smile, but an earnest one. "This will be good for you. Who has ever heard of a prince who doesn't know how to use a weapon? You hold the weight of a kingdom on your shoulders, Mazen. You cannot protect it with just good intentions."

His father had a point. Never mind the fact that Mazen could barely pick up a blade for fear of having to plunge it into some living thing, or that he detested violence. He was glad, at least, that it would be Omar who bore the bloody weight of their kingdom in the future. Mazen had never wanted anything less than he wanted the throne.

"If it is boredom you fear, do not worry." The sultan blew on his coffee. "We will fill your days with productive work. I have already told the councillors you will start attending our meetings. I expect to see you at our afternoon gathering tomorrow. Understood?"

Ah, so swordplay and politics were to be his routine for the foreseeable future. But Mazen would not step into that life—not yet.

"Yes, yuba," he said softly.

That was how he said goodbye to his father—not with a hug or a kiss to the forehead, but with an admission. When he left the diwan, his heart was heavy with everything left unsaid.

—⁂—

It was the fifth hour of sunrise when he made it to Hakim's study. He'd been preparing for his journey, packing clothes that were not his and conversing with Omar about things he needed to know as the King of the Forty Thieves. His brother had given him most of his possessions—everything except for his crescent earring, which he refused to part with. It was also the only thing missing from Mazen's disguise now as he stood outside Hakim's door.

Hesitantly, he rapped on the wood in the pattern he always used, and entered when Hakim bade him to do so.

Hakim's room was unchanged, still full of tomes and shadows and maps. "Mazen? You're unusually quiet today." Hakim swiveled on his chair. The moment he saw Mazen, he tensed. "Omar?"

Mazen hated watching his normally composed brother become uncomfortable at Omar's appearance. It was, Mazen knew, his fault. Years ago, after his mother had told him about Hakim's existence, he had begged his father to bring him back to the palace he'd been banished from. He'd wanted someone to play with, someone who would treat him like a brother, unlike Omar. And so, begrudgingly, the sultan had tracked down Hakim's mother's tribe and brought him to the palace. For Mazen, he'd given Hakim the honorary title of prince, even though he was not of his blood.

Hakim, two years younger than Omar, had been closer in both age and temperament to Mazen. His arrival had marked the beginning of a more peaceful time. At least, until Mazen's mother died and the sultan locked Hakim in his room and allowed Omar to belittle him.

My fault, my fault. Mazen felt a stab of shame, knowing he'd been the one to separate Hakim from his tribe. As a child, he'd insisted Hakim was *his* family. He'd realized only in retrospect, once his brother was trapped here, how selfish he'd been.

He forced the thought to the back of his mind as he pulled the bangle from his wrist, and managed a weak smile when Hakim startled. "Salaam, Hakim."

"Mazen!" Hakim fell back against his desk. "You nearly gave me a heart attack."

"My apologies. I haven't had the opportunity to take this damned thing off until now."

"Is there a reason you're using magic to masquerade as Omar?" Hakim eyed the bangle. "Is that . . . a relic?"

"Yes and yes." Mazen's smile fell as he drew closer. The map the sultan had presented to Rasul and Loulie lay stretched on Hakim's desk. His brother had added more traveling routes.

He could feel Hakim scrutinizing him. He expected a gasp, a grumble, but when Hakim next spoke, his voice was calm. "You plan on taking Omar's place today."

Mazen swallowed. "You remember the favor I owe him? This is it. He wants me to accompany the merchant, pretend to be him."

"And you're going to do it?" Hakim stood abruptly. His broad shoulders and impressive height made Mazen feel small and insignificant. "You would willingly head into a desert filled with cutthroats and jinn just to keep your secret safe from the sultan?"

Mazen stepped back and out of his brother's shadow. "But if he knew—"

"He *loves* you, Mazen! You are his favorite. He would never hurt you."

Mazen almost laughed. *Me? His favorite?* How could Hakim think that? His father never *listened* to him. He did not even trust him; he gave all the important responsibilities to Omar. But Mazen knew Hakim would argue with him until the sun set, so he humored him.

"Then his love blinds him. He never sees reason with me."

"Is it so wrong that he wants you to have an escort outside the palace?"

Mazen shook his head. "Now I am to be trapped in the palace at all times." He paused, realizing how spoiled he sounded. Hakim wasn't even allowed to attend palace events without the sultan's permission. And here he was, complaining.

He wished he could take the words back, but he couldn't bring himself to speak into the awkward quiet. He busied his hands instead, reaching into his satchel to withdraw his mother's scarf, which was vibrant even in the gloom of Hakim's dark study.

Hakim fell back onto his chair, shoulders slumped. "You're not just leaving because of the sultan, are you? It's for the Midnight Merchant. And because you want to escape the palace."

Mazen swallowed. He *did* want to leave Madinne. He *did* want to help the Midnight Merchant, even if he wasn't sure he was up to the task. He owed her.

Hakim chuckled, a soft sound that made Mazen's heart sink. "I know you better than you know yourself." He held out his hand. "I know you brought the scarf because you want me to keep it safe. And I know your mind is made up. You have the sultan's stubbornness in you."

Mazen wanted to object, but Hakim had a point. "As always, you see right through me."

"You wear your heart on your sleeve." Hakim took the scarf from him and began to roll up his map. "Who else knows of this switch? Your servants? Karima?"

Mazen shook his head. "No one. I cannot risk sharing this secret."

"What about the Midnight Merchant? Do you not think she would be more willing to travel with you if she knew your true identity?"

Mazen's heart twisted with guilt. He hated lying to Loulie al-Nazari, but what choice did he have? She despised the sultan. If she found out Mazen's secret, what was to stop her from using it as blackmail against his father? If that happened, the sultan would never forgive him.

Mazen liked Loulie, but he feared his father more.

Hakim nodded solemnly when Mazen told him this. "Then I alone will keep an eye on Omar." He frowned. "It bothers me that he would put his own personal business before the sultan's. And that he would send you on such a dangerous journey."

It was bothersome, but not surprising. As a child, Omar had dared Mazen to do all sorts of dangerous things, only to laugh when he injured himself.

"I have marked the most well traveled routes on the map." Hakim handed it to him. "The fastest route will take you through Dhyme and Ghiban."

Mazen smiled wryly. "Ah yes, exactly what I need: cities full of people to act for."

Hakim said nothing, only stared at him quietly, his bright eyes shadowed in the dim firelight. Mazen clutched the map to his chest, heart suddenly tight. He had no right to lament his trickery in front of his brother. His brother, who was trapped here because of him. "I'm sorry, Hakim." The apology came out whisper thin.

Hakim blinked. "For what?"

Mazen gestured feebly around the chamber. At the towering stacks of tomes, at the maps pinned atop each other on the walls because there was no *space*. If it weren't for him, Hakim would be out in the desert drawing his maps. Instead he sat here, a prisoner, handing Mazen the key to *his* escape.

The shadows on Hakim's face shifted when he smiled, drawing dark crescents beneath his eyes that made him look much older than his twenty-five years. "I told you before: you owe me no apologies. Besides, now is not the time for them."

Mazen swallowed the knot in his throat. *No, now is the time for goodbyes.*

Hakim stood and embraced him first, and it was all Mazen could do to return it without trembling. When Hakim drew away, his eyes glistened with unshed tears. "May the stars guide your path and the gods keep you safe. And remember, Mazen." He clapped a hand on his shoulder. "When in doubt, there is no better person to be than yourself."

Mazen forced himself to smile. "I would never hope to be anyone else."

He did not tell his brother that on this journey, he would be useless as himself. And that, deep down, he'd begun to fear this would always be the case.

18

LOULIE

Typically, Loulie's departures from Madinne were quiet affairs. She and Qadir would rise with the sun, share chai with Dahlia, and then head out on horseback with their supplies in the bag of infinite space and the compass in hand.

Today was different. Today, everyone in Madinne was here to watch her leave. Or so it seemed. Loulie had never seen the thoroughfares so crowded. She'd known she had a reputation, but she had never expected *this* many people to know of her. It was strange that they were still enchanted by her, even though she looked far from mysterious standing upon the sultan's hastily erected stage in her midnight-colored robes. Normally, she left Madinne in her brown shawls; there was no reason for her to draw attention to herself in the desert.

But now here she stood—the elusive Midnight Merchant, revealed at sunset.

Rasul al-Jasheen, the merchant, stood by the edge of the stage, trying to catch her gaze. Loulie ignored him. *He* had gotten her into this mess, and she would not forgive him for it.

She faced the crowds as the sultan's speech came to a close. Their applause pulsed like a heartbeat in her body and thudded painfully through her head. Her stomach churned, and she could not tell if it was a consequence of the alcohol from last night or her own anxiety. Everything was too loud, too bright. The cheering was the worst—it was proof these people approved of her journey, and that they would not forgive her if she fled.

On the sultan's command, Loulie mounted the chestnut-brown mare waiting at the head of the procession. She forced herself to sit upright as he came to her side with well-wishes that were clearly sugarcoated threats. Though she refused to do more than acknowledge him and his sons, her eyes lingered on the youngest prince as he turned away.

"Prince," she said beneath her breath. "The jinn attacks were not your fault." She had been meaning to say that to him ever since their conversation in the courtyard.

The prince angled his head and smiled. "Shukran. Safe journeys, al-Nazari." He followed after the sultan and his brother. She blinked, startled by his curtness and the lack of sincerity in his voice.

She tamped down her irritation as she guided her mare forward, fighting dizziness as the world lurched. Prince Omar and his frowning thief, Aisha, were waiting for her, along with Qadir, who rode atop a broad stallion with his bow and quiver strapped to his back. Loulie was surprised to see the shamshir from their rooms sheathed at his hip.

"Feeling sentimental, are we?" She grinned. "And here I thought the shamshir would only ever be a pretty display."

He turned as she approached. "It would be foolhardy to venture into the desert without a blade, no?" His eyes twinkled with humor. "It was collecting dust on the wall; I figured I may as well bring it with me in case I finally had a reason to use it."

Hopefully there will never be *a reason.* Loulie held back a sigh as she joined him.

Qadir leaned back in his saddle, nodding toward the townsfolk. "I had no idea you were so popular in the land of the living." His eyes skimmed the screaming, cheering crowds.

"You make me sound like a ghost."

"Or a legend." Qadir caught her eye.

She sighed. "And here I thought I was living a simple, humble life."

He turned away with a snort. Loulie looked at him out of the corner of her eye, considering. There was a lot she still needed to ask him. About the lamp, the journey, and...

The cutthroats. She had not forgotten the shadow jinn's warning. That in order to seek revenge, she would need to close off her heart. Those words had to mean something. And she would discuss them with Qadir as soon as they were able to steal a moment alone.

But who knew when that would be? Even now, she could feel Prince Omar smirking at her. She had never felt so great a desire to slap a smile off someone's face.

She looked past Omar at his thief: a tall, graceful woman with dark braided hair that brushed the small of her back. Loulie felt insignificant beneath her glower, like a beetle being crushed beneath the heel of a boot. She was certain she had never been in worse company.

At least I still have Qadir. She held on to the thought as they started forward.

Her headache built into a painful throb as all around them the crowds hooted and trilled. Children waved decorative streamers from rooftops, women ululated and cheered, and men threw copper coins that glittered on the thoroughfares. The sultan's soldiers stood sentinel at the edge of the road, stoically watching the proceedings while they kept an eye on the masses.

Though Loulie was accustomed to crowds, this was the most people she had seen together in one place, and the sight nearly made her freeze up. But then she remembered Dahlia's words: *A person's reputation is determined by how they interact with others.*

Loulie's identity was a thing crafted from mystery, and she intended to keep it that way. She forced herself to straighten in her saddle and lift her head. She'd nearly made it to the souk entrance when a familiar voice called her name, and she turned before she could help it. Rasul al-Jasheen was pushing past people as he waved at her.

He drew close enough to touch her. "I had no choice," he said.

Loulie said nothing, though her hands trembled on the reins. Rasul's eyes darted back and forth, seeking guards who were already approaching. "It was my tribe. I could not—could not risk them."

Her heart beat so wildly she could barely hear herself think. *Tribe.* The word sounded like home and heartbreak. If she had been able to save her tribe all those years ago by destroying the lives of others, would she have done what Rasul had?

"Do not disobey him," Rasul murmured as he stepped away. His green robes blended into the vibrant hustle and bustle of the souk, and between one blink and the next, he was gone.

Loulie was shaken when she turned to the gate. Her gaze wavered again, without her permission, and she saw Dahlia standing at the outskirts of the crowd, bulky arms crossed as if in defiance, amber eyes narrowed against the sun. The minute their gazes caught, Dahlia placed a hand over her heart and bowed.

Loulie loosed a soft breath and nodded back.

Goodbye, Dahlia.

—⁂—

"You're sure about this?" the tavernkeeper said.

Layla grinned. "Completely. You told me I had to earn my keep somehow."

Dahlia scoffed. "What I said is that I don't take in freeloading orphans. Your errand running is more than enough payment. I never suggested you wander the desert looking for relics that may or may not exist. How do you even plan on finding these things?"

Layla glanced at Qadir, who was spooning sugar into his cup. Without batting a lash, he raised the cup and drank. Layla had to bite down on her lip to keep from laughing. She doubted Qadir knew she'd discovered his secret—that he was only pretending to spoon sugar into his chai. His cup was empty. Qadir drank the sugar plain.

She waited patiently for him to finish, then held out her hand for the compass, which she presented to Dahlia. The tavernkeeper eyed it skeptically. "An ancient compass?"

Layla tapped the glass surface. The red arrow shuddered. "A magic *compass."*

Dahlia looked unimpressed. "Come back in thirty days with these relics and I'll believe you. One day longer and I'll send out a search party."

Layla raised her brows. "If I didn't know any better, I'd think you were worried *about me, Dahlia bint Adnan. And here I thought you had no heart."*

"I'm worried about you as an investment, girl. You're worth more to me alive than dead." Her gaze softened. "You'll be careful, won't you? The desert is dangerous."

"I know." Layla passed a cup back and forth between her hands. "I miss it."

"You Bedouin and your wanderlust." Dahlia sighed, but she was smiling. "Well, make sure you return. You still owe me gold for rent."

"I'll do better than that." Layla leaned forward, held up her cup. "I'll bring back enough relics to sell for a small fortune. And then I'll split it with you."

Dahlia laughed as she raised her cup. "To small fortunes, then."

They clinked their cups together. "To small fortunes," Layla echoed.

19

MAZEN

The first time Mazen had ventured into the desert, he'd been learning how to ride a horse. Though there were fields in the noble quarter that had been cleared for such practices, the sultan insisted the best place for him to learn was in the terrain where he would be doing most of his riding. Mazen could still remember his wonder then, when he'd stepped beyond the city gate for the first time and witnessed the majesty of the desert up close.

He remembered the air shimmering with particles of dust so fine they looked like twinkling stars. He remembered the landscape—a tide of sand that shone gold beneath the setting sun—and the wind, which tugged playfully at his clothing.

The lessons had been difficult, but Mazen had nonetheless enjoyed them. Back then, things had been simpler. He'd been just a child, looking forward to the important business trips he would one day accompany his father on. He had imagined adventures where he rode across dunes and ran into legendary creatures he would brag to his mother about.

And then his mother had died, and those days had never come.

A strange nostalgia swept over him now as they followed the travelers' path out Madinne's front gate. He was struck with the peculiar feeling that he was riding into the past rather than the future; there was that same sunset painting the distant dunes a golden red, and there was the dust that glittered faintly in the air, carried on a gentle breeze. He looked down, noticing yellow wildflowers shooting out from the sand, and wondered if someone had planted them there or if even this small offshoot of greenery had sprung from jinn blood.

He would have asked the question aloud if he had been himself.

He shifted, hopefully discreetly, in his saddle. It had been a long while since he'd been on a horse; he was still remembering how to relax his body. No, how to relax *Omar's* body, which was much heavier—sturdier—than his. Thankfully, none of his traveling companions paid his restless movements any mind. In fact, none of them spoke at all. Mazen tried to be optimistic about the silence. At the very least, it gave him time to appreciate the journey.

The remarkably *short* journey.

When the rock-lined path quickly disappeared, the merchant took out a compass and used it to guide them in the right direction. From there, they had only to follow the tracks of other travelers for a couple of hours until they came to the first stop on their map: an outpost not far from the city, a spot visitors called al-Waha al-Khadhra'a, the Green Oasis. It was more a retreat than a stopover, a miniature town made up of clay buildings and colorful stalls. At the heart of the outpost was the oasis, a large body of water surrounded by yellow grasses, sloping date trees, and tents. Mazen could not help but wonder how many jinn had died to create it.

The morose thought hung above him like a dark cloud as they entered the outpost and Loulie al-Nazari turned to address them. "We camp here tonight," she said stiffly, and then she rode on ahead without waiting for a response. Mazen watched her stifle a yawn as she and her bodyguard headed for the space by the water reserved for overnight camping.

He wondered briefly at her exhaustion before turning his attention to the new and unfamiliar sights around him. He took in the women walking with woven baskets on their heads; the men leaning against trees, munching on skewers of lamb; and the children darting behind stalls, giggling as they hid from each other.

The scene brought the briefest of smiles to his face before he realized he was meant to be Omar, and Omar would not gawk at such things. He pushed his horse forward, beating dust from his clothing as he followed after Aisha bint Louas, who had paused a short distance away. She had not said anything on the journey. In fact, she had not spoken to him at all, except to tell him to stand taller at the procession.

The silence between them persisted as they set up their tent. Loulie al-Nazari did not speak to them again for the rest of the night, though Mazen spotted her wandering the outpost stalls. She spent every waking moment with her bodyguard, who loomed behind her like a shadow. Every time Mazen thought about approaching her, the bodyguard—Mazen had overheard her call him Qadir—would frown at him from a distance. Mazen found his deadpan stare even more disconcerting than Aisha's permanent scowl.

By the time midnight rolled around, Mazen had barely spoken to any of the travelers around the outpost, save for a few who recognized his face beneath his hood. It was a strange thing, to be recognized as his brother. An even stranger thing when people smiled at him with stars in their eyes and referred to him by titles that did not belong to him.

King of the Forty Thieves, they called him. *Hero.* But strangest was the third title, which he'd never heard before: *the Stardust Thief.* It was worse than the other titles because it was proof that everyone knew what Omar truly was: A man who stole jinn lives. A killer dressed in silver blood.

He was still thinking about the title when he fell asleep in his tent that night. It passed into his nightmares, a whisper on his lips when Omar approached with his black knife. *Spare me, Stardust Thief. Spare me.* But Omar, terrible, smirking Omar, had no mercy. He brought the knife down and—

Mazen awoke with his heart in his throat. At first, he couldn't breathe, could only sit there in shock as he took in the unfamiliar cloth walls surrounding him. He was in a tent, he realized. Not his bedroom. Not the palace. He ran his hands shakily through his hair—only to realize his curls were gone, replaced with coarse, cropped strands.

"Something wrong, Prince?" Mazen looked up and saw Aisha stretched out on the bedroll across from him. She had propped herself up on an elbow and was frowning at him.

Gods, the fall of a feather could wake her.

"It's nothing," he mumbled. "Just a nightmare."

Aisha raised a brow. "Need me to sing you a lullaby?"

Mazen blinked. This was the first time she had responded to something he'd said. Exhausted, he shook his head and stood. Aisha continued to watch him.

She was very pretty, Mazen thought, even if she was more than a little terrifying. She had alluring eyes that were a brown so dark they were nearly black. Her hair, which had been braided earlier, now fell in a silky curtain around her shoulders. Her face was all angles: sharp cheekbones and nose, slanted eyebrows, and a pointed chin. If the legends were true and humans had been made from the earth, then Aisha bint Louas had been sculpted from the toughest, harshest stone.

"I'm going to get some fresh air."

He was on his way out when the thief said, "The nightmares are normal. I had them too when I first fought jinn. They'll go away." She eased herself back down onto her bedroll and turned away from him with a sigh. "Eventually."

Mazen's heart lifted at the reassurance, brusque as it was. "I'm relieved to hear it."

Aisha didn't respond, but he was unoffended. Now that the silence between them had broken, it no longer seemed so heavy. A smile touched his lips as he pushed open the tent flap. "Tesbaheen ala khair," he murmured.

"Wa inta min ahlah," came the grumbled response as he exited.

Earlier, the area outside had been lively, filled with visitors sharing food and gossip. Now it was quiet, the campfires had been put out, and the only light came from the distant torches surrounding the perimeter of the encampment. At first, the darkness was suffocating. It hissed and whispered, drawing Mazen back into his nightmares.

But then he saw the sky. There was no smoke, no trees, no buildings—just that infinite expanse of midnight blue, punctuated by scintillating stars.

He thought of Hakim, who, years ago, had taught him to see constellations. As a boy, Hakim had learned to navigate by them. Mazen had thought he'd be able to do the same once he left the city, but if the stars were a compass, they were one he did not yet know how to read.

The wind gently pulled at his clothing as he wandered to the oasis at the campsite's center. As he circled the water, he observed that the breeze did not permeate Omar's skin the way it did his. In Omar's body, he felt warmer, lighter. And though he was still learning the equilibrium of his brother's body, he realized he nonetheless felt more confident in his skin. More *capable*. The best part of their switch, however, was that the injury from the shadow jinn had ceased to exist, which made it possible for him to forget he'd fallen prey to her.

Until the nightmares return. Dread coiled in his chest. When next he was able to coax Aisha into speaking with him, he would have to ask her how long it had taken for *her* nightmares to subside.

He sighed as he returned to the clearing where their tent was. A campfire he was sure had not been there before crackled at the center. He stared at it. Surely someone would have thought to put it out by now?

"Lost, Prince?"

Mazen jumped at the sound of the voice. By the fire, where he was sure there had been nothing before, he suddenly saw a shadow of a man. A dark-skinned phantom with burning embers for eyes. Mazen nearly fainted at the sight of him. *Not a jinn.* He took a deep breath to calm his heart. *Not a jinn.*

He stepped forward and the vision dissipated. Shadows gave way to light, and Mazen saw a familiar man sitting by the firelight. Qadir, the Midnight Merchant's bodyguard.

Mazen swallowed his nerves and chuckled. "Me, lost? What an amusing thought."

"Hmm." The bodyguard looked away, turning his attention to something balanced on his knee. A compass. Even in the dark, Mazen could see the arrow swaying back and forth. He wondered if it was the compass the merchant had referred to during their ride. It certainly looked the same, though it didn't look particularly dependable now.

Mazen raised a brow. "A broken compass?"

Qadir didn't even spare him a glance. "Not broken, just precise."

"Precise?"

The bodyguard offered no response. Mazen waited for a while, but he could not fashion the quiet into a weapon like his brother could. In the end, he walked away. He was curious, but he was also tired. He hoped that this time, he'd be able to sleep.

20

✦

AISHA

After weeks in Madinne, Aisha was glad to be back in the desert.

She was not, however, glad to be here with the present company. She was accustomed to working alone or, on rare occasions, with Omar or another thief. Camping with near strangers was exasperating.

She grumbled to herself as she leaned over their campfire. Things could be worse, she supposed. At least the bodyguard and the merchant weren't inept. On the contrary, Qadir was good with a bow, and Loulie knew how to skin and cook the game he brought back. For the last three days since they'd left Madinne, they had helped set up camp and chart the way to Dhyme. All in all, Aisha could admit that they had been decent traveling companions.

And then there was Prince Mazen. Though he was familiar enough with Omar's mannerisms to be a decent actor, he was dead weight. All she had managed to teach him so far was how to make a fire. Every other task she handled by herself. It would not have been so terrible, she thought, if she hadn't been pretending to serve a man who was not her king.

Aisha plucked a branch from the edges of the fire and absently began to draw shapes in the sand. It was not until Loulie al-Nazari joined her and glanced at the lines that Aisha realized she was scratching flowers into the dirt. She brushed them away with feigned nonchalance.

The merchant pulled her knees to her chest. "Hobby of yours?" she asked.

"None of your business," Aisha said.

"Not one for talk, are you?"

"Speak for yourself. Do not pretend you have not been avoiding us."

The merchant shrugged as she leaned closer to the fire. "And? You've been avoiding *us*." No sooner had she begun to warm her hands than a gust of wind rushed through, unsettling the sand and making the flame flicker. The merchant flinched back. Aisha suppressed a shudder as she pulled up her hood. It always took her a few nights to acclimate to the harsher winds when she returned to the desert.

Footsteps sounded behind them, and moments later, Prince Mazen and Qadir appeared. The prince with the map she'd insisted he study, and Qadir with a bag of dates he'd apparently purchased at the oasis two days ago. Mazen seated himself a few feet away while Qadir settled himself beside the merchant. She shifted closer to him, close enough to steal the bag of dates off his lap. Qadir didn't seem to mind when she started munching on them.

"I see there's been a shift in the weather," he said.

Mazen smirked. It was a disconcertingly perfect mirror image of Omar's usual smile. "What an astute observation."

Aisha glanced up at the sky. The full moon looked hazy, almost like a mirage. She saw no encroaching clouds, so it was unlikely a rainstorm was coming. What, then? Was the bodyguard just referring to the colder winds? That was not unusual for this time of year.

"It is hardly noteworthy." She returned her gaze to the merchant, who looked like she was fighting a chill with her arms crossed beneath her cloak. Qadir, on the other hand, appeared completely unperturbed by the cold. And Prince Mazen—Aisha could tell by the way he clenched his jaw that he was trying to keep his teeth from chattering.

"Shift or no shift, we'll arrive at Dhyme tomorrow," he said. "We will not have to fear the weather being a hindrance when we are within the city walls."

The merchant raised a brow. "What an *astute* observation, High Prince."

Mazen blinked, looking stupefied.

Aisha pointedly cleared her throat and diverted the conversation. "Do not forget about the wali of Dhyme, sayyidi. He will be expecting us to pay him a visit when we arrive in the city." Omar never passed through Dhyme without visiting the city's guardian.

It was a small reassurance that Mazen would already know Ahmed's demeanor. Mazen was a prince, after all, and he'd doubtless met the wali when he visited Madinne on business.

The prince sighed. "Of course. I could never forget Ahmed. He's too dramatic for that."

Loulie al-Nazari flinched. It was a slight motion but noticeable, given her silence. *She knows him*, Aisha thought. But her curiosity sparked and died in the same breath. She could not read the merchant's feelings off her face, and she did not care enough to pry.

Silence encompassed the area. They all stared solemnly, quietly, into the fire. And then the merchant threw a stray stick into the blaze. The flames crackled and flared, painting her face with shadows that made her scornful gaze look even harsher.

"Well," she said. "Where the weather is concerned, I suppose there's nothing to do but wait and see what tomorrow brings."

—✺—

The next day brought a godsdamned dust storm.

Tenacious winds cleaved at the landscape, and harsh gusts tore at their clothing and whipped at their skin. One needed only to glimpse at the eerie orange sky to know they were in the middle of a sandstorm. The city of Dhyme, which ought to have been a few hours away, was nothing but a blurry shape barely visible beyond clouds of dust. The single indication they were going in the right direction was the merchant's compass, which dutifully pointed north.

Or so Aisha assumed. The merchant and her taciturn bodyguard had disappeared into the haze, and she could no longer see them.

The wind howled in her ears, throwing so much dust in her face she had to conceal it behind her scarves. She cursed as the world collapsed into sand and wind and gloom. The sand was there even when she squeezed her eyes shut, sticking to her lashes and prickling the backs of her lids. It was in her throat, turning every exhale into a painful, wheezing cough.

She wanted to kick herself for not realizing the foggy sky had been a precursor to this. She had foolishly expected tamer traveling weather because it was the beginning of the Cold Season, but she ought to have known by now that desert weather was a fickle thing.

She chanced a look at her surroundings as the wind's shriek died into a mournful moan, squinting into the dust for any sign of human motion. The Midnight Merchant was still absent from sight, but Aisha could see another figure approaching. His face was covered, but she would have recognized Omar anywhere.

Even when he was not himself.

Aisha urged her mare toward the prince. Closer and closer—until the wind picked up again and a thick curtain of dust descended upon them. Her vision went black.

Time ceased to exist in the darkness. It was useless to push forward, so Aisha gripped her reins, ducked her face into her scarves, and retreated into the calm of her mind. The wind battered her so heavily from every side that she soon lost all sense of direction. She simultaneously felt as if she had been flung into the air and also like she was being buried. It became difficult—nearly impossible—to breathe. Only one thought kept her anchored to her saddle: *I will not be bested by a storm.*

Long minutes passed, and she repeated the words over and over again until, eventually, the wind abated and the sky lightened to a dim red. Taking advantage of the break in the storm, she pulled down the cloth covering her stinging eyes and looked up. Sand trailed down her cheeks like tears as she examined the desert.

The landscape was empty. No prince, no merchant, no bodyguard. Nothing but sand.

The dread hit suddenly, with the force of a punch to the stomach. Aisha keeled over in her saddle. She clenched her reins with trembling hands. Omar had given her this single, simple job. If she confessed to him that she had lost his brother simply because she'd underestimated the storm and hadn't taken the proper precautions, that she hadn't even bothered to rope their horses together...

No. She bit her cheek, hard. *Self-pity is for failures.*

She *would* find the prince. It was her mission to protect him, and she would not fail. She focused on her breathing, exhaling slowly and deeply into her scarf to settle her thudding heart. The merchant and her bodyguard had been heading north, probably toward some kind of shelter. If she could find a way to reorient herself in that direction...

"Aisha!"

The call was barely a murmur, but Aisha could still discern the direction it was coming from. Her heart simultaneously leapt and sank with relief when she turned in her saddle and saw the shadow of the prince waving at her from a distance. She waved back—one curt motion to let him know she saw him.

The prince raised his hand and pointed east. Aisha veered left, mirroring his progress from afar as she worked to close the gap between them. But it was a sizable distance, and the wind was beginning to pick up again, bringing with it a thick layer of sand that made it difficult to tell whether he was miles or feet away. In this visibility, she couldn't even see his face.

Aisha leashed her frustration and focused on her progress. Never mind that there was sand in every crevice of her body, or that every one of her breaths was a rasp because there was so much of it in her lungs. Never mind that the wind was unraveling her shawls and that its howl had softened into a whisper that sounded, oddly, like a voice...

Ya Awasha, that glower will stick to your face if you don't lighten up!

Aisha tensed. Unbidden, her eyes wandered to a smear of color at the edge of her vision. She inhaled sharply at the impossible sight before her: a man, standing in the middle of the storm and waving at her with a crooked smile on his face.

But...no, she was mistaken. There was no storm. There was only her brother standing in the fields of Sameesh, teasing her because he knew it was the best way to spark her motivation. *I know you, dear sister. Deny it all you like, but I know that it is spite that best fuels you.*

The longer she stared, the clearer her brother's visage became: the angular face, the dark eyes, the stubble he had never had the chance to grow into a beard...

A door slammed shut in Aisha's mind, and her brother suddenly vanished. She tightened her grip on her reins and thought, *The dead do not speak.*

Normally, being self-aware was enough to overcome the heat-induced hallucinations of the desert. But these mirages were just as persistent as the storm. Every time Aisha turned away from one, another materialized before her eyes. She saw her mother, beckoning to her from beneath a date tree as she worked on one of her baskets. She saw her uncle, leading a herd of sheep to pasture.

Aisha dug her nails into her palms hard enough to make the skin tear. "The dead do not speak," she murmured to herself. "The dead do *not* speak."

"How curious, that you can silence their voices."

She whirled, and suddenly there was her brother, inexplicably riding beside her on the prince's horse. No, not the prince's. The shadow she had thought was Mazen was not him at all.

"Tell me, killer. Does it ease your conscience to silence your victims?" The phantom's eyes darkened with his smirk, the pupils bleeding into the whites until they were as black as coal. "Typical hunter, thinking you are above death."

Jinn magic. The epiphany burned through Aisha like fire. She moved on instinct, sliding a knife out from her sleeve and throwing it at her brother's face. The mirage that had been her flesh and blood crumbled to dust, and the horse vanished with it.

But Aisha was no longer alone.

Beneath the layers of wind and dust, she could make out a dune. And at the top of the dune was a lone, grinning shadow. *Find me, jinn killer*, it whispered in her mind. Aisha's possession-resisting rings burned; it was all she could do to keep from prying them off.

She knew she should turn around. That she should try to find the prince again. Trying to fight in this storm was madness, and the jinn was clearly taunting her. But this creature had looked into her mind. It had thought to *fool* her. And Aisha refused to be deceived by a jinn.

A deadly calm washed over her as she spurred her mare forward. She would deal with this monster and its illusions, and then she would resume her search for the group. It would not take long to dispatch the creature; she had faced many like it before.

The shadow never moved, just stood there smiling at her from a distance. *Find me*, it whispered. *Find me. Find me.* By the time Aisha had dismounted, the voice was a relentless jeer, urging her onward and making her vision beat red with rage.

Aisha climbed the dune. Even when the wind battered her from every direction and her world descended once more into darkness, she climbed. She pressed her lips together—sand crunched between her teeth—and put one heavy foot in front of the other. Over and over and over again—until her heel met air.

There was a moment of suspension. And then Aisha stumbled, gracelessly sliding down the slope of sand on nerveless legs. One of her scarves flew loose, and by the time she'd reached the bottom of the dune, her throat was so full of sand she could barely breathe.

Irritated and shaken, Aisha cursed as she reached for her blades. She was relieved to feel both still sheathed at her hips.

Good. Her eyes were burning and her body was sore, but at least she had her weapons. She wrapped her fingers around the hilts as she squinted into the dust. That was when she saw the chasm: an ominous darkness partially hidden behind a curtain of sparkling sand.

Aisha threw a look over her shoulder at the desert. The storm still raged behind her, vicious and blinding and relentless—just as impenetrable as the void before her. Aisha knew a trap when she saw one. The jinn had orchestrated this so that regardless of which way she turned, she would be lost.

Find me. The taunt echoing from the darkness had the cadence of a song.

She faced the gloom with a glare. She had no way of knowing if the jinn was the cause of the sandstorm, but it didn't matter. It was her job to exterminate the creatures. What kind of hunter would she be if she let this monster escape to wreak havoc on unsuspecting travelers?

She would deal with the jinn first, then she would find the group. Simple.

Aisha stepped forward. "Prepare yourself, jinn."

She began the hunt.

21

LOULIE

Loulie saw Qadir's fire first: a bright, nearly blue flame that flickered fiercely in the distance. It was the single guiding light in this pitch-black sandstorm. She rode toward it, stopping only when her horse's hooves clicked rather than crunched.

Then Qadir was at her side, leading her horse into the cave. She cursed as she unwrapped the shawls from around her face. Her eyes burned like hell, and there was sand in her teeth. Qadir wordlessly handed her the waterskin as she dismounted, and she drenched both her face and throat with water before shaking off the thick layer of dust that had settled onto her clothing.

"No sand in your lungs?" Qadir said.

She coughed. "Only a little more than usual."

Not long after Qadir tethered her horse, the prince entered the cave through a curtain of dark sand. His eyes were cracked with red as he slid off his saddle and unwound his scarves. Loulie expected a smirk, not the haunted look on his face. "Has Aisha arrived?" he asked. Loulie glanced at Qadir, who shook his head. The prince cursed. "I lost her in the storm."

Though he made the proclamation calmly, Loulie saw his panic in the way his throat bobbed and in the way he looked not once, but twice over his shoulder, as if he expected his admission to summon the thief. Before Loulie could say anything, he went to stand at the cave entrance. Sand assaulted him from various directions, but the prince stood tall and still as he stared out into the dark void that had become the desert.

"Gods," she heard him murmur. She was taken aback by the emotion in his voice.

"We'll search for her after the storm clears." Qadir approached the prince's horse and patted the dirt from its muzzle.

The prince whirled. "But Aisha—bint Louas…" He looked at a loss for words.

She almost—*almost*—felt sorry for him. Mostly, though, she was disappointed that he too had not disappeared. That she could not lose him and flee this terrible quest.

Abruptly, as if he realized he'd let his mask fall, he turned away from the entrance and sighed. "Fine. We wait for the storm to clear."

And wait they did. When evening came, they broke bread over the fire and took turns watching the mouth of the cave. There was barely any conversation between them, and Loulie was glad for it. She did not want to talk about the lost thief. And she did not want to talk about Dhyme again—especially when the topic was Ahmed.

She had been trying to forget him since he was mentioned last night, but now the conversation was etched into the back of her wandering mind: a reminder that she too would have to visit him. A reminder that, for all her convoluted feelings about the wali, she *wanted* to visit him. Loulie absently turned the thought over in her head. It faded only when she slept, once more dissipating into a problem to be addressed later. Always later.

The storm did not subside until early morning, at which point they packed their supplies and left to search for the missing thief. Loulie assumed Aisha had found refuge in some other place, but she saw nothing nearby that would pass for shelter. There was also no sign of her horse. Loulie thought about using the compass to track her but ultimately decided against it; she did not want to reveal its magic to the prince. He was a thief, after all, and she did not think it beneath him to steal it.

Retracing their steps from the previous day was impossible—the storm had covered their tracks completely. It was impossible to tell where they had lost Aisha; except for the occasional cactus or shrub, the desert was just a landscape of rolling dunes, steep valleys, and squat cliffs. The only nearby civilization was Dhyme, which seemed farther than it had yesterday. It was nothing but a speck on the horizon, visible only when they gained elevation.

Loulie groaned as they passed a scraggly yellow shrub they had most certainly walked past earlier. Perhaps she *should* use the compass...

"I think I see another cave in the distance," Qadir said. He pointed, and though Loulie saw nothing but smudges, the smudges were gray in color, and that was promising in a landscape of golds and reds. "I'll ride out and check." He looked at her and raised a brow. *Wait for me*, the look said.

Loulie hesitated. She and Prince Omar, alone? The thought made her nervous. Not because she was *scared* of him, no, but because she abhorred the idea of having to exist in the same space as him without Qadir. But...

She cast a surreptitious look at the prince. He was sullen, lips pressed together in a grimace that was more anxious than angry.

He is tolerable like this, she thought, and nodded at Qadir to say so.

The minute Qadir took off, the prince slid from his saddle and began climbing the nearest hill of sand. Loulie frowned at him. "What are you doing?"

"Trying to get to a vantage point." He hesitated as the sand shifted beneath his feet, then turned to look at her expectantly. Loulie bristled. She refused to be looked down on—figuratively *or* literally.

Her legs were sore by the time they reached the top, but she was reinvigorated by the view. To the east: the shadow that was the city of Dhyme. And to the west, she saw a speck that was Qadir. He was heading for the gray smudge, which from here she could see was indeed a cave. In the distance she saw a line of shadows that might have been a caravan, but they were too far out for Aisha to have reached in a single night.

Loulie glanced down. The hill they were on dropped into a small, steep valley on this side, one surrounded by slopes of sand. It was a spectacular if eerie sight.

"I see something," the prince mumbled. He pointed, and Loulie followed his gaze to a sliver of color below. From this distance, it looked like a crumpled shadow without an owner.

Loulie slid down into the valley ahead of him to investigate.

She dug through the sand to unearth the shard of color. Her heart dropped as she held it up.

It was a velvet scarf.

Omar snatched the lightweight cloth from her hands. "This looks like one of Aisha's."

Loulie stood and glanced around them. If this scarf *was* one of the thief's, and it was here between the dunes, did that mean she had stumbled into this valley? Or had the wind simply carried it here?

Beside her, Omar inhaled sharply. He whirled in place, eyes narrowed. "What is that..." His gaze seemed oddly unfocused. "*Infernal* sound?" Loulie strained her ears, but all she could hear was the distant cry of a hawk.

"There's a voice." Omar stepped toward the dune. He paused, tilted his head. "A woman's voice?" He pressed his palm to the gigantic hill of sand. For a few moments he just stood there, squinting. Then he began to claw at the dirt.

Loulie stepped back, away from the falling dust. "Ah, what a great idea, High Prince. I hadn't even considered the possibility of Aisha burying herself in sand!"

The prince just kept digging like a man possessed, sending more dust at her face. She gasped—a terrible idea. She inhaled a fistful of sand and choked on her own breath. By the time the air cleared, her throat was on fire.

She spun on the high prince, a curse on her lips, but it died in the same breath. Despite all of the falling sand, the dune looked exactly as it had moments ago.

And Omar was gone.

She half expected him to jump out at her. But no such thing happened, and the prince did not respond when she called his name.

Magic?

There was only one way to find out. She reached into her robe and pulled out the compass. She knew even before looking at the arrow what it would show her. The instrument was humming the way it did every time an undiscovered relic was close.

Sure enough, the red arrow was pointing straight at the wall of sand, quivering as if with anticipation. Loulie eyed the dune warily. It was not rare for a relic to manipulate the space around it. The stronger the relic, the more powerful the manipulation. But—a dune?

She put her hand to the hill and startled when her rings warmed. Indecision seized her as she looked at the compass. She had never gone searching for a relic without Qadir. Had never left him without a way to find her. But...

I just need to grab the prince and get out. I'll be back before Qadir returns.

She tucked the compass into her pocket and stepped forward. This time, the magic did not hide itself from her. The sand gave away, revealing an entrance that hadn't been there before. Loulie stepped into the darkness and disappeared from the valley.

22

MAZEN

The corridor was glorious, shining from floor to ceiling with beautiful mosaics. Stone pillars held up a domed ceiling covered in decorative stained glass. Skull-shaped sconces hung from the walls and contained flaming white candles that made the tiled floor flash a brilliant cerulean blue. It was, despite its eeriness, the most beautiful corridor he'd ever seen.

Mazen had absolutely no idea how he'd gotten here.

He could vaguely remember seeing a dune. Digging into the dune. Falling into the dune. Once inside, screaming at the pitch black of the dune. He remembered panicking, beating his fists against dark walls in an effort to find the exit. But after that, his memory was a blur.

He took a deep breath as he turned to the cracked image on his right. He beheld a clustered, chaotic depiction of what he guessed were the seven jinn kings. One jinn was half bird and half man, sporting a human torso and legs but bird wings and a falcon head. Mazen wondered if it was a depiction of the jinn king imprisoned by Amir.

The second jinn was portrayed midspin, its features hidden behind a veil of mist. The third jinn held a skull in one hand and a scepter in the other; the fourth had fins sprouting from its back and scales shining on its flesh. The fifth: a jinn wearing a dara'a cut into two halves—one glittering with jewels and the other black and torn. The last two jinn were the strangest; one was crafted from wood and had flowers growing between its fingers, while the other was a fanged shadow with glittering red eyes.

Mazen stepped back at the sight of it, heart pounding in his ears. It reminded him of the shadow jinn. But...no. Surely she had not been a jinn king?

He stifled a nervous laugh and forced himself forward. Every footstep echoed too loudly in the silent hall, and the jinn on the walls seemed to follow him with their eyes.

Don't panic. He plucked a dagger from Omar's belt in the hope that it would make him feel braver. The ruins were so quiet he could hear the rustle of his clothing, the frantic pounding of his heart. Usually, even silence had a sound—some underlying cadence that went unnoticed until all other noise disappeared. But this absence was absolute. Unnatural.

Don't panic. He forced himself to walk. And walk. And walk.

His stomach jumped into his throat when he again saw the image of the seven jinn. He knew it was the same because the stone was chipped in the same places. He wasn't walking down an endless corridor—he was walking in place.

The fire nearby wavered. Mazen's grip on the blade tightened. His muscles tensed, his breathing hitched, and he thought, *Oh gods, please don't let me be possessed please—*

"Salaam."

He turned and thrust the dagger forward. It sliced through nothing. The stranger was far enough away that the blade never even brushed her skin.

Mazen froze. He knew this woman.

Long hair that gleamed like polished wood, freckled olive skin, gold eyes flecked with uneven brown—Mazen lowered his blade. Those were *his* eyes. His mother's eyes.

"Uma?" He blinked and somehow, impossibly, she did not disappear.

"Habibi," she murmured. He flinched but did not pull away when she placed a hand on his cheek. Her skin was cold, so very cold. But her hand was so *soft*. When she pulled it away, Mazen felt as if she'd unwound some vital thread from inside of him. He blinked, and his mother wavered on the spot like a mirage.

"Uma—" His fingers swept through air.

"Habibi."

He turned and saw her standing farther down the corridor, holding a lantern that glowed with the same garish light as the candles in the sconces. She gestured him forward, a soft smile on her face. "Follow me."

He stepped forward. "Where are you going?"

But Shafia did not answer. She turned and walked away, and the flames in the sconces flickered and died as she passed them. Darkness nipped at Mazen's heels. *Inconsequential*, it whispered. He shrank away from it and chased after his mother.

His heartbeat drummed in his ears and throbbed behind his eyes. He was vaguely aware of the sudden heaviness of his body and the strange pressure building in his head. He felt the iron rings, too hot and tight on his fingers—and then nothing. Every time he blinked, his mind grew foggier, until it was empty of everything save for a gentle humming. The corridor ceased to exist. There was just his mother, singing a song beneath her breath.

The stars, they burn the night
And guide the sheikh's way..."

Mazen did not recognize the lyrics, yet he found himself humming along with his eyes half-closed, relishing the strange feeling of nostalgia that washed over him.

They passed through chambers that flourished before his eyes. One moment they were filled with cobwebs and dirt, and the next, elaborate tapestries stretched across the walls and rich rugs unrolled beneath their feet. They entered what appeared to be a diwan, where skeletons sat hunched over cups filled with beetles. But as Mazen passed, the skeletons became living people who raised their cups to him and cried, "Savior! Savior!"

More than a few times he wondered if he ought to voice his concerns. *What am I saving you from?* he wanted to ask. Or perhaps, *How are you alive, uma?* But the urge faded every time his mother sang.

The song was still echoing in his mind long after she stopped, still numbing his thoughts, when his mother spoke into the quiet. "Do you know the story of the Queen of Dunes, Mazen?"

Mazen heard her words but for some reason was unable to grasp their meaning. He smiled, hoping it was the appropriate response.

His mother smiled back. It was the same bright smile she'd always worn, the one that made dimples appear at the corners of her mouth. "She can make all of your wishes come true. Even the impossible ones." She paused at the bottom of a staircase that spiraled up into a dark tower. She mounted the rickety wooden stairs. "But all wishes have a price," she continued. "The queen will make a request of you. You must accept before she will give you your heart's desire."

If you wish it, I can even raise the dead. A deep but gentle voice caressed his mind.

Mazen's heart lurched at the sound of it. His vision blurred and his mother vanished. In her place was a gangly pale creature with long limbs and gaping holes for eye sockets. It spoke to him in his mother's voice. "You'll help me, won't you, Mazen?"

Mazen opened his mouth—to gasp, to scream—but then the humming began again and smoothed his fears away. The creature disappeared, and it was once again his mother standing before him, brows scrunched with concern.

Of course I'll help you, uma.

She beamed. "I knew I could count on you, Mazen."

He blinked, not realizing he'd said the words aloud. But he supposed it didn't matter. His mother had always been good at deciphering his expressions—

He stopped. He'd forgotten he was in Omar's body. How did his mother . . .

"We've arrived." She gestured ahead, to a set of bronze doors at the stair landing. "Remember what I said. Nothing sacrificed, nothing gained."

Mazen hesitated. That strange fogginess was invading his mind again, making it impossible for him to grasp his thoughts. But then his mother set a hand on his shoulder, and his focus shattered completely. "Have faith, Mazen." Her words were soft, a conspiratorial whisper. "Not everything that is stolen from us must remain so."

Mazen turned away. He breathed in. And then he slowly approached the doors.

He knew all about loss. He had lost his mother. He had lost his freedom. Now he had even lost his identity.

I can bring her back, the humming voice said in his mind. *I can bring back your mother.*

The doors opened into a circular chamber lit by fading torchlight. A deft wind blew through cracks in the decrepit walls, ruffling maroon-colored drapes. Save for the rustling, the space was disconcertingly quiet. An empty circular chamber made up of cracked walls.

And then Mazen heard a crunch as he stepped into the room.

He looked down and saw bones on the tiled floor. He recognized, vaguely, that this discovery ought to be upsetting. That it was probably cause for concern. But he did not have time to worry, so he tucked the realization away to be evaluated at a later time and continued toward a stone dais rising above the sea of bones. Sitting atop the dais was a circlet—a ring of intricately carved golden skulls. Some distant part of him wondered why he gravitated toward it, but he did not allow himself to linger on the thought, for he knew this circlet would make his wishes come true. He had only to possess it and...

Then I will be queen once more.

Mazen began to hum as he stepped up to the dais. The bones whispered as he reached for the crown. *Queen, queen, queen.* The word pulsed through his body. Through his fingertips.

He grasped the circlet of bones.

23

LOULIE

Sweet Fire? Wake up, Sweet Fire.

It was as if the world had been reduced to black ash.

Loulie! Lou-Lou-Loulie!

Loulie startled. "Baba?" No one else used that ridiculous call except for her father. She groggily searched the darkness for him.

I am here, Sweet Fire.

The strange darkness abruptly receded, revealing a corridor filled with elaborate mosaics and eerie skull-shaped sconces. She squinted into the dark but perceived no end to the hallway. A thick silence hung in the air, making her uncomfortably aware of her breathing. But it shattered before she could ponder it.

"Over here, Loulie."

She saw him in the distance then, silhouetted in the blue light emitted by the candles: her father. Broad shouldered and tall, with deep-brown eyes that twinkled with permanent amusement. In one hand he held a lantern. With the other, he beckoned her closer.

"Baba?" Her heart thudded. Once. *It can't be.* Twice. *You're dead.*

She moved toward him in a daze. Or at least, she tried to. But every time she stepped forward, he appeared farther away. "Sweet Fire," he called from a distance. "Come. Follow me." He turned, and his robes—the same robes she wore as the Midnight Merchant—brushed the ground with the motion.

She hesitated. This was clearly a trick. She did not have time to chase mirages down dark corridors. She turned around, searching for the entrance—and saw only a dead end.

The sight filled her with exasperation. *Wonderful.*

"Hurry!" the phantom called. "Unpleasant things roam the dark, Sweet Fire."

Sure enough, she became aware of shifting, of whispers in her ears. She suppressed a shudder and started walking. She began formulating a plan. Step one: avoid getting devoured by sentient darkness.

But while she could escape the dark, she could not run from the voices. The closer she drew to the mirage of her father, the louder they became. She gritted her teeth and touched her rings, focused on the burning at her fingertips. *None of this is real. This is magic. This is…*

Her father began to sing. *"The stars, they burn the night and guide the sheikh's way."*

Loulie startled. Where did she recognize that song from? The more she thought about it, the cloudier her mind became, until only the lyrics remained. The song filled her with warmth and longing. It made her feel like she was coming home.

"Yes," her father said softly. "We are going home."

"Home?" The word was faint on her lips. She had given up returning long ago, because… because something had happened. She remembered fire and pain and death. She remembered loss and the denial of loss. She remembered not wanting to remember.

"Home," her father said gently. "But first, we must bring everyone back."

Loulie nodded slowly, deciding this sounded reasonable. Plausible, even. She could trust her father; he had never steered her in the wrong direction before. Had never…

A memory surfaced. Shattered and fragile, like broken glass. In it, she sat by a campfire, knee-to-knee with her father. He reached into his pocket and pulled out a flat disc made of wood and glass. A compass. *There are many mysterious things in the desert, Sweet Fire. If ever you find such items, you must take great care of them, for they may be relics enchanted by jinn.*

She remembered the warmth of his hands as he set the compass in her palms. *Is this compass filled with magic, then?* she'd asked.

He'd laughed. *It does not work for me, but perhaps it will guide your way.*

The memory dissipated. Loulie squinted, renewed her focus. They were just about to turn a corner when her eyes snagged on a particularly gruesome mosaic. In it, sailors sank beneath a blue-black ocean and reached fruitlessly toward the sky. Their mouths were agape, and their eyes bulged grotesquely from their skulls. Loulie arched her head and saw the god they were reaching for: a woman with unnaturally pearl-white skin and black eyes that gleamed like ink. Her hair was a mess of ashy flakes that burned like embers as they fell to the ground. A collar of golden bones circled her throat.

"Loulie?" her father called, but his voice was far away.

She put her hand to the mosaic. It was cold. Cold enough to remind her of her burning rings. Reality came crashing back. She remembered, suddenly, where she'd heard the song. *Qadir. This is the song Qadir sings.*

She turned, but the mirage had already gone on ahead. The light was a pinprick of blue in the darkness. And then it was gone. The fire died, and her surroundings vanished.

The humming in her head became a shrill buzzing that made her ears pop and her knees tremble. She tasted metal—blood on her lips. She was bleeding from her nose, and her head was pounding so hard she was beginning to feel faint.

Run, she thought, and the voice was sharp, like Qadir's. *Run or you die.*

She turned and bolted without another thought. The darkness gave chase. It fell on her shoulders and grabbed her ankles and screamed in her ears. *Jinn killer! Murderer!*

She was too terrified to object.

If only the glowing orb hadn't been shattered in the sultan's diwan! It would have been useful now, would have at least illuminated her enemy. But no, she was alone; she was—

Suddenly pinned beneath something full of sharp edges and angles. She panicked and swung out with her elbow. There was a crack, and the thing hissed and drew back. She rolled to her feet and ran. When she looked back, the darkness had swallowed her assailant whole.

She was still running when the blackness fractured into fragments of blue gold. Too late, she realized it was someone holding a lantern. She crashed into them, and they both tumbled to the ground in a mess of limbs.

Loulie untangled herself and sat up. She was shocked to see Aisha bint Louas crouched in front of her, eyes shining like daggers. She had a blade angled toward Loulie's neck but lowered it when she saw her face. There was a moment of tense uncertainty.

Truth or illusion?

Before Loulie could decide, Aisha raised her arm and threw the dagger.

It sailed past her shoulder. Loulie heard the sound of tearing cloth and then a shriek. Her bones rattled with the sound. It was a sound she'd never heard, and yet she recognized it.

It was her father's scream.

She turned in place and saw the thing shrieking in her father's voice. A doomed, sinewy, human-shaped creature with hollow eyes and tattered flesh, with too-long limbs and creaking bones that jutted from its too-thin skin like knives.

A ghoul.

Not my father. The thought sounded like an alarm as she pulled out Qadir's dagger and rushed the ghoul. Her panic made her vicious, and she rent bloodless flesh from bone without stopping to breathe. She stabbed and slashed and smashed until there was nothing left to destroy. She was trembling as she crushed the last of the shattered, bloodless bones to dust.

She had faced ghouls before, but never one like this, never one warped by illusion. She had only ever known ghouls to be trackers: near-blind creatures that smelled magic from a distance and chased the humans bearing its source. They were stealthy creatures; muting sound was their most lethal ability. Often, an unnatural hush came over the desert at their approach.

Now, at least, she knew why the corridor had been so quiet before.

Aisha bint Louas walked past her with a sigh. "Salaam, al-Nazari."

Loulie startled at her calm. A layer of sand still glittered on Aisha's cloak and hair from the storm, but she was otherwise unbattered and uninjured. Loulie could not help her irritation. She had come here to *save* this woman, and she had the audacity to sigh as if Loulie had been the one to inconvenience her?

"Where in nine hells have you been? We've been looking all over for you!" Loulie didn't bother softening her voice.

Aisha slid the knife into her belt. "I'd think the answer was obvious. I've been hunting a jinn. It was even nice enough to welcome me into its home."

Loulie recalled the strange look on the prince's face when he'd stood before the dune. He'd said something about hearing a woman's voice. It occurred to her that maybe he had been under the voice's spell before she had, and that there was a chance he still was. But it seemed unlikely. The Omar she knew was a killer, not a victim.

"Is that what you say when a jinn traps you in a buried ruin?" Loulie scowled. "It's *welcoming* you into its home?"

Aisha frowned. "Careful, merchant. I have little patience for your snide remarks."

"And I have little patience for thieves whose egos are so big they refuse to admit they're *lost*. If you're such a good hunter, why haven't you already tracked this jinn?"

When Aisha turned and walked away, Loulie trailed after her. "Well?"

She was just about to reach out and grab Aisha's shoulder when she paused, noticing the marks on her arms. Aisha usually wore her cloak closed, so Loulie had never noticed the henna patterns trailing up her arms: intricate floral designs that wrapped around her elbows and swirled past her shoulders. She would have thought them uncharacteristic if they had not featured so many thorns and razor-sharp leaves.

But it was not the pattern that gave Loulie pause, but the marks beneath the henna—layers of scars simultaneously veiled and accentuated by the ink on Aisha's skin.

The thief turned. "Is there something you want to say, merchant?"

"It seems pointless to ask you another question when you didn't answer my first."

She and Aisha frowned at each other. Loulie forced herself not to blink.

Finally, Aisha turned away. "You want the truth? Yes, I'm lost. I got lost in the sandstorm, and now I'm stuck in this hellhole. I've been unable to find my way out since I was pulled in. If you're so full of great ideas, why don't *you* show us the exit?"

Loulie flushed. Other than the knife, she had only two other items on her. She supposed if there was any time to use them, it was now.

She took out the compass first but quickly abandoned the idea of using it when she saw the arrow spinning in a frenzied circle. Even a silent command would not calm it. The coin only ascertained that she was, indeed, lost and that yes, there was an exit. Somewhere.

Aisha snorted. "So even the legendary Midnight Merchant is at a loss."

"Can you be quiet? I'm trying to think."

Loulie thought about the ghoul masquerading as her father. He'd been trying to lead her someplace before she broke out of her trance; she was sure of it.

She looked at Aisha. "Did a ghoul try to take you somewhere?"

Aisha's mouth twisted into a grimace. "It didn't get very far, but yes."

Looking at the thief's harsher-than-normal scowl, it occurred to Loulie that she must have also seen a ghoul warped by illusion. She wondered—who had she seen? Had it been someone from her family? Her despicable jinn-killing master?

Aisha looked at her, deadpan. "You were saying?"

Loulie imagined that her curiosity was a flame and extinguished it. The last thing she needed was to become more involved than she already was with jinn killers. She shook her head. "I think the ghouls are our key to finding our way through this place."

Aisha raised a brow. "The only way to make it through here is to have a ghoul guide?"

Was that what she was saying? Physically, there was nothing the ghoul possessed that they did not. It had carried a lantern, but they had one too. It had walked the corridors, just as they were walking them now. And it had been . . .

"Singing." The realization hit like a thunderclap.

Aisha crossed her arms. "I suppose, if you want to call that wail a song. What about it?"

A ludicrous idea came to her. So ludicrous that she nearly laughed aloud. But the song was the only thing missing, so why not try to sing it?

She faced the infinite dark and took a deep breath. Ignoring the heat in her cheeks and the twisting in her stomach, she let Qadir's song settle in her mind. She focused on the words, ignoring the fact that Qadir had sung them.

"The stars, they burn the night
And guide the sheikh's way."

The words came, slow at first, then faster, a still lake transformed into a fast-moving stream. She blocked out Aisha's laughter and focused on the song.

"Go to her, go to her, they say,
The star of your eye.
Go to her, go to her,
The compass of your heart."

She felt like she was floating. The song had become a map, the lyrics a path through a foggy, unfamiliar memory. As she sang, the ruins around her blurred and re-formed into a magnificent palace of marble and gold. Everything was gloriously bright.

"The sun, it warms the sand
And sets the sheikh's heart aflame.
She waits in the shade, the sun says,
The beloved of your dreams.
She waits in the shade, the shade."

Loulie's feet moved on their own, guiding her down a road that twisted through past and present. She wandered through rooms simultaneously filled with and deprived of color, through court-yards crawling with plants and filled with ash. They passed through chambers filled with buoyant dancers one moment and inanimate skeletons the next, and corridors shining with newness and dull with age. And then, at last, they came to a fragile-looking staircase.

A voice spoke loudly in Loulie's mind, scattering her thoughts.

Welcome, my guests! It was a woman's voice, deep and sonorous. *Deceitful jinn killers! Murderers of highest esteem! Have you come seeking glory? Power beyond your wildest imaginations?* The voice laughed, and somehow, despite it being in their heads, the sound made the walls tremble. *I am afraid you are too late. Someone has already claimed those honors. But since you've come all this way, please, by all means, come to my chambers. What kind of hostess would I be if I did not entertain my guests?*

"Omar?" Aisha murmured at the same time Loulie thought, *The Queen of Dunes.*

Loulie rushed up the staircase, all the while thinking of the woman from the painting, the one with the ghoulish white skin and the black holes for eyes. The Queen of Dunes. Old Rhuba's tale of the jinn queen poured through her mind like quicksand.

The Tale of the Queen of Dunes

Neither here nor there, but long ago . . .

There once lived a slave named Naji, who was indentured to a cruel merchant. Every day and night, Naji suffered at his hands, for he beat her ruthlessly and without reason. She spent many torturous years serving him until one day, she fled in the middle of a sandstorm. She ran until she could run no more, then collapsed in a secluded valley and prayed to the gods for help.

Much to her surprise, one of the gods responded and, in a silk-soft voice, goaded her farther into the valley, to a wondrous palace concealed behind a veil of sand. Naji was so starstruck she forgot her exhaustion and explored the palace with the giddy innocence of a child. Eventually, she came to a throne room that was so filled with splendid décor it made even her master's wealth pale by comparison.

At the back of the room was a beautiful throne, and sitting atop it was a woman with porcelain-white skin and midnight-black eyes. "Welcome, my esteemed guest!" she cried, and Naji recognized the voice that had led her to the palace. "Please, stay and rest awhile, habibti. I will prepare food and entertainment for you."

Naji was so grateful she could have cried. But no sooner had she beheld the performers than her good cheer vanished, for what she saw was a mockery of life. The dancers were nothing but human shells with hollow eyes. Like puppets, they danced and sang on the command of Naji's hostess.

When they were done, Naji collapsed to her knees and clasped her hostess's cold hands. "You have been so very kind to me, sayyidati, but I must beg your leave. I am being chased by a dangerous man, and I do not want to bring him to your palace."

"Do not worry for me, child. I fear no man. No, it is *they* who fear *me*." Her hostess smiled warmly. "Would you like me to dispose of this monster for you?"

Naji was so in awe of her hostess's courage that she forgot about her unnatural performers. "Could you truly stop him from pursuing me?"

"Oh, I can do that and much more! I can make all your wishes come true, even the impossible ones." Her dark eyes glittered with distant stars. "Of course, all wishes have a price. In order for me to perform such a feat, I will require something from you."

Naji was so desperate she immediately lowered her head and asked how she could serve.

This is what her hostess told her: "In order to perform my magic, I must leave this place, and for that I require your body." She lifted a circlet of golden bones from her head and handed it to Naji. "Clasp this around your neck, and I shall give you the power to destroy your nightmares."

Naji did as commanded, and while her hostess withered away to smoke and ash, Naji was filled with a fearsome, terrible power. Her hunger and thirst vanished, replaced by an insatiable desire for revenge. She returned to the desert, traveling miles until she reached the campsite of her cruel master. He had hired mercenaries to help track Naji down and was shocked when she appeared before them.

"So you've returned, slave!" The merchant approached, holding a whip. "Will you beg me for forgiveness, or will I have to punish you?"

Naji raised her head and looked her former master straight in the eyes. "I will never beg you for forgiveness again." She lifted her arms and called to the dark magic in her veins.

Creatures made of torn flesh and bone answered her call, emerging from the sand with howls of rage. When the merchant and his men fled, the ghouls chased after them like hounds, breaking their bones and shredding their hearts. Afterward, Naji called the creatures back to her. She was shocked when the corpses of the slain men rose and shambled toward her too.

She stepped back with a cry. "What foul magic is this?"

Her hostess laughed inside her mind and said, "My dear girl, this is the magic of the Queen of Dunes. *My* magic. And now that I am free, you have unleashed it upon the world."

Naji had never known a fear as deep as the one she felt then, for the Queen of Dunes was no mortal woman; she was one of the seven jinn kings. She tried to pry the circlet of bones from her neck, but to no avail. The Queen of Dunes laughed. "Our deal is not yet done, habibti. I have destroyed your nightmares, so now you are obligated to hand your body over to me. Do not mourn, dear girl! Together, we will be indestructible."

Then the wicked Queen of Dunes snuffed out Naji's thoughts as easily as one extinguishes a candle, and began to plot. She led her army through the desert and to a brilliant human city, where she met with the wali who governed it. She promised the city's guardian power the likes of which he had never seen if he provided her with shelter. The greedy man accepted her deal and did not mourn when she killed his soldiers, for she reanimated their corpses and made them into a fearsome, undying army.

The wali was so in awe of the queen's magic that he forgot to be afraid. This was his most dire mistake. Weeks after she took over his armies, the Queen of Dunes murdered him on a barren battlefield. "A heartless man needs no heart," she proclaimed, and she tore the man's beating heart from his chest before commanding his corpse to follow her.

The Queen of Dunes wandered the desert for many years, building her army of the dead. They built her a palace, one even more magnificent than the ruins Naji had found her in. It was there that she resided for years, content to be worshipped and feared.

Then came Munaqid, a peasant from a nearby settlement. He, unlike the rest of the townsfolk, refused to worship the queen. "The jinn are blasphemers banished by the gods for their wickedness," he told the others. "And the seven kings are the worst of all, for they are the root of that evil." He sought a way to end the queen's reign of terror. His plan brought him to her palace, where he prostrated himself before her and offered false prayers. Day after day he returned and showered the queen with praise.

The Queen of Dunes was bemused by his dedication and decided to let him stay at the palace so he could serve her. She kept him alive, for she liked to see his expression war between adoration and fear. Over time, she began to trust him.

One day, as they were walking through her dust-filled courtyard, Munaqid asked about her appearance. "You possess the divine beauty of a goddess. What inspired your form?"

"I am but a shadow of what I once was. In order to exist in this world, I require a vessel. This body was an offering." She smiled fondly as she stroked the bones at her throat.

Munaqid understood what he had to do. When nighttime came, he made his way to the queen's bedroom, silencing any ghouls who stepped in his path. He found her slumbering in her bed and pried the circlet from her neck before she woke. What had been impossible for Naji was possible for Munaqid, for he was not bound by magic. He threw the circlet to the ground, grabbed Naji, and ran from the palace even as the queen's ghouls gave chase.

He was bleeding and exhausted by the time he escaped, and still he heard the queen's voice in his mind. *Traitor!* she cried. *Terrible traitor!* Munaqid was beginning to fear he might have to suffer her voice forever when a sandstorm hit and drowned out the sound. He sought shelter in a cave and held Naji to him as the storm raged. When it was over, he stepped outside and saw that where the palace had been, there was now nothing but a huge hill of golden sand.

"The gods have heard my prayers," Munaqid whispered. "They have buried the Queen of Dunes once more. Now we are all free."

Munaqid returned to the cave and found yet another miracle: Naji, revived. He took her hand, and together, they walked back to the settlement. Munaqid's victory was celebrated all across the desert kingdom, and the people once again knew peace. Hundreds of years have passed since his resounding victory. But beware, fair desert folk, for peace is a fragile promise. If ever you come into the desert and hear a voice from your memory offering you your greatest desires, turn away from it. That path is filled with broken and deadly lies.

24

MAZEN

The moment he touched the circlet, a tantalizing warmth rushed through his veins. It was power, intoxicating and overwhelming, and Mazen nearly caved beneath its weight.

Let go, said a gentle voice in his mind.

His hand was shaking as he held up the crown. He could discern another feeling beneath the heat: an electric cold that numbed his bones even as his iron rings burned against his skin in resistance to the magic. His fingers curled tighter around the crown as he brought it to his... neck?

Not a crown, he thought. *A collar.*

He froze. A shadow-drenched memory flashed before his eyes: a phantom with ruby-red eyes stood before him, glowing unnaturally in the dark. He gasped as she approached, collapsing into smoke and entering his lungs and—

"No." The gleaming collar was inches away from his neck.

The terrible humming in his mind said, *Yes.* It was a whisper and a wail and a scream. *Let go*, it said. *Let go let go let*—

"Fine," he said through gritted teeth. He raised the collar. Higher, higher—and then he threw it away. He refused to be possessed again.

Many things happened then. The humming ceased, the collar

started *screaming*, and the sea of bones surged up in a wave, howling with rage. Mazen saw flashes of reanimated bone, severed skin, and flashing blades. The ghouls formed so quickly he didn't realize they'd come to life until they stood before him in all their gruesome glory.

If you will not succumb to me, then you will serve me, the humming voice said.

The fear was immediate. It shot through Mazen's veins like lightning, pulsing at his fingertips as he reached for his knives, which were slippery in his sweat-coated palms.

By the time he'd finally grabbed one, the ghouls were close enough to stab him. They smelled like dirt and rot and decay—a scent that made bile rise in Mazen's throat. He swallowed it down as he tried to focus on anything beyond the ghouls' mutilated faces. But he could not stop looking at the sharpened teeth. The sunken eye sockets. The crushed noses.

One of the ghouls growled deep in its broken throat and reached for him. Mazen's body jerked in reaction. He swept the blade forward in a wild, desperate arc.

Amazingly, the ghoul backed away, hissing at him through cracked teeth.

That blade! The voice lanced through his mind, sharp as a knife. *Abomination! Jinn killer!* Each word stabbed Mazen in the heart. How many times had they been hurled at him when they were not even the truth?

You are not worthy of being my servant. Mazen had the distinct impression the voice was turning away from him. *Kill him*, it said. *Destroy everything, even his bones.*

This time, the ghouls did not hesitate. They rushed him, and Mazen's only instinct was to desperately swing his blade through the air in the hope it would keep him alive. In Omar's body he was faster, stronger, but fear still scrambled his mind.

The ghouls were relentless. Though they lacked the coordination for an organized attack, they came at him from every side. An arrow whistled past Mazen's ear as one ghoul rammed into him. He stumbled, only to have another ghoul slam the flat of its blade into his stomach. One sword tore through his sleeve while another just barely missed his leg.

Mazen staggered back. Landed hard on his heel. Pain shot through his ankle, making him cry out. He clenched his teeth against the ache as he sidestepped one blow and swerved to stab another ghoul in its eyeless sockets.

He startled when it burned to white ash and fell to the ground.

Mazen glanced at Omar's blade. Vaguely, he recalled the Midnight Merchant's comment about the knives being enchanted. But he had no time to think about what that meant. He readied himself for the next wave of ghouls.

That was when he saw a blur of color in the landscape of white. He glanced to the entrance of the room and saw nondescript brown robes. Loulie al-Nazari glowered at him from a distance. Moments later, she was joined by Aisha bint Louas, who sighed when she saw him.

Her exhale shattered the eerie silence. The ghouls scattered, some heading for the doors, others for the pedestal where Mazen was still standing. Mazen focused on staying alive. He sliced his blade through the air, sometimes hitting flesh and bone. Whatever he touched disintegrated to ash, and he soon realized all he had to do to destroy the ghouls was nick them with the blade.

The knowledge did not make him invincible. Nor did it stop the trembling in his hands or clear his head. But it was better than being helpless, so Mazen leaned desperately into every strike, hoping it would carve out an escape. An end.

Moments or minutes or hours passed. When Mazen finally looked up and beyond the ashy carnage in front of him, he saw the merchant and the thief. Aisha was relying on speed rather than power, knocking down ghouls and severing their limbs before they could give chase. Loulie al-Nazari was at the opposite end of the room, using the curtains as cover. She had just disappeared behind one of them when he heard a snap.

When the merchant reappeared, her knife was on *fire*. She was grinning triumphantly as she swept the blade through the air and set the ghouls aflame. Mazen watched as one of those ghouls collapsed with a wail, its hands outstretched as if reaching for something. He tracked its gaze and cursed when he saw the collar lying on the ground.

The Midnight Merchant paused to look at the relic. For moments, she was absolutely still, head cocked as if she were listening for something. Mazen approached her on shaking legs.

"Al-Nazari." He forced her name out through cold lips. She ignored him. "Midnight Merchant!" She began to walk slowly toward the collar, fingers outstretched.

"Stop, al-Nazari!"

She reached down to pick it up.

Mazen collided with her headfirst, knocking the thing from her hands and tackling her to the ground. He gasped as she drove a knee into his stomach, but forced himself to hold tightly to her wrists as he gritted his teeth against the pain. He pinned her to the ground. "Snap out of it!"

The merchant dug her fingernails into his skin. Mazen pulled back with a yell, and she used the opening to slash at him with her dagger. He flinched away from the flaming blade, eyes closed—and felt only heat on his skin. When he eased his eyes open, the dagger's blue flame danced before his eyes, bright but harmless. The merchant gave him no time to ponder why he hadn't been scorched.

She punched him in the face. Stars danced before his eyes as she rose. Mazen blinked to clear his vision. The darkness receded enough he could see the smudge of Loulie's brown robes as she turned away. Instinctively, he stretched out a leg and tripped her. She fell, hard.

They struggled against each other until they were nothing but an entangled mesh of bodies and blades and curses. The next time Mazen saw the merchant's face with clarity, she was looming over him with the flaming blade angled at his face.

Desperation took over. Mazen just barely rolled away from her incoming strike and drove his dagger down into her hand. Loulie fell off him with a raw, animal cry. His stomach clenched with guilt when he saw the gaping wound—the deep, weeping gash *he* had left.

"Prince!" Mazen turned and saw Aisha standing behind them, covered in white dust. Her eyes flickered to Loulie's wound and then back to Mazen. "We have to leave. Where is the jinn?" Her eyes snagged on the collar before he could respond. A perplexed frown tugged at her lips. "It's...a relic?"

No! Before he could reach for it, Aisha grabbed it and tucked it into her satchel.

The moment it vanished, the room shuddered and groaned as if in danger of giving way beneath some gargantuan weight. The remaining ghouls bled to sand, and the flames on the merchant's blade died into smoke. Above them, the ceiling began to crack, and sand rushed in through the gaps.

No one said anything. Aisha ripped off a part of her shawl, wrapped it around the merchant's hand to stanch the bleeding, then grabbed her by her good arm and hauled her up and off the ground. The three of them ran—the merchant stumbling behind them with blood dripping between her fingers.

They made it down the crumbling staircase and onto the ground floor before a wall collapsed and a torrent of sand crashed down through the fissure. The force of the impact knocked Mazen off his feet. He fell hard on his hands and knees, hissing in pain. When he regained his footing, the corridor was dark with a dense layer of falling dust. The walls creaked, the mosaics bled colorful dirt, and the floor trembled.

Someone shoved him forward. Aisha, already hurrying ahead with Loulie.

There came a terrible groan. An ear-piercing screech as stone scraped together. And then the ceiling above them shattered, and sand engulfed the world, rushing toward them in a wave.

Mazen fled.

He chased after Aisha and Loulie, sprinting through sinking halls and weaving past falling rubble until the labyrinth narrowed into a single hall and light—glorious, gods-sent light—poured in from the exit at the end.

The ruins, as if aware of this fact, began to fall faster. The walls pressed closer; the ceilings loomed. A tremor ran through the building, strong enough to send a jolt through Mazen's body and cause him to lose his balance. He stumbled into a wall, knees shaking.

Pressure built on his shoulders and weighed down his limbs as the building groaned and tipped. There was sand, sand everywhere. In his eyes, his ears, his lungs.

He couldn't breathe. Could barely run. But—

Almost there.

He lurched to his feet. The floor slanted sideways. He slid. Quickly regained his footing.

Almost there, almost there.

He sprinted until the light was no longer distant, until it overwhelmed his senses and he was stumbling blindly, madly through the exit after Aisha and Loulie. There was a curtain of dust. A gasp of fresh air. And a whisper, quavering with excitement.

Finally, the Queen of Dunes said. *I am free.*

25

LOULIE

Loulie dreamed of fire.

In her dream, the sand was ash and the sky was filled with crackling embers. Her tribe's campsite burned in the distance, engulfed in so much smoke it was impossible to tell victim from killer. When Loulie attempted to approach the slaughter, the embers in the sky blew harder, and the ground beneath her feet began to burn.

One of the shadows emerged from the smoke, garbed in robes the color of darkest midnight. His charcoal eyes locked on her. Vermilion blood glinted on his knife as he stepped toward her. *Do you desire death or slavery, girl?*

—※—

Loulie came back to the world of the living swallowing a scream. The memory of the burning campsite was already fading as she brushed beads of sweat off her forehead. The movement made her aware of the pain in her hand, and she remembered, suddenly and with great clarity, the wound the high prince had inflicted upon her.

"Finally, the dead has awakened."

Loulie looked up and saw Qadir sitting beside her, frowning. A lantern sat on the desk beside him, flickering an ominous green. It contoured Qadir's face with shades of shadow, making his frown appear deeper, more severe.

She eyed him warily. "You're not an illusion, are you?"

When he simply raised a brow, she sighed. Qadir's calm, no matter how skeptical, always put her at ease. Her eyes traveled to his hand, where she saw a familiar strand of beads wrapped around his fingers. The sleep-inducing relic. "To help you sleep," Qadir explained. "You were in so much pain riding to Dhyme I thought it better for you to enter the city passed out."

We've reached Dhyme?

She paused to take in her surroundings. She recognized the room at the Wanderer's Sanctuary, where she and Qadir stayed every time they came to the city. It was small, containing only a single bed and an unimpressive writing desk. The bag of infinite space and Qadir's shamshir had been tucked into a corner, right next to an alcove that was home to a set of small stone idols. Sometimes Loulie amused herself by rearranging those idols to make it look like they were fighting a mock battle. Now they stood in a straight line, looking at her. Even faceless, they looked judgmental.

She turned her attention to her hand and flinched when she saw the blood-drenched cloth. Now that she was awake, it was impossible to ignore the sharp ache beneath her skin. She remembered Aisha wrapping the wound, pulling her through the crumbling ruins.

"What happened?"

"What happened was you were impulsive and nearly died," Qadir snapped.

Loulie looked up at his tone of voice. She cringed when she saw his eyes. They had gone from their usual brown to a startling blue silver that flickered like fire.

"How many times must you nearly die before you realize you are not invincible, Loulie?" He leaned forward, eyes shining so bright they were almost white. "First you attack the shadow jinn without provocation, then you walk *straight* into a deadly illusion without thinking about the consequences."

Loulie's shame was a knot in her throat, and it stopped her from forming words. *You don't need to coddle me*, she wanted to say. *I'm not weak.* She clenched her good hand and faltered when she felt the coldness of her rings against her skin. They had been useless in the ruins. She had fallen to the Queen of Dunes, had nearly given in to her…

Not weak. No matter how many times she thought the words, they rang hollow.

"I'm sorry." It was an effort to keep her voice from shaking. "I only meant to bring the prince back." She could already hear Qadir's retorts in her mind. She knew that if he wanted to, he could use his words to slice through her bravado.

But that was not his way.

Slowly, the white in his eyes faded, like ice melting in the sun. His scowl softened as he took her injured hand in his. Though he was gentle, pain still shot through Loulie's fingers as he raised her palm, and she had to bite her tongue to stop a whimper from escaping her lips. She watched as he unwrapped her bandages, revealing the hideous injury caked in dried blood, the gash at its center so deep she could see bone. Her stomach lurched at the sight.

Qadir slipped a dagger from his belt and sliced his palm. Loulie stared as silver blood rose to the surface of his skin. He gave her no time to ask questions, simply set his bloodied hand down on her wounded one and said, "Tell me what happened."

She gasped. It had been a long time since she'd felt his blood magic in her veins. Qadir rarely healed her. He did not believe in mending minor injuries—especially not the ones she suffered because of her own "rash" decisions. The magic was an unpleasantly cold and prickling feeling beneath her skin, one that alternated between pain and numbness. Even more disconcerting: she could *feel* the torn tendons in her hand sewing themselves back together.

"Tell me." Qadir's voice was soft. She knew he was trying to distract her.

She humored him. She told him about the prince's disappearance and wandering the ruins. She told him about the song, the voice in her head, the ghouls, and the collar. When she tried to remember her fight with the prince, there was only the lingering sensation of pain.

The shock of waking from a nightmarish sleep. The last thing she remembered was stumbling out of the ruins and then—the warmth of Qadir's chest and the intoxicating lull of sleep.

By the time she'd come to the end of her account, her mind was fuzzy with pain. Still, she forced herself to focus so she could ask the questions whirring through her mind. "What happened to the relic?"

Qadir grimaced. "The high prince's thief refuses to hand it over. She believes that because the prince located it, it belongs to him." His frown deepened. "I do not know how, but we must find a way to take it back. It is . . . special."

He pulled his hand away, and where the terrible gash had been there was now a faintly glittering scar. Loulie knew she would have to bind the wounded hand again after she cleaned it; she could not let the prince and the thief see it healed so soon.

"Shukran," she mumbled as she ran her thumb over the sensitive skin. "For healing my injury." She looked up and caught his eyes. "And for helping me in the ruins." Even from a distance, he'd been watching over her.

Qadir simply nodded as he turned to the window, eyes locked on the stars hanging in the ebony sky. Loulie knew that if she let him, he would sit there all night, stargazing. It was what he did every time he wanted to avoid speaking with her.

She pushed off her covers and threw her legs over the side of the bed so that she could face him. "Are you going to tell me why the relic is special? Does it have something to do with it belonging to the Queen of Dunes?" Even the name was a question.

Qadir sighed. "Meaningless titles aside, yes, the jinn you ran into in the ruins is an ifrit who specializes in death magic. It is what allowed her to influence the movements of the ghouls."

Loulie probed her injury and flinched at the dull pain that shot through her limbs. She could feel Qadir's eyes on her. "And the song she sang?" she asked softly.

"It is an old song." His eyes dimmed as he leaned back in his chair, away from the fire. "A nostalgic song, one passed down by jinn who call Dhahab their home."

Home. She had felt that insatiable longing for it in the ruins. She wondered if the reason she had seen her father was because he was a manifestation of what *home* meant.

"I never knew it had the power to *possess* people."

Qadir smiled wanly. "The ifrit did not use lyrics to ensnare you. She used magic." The smile faded. "That is why the ifrit are dangerous: their manipulation is subtle but powerful. Worse, they can possess people from a distance, through just their relics."

"And what happens when we somehow manage to take this relic back from Aisha?" Loulie paused. "What if the ifrit possesses her before we can get it back?"

"The relic seems to have gone silent for now, but yes, time is of the essence." He crossed his arms. "Once we have the collar, I will keep it until we figure out what to do with it. As a jinn, I am immune to ifrit possession."

"And you call *me* cocky." She regretted the words immediately after saying them.

But, much to her surprise, Qadir gave her—well, not a smile, exactly, but the edges of his lips had curled into something vaguely resembling one. "I know my limitations, unlike you." He turned to the lantern, and the light dimmed. Qadir faded into shadow, and then he disappeared. Loulie spotted him curled around the base of the lantern in his lizard shape. He rested his head against the metal and closed his eyes.

"There's a hammam at the end of the hall," he said, his voice a whisper. "You should wash your hand, then get some sleep."

Loulie groaned as she slid out of bed. She had nearly made it to the door when she stopped, eyes on her healing hand. "Qadir? You heard the tale of the Queen of Dunes; do you think the ifrit in the relic is the queen from the story?"

Qadir spoke softly into the darkness, as if afraid of being overheard. "Who knows? Humans make up tall tales all the time, but even lies stem from a kernel of truth."

It was a dubious answer, a very *Qadir* answer, and it did little to assuage her worries. *Well,* she thought as she opened the door. *At least now I can worry in earnest.*

26

LOULIE

When Loulie woke, Qadir was reading a letter that had arrived for her that morning. She knew even without looking that it was an invitation to the wali's residence. Ahmed bin Walid was a man of habit; he and Loulie executed the same song and dance every time she came to Dhyme. The only difference was that this time, she had not alerted him to her arrival.

Great. She rubbed at her sleep-crusted eyes. *Now my reputation really* does *precede me.*

"Ahmed?" she asked Qadir.

He crumpled the note in his fist. "Ahmed," he confirmed. "There's to be a social gathering in his diwan tonight."

"Try not to look too excited to see him."

"Speak for yourself. You're smiling like a fool."

Too late, Loulie realized she was blushing. She stood up and, scowling, made her way out of the room and to the hammam. When she returned, she was clean and dressed in her plain brown robes. "Well?" She looked at Qadir expectantly. "Are we getting iftar or not?"

In daylight, the city was lively and colorful, the winding streets filled with laughing children and gossiping adults wearing all manner of colorful robes and clothing. Pale, box-shaped houses loomed above them, their circular windows crisscrossed with latticed patterns. Clothing lines stretched between the upper floors, providing a temporary—and likely unintended—reprieve for migrating pigeons. On the ground, the city's dirt paths were lined with palm trees and carts, the latter of which had sides decorated with bright paintings.

The shop Loulie purchased her pita and labneh from was in the main square and featured paintings of bakers spinning bread in the air. She admired it from afar as she broke off pieces of bread and offered them to Qadir, who sat on her shoulder. They had settled at their favorite eavesdropping spot, a simple fountain that had the names of famous poets carved into the stone. Loulie sat cross-legged on the lip, absently munching on bread as conversations drifted past her.

She caught many snippets of gossip, some pertaining to her. It did not surprise her that Dhyme's citizens knew she was traveling with the prince—the cities received their news from hawks that traveled much faster than horses. The moment she'd left Madinne, she had been resigned to the fact that she would be expected in both Dhyme and Ghiban.

She had just scooped up the last of her labneh when she caught wind of a conversation that made her hold her breath. "...taken to calling him the Hunter in Black," a turbaned man was saying to his mustachioed companion.

The mustachioed man laughed. "Nameless, is he? How enigmatic."

"Melodramatic, if you ask me. But what's important is his tally. His *technique*. They say he's killed more jinn than the high prince."

The mustachioed man slapped his friend on the neck. "Shh! If someone hears you..." His voice dipped into a whisper. Loulie strained to catch the rest of the conversation, but to no avail. *The Hunter in Black.* What if he was one of the cutthroats the shadow jinn had been referring to? What if he was one of the killers who had murdered her tribe?

"Al-Nazari?"

She whirled. The high prince stood behind her, looking bemused.

"You look awfully suspicious. You aren't plotting something nefarious, are you?"

Loulie bristled. "What do you want?"

The prince's smile faded as he glanced at her injured hand. Loulie stuffed it into her pocket without thinking. She had bound it with fresh bandages this morning, but bindings would not hide the flexibility of her fingers.

Omar cleared his throat. "I wanted to apologize for injuring your hand."

Loulie blinked. "What?"

His brow furrowed with something that looked startlingly like concern, but the expression was gone as quickly as it had appeared. The smirk returned. "I said—"

"Apology accepted." She turned away, heart thudding. The truth was that the prince had saved her from herself. He had saved *himself* from her. She could hardly expect him to apologize for that. *But I won't thank him. No one in his crooked family deserves my thanks.*

She was already walking away when he called after her, "See you tonight!" Loulie did not respond. *Of course* Omar had been invited to tonight's gathering. She was filled with dread at the prospect of having to navigate a conversation with Ahmed bin Walid while he was there.

She made it to the inn before she realized she'd forgotten to follow the gossipers in the souk. Qadir sighed in her ear. "Off to a great start, aren't you?"

—⁓—

Her mood had not improved by the time evening rolled around, and it only worsened when she stepped into the wali's courtyard. It was both the most beautiful and the most grotesque garden she'd ever laid eyes upon—an evergreen labyrinth filled with flowering trees and glittering ponds. Lantern-lined bridges curved over the water while marble statues posed in various locations across a grassy field. She had no doubt Ahmed's visitors thought it a serene place. But

Loulie could never think it peaceful when the land was soaked with silver blood.

And the statues—they were awful. Sculpted to look like dying jinn, they were the most tasteless décor she'd ever seen. They seemed to reach toward her desperately, eyes bulging, mouths open in horror. Loulie was reminded of the drowning men in the mosaic from the ruins. She tried not to look at them as the wali's guards led them through a jinn-made forest to the diwan. She did not want to mull over the fact that back when he'd been alive, Ahmed's father had created the statues to commemorate his kills. Though Ahmed himself always grieved his victims, the statues were a reminder of the murderous legacy he carried on.

She glanced over her shoulder at Qadir, who openly wore his contempt on his face.

Even the forest, for all its beauty, had an oppressive air to it. There was something about the trees, which had grown so close together they all but blocked out the moonlight. And then there was that damned sound the wind made as it passed through the leaves: an ominous rattling moan that always made her skin prickle. Loulie was relieved when they finally emerged and came to the diwan in the center of the courtyard. A set of stairs led up to a large wooden platform nestled between two flowered hedges, and balanced atop them was a wood ceiling with an opening in the center that offered a view of the stars.

More than once, Loulie had sat beneath it with only the wali for company, eyes closed as she leaned against his shoulder and told him of her relic-finding adventures. She had shared stories about the ghouls she'd faced with Qadir, of the cliffs she'd scaled and the oceans she'd crossed. Ahmed was a good listener and always enthusiastically asked for more details. Loulie hated that he was so easy to confide in. He was a damned hunter; he did not deserve her trust.

With a conscious effort, she pulled herself out of the memory and focused on the diwan. The room was filled to capacity with decadents reclining on cushions and exchanging gossip over luxurious foods and wine. Loulie sighed into her scarf as she entered. A rawi

reciting poetry went mute, and the musician onstage stopped playing his oud. Loulie ignored the quiet and focused on the wali, who
rose from a divan close to the stage.

Ahmed bin Walid was dressed in layers of vibrant red and orange.
His handsome face was uncovered, revealing features that glowed
under the lantern light. Stubble shadowed the bottom half of his
face, sketching his quirked lips in stark relief, and he had outlined
his brown eyes with kohl, which made them seem bigger, brighter.

He approached her with a dazzling smile. "Ah, our most important guests have arrived!" Loulie's heart fluttered with nerves as he
stepped toward her. *He is just a man*, she thought. *He has no power
over me.*

Qadir set a steadying hand on her shoulder. "It is a pleasure to see
you again, bin Walid."

Ahmed clucked his tongue. "Ya Qadir, you treat me like a
stranger! We are friends, no?" Ahmed clapped him on the back
before turning to Loulie, a familiar question burning in his eyes.
One she had left unanswered for months.

Let him wonder. He would not be receiving an answer tonight
either.

"It's good to see you again, sayyidi."

"The pleasure is always mine, al-Nazari." He never stopped smiling as he turned to his guests. "Why so serious, my guests? Be merry,
for tonight we have the sultan's very own Midnight Merchant with
us!" Uproarious applause went up at the proclamation, and Loulie
fought the urge to shrivel into herself.

The *sultan's* Midnight Merchant? Were people really calling her that?

The room unfroze after the ovation. Conversations resumed in
earnest, the rawi began another poem, and the oud player started a
song. Ahmed led Loulie and Qadir to the area by the stage, where
the high prince and Aisha sat cross-legged on cushions, snacking on
rose lokum and looking out of place. But then, Loulie felt the same
way. Though Ahmed had orchestrated various meetings between
her and other businesspeople, he'd never invited her to a large celebration like this. He knew she despised them.

There were two free cushions—one beside Ahmed and another between Omar and Aisha. Qadir saved her from her indecisiveness by taking the one by Ahmed.

"I'd have thought someone who hated attention would avoid arriving late," Omar said by way of greeting as she sat down.

"*Some* of us have other, more important things to do," she snapped back.

Ahmed laughed as he waved a servant over. "The Midnight Merchant is a busy woman. I am lucky she visits me at all."

Aisha raised a brow. "I had no idea you were so well acquainted with a criminal, sayyidi."

"*Criminal* is such a base title! I find *bold entrepreneur* much more fitting."

Loulie wondered if it even mattered whom the wali associated with. The sultan doubtless had his own illegal connections, her included. Why would he care about the wali of Dhyme's?

The servant began to pour a sparkling wine into their cups. Knowing Ahmed, it was probably the most expensive alcohol on the market. As the city's sultan-appointed guardian, he was one of the wealthiest people in Dhyme—and *was* the city's most powerful government official. He had told Loulie once that flaunting his wealth in front of influential people was not just a privilege, but a necessity to maintaining power. Or so he claimed, anyway. Loulie was always skeptical when he broke out his opulent bottles of wine.

The servant had just reached for Loulie's cup when Ahmed waved her away. "Please." His eyes twinkled with mirth as he stole the bottle and poured the last cup himself. "Tonight, let me serve you." He held the cup out, and Loulie fought to keep her expression blank when their fingers brushed. Her heart was beating so loudly it seemed a miracle no one else could hear it.

Conversation had thankfully not yet sparked between them when another servant came by and told Ahmed he had a guest asking for him. The wali came to his feet with a smile. "Please," he said to their entourage. "Make yourselves at home." He flashed them all a smile before striding away.

Omar sighed into his cup of wine. "Does that man know how to *not* smile?"

Loulie cleared her throat. She was resolved to avoid talking about the wali while he wasn't here. Besides, now that he was gone, she had an opportunity to speak with the thieves alone. "Never mind the wali. I have something important I must discuss with you. It's about—"

"The relic?" Aisha scoffed. "You will not convince me to give it to you."

Loulie paused. Her eyes flickered to Omar, who watched her quietly. "It's dangerous," she insisted. "You saw what it was capable of."

"Of course. How could I forget you trying to kill me?" He chuckled when she flushed. "I hope you remember that it was *you* who was possessed, merchant."

Loulie was disgruntled. In the ruins, the prince had been afraid of the collar. And now the smug bastard was acting like he had been in control of the situation the whole time? She wanted to protest but realized she had no way of knowing if he or his thief had fallen under the ifrit's spell. She had never found out what happened to them in the dune.

"It was lucky that your flaming blade did not burn my face," Omar said. "Such an assault, even accidental, would have been difficult to forgive."

Loulie pressed her lips together. Thank the gods for Qadir. His control over his fire's heat—even from a distance—was astounding. But she could not tell the prince that when he thought her blade a mere relic. "Magic fire distinguishes friend from foe," she murmured.

Omar raised his brows. "Impressive."

Loulie cleared her throat. "As I was saying, I have a way of neutralizing the magic." She glanced at Qadir, hoping he would jump in to assist her, but he was staring broodily across the diwan at the wali, who spoke animatedly with a band of musicians.

"Neutralizing?" The prince tilted his head. "Do tell."

"No, don't," Aisha said sharply. Loulie did not miss the frown the prince cast in her direction. "There's no point trying to convince me. I told you: I don't plan on handing over the relic. It was found by my prince, and it belongs to him."

Loulie narrowed her eyes. "If that's the case, why do you keep talking as if it's *your* decision to make?"

Loulie ignored the thief's cutting look and calmly sipped from her wine as she considered her next words. She could keep down this path and try to get the prince on her side, or—

Sudden applause broke her from her thoughts. She looked up and saw that the diwan's occupants were clapping for the musicians Ahmed had been speaking with. "Now!" the wali cried onstage, clasping his hands. "We have a very special performance!" A flurry of lively music broke out at his words, and the diwan was filled with the whistle of the nay, the beat of the riqq, and the *dum* of the tabl baladi.

The room vibrated with an intoxicating energy, the kind that inspired strangers to seek out dance partners. This was how Loulie found herself pulled into the crowd by a cheery young man who'd clearly had too much wine. She glanced back at Qadir, but he just watched her, amused, while Aisha and Omar retreated through the crowds.

Cowards. Loulie scowled. *Fleeing before we could finish our conversation!*

At first, she tried to run. But every time she fought the crowd, it pulled her back in. So she gave up and begrudgingly started to dance. Self-consciously at first, but then, as she became attuned to the rhythm of the melody, with more confidence.

The music became a current, carrying her through the steps of the debka and from one partner to the next. She was so immersed in the motions that she barely noticed her partners' faces. It was not until she saw the flash of a familiar smile that she looked up and saw Ahmed bin Walid approaching. He swept toward her gracefully, clasping their hands—his left hand and her "good" one—and raising them above their heads before she could slip away.

He beamed at her. "Well met, Loulie."

She distanced herself as they circled each other. "*Midnight Merchant* will work just fine," she murmured. The last thing she needed was for anyone to notice his overfamiliarity.

Ahmed laughed. "My apologies. Tell me, Midnight Merchant, have you given my proposal any thought since our last meeting?"

Loulie stepped down too hard and stumbled over Ahmed's foot. He gripped her hand and caught her before she fell. She looked away from his face as he helped her up, and caught sight of the letters tattooed around his wrist like a shackle. Four letters: a meem, a kha, a lam, and a saad. *Mukhlis*—loyal. Loyal to his gods, he had once told her. And then he had looked at her and said, *And if you will have me, loyal to you.* He'd shown her the tattoo when he proposed to her, and now she could not stop looking at it, *searching* for it.

Four months ago he had proposed, and for four months she had not answered him. It was cruel of her to leave the question unanswered for so long. Even crueler to try to forget it when she was not in Dhyme, but—Ahmed bin Walid was a jinn hunter. A *politician.* He was everything she hated. And yet she found herself inexplicably drawn to him. *You and I are the same,* he had once said. *We suffer from wanderlust and find excuses to leave home.*

Only, while Loulie searched the desert for treasure, Ahmed hunted jinn. He killed them because it was his duty, he said. It was for his gods, his people. He even prayed for his victims. Loulie had always told herself he meant well, that she could make him see the error of his ways. She hated that she thought he was worth the effort. That on those nights when it was just the two of them trading stories, she saw him not as a hunter, but as a kindred spirit. A man, not a monster.

"No." She could barely say the word, tight as her throat was. "Not yet."

Ahmed was, as always, emotionally unscathed. "I understand; you've been busy." He pulled her closer as another pair of dancers swept by.

Loulie caught hold of his sleeve to keep her balance. The motion turned her toward him, and she realized, suddenly, how close they were standing. Close enough she could feel the heat radiating off his body. Close enough she could have reached up to cup his face and—

Her heart hitched. She quickly readjusted herself to stand beside rather than in front of him, then refocused on matching his steps.

Cross, kick, stomp. Cross, kick, stomp.

Her legs felt unsteady, like they might give way beneath her at any moment. It was impossible not to fixate on the warm press of his palm, on the firm but gentle curve of his fingers through hers.

"Midnight Merchant." Ahmed leaned in close enough to whisper in her ear. She shuddered at the warmth of his breath against her neck. "I hope you know I do not mean to be overbearing. If ever you wish to speak to me about this or anything else, my doors are always open. Remember that my home is your home, if you wish it."

Your home. Loulie swallowed. "You are too kind."

Perhaps someday, she would find the confidence to reject Ahmed bin Walid outright and stop hoping for something that tore her heart in two. But—the thought of losing her connection with him was just as terrifying as putting a name to it in the first place. She'd always told herself it was easier to walk away from someone when she buried her feelings for them; she couldn't lose anyone she didn't commit herself to.

And yet for months, she had been reluctant to cast off Ahmed.

Loulie was so distracted by her thoughts she did not realize the other guests had swapped dance partners until she noticed them eyeing her and Ahmed, curiosity plain in their raised brows and upturned lips. Loulie was accustomed to attention, but not *this* kind of attention. She abruptly pulled her hand out of Ahmed's and stepped away.

Concern flashed over the wali's face. "Lou—?" He paused, suddenly noticing her bandaged hand. "What happened to your hand?"

Instinctively, she hid it behind her back. "Just a minor injury," she mumbled.

His eyes warmed with hope as he stepped toward her. "Tell me about it? We can catch up tonight, once everyone is gone?"

For a few moments, she hesitated. She considered staying and recounting her quest to him. She would tell him about the shadow jinn and the Queen of Dunes, the sandstorm and the sinking ruins. And then she would grow drowsy enough to let her guard down. She would lean into his touch and soak in his warmth without feeling ashamed.

And she would wonder, as she always did, what it would be like to accept his proposal. To share a life with someone and be so open with them that they knew all her secrets and feelings.

The musing made a wild terror rise up inside her. "No," Loulie said. It was her longing for that fragile, frightening vulnerability that pulled her away. "Not tonight."

She rushed through the crowds and out the diwan before he could call her back.

27

MAZEN

Mazen had never liked Ahmed bin Walid.

His dislike went back many years, to the first time Ahmed had come to Madinne with his father, the then wali of Dhyme. Mazen, only ten years old at the time, had been commanded by his father to watch over Ahmed. He'd taken the responsibility very seriously. Ahmed, who had been a scrawny child of thirteen years with a too-wide smile, had not. Mazen had quickly discovered Ahmed was what people called a free spirit, a sprightly boy who preferred to do anything other than what he was ordered.

Unlike Mazen, who got in trouble for disobeying his father's orders, Ahmed was never chastened. Every time he disappeared and Mazen tracked him down, the older boy would smile innocently and say, *Ya Mazen! I thought you were behind me this whole time! Where have you been?* Later, when Ahmed offered that explanation to the adults, they forgave him and turned their ire on Mazen.

Smiles were Ahmed's preferred currency. With them, he could buy anything he wanted: affections, possessions, even connections. Everyone was taken in by his smiles—everyone except Mazen.

Even now, sitting before Ahmed in Omar's body, he could not shake his dislike. It was the wali's godsdamned smile. It was too wide, too bright—a strained, jovial mask. He was wearing that smile now as they sat in his diwan the morning after the gathering and spoke at length about things Mazen did not care about. "You remember the hunter with the sweet tooth? Issa? He came to see me before he traveled north."

Mazen supposed if he were Omar, he would know what Ahmed was talking about. This was why he pretended to listen, nodding his head and offering a comment when he thought it safe. But his mind was elsewhere. It had been ever since the incident in the dune. He could not stop thinking about the collar. He was still trying to convince Aisha to dispose of it.

Earlier, when he confessed to her that he'd nearly been possessed, Aisha had just rolled her eyes and said, "You are *always* almost possessed." She told him that collecting relics for Omar was part of her responsibilities as a thief. And then she ignored him. She was still ignoring him, which was why she had opted to wait for him on the diwan steps rather than join him inside.

"But enough about me." Ahmed reclined on his divan, lips curled in a satisfied smile. "Tell me about *your* recent journeys, sayyidi. I see you've found a new relic?" Mazen nearly choked on his breath when he realized Ahmed was eyeing the enchanted bangle on his arm.

"If only." He pressed his fingers to it. "I'm afraid this is just a flashy family heirloom."

Ahmed laughed—a soft, breezy sound that made Mazen bristle. "And here I thought you favored utility over sentimentality. The only flourish I've ever seen you allow yourself is your earring." He tapped his ear, raised a brow. "Have you traded one piece of jewelry for another?"

Mazen swallowed a nervous laugh. Omar had insisted no one would notice the missing earring, but *of course* the annoyingly attentive wali of Dhyme was an exception. "You are as sharp-eyed as always. I removed it when we were traveling to the city; we had to weather a sandstorm, and I thought the earring was safer where the elements couldn't reach it."

It was a spontaneous and shoddy fiction, so Mazen was relieved when the wali grinned and said, "Ah, a sandstorm. A great way to start a quest, to be sure. I hope the rest of your journey has been more pleasant?"

It's been hellish. Mazen cleared his throat. "It's been, ah, tedious."

"Oh?"

"I told you yesterday. We ran into some trouble on our way here."

"You told me you had to deal with a troublesome jinn, but didn't elaborate." Ahmed leaned forward, arms draped across his knees. Somehow, he managed to make the slouch look refined. "But you must enlighten me! What happened?"

Mazen hesitated. What was the danger in bragging? He had overheard his brother boast to Ahmed about his kills before, after all. He reached into his satchel for the relic, which Aisha had packed with the rest of his belongings in case questions of ownership were asked. They both knew Omar would never have yielded a relic to one of his thieves for safekeeping.

Of course, that didn't stop Aisha from holding on to the satchel when they *weren't* in someone else's company.

"It's quite the story…" He gave Ahmed the short version, omitting the bits about him and Loulie being possessed. At the end, Ahmed released a low whistle and eagerly held out his hand for the relic. Mazen handed it over.

"Amazing…" Ahmed turned the collar over in his hands. "To think such a small thing could contain such power."

Mazen shrugged. He hoped it looked characteristically nonchalant. "Isn't that the way it always is with relics? It is impossible to tell their worth through appearance alone." He could not stop his eyes from wandering to the bangle as he spoke. It was hard to believe his own body was a hair's breadth away, that all he would have to do to be himself was remove it.

Ahmed looked thoughtful. "True enough. Though I can't say I've come across enough of them to know for certain." He laughed as he set the collar on his lap. "I'm amazed the Midnight Merchant hasn't tried to barter this off you."

Oh, she's tried. Her and her bodyguard both.

He quickly changed the subject. "You seem to know al-Nazari well. Do you do business with her often?"

"I have seen the Midnight Merchant on many occasions, but no,

I have never purchased anything from her. I prefer not to rely on jinn magic I do not understand."

Mazen raised a brow. "What point is there in meeting with a merchant if not to buy something from them?"

Ahmed smiled. "I enjoy her company."

Mazen opened his mouth to say something. And said nothing. Ahmed chuckled at his confusion. "Is it so strange I enjoy spending time with her? Loulie al-Nazari is like a candle; she lights up even the darkest of nights with her smile."

Loulie al-Nazari, *a candle in the night*? She had seemed anything but warm to Ahmed at the gathering last night. Was the man simply in denial?

Ahmed either didn't register Mazen's shock or ignored it. "I think the two of us are well matched," he said with a dreamy look on his face. "At least, I like to hope so."

Mazen tried to imagine Loulie al-Nazari, perpetual storm cloud, standing beside the ever-shining Ahmed bin Walid. He did not realize he was laughing until the smile faded from Ahmed's face. "Does something amuse you, sayyidi?"

"*You* amuse me, Ahmed. Loulie al-Nazari is a wanderer. If she's married to anything, it's the desert."

The look on Ahmed's face was uncharacteristically stoic. "You speak as if you know her, sayyidi, but is she not just a pawn for you, a means to an end?"

Mazen stared. How did he respond to that honesty? How did *Omar* respond to it?

"My relationship with the merchant is none of your business." He did not have to put effort into making the words icy. "What does this have to do with *your* infatuation?"

Ahmed considered him for a few moments before leaning back and loosing a breath. "Nothing. I only meant to imply she has other sides of which you are unaware. If you knew about them, you would not find our relationship so strange." He smiled, but it was a smile that did not reach his eyes.

The awkward silence that ensued was proof that neither of them was eager to continue the conversation. It was the opening Mazen had been waiting for. He stood with a sigh, stretching slowly to make it seem as if he had not been anticipating this moment since his arrival. "I am too restless for these domestic scenes, I think." He flashed what he hoped was a convincingly Omar-like smile. "I thank you for your hospitality, but I'm afraid I must be going now. I need to map out our travel route before we leave tomorrow."

Ahmed's responding smile was stiff. "Of course, sayyidi. Will you at least be able to attend the meeting with the other hunters tonight?"

The meeting of the jinn hunters was apparently a monthly gathering in Dhyme. Aisha had provided an explanation last night after Ahmed personally invited them. Neither Mazen nor Aisha was keen on Mazen's attendance. Mazen because the last thing he wanted was to listen to killers brag about the blood on their hands, and Aisha because she doubted his ability to lie convincingly about having that blood on his hands.

Mazen settled for a noncommittal answer. "Time permitting, I will be there."

A dent appeared between Ahmed's brows at the response. Mazen cringed. *Stupid! Why would Omar pass up the opportunity to flaunt his prowess?* But it was too late to take the words back, so he did the next best thing: he fled before he could dig himself into a deeper hole.

28

AISHA

When Aisha and the prince returned to the Wanderer's Sanctuary tavern, the small room was packed with marketgoers and travelers and filled with the sounds of clinking glass and ringing laughter. The chaos made her miss the quiet, safe solitude of her bedroom. Now she could not afford to let her guard down. The prince—and the damned talking *relic*—were a constant concern. She was beginning to wonder if staying in Madinne would have been the less annoying choice after all.

They had just stepped into the tavern when the prince froze. Aisha followed his gaze to the staircase, where Loulie al-Nazari was descending in her brown robe. Her face was unpainted, her eyes cracked with red as if she hadn't slept. Her bodyguard was nowhere in sight.

Aisha glanced at the prince. The expression of longing on his face was almost embarrassing to witness. When the merchant approached, he opened his mouth as if to say something but then just ended up offering a cordial nod as she walked out the door without acknowledging them. He looked crestfallen.

Aisha nudged him. "Your lovesickness is showing, sayyidi."

The prince flushed. "I'm not..."

But she was uninterested in his excuse and already walking

toward the stairs. By the time he caught up to her, she'd used a spare key to enter his room, and spread Prince Hakim's map on his bed. "I hope you didn't embarrass yourself too badly in front of the wali." She pointed to the room's desk, and he set his satchel atop and sighed.

"If you were so worried, you should have been there," he mumbled. "It would have been more productive than sulking on the stairs."

"Omar did not send me here to babysit you."

"No? That's what he told me. 'Leave the fighting to Aisha,' he said. 'She'll protect you.'"

"I think you're confusing bodyguard with nursemaid. Now, come." She patted the edge of the bed. "Let's get this over with."

The prince obediently sat as she outlined what would be the fastest route to their final destination. She started by pointing out settlements and Bedouin campsites they would be able to rest at during their upcoming ride to Ghiban, the city of waterfalls. Aisha was impressed; Prince Hakim's renderings of the cliffs and rivers were so detailed they could have been pulled from her memories. She paused, finger hovering over Ghiban. "Interesting."

Prince Mazen looked up. "What is?"

"Your brother." When the prince simply blinked at her, she raised a brow and said, "How is it that a trapped man knows the desert so well?"

The question seemed to take him by surprise. He squinted at the map as if he could unearth an answer from between the layers of lines and colors. Then, softly, he said, "Before my brother came to Madinne, he traveled the desert with his mother's tribe. He's seen much more of the world than I." A fond, distinctly un-Omar-like smile tugged at his lips.

Aisha looked at him skeptically. It was impossible for a map-maker to draw from memory when the landscape changed so often. After all, new oases sprang from the blood of slain jinn every day, and human villages were wiped off the map in the blink of an eye. Once, before it had been burned to the ground, her own village had been on a map like this.

Aisha shook off the memory of Sameesh before it could settle. Prince Hakim's cartography skills were none of her concern. All that mattered was that his map was reliable.

She returned her attention to the route. "There will be fewer oases once we leave Ghiban, but there are caves built into the cliffs that will provide good shelter." She traced the cliffs to the outskirts of the Western Sandsea. "The last outpost is right here, at the edge of the Sandsea." She circled the area with her finger. "Your brother has marked caves that might lead beneath the Sandsea, but there's nothing conclusive. We'll have to search by foot when we arrive."

The prince nodded absently. He was taking in the map like a starving man took in a feast. She forgot that while this trip was just another journey for her, the prince had never ventured far from Madinne. That this was, more or less, an introduction to a whole new world for him.

"So if Dhyme is here"—he pinned the city with his finger—"then the ruin where we found the relic is—" He abruptly went silent, expression morphing from one of wonder to horror.

Aisha was immediately suspicious. "What's that expression for? You look guilty."

He swallowed. "Guilty? No, the only thing I'm guilty of is injuring the merchant, and she's fine now."

Aisha watched him carefully. "You're *still* thinking about that? It could be worse than injuring someone, you know." She raised her brows. "You could be expected to kill them."

"That's different. You choose to kill jinn."

The comment, said so flippantly, should not have bothered her. But perhaps because the memory of Sameesh was so raw, the words caused her thoughts to scatter.

In her mind's eye she saw green-gold fields. She saw her sisters twirling through the high grass, her aunts lounging beneath the date trees, and her mother standing at the front door with a plate of luqaimat and calling everyone inside for dessert.

And then she saw everything—the fields, the house, the bodies—burned to cinders.

"What a foolish thing to say." The words were soft when they left her lips, as faded as her visions. "Not all killers choose to wield a blade. Some of us do it out of necessity."

The prince looked taken aback. "I thought Omar's thieves sought him out because they wanted to kill jinn?"

Perhaps she ought to have been annoyed that the prince was probing for information, but it had been a long time since someone asked about her life before Omar, and she found she *wanted* to talk about it. Her past had never been a secret; maybe that was why no one found it valuable enough to steal from her.

"Perhaps." She shrugged. "But it's not as if I grew up desiring to wield a blade. I lived on a farm in Sameesh; the only sharp thing I was meant to handle was a sickle. But expectations change when your village is slaughtered by jinn. Farming tools didn't keep me alive; a blade did."

The prince looked at her dolefully. "I'm sorry," he murmured.

She looked away, unnerved at seeing such honest sympathy on Omar's face. "I don't need your apologies. If there's one thing I've learned since picking up a sword, it's that empathy is weakness."

"You speak like..."

"Like a killer? You'll get used to it."

She fell back against his bed and closed her eyes. Her cloak flared open with the motion, and she deduced by the prince's silence that he was looking at her scars. "It's rude to stare," she said without opening her eyes.

"I was just looking—"

"At my scars? Are they really so fascinating?" She sighed. "Some people hide their scars; I prefer to wear mine like badges. They remind me of everything I survived, and of who it is I must seek revenge against."

Beneath the darkness of her lids she saw Sameesh again: bright, burning, dying. And she saw the smoky creatures standing amidst the destruction, eyes burning with hatred. The jinn travelers they had welcomed into their home—repaying hospitality with violence.

The prince's voice was faint. "The jinn from Sameesh—"

"They are gone, but my bloodlust is not. That is why I am here, Prince." She pried open an eye. "Don't you have better things to do than gawk at me?"

The prince stood so abruptly he bumped into the table and nearly knocked over the satchel. His gaze darted to the window, to the sky now glowing with stars. "I forgot something in Ahmed's residence," he muttered. "I'd like to retrieve it before his meeting starts." He walked off but hesitated at the door. "Aisha?" He glanced over his shoulder, eyes glimmering with...hope? "Thank you for opening up to me. I appreciate your honesty."

Laughter burst from Aisha before she could help it. How amusing, that this prince thought her sharing her past with him—a past that was so clearly written on her skin—meant anything. She was still chuckling to herself long after the prince's footsteps faded down the corridor. When she reached for his satchel and, out of habit, searched inside for the relic.

The laughter died in her throat when her fingers brushed against nothing.

29

MAZEN

He had forgotten the relic in Ahmed's diwan.

The weight of his guilt was so heavy it nearly knocked him off his feet as he burst out of the inn. It was all he could do to keep himself from sprinting outright toward the wali's manor. Maybe if he moved quickly enough, he could retrieve it before Aisha realized it was missing. He did not want her to think him more incompetent than he already was.

Ahmed is fine. He's a hunter; there's no way he'd fall under a jinn's spell.

Aisha had picked up the collar in the ruins without flinching, after all. When Mazen had asked if the jinn tried to manipulate her, she'd scoffed and said, "*I* am not gullible like you."

Still, the closer he drew to Ahmed's residence, the more fearful he became. His dread became an anchor, pulling him back down into the dark waters of paranoia he'd been trying to surface from ever since his encounter with the shadow jinn.

As he hurried through Dhyme's labyrinth-like streets, he became aware of the darkness twisting on the walls. Of the shadows with red eyes wrapped around palm trees and draped across lantern-lit pathways. *Gullible*, Aisha had called him. But how could his naivete be the cause of such morbid visions? Everywhere he turned he saw darkness encroaching. *Inconsequential*, it murmured in his ears.

Mazen tried to convince himself that he was hallucinating, that his nightmares were bleeding into reality, but the shadows would not leave him alone.

You thought you could escape. But I know your blood.

He was only streets away from the wali's manor when a sudden nausea took hold of him and he was forced, on shaking legs, to make his way to the nearest alley so he could collapse against a wall. Sweat beaded his forehead, and he could feel his heartbeat in the soles of his feet.

And then the dark was pressing on him, clinging to his heels. *Jinn killer!* it screamed. *You are not worthy of being my servant!*

"Not real." Mazen breathed out slowly. "Not real."

He closed his eyes but succeeded only in plunging himself into a different darkness, one illuminated by the mosaics of the seven jinn. The shadow with the red eyes grinned at him. Mazen turned away from the image only to face another, more haunting depiction. He saw the third jinn: a woman holding a skull. *The Queen of Dunes.*

In the buried ruins, he hadn't been thinking of Old Rhuba's tale; it had not been until after that he connected the two jinn. He hadn't brought up his suspicions to Aisha. She would think he was crazy.

I'm going to take my time with you, lest your suffering be over too quickly.

Mazen pressed his hands to his ears, but the voices could not be blocked out. He dug his fingernails into his palms, and when the pain became too intense, he pushed them through the dirt instead.

The ground *creased* beneath his touch.

The feeling was so unexpected he opened his eyes and looked down.

And saw his shadow, crinkled beneath his fingers like satin. He stared, pulled his hand away. The shadow flattened back into the ground like an ink stain. It did not attack him. It did not even move.

Slowly, cautiously, he reached for it again. When it rippled beneath his touch, he took a deep breath, then *plucked* it from the ground. The moment the shadow enveloped his hand, it disappeared from view.

Gods. I really am *going crazy.*

For a few minutes, all he could do was stare warily at his hand—or the lack of it. Then, slowly, experimentally, he slipped other parts of his body through the shadow fabric. He watched in amazement as it all disappeared. His hand, his arm, his leg—anything beneath the pall of shadow vanished.

It was magic. It had to be. But where had it come from?

He twisted the shadow in his hands and marveled at the way it faded in and out of existence. One moment it had the appearance of a deep-black fabric, and the next, it—and the skin beneath it—disappeared completely.

My shadow is magic. The thought was so ridiculous he burst out laughing.

A couple passing by the alley paused and, when Mazen looked up, hurriedly walked away. An idea occurred to him. He grabbed the shadow and, making sure the thing was covering every part of his body, stepped out of the alley.

No passersby gave any sign of seeing him. Sometimes they glanced at the wall, as if sensing his gaze, but never directly at him. He was a shadow. He was invisible.

Mazen's mind whirred with questions long after he doffed the shadow and let it trail behind him. He wondered if this was a curse set on him by the shadow jinn. Maybe it was the reason she haunted his dreams.

Or maybe, Mazen thought with a shudder, *it's an omen.*

30

LOULIE

"If looks could kill, you'd have murdered everyone in the souk by now," Qadir said as he ate the last of the falafel they had bought. He crumpled the falafel bag in his fist and, when Loulie did not respond, bounced it off the top of her head. She caught it and threw it back at him. She knew he was only trying to goad her into sharing her troubles—he'd been trying to improve her mood since their afternoon walk earlier—but she did not care for his antics right now. Not when she was busy fretting over her meeting with Ahmed.

Even the chaos of the souk could not distract her. The lanterns hanging from the palm trees cast a too-lurid light, and the once appealing designs on the colorful carts now seemed garish. Though the souk was emptier than before, its many twisting streets made it more claustrophobic than Madinne's souk. Loulie felt suffocated.

Qadir pressed closer. "Are you sure you do not want me to accompany you tonight?"

Loulie glanced at a gaggle of children sitting on a nearby rooftop. She smiled when they pointed at her and began whispering excitedly. "I'll be fine. Ahmed is harmless." Even without looking at him, she knew Qadir was raising a brow. "Last night was..." She faltered. She'd been overwhelmed, embroiled in self-loathing. Tonight would be different. Tonight was not about her and Ahmed. It was about her business.

She had woken to yet another invitation this morning, to the promise that Ahmed would introduce her to friends of his—potential clients—before she left. Loulie didn't care about collecting blood-stained gold from jinn killers. In fact, she avoided selling to them when she could. No, there would be no sales tonight. She just missed having the freedom to refuse a deal that didn't strike her fancy. Tonight, she would wrest back some control of her life.

Qadir sighed. "Last night was pathetic." When Loulie glared at him, he snorted and said, "There it is again. The murderous look. You don't *look* fine."

"I don't believe I asked for your opinion." They rounded a corner and entered the jewelers' street, where merchants showcased gold and silver trinkets beneath glass cases. Loulie's eyes flickered absently over necklaces and rings inlaid with sapphires and rubies, over large golden bangles and precious chains that held tiny pearls. Each display was dazzlingly bright beneath the lanterns, enticing up until the moment the jeweler named their absurd price.

Gods help the poor fools who don't know how to haggle, she thought.

They were nearing the center of Dhyme, where Ahmed's residence was located amidst a cluster of pretentious mansions, when Qadir stepped in front of her. "This is your last chance. Are you sure you do not want me to accompany you?"

"Yes." She crossed her arms. "I don't need you here for a *civil* discussion, Qadir. I'd much rather you track those rumors about the assassin in black."

Qadir sighed. "Rumors that will no doubt amount to nothing."

"It's still a better way to spend your time. You don't have to coddle me." It was what she had been telling him all day. To convince him or herself, she wasn't sure.

Qadir gave her a hard look. When she didn't break under his stare, he eventually relented. After he left, she turned toward Ahmed's residence and took a deep breath.

Ahmed bin Walid is just a man. I don't need *him.* She repeated the words in her mind as his guards led her through the courtyard. She heard Ahmed's guests before she saw them. There were a dozen of them seated around a carpet in the diwan—hunters dressed in expensive silks and jewelry. All wore weapons beneath their layers of finery.

Loulie spared a glance at her surroundings and noted the space had been cleared in her absence. Gone were the stage and the luxurious furniture from the night before. Now there was only the carpet and the decadent killers who sat around it. Ahmed bin Walid sat at the farthest end of the rug. He was in modest clothing today: a simple beige tunic and pants, with a dark blue scarf draped across his shoulders. When he saw her, he smiled—the same familiar smile that made her heart sink and leap. "And so the guest of honor arrives. Welcome, Midnight Merchant." He gestured to the vacant cushion to his right.

Loulie forced herself to relax as she strode toward him. With an effort, she shoved aside the memory of their intertwined hands and his breath on her neck. She lowered her shoulders and exhaled, releasing a sigh thankfully muffled by the scarf over her mouth as she plopped down on the cushion beside him. "As always, it is a pleasure." The hunters surveyed her with varying levels of curiosity. One of the men—the youngest, by the look of his face—squinted at her suspiciously. Loulie frowned. "Is something wrong, ya sayyid?"

The hunter flushed. "Forgive me, merchant. You are younger than I expected."

Loulie resisted the urge to roll her eyes. She knew it was not just a matter of youth. Men were praised for being successful at a young age, but a successful woman was a perplexing puzzle. Most men did not know how to respond to her confidence.

She raised a brow. "No, forgive *me*. I should not have spoken so sharply to a child."

The hunter's face burned a deep red when he glared at her. Loulie enjoyed his anger, but she relished the laughter of his companions even more. Even Ahmed was grinning. "One thing you should know about Loulie al-Nazari is that she suffers no insults. Not without reciprocation, anyway." He glanced around the circle, eyes sparkling. "Well then, it seems we are all here."

"What of the high prince?" one of the hunters, a grizzled old man with more than a few scars on his face, asked.

Ahmed sighed. "I invited him, but I assume he was too busy to attend."

Murmurs arose from the group. Loulie wondered at their disgruntlement. Was the prince so close with these men that they expected his presence? Or did they see him as a celebrity?

Ahmed clapped his hands, quieting them. "At ease! We don't need the high prince to have a good time." He waved a hand, and the servants waiting in the wings laid out a feast. Loulie's stomach growled as they set down plates of halloum and pita, bowls of baba ghanoush and fattoush, skewers of chicken and lamb shish tawook, and dolmas stuffed with rice and onions.

"Please, let us eat and talk! You are in good company tonight."

Loulie was happy to oblige. Without Omar bin Malik there, she was apparently the most interesting person, and the hunters asked her constant questions. They asked her about her goods and her travels, her bodyguard—Loulie snorted when they called him *mysterious*—and her history. She told them an echo of the truth, a flimsy but interesting half lie.

Then, when they'd devoured the food and moved on to dessert, she showed them her relics. There were only a few—she had sold most of them in Madinne's Night Market—but there were enough to sate their curiosity.

"How in the world do you find enough relics to sell them?" This question came from the scarred hunter as plates of baklava and kunafah were served. Loulie declined the latter and took two plates of the first. Baklava was her favorite, and the treats prepared at Ahmed's manor were some of the best she'd ever had.

She turned to the hunter and, speaking around mouthfuls of honey and dough, said, "I'm afraid that's a trade secret."

"Hmm." Another hunter—Snub Nose, Loulie called him— thoughtfully ran the sleeping beads through his fingers. "Why sell them at all when you could have the most valuable collection in the country?"

"Collections are a hobby." Loulie raised a brow. "I run a business."

Besides that, what point was there in gathering enchanted items that would simply sit on her shelves and collect dust? It was the relics' uses that made them valuable—and which allowed her to make a living. A forbidden collection would gain her nothing.

The irritable young hunter cocked his head. "Isn't what you're doing illegal?" He glanced at Ahmed, and as if on some invisible cue, the other hunters looked at him too.

Loulie scowled. "I can speak for myself, shukran." Still, she glanced at Ahmed, curious about his response. She was taken aback by the steeliness of his gaze.

The look did not go unnoticed by the others. The irritable hunter frowned. "Ahmed?"

"Is something amiss?" said another hunter.

Ahmed blinked. He had the look of someone coming out of a dream. "Mm? Oh, no. I apologize; I was a prisoner to my thoughts." He smiled, but it was only a halfhearted twitch of his lips. "We were talking about relics, yes? Collecting and selling them as if they were tools?"

Loulie frowned. "They *are* tools."

"Do you truly believe that?" The wali's feeble smile disappeared. "Have you at all considered, merchant, that your business capitalizes on suffering?"

His barbed words made her flinch. Relics were items that had been enchanted by jinn and forgotten in the desert. Where was suffering involved?

"I'm afraid I don't understand what you mean." She felt a twinge of unease as she slid away from the wali, wary of the blankness that had settled across his features. She had never seen that look before. Unthinkingly, she clasped her hands—and cringed when she felt the heat of her rings through her bandages.

Ahmed laughed. A soft, humorless chuckle. "Of course you do not." He turned his attention to the circle. "Tell me, friends." His lips twisted into a sharp, slanted smile—an awful, foreign grin that made Loulie's blood freeze. "Do you kill jinn because you hope to steal their magic? Or do you do it for the blood? For the thrill of the kill?" He held up a hand. "No, do not speak. The answer does not matter."

Loulie stared at the wali, nonplussed. Who was this grinning stranger sitting before her?

A seed of fear took root in her chest as she watched the hunters reach for concealed knives and weapons. Instinctively, her hand went to the compass in her bag—her guiding relic. "Sayyidi?" she said softly.

He set a hand on his scarf, smiled. "Hello again, jinn killer. Would you like to sing with me?" He began before she could respond, singing a song she recognized. A nostalgic song, Qadir had called it. But to Loulie it sounded like a lamentation for a never-ending, fruitless journey.

She was only vaguely aware of the singing. It was becoming difficult to focus. She recognized the voice of one of the hunters. Saw something flash through the air—a blade, perhaps—but then her vision was gone and there was only her heartbeat, growing louder and louder, and it was strange because it almost seemed as if it were coming from the compass and...

She was barely able to breathe as the hunter clasped the iron shackle around her throat. Pain, hot and sharp, lanced through her veins and punctured her bones.

The hunter stepped closer, dark eyes narrowed. "How old do you suppose this one is?"

"At least a hundred years," said his companion. "Perhaps older."

"An ancient monster," the hunter mused. "I expected her to put up more of a fight."

The hunter's companion moved to stand beside him. The only feature she could make out on his veiled face was his eyes, which looked like shards of gold. "Can you speak, monster?"

She did not bother responding. She'd heard stories of jinn who had their tongues removed for speaking. She lowered her head and started praying. She tried not to think of the grass beneath her feet—of the blood the hunters had spilled from her veins to make it.

She forcefully altered the pathway of her thoughts until she was thinking about Him instead. If He woke and saw her with these humans, He would, He would... well, He would try to save her and die. And she had not resigned herself to this fate just for Him to perish. She had freed Him. She would not let Him be captured again.

When the hunters realized they would not be able to make her scream, they secured the chains holding her to the boulder and unceremoniously pushed her into the lake. Even then, as death drew nearer, she did not stop praying. Did not stop remembering.

She thought of the haunted look in His eyes, the blood on His hands. The way He had stood, back so straight, when they tortured and scarred Him.

And then she thought of His future, which unfurled in her mind like a map. She saw a desert camp. Robes glittering with stars. A band of killers. Him, shifting through the flames like smoke, approaching a crying girl with a compass in her hands. And she knew, suddenly, that the compass was hers—was her. She felt the weight of it in her pocket and thought, If I cannot guide Him through the desert hand in hand, then I will use this arrow to point him toward His fate. *She held the shape of Him in her mind as the last of the air left her lungs. And then...*

Loulie opened her eyes with a gasp. The world before her was tilted on an axis. She shifted her suddenly heavy head and realized she was lying on the ground, clutching the compass. Every time she breathed, she heard the echo of her heartbeat in the wooden instrument.

No, not *her* heartbeat. The relic—it was a living thing.

Not just a compass, but a soul. A *life.*

Her mind drifted, and for a few moments she was back beneath the water, *unable to breathe, dying.* She released the compass. The vision collapsed, plunging her back into a reality where Ahmed bin Walid loomed above her with a dagger, eyes shining with hatred. His scarf hung askew on his neck, revealing the gleam of a golden collar at his throat. "Now you know how it feels for my kind to die," he said. "But it is not enough to redeem you."

Loulie squinted against the blurriness of her surroundings. She saw the other hunters sprawled nearby, looking just as bleary-eyed.

"How many jinn have you killed? All so you could steal our magic and paint your world with our blood?"

None, she thought. *I have killed no jinn.* But her lips refused to form the words.

She felt Ahmed grip her arm. Felt him lift her up.

"No more." His voice was heavy with grief. "Goodbye, jinn killer."

He pressed the blade to her throat.

31

MAZEN

Mazen was still thinking about his shadow when he stepped through the gates to Ahmed bin Walid's residence. The guards did not bother leading him to the diwan. Doubtless, they trusted the high prince to find his way there on his own.

Paranoia tightened his lungs as he walked through the empty courtyard. He could not stop his gaze from wandering to his shadow. It *looked* like a normal shadow, but every time he nudged it with his foot, it caught against his boot.

How is this possible? He considered the question as he wove through the evergreen garden. Even in the dark, the courtyard was beautiful. And...different?

The trees seemed closer, as if they had moved to block his path, and the howl of the wind was strangely mournful. The moonlight filtering through the canopies was an eerie silver, and he found himself ducking through the trees to avoid it. He felt like he was being watched.

He shook the thought away as he approached the diwan steps. As his legs slowed and his eyes drooped and the world blurred. He had only just become aware of his sluggishness when a song—a soft, terrible song he recognized—speared through his mind.

Mazen staggered. He did not realize he'd collapsed until he felt the softness of his shadow beneath his fingertips. He became aware of a second sound, a thrumming in his arm, his feet...all around him? He paled.

My shadow has a heartbeat. His stomach knotted with fear.

Before he could pull his hand away, he *felt blood dribbling down her lips as she coughed. "How...?" She gasped as the knife was pulled from her shoulder. Gritting her teeth against the pain, she turned, hand over her gaping wound. She was stunned by the apparition before her.*

"Impossible." She stepped back. "You...I killed you!"

He had to be a mirage. A hallucination. He could not possibly be alive, not after she had suffocated his heart with magic. Not when she had watched the life fade from his eyes. Not when every human in the diwan had seen him collapse, lifeless.

And yet—the hunter stood before her with his terrible black knife, grinning.

"You, kill the King of the Forty Thieves? What a conceited notion."

"No!" She stepped back. If she perished here, there would be no stopping him from making her into his slave. He would kill her, just as he had killed her beloved, and then he would steal her magic. Her eyes shifted to the shadows—what might be her final escape.

But there was no running from the hunter. In moments, he was upon her, sinking his cursed dagger into her heart, and...

He was barely breathing as the vision of the shadow jinn faded. The world—*his* world—returned in all its starlit chaos. He could make out sounds from the present, the most recognizable of which was a voice. He had spent enough time despising its lulling cadence to know it by heart, even if it was uncharacteristically soft.

Ahmed. Mazen stumbled toward the stairs. Dark spots danced before his eyes, threatening to pull him back into a memory that was not his. Desperate, he reached for his rings. Heat shot through his fingers. It burned like hell, but—it was enough to root him in the moment, to remind him of the uncharacteristic softness of Ahmed's voice. The Ahmed he knew did not speak in conspiratorial whispers. The Ahmed he knew did not abide silence; he shattered it.

"How many jinn have you killed?" the wali said in his strange, stiff voice. Beneath his cadence was another voice, so soft it was barely audible. "All so you could steal our magic and paint your world with our blood?"

Mazen stepped into the diwan.

Ahmed's guests lay on the floor, staring unresponsively at their surroundings. It appeared as if they had been in the middle of a feast, for food and drink lay scattered across the floor, staining the rich carpet and tile. Ahmed stood at the center of the mess, holding the merchant up by the collar of her robe. She was limp as a rag doll in his grasp.

"No more." The wali raised his hand. Mazen saw a flash of silver. "Goodbye, jinn killer."

Mazen did not think. He moved.

One moment he was standing unseen at the diwan entrance, and the next, he'd tackled Ahmed to the ground. Ahmed lay stunned for a few moments, face paling as he took in Mazen's—Omar's—sudden appearance. "*You*," he choked.

Mazen's eyes flitted to the scarf hanging loosely on the wali's neck, to the band of golden bones no longer concealed beneath it. He reached for the grimacing skulls.

But before Mazen could grab the collar, Ahmed seized his wrist and wrenched it sharply to the side. Icy pain rippled through Mazen's arm. He bit back a yell as the wali threw him off. For a heartbeat, he lay stunned on the floor, overwhelmed by the pain shooting through his bones. But then the adrenaline kicked in, and he was able to push himself up.

It was just in time to watch a groggy-looking hunter approach Ahmed with a blade in hand. "Foul creature!" the hunter cried. "Leave the wali be!"

Ahmed reached for one of his daggers as the man rushed toward him. Their blades met with an ear-piercing screech. The standstill lasted a heartbeat, two. Then Ahmed slid past the hunter's guard. The man lost his balance, and Ahmed used the opening to aim a hard kick at his legs. This time, the hunter toppled, and the wali fell on him with the dagger.

Mazen had been audience to mock battles before. He had watched palace soldiers cut flesh and draw blood as they outmaneuvered each other. But there were no artful tactics in this struggle. There was only life-ending defeat as Ahmed carved a crescent into the hunter's neck. The dying man's scream faded to a choked gurgle and then into a horrible, broken wheeze as Ahmed rose to his feet. When he turned, his robe was drenched with blood.

Mazen did not hear his own scream over the uproar that followed, but he felt it tear through his chest as he scrambled away from the gore. A yell on the other side of the diwan drew his attention, and he looked up to see another hunter—a grizzled man with scars on his face—come at the wali with a sword. Ahmed slid past his reach and plunged a dagger into the back of his neck as he swept past.

The hunter toppled with a gasp, red bubbling at his lips.

Immediately after, a pair of hunters came at Ahmed from either side of the diwan in a pincer movement. The wali sidestepped one man and lunged to catch the other's wrist midstab. There was a moment of shock as the hunter tried to free himself. But he was too slow.

Ahmed threw him into his fellow, and the two collapsed in a heap. The wali stepped hard on one man's back, eliciting a crack so loud it could be heard over the yelling, and then he leaned down and, in one swift motion, slid a dagger out from his sleeve and plunged it into the other man's throat.

Mazen watched the massacre unfold like a stunned spectator, barely breathing as Ahmed cut down hunter after hunter. He watched bones snap, bodies break, blood splatter, and all he could do was blink back panicked tears. If Ahmed turned on him, he would not be able to run.

But the wali had eyes only for the men who faced him like warriors. The next opponent he confronted was the youngest Mazen had seen yet: a boy with determination sparking in his round, frightened eyes. The boy and Ahmed faced each other over a corpse.

The boy struck first. Ahmed parried. Their blades connected, slid, and clashed in midair.

There was a moment—Mazen's heart beat with frantic hope—when the boy managed to catch Ahmed off guard and push him away. Ahmed stumbled as the boy raised his blade.

The corpse beneath them shuddered.

Mazen shot to his feet and yelled, "Watch out!"

Too late.

The corpse gripped the ankle of its still-living companion and pulled. The boy fell. Ahmed was prepared—he caught the youth in the chest with a purloined blade. By the time the boy hit the ground, his eyes were glazed over.

Mazen crumpled against the wall, shaking with terror as an eerie silence washed over the diwan. The wali's eyes slid over him as he turned toward the remaining six hunters surrounding him in a broken half circle. At the sight of his bloodstained face, they stepped back, weapons drawn like shields.

A twisted smile creased Ahmed's lips as he reached down and plucked a sword from one of the corpses. "What's wrong? I thought hunters did not fear death. Will none of you face me?"

When no one rose to meet his challenge, the wali snorted and snapped his fingers. Like puppets yanked up by invisible strings, the corpses on the ground shambled to their feet, eyes glazed and unfocused. "Fine, then. I will force you to look death in the eyes."

The undead surged forward, and the hunters retreated into the forest. Mazen was numb—so numb that when Ahmed faced him, his legs would not move. Dread had frozen his limbs.

"I thought you were brave," said the jinn wearing Ahmed's skin. "But you're a coward like the rest of them, aren't you?" He stepped forward.

Move, Mazen commanded his body. *Move, move!* But it refused to obey him.

Ahmed pulled his blade back—and froze as the sound of crackling fire suddenly filled the diwan. Loulie al-Nazari had regained her footing. She stood behind them, holding up a dagger. A dagger that was, conspicuously, on fire. She stepped forward, and Mazen saw the fire from her blade reflected in her eyes. "I don't know how you dug your claws into him, but the wali does not belong to you. Leave him be."

"He does now." Ahmed matched the merchant's steps. When she sidestepped, he moved in the opposite direction, so that they were circling each other.

"Leave him now, or I'll carve you out of him," she hissed.

Ahmed blinked. Laughed. "Foolish girl. You cannot exorcise me with fire."

The merchant shot forward like an arrow, embers trailing in her wake. Ahmed caught her dagger with his sword. But though he stopped her blade, he could not deflect the fire, which spat and hissed and *stretched* toward him. He drew back with a growl as it scorched his wrist.

"*You* might be immune to fire, but humans are not."

"You would hurt the man you want to save?" Ahmed laughed. The sound was high pitched, almost desperate. "You humans truly are heartless."

"No more heartless than a jinn who does not let the dead rest."

The skirmish became a blur, a cacophony of metal shrieks. Ahmed was the superior fighter, but the merchant had fire. It burned brighter with each strike, and then it burst. Ahmed pulled back quickly enough to avoid the center of the blast, but the hem of his sleeve was burning so fiercely he had no choice but to lower his sword and focus on putting it out.

Instinctively, Mazen reached for his shadow on the wall and draped it over his head as the wali drew closer. Out of sight, he finally relaxed enough to retreat. He noticed two things as he inched away. First, that though Ahmed's sleeve was aflame, his skin was unburned. It was as the merchant had said: *Magic fire distinguishes friend from foe.*

Second: the merchant was, impossibly, wielding her dagger with her injured hand.

But these were fleeting realizations, ones Mazen forced away as the fight took an abrupt turn. Ahmed was no longer rushing toward the merchant; he was running *away* from her, taking the diwan steps two at a time as she chased after him.

What are you waiting for? his inner voice screamed between panicked palpitations of his heart. *You're the Stardust Thief! You have to go after them!*

The voice was wrong. He was not his brother, the fearless jinn hunter. He was Mazen, the coward prince, and every fiber of his being was screaming at him to run. But when he tried to run, tried to *move*, he saw the blood splattered on the floor and froze, heart rising into his throat.

He clenched his fists. Forced himself to breathe out.

There didn't need to be any more killing. He just had to get the collar off Ahmed's neck.

He forced himself to move, to follow the sounds of battle into the cluster of trees that formed the jinn-made forest. Adrenaline pushed him forward, through the trees with twisted, sharpened branches and past the skirmishes between the living and the dead. Every fight was a desperate clash; the living fought to stay alive while the dead single-mindedly sought to kill. Watching the fighting made Mazen feel as if he were in the middle of some morbid, deadly dance. One where everyone but him knew the steps.

He ran into the next clearing so fast he nearly put himself in the center of Ahmed and Loulie's fight. He just barely dodged the merchant's strike as she carved a flaming arc through the air. It was evident from the way she moved that her strength was flagging.

No sooner had Mazen thought this than she stumbled and Ahmed raised his sword.

Mazen said a prayer to the gods and threw himself at Ahmed, feeling the shadow slide from his shoulders as he grabbed the man from behind. Had Mazen been in his own body, Ahmed would have easily been able to throw him off. But beneath Omar's weight, he stumbled.

"Grab the collar!" cried Mazen as the wali gasped beneath his grasp.

"How did you—" The merchant blinked, then waved her flaming dagger at him. "*You* grab the collar! You're the one strangling him!"

By the time Mazen thought to get his fingers around the wali's throat, Ahmed had regained his footing and heaved him back into a tree. The impact drove the air from Mazen's lungs. He collapsed to the ground, breathing hard, as the wali turned.

When he lunged, Mazen ducked sideways, but Ahmed's sword still sliced across his shoulder, cutting fabric and flesh. Mazen yelled in panic before he could help it.

"You are an abomination," Ahmed hissed. When Loulie rushed toward him, he deftly turned and deflected her strike. "It is because of humans like you that my people suffer. Because of you that they are *slaves*, even beyond the grave." He shoved the merchant away— or tried to. The fire on her dagger flared, and Ahmed was forced to pull back.

Mazen put a hand to his wound and felt blood beneath his fingers. Though the cut stung, it was thankfully just a flesh wound. The pain was unimportant. He rose to his feet, drew a blade, and ran at Ahmed.

He and the merchant both missed. Ahmed stepped back, a triumphant grin on his face.

That was when Mazen heard a rustle in the trees. Saw movement in the shadows.

Before Ahmed could turn, a figure darted into the clearing and jumped him from behind. Mazen recognized her voice, even pitched at a scream. In combat, the scowl on Aisha bint Louas's face was lethal as a knife. Mazen saw it only briefly before she pinned Ahmed to the ground and clawed at his neck.

"Aisha—" Mazen said, breathless. He approached slowly, hand over his injury.

Aisha paused, collar in her hands, eyes cloudy. Mazen rushed toward her. She startled when he grabbed at the collar. It was that moment of surprise that allowed him to pull the relic away. He threw it at the merchant, who barely caught it before it fell.

"Keep it," he wheezed. "I expect you to *neutralize* it however you see fit."

An eerie silence hung over them, punctuated only by the harsh sound of their breathing. Aisha looked at Mazen. Mazen looked at Loulie. Loulie looked at the collar, face ashen.

And then there was a sound: a shuddering inhale from Ahmed, who was crying. "I'm sorry," he said, voice laced with such shame Mazen had to look away. "I'm sorry. I'm so sorry."

It was the merchant who went to him first, who tried to console him when the other hunters arrived covered in blood and grime. It was she who walked with him when the guards took him away. Aisha was about to follow when she noticed Mazen holding his shoulder.

"It's fine," he said weakly. "Only a flesh wound. I'll catch up with you in a moment."

Aisha turned away without another word. It was not until she and everyone else left that the numbness faded and Mazen was finally able to consider his injury. He pulled his hand away and looked at the blood. He blinked. Again and again, but the impossible sight did not vanish.

His blood was black.

32

LOULIE

"This isn't the way to Madinne, is it?" Layla glanced over her shoulder at the looming city in the distance. The compass had been pointing them toward it for the last week, and they were close enough now that she knew it was not a mirage.

The sight was a relief. After weeks of traveling with a hollowed-out heart, Layla yearned for a place to rest. It had been less than a month since she'd lost her family, and the jinn insisted the liveliness of the city would help fill the yawning emptiness inside her.

But now Qadir's attention was focused not on the city, but on the compass, which pointed south. "Sometimes we must make necessary stops before we reach our final destination."

Layla grumbled as she followed him to a date tree. Qadir glanced from the compass to the short still-young tree, brows scrunched. Then he tucked it away and began to climb. Layla knew better than to question him.

When Qadir climbed back down, he was holding a swath of silk. A shawl.

"Do you think a traveler lost it in a sandstorm?" she asked.

In answer, Qadir threw the scarf at her and said, "Put it on."

"Why?" She eyed it suspiciously.

Qadir gave her The Look. The one where he raised a brow and

made a straight line with his mouth and stared at her so hard it made her want to wither away. Layla wound the shawl around her neck—and noticed the change immediately. The silk was cool, so chilly against her skin it felt like a contained breeze. "Did you enchant it?" she asked, voice soft with wonder.

He shrugged. "It was already enchanted when I found it. All relics are like this."

Layla tilted her head. "Relic?"

"A relic…" He paused, as if trying to find the right words. "A relic is an item enchanted by a jinn. It contains their magic." He held up the compass. "Like this compass."

"Did you enchant the compass?"

A wry smile pulled at his lips. "No, it was already enchanted when I received it."

"And this shawl?"

Qadir shrugged. "It most likely belonged to a jinn traveler."

"Do you think they'll come back for it?"

Silence. Some emotion flickered across his face but quickly faded. "No," he said after a few moments. "Why would they, when they could easily enchant another?"

It was a good point. Tools were easily replaced. Still…there was something awfully sad about this fabric fluttering on the tree, forgotten.

Qadir turned and began to walk toward the city. Layla followed, still grasping the shawl. "Why are they called relics? It makes them sound ancient."

Qadir spoke without turning to look at her. "Jinn are ancient. Is it any surprise the things we enchant are just as old?"

———

Qadir had lied to her.

The realization festered like an open wound, growing more tender until, by the time Loulie left Ahmed's diwan, it was causing her physical pain.

The city was dark by the time she returned to the Wanderer's

Sanctuary, its bright buildings dulled beneath the pall of deep night. Most of the lights around the souk had been put out, but this did little to dissuade miscreants from sneaking through the shadows.

Miscreants like me, she thought dourly.

Loulie found Qadir sitting on the inn's sloped roof, looking quietly at the stars. She used the crates in the alley to climb up and, swallowing her anger, carefully inched her way toward him. She tried not to think about the helplessness she'd felt when the ifrit wearing Ahmed's skin put a knife to her throat. Tried not to think of the way his—her—eyes had burned with accusation when he said, *Do you kill jinn because you hope to steal their magic?*

She tried not to think of the pain that had racked her body when she had been stuck in the memory that was not hers, of her horror when she pieced together the meaning behind it.

The ifrit's words pounded through her mind. *Have you at all considered, merchant, that your business capitalizes on suffering?*

Long ago, Qadir had told her relics were enchanted items. But charmed objects did not have memories of being *alive*. It had taken an ifrit with death magic to help her realize that truth.

Qadir lowered his gaze to meet her eyes as she stopped in front of him.

"I believe you owe me some answers," she said. Each word was cold, brittle.

Qadir patted the space beside him. "There was no news of your assassin in black."

Loulie bristled at his deflection. She had always abided Qadir's secrecy because she understood the comfort in being enigmatic— *Qadir* had shown her that appeal—but a secret history that had no bearing on her life was different from one that shaped her morals.

"Are you going to sit, or do you prefer glowering at me with your neck craned?"

She did as Qadir suggested, though she sat far enough away he could not reach for her. Qadir appeared unoffended. He looked at her expectantly. Loulie tried to speak but found that all her accusations were lodged in her throat. *This is my fault*, she thought. *I* let *Qadir lie to me.*

"You want to ask me about what happened tonight." He spoke slowly, as if he were speaking to a child moments away from a tantrum.

On impulse, Loulie reached into the bag of infinite space she'd lugged with her, pulled out the compass, and held it over the roof. "What would happen if I broke this compass?"

Qadir's calm never vanished, but Loulie saw a muscle feather in his jaw, betraying his panic. "You would release the soul inside it, and the item would lose its magic."

"What's this about a soul? You told me relics were enchanted items."

Qadir's eyes flickered between her and the instrument. "They *are* enchanted items." He inched closer to her, closer to the compass.

Loulie held it out of his grasp. "No, this is a prison."

"No." Qadir was so tense he could have been made of rock. "Not a prison. We jinn live on in the items most precious to us. It is how we guide the living, even after death. You should understand—you humans leave behind valuable heirlooms for your loved ones too."

"We don't live in those items!" Loulie's voice pitched higher without her consent. "You told me relics were magical objects—replaceable trinkets with enchantments. Do your dagger and the two-faced coin contain souls as well?"

Qadir held up his hands in a placating—or perhaps a defeated—gesture. "You humans use the word *relic* to refer to all magical items, but it is no lie we can enchant objects. Like the dagger and coin." He shifted closer. "But enchantments are temporary and fade upon death. The only way to keep our magic alive forever is to contain it in what *we jinn* call a relic: an object to which we bind our souls so we can live on after our mind and body have perished. That is what the compass is."

Loulie turned away from Qadir's pleading gaze with a sinking heart. She did not need him to tell her the obvious: if enchantments faded after death, then the chances of them running into magical possessions left behind by still-living jinn were extremely slim.

"Loulie." Qadir was close enough to brush shoulders with her.

Loulie leaned farther over the edge of the roof. The jinn froze. "Loulie, please," he said, voice so soft it made her tremble. He had never begged her like this before. It made something in her crack. "That compass—it contains the soul of someone who is precious to me."

"And what of the souls in other relics?" Her hands were shaking. "Are the lives of other jinn so worthless that you would let me sell them like they were mere tools? I'm no better than a slaver!"

This whole time, she had been selling captive souls.

"Loulie." Qadir set a hand on her wrist.

Her pulse jumped. "Don't *Loulie* me. Lying by omission is still lying, Qadir."

"I wanted to give you a purpose. Do you remember when we came to Madinne? Dahlia was having you deliver messages to earn your keep, but it wasn't enough. You said the city was too small for you, that you wanted to go back into the desert." He took a deep breath. "Before I met you, the compass was leading me to jinn so I could give them a place to exist after death. I knew what it felt like to be lost; I did not want others to suffer my fate, not even as relics. I thought you could help me keep their legacies alive while reaping the benefits."

"You told me I would be a treasure hunter." Loulie could feel the prickle of tears in her eyes; she rubbed furiously at them with her bandaged hand. "But these are more than lost treasures, Qadir. They're priceless, living artifacts. And I've been affixing prices to them like they're nothing but convenient tools."

"It was wrong of me to keep that truth from you, I know. But think: the relics the compass leads us to belong to jinn like me— people who fled my world because they feared for their lives. There is no going back for them. Do you think it would have been better to leave them in the desert, abandoned and alone? At the very least, we can find them new homes, places with folk who understand and appreciate their magic."

Loulie swallowed. Long ago, her father had given her a compass— a relic. He had not known the nature of its magic, only that it was valuable. He had thought it would guide her. And it had. Through it, Qadir had found her. But she was not so naive as to think all her customers would cherish relics this way.

"And who is to say those jinn would rather help humans than remain lost?"

Qadir smiled sadly. "No one knows what the dead want, Loulie. All we can do is honor them in the ways we understand. Where I come from, we cannot decide who our relics are passed on to, but we hope they will nonetheless guide the living. In your realm, I believe this is the form that remembrance takes. I do not believe what we are doing is wrong."

Loulie knew Qadir was trying to win her over with reason, trying to soothe her frayed edges until she forgave him. He always did this—always backtracked after he made some mistake. And she always forgave him.

What if he lies to me again?

But—Qadir had saved her. When her tribe had perished and she alone was left to die, Qadir had appeared with his magic fire and rescued her. *Layla Najima al-Nazari*, he had said, *it seems saving your life was my destiny.* He had gestured to the compass she was holding—had shown her the red arrow pointing directly at her.

Qadir had done more than rescue her; he had given her life a purpose.

Her voice was thick with tears when she said, "You decided the course of my life without telling me the full truth. Had I not seen the ifrit's magic tonight—had I not *come* to you with these concerns—would you have ever told me all of this?"

Qadir fixed his eyes—eyes smoky with desperation—on her and said, "Yes. When the time was right."

"And when would the time ever be *right*?"

Qadir shook his head. "I know it was wrong of me to lie to you, Loulie, but you must understand: I am not accustomed to facing my mistakes. Always, I have run from them."

She remembered words he'd spoken to her long ago: *I was lost in your human desert and could not return home. That is why, when I tracked the compass to you, it saw fit to guide me down a different path.*

Your path. And when she had asked why he could not return, he'd simply said, *Because I am no longer welcome there.*

The last of her resistance snapped when he said, "I apologize. You deserved the full truth. I initially thought the compass had guided me to you because you were a way for me to fulfill my purpose."

"And now?" She lowered the compass to her lap.

Qadir visibly relaxed. "You are not a tool; you are my charge." He seemed to hesitate, then added, "If you disagree with this lifestyle, relinquish it."

"Easy to offer me the alternative *after* it's become my life." She was the Midnight Merchant: seller of rare, magical items. Without the relics, she was nothing.

"I know it's wrong. But it's all I can offer. What we're doing is not immoral, Loulie."

"Says who?" She was suddenly tired. So very tired. "The compass? Do you let the jinn in here decide the morality of your actions too?"

"She is the most moral person I know," Qadir said, unscathed. He held out a hand. Reluctantly, Loulie handed over the compass. But Qadir surprised her by gripping her hand. "The jinn in this compass was my savior. She freed me from a terrible fate and guided me through your desert so that I would not perish. I owe her everything, including my life."

Loulie pulled her hand away with a glare. "You do not owe her *my* life."

"Yes." Qadir looked away, brow furrowed as he gazed at the stars. "Of course."

An uncomfortable silence hung between them, filled with questions and accusations. Loulie closed her eyes in an effort to calm herself. When she did, she was assaulted by memories that were not hers. She was shackled to a rock, preparing to die, thinking of *Him.* Qadir, she now realized.

"What happened in the diwan was only possible because you were dealing with an ifrit." She opened her eyes and glanced at Qadir, who was speaking to the stars. "I told you before she can use death magic, which is what allowed her to show you the memories of the jinn in the compass. Only an ifrit would be powerful enough to interact with souls while confined in a relic."

A breeze brushed up Loulie's arms and made her shiver. She felt, very acutely, as if they were being watched. Qadir seemed to sense this as well. He reached into the bag of infinite space and pulled out the collar Omar had surrendered. The moment he held it in his hands, it flashed a muted silver and the feeling vanished. Loulie did not realize she had been holding her breath until she released it through cold lips.

"It is a good thing you found a way to steal this back. Doubtless, the ifrit would have possessed someone else if given the opportunity. With us, the relic can do no harm."

"What did you do?"

"I bound its magic."

"And you couldn't have done this earlier, before..." *Before Ahmed was forced to kill his comrades?* She would never forget the agony in his eyes.

"No, even if I had been able to seal it, the relic needs to stay close to me. You saw how powerful the ifrit was. It will take great concentration to keep her contained." Qadir patted the bag of infinite space. "From now on, this stays with me."

Loulie stiffened. The bag was a lifeline to her business, and if Qadir had lied to her before, then maybe he had lied to her about other things. She'd opened her heart too much this day. "No," she said sharply. "Find another way to carry the collar. I'm keeping the bag."

She frowned at Qadir until he relented, pushing the bag back to her. "If you insist."

"Forgive me for not trusting you after suffering your lies."

Qadir's expression fell. "Loulie, I'm—"

"Yes, I know. You're sorry." She hefted the bag over her shoulder. "I am returning to the wali's manor. I told him I would be back, and..." She sighed. "I need some space to think, Qadir."

She walked away without waiting for his response.

33

MAZEN

Mazen was listening for his shadow's heartbeat when Aisha burst into his room like a storm cloud. He flinched back at the glare on her face. Though he'd mentally steeled himself for her rage, he was not prepared for the shame that suddenly overwhelmed him.

Yesterday, he'd been too mortified to admit to her that he'd forgotten the relic in Ahmed's diwan. And after the battle, he'd been so alarmed by the sight of the black blood oozing from his skin that he'd fled to treat his wound in private. The doctors hadn't batted a lash when he'd stolen some of their bandages—they'd been too busy dealing with potentially fatal injuries.

He'd managed to avoid Aisha last night, but he couldn't ignore her penetrating gaze now.

"You gave away a priceless relic yesterday," she snapped.

"It was never ours."

"*You* found it—"

"And I gave it away to the merchant. I would rather not be possessed by a vengeful jinn, shukran."

"You're a coward."

The accusation startled him. It hardly mattered that it was the truth. "You weren't there when the wali was first possessed. Not even a sliver of his consciousness remained. You would risk that danger?"

"Yes." Her response was so immediate and sure it shocked him into silence. "I am one of the forty thieves. It's my *job* to collect relics for my king."

King. Mazen hated that title. It gave his brother an authority he did not deserve. He glanced at his shadow and thought of the dream that had plagued him since the shadow jinn's demise, the one he now recognized as her memory. His brother had killed her—ruthlessly. And the part of her that remained had somehow attached itself to his shadow. Had somehow changed it into a *relic*.

After witnessing the shadow jinn's memory and hearing the Queen of Dunes' words, he had no doubts. He didn't know how jinn magic worked beyond the miracle of their blood, but this at least explained his new power. He'd briefly contemplated telling Aisha about the shadow, but now he reconsidered.

If she knew it existed, she would try to steal it. Never mind the impossibility of the act. If anyone could find a way to steal a shadow, it was Aisha bint Louas.

He looked at her now, trying to gauge her awareness. "Do you know what they are? The relics you're collecting for my brother?"

"Speak plainly, Prince."

Haltingly, he told her about what he'd realized in the diwan. Aisha was completely unfazed by his explanation, which meant she thought he was lying, or...

"So you know," he said softly.

"Of course I know." She rolled her shoulders in a shrug. "Our king is the most accomplished hunter in the desert. Do you know how many relics he's stolen off corpses? He surmised there were souls in them long ago."

Mazen stared at her, horrified. "Do all hunters know?"

"None that I've met. But a wise one would know to check a corpse for magic regardless."

He must have been wearing a gloomy expression, because she sniffed and said, "Wipe that sour look off your face. The jinn are monsters. We use their blood to return nature to the world; what does it matter if we use their soul magic too?" She leaned against the door, pinched the bridge of her nose. "Do you ever think things through?"

He bristled. "At least I am not single-minded like you." The words stunned him nearly as much as they did Aisha. When had he become so blunt?

The thief recovered her composure quickly enough. "I, at least, know how to take my obligations seriously. *I* don't go around forgetting relics in other people's homes."

Mazen flinched. Because of his forgetfulness, people were dead. The epiphany was so heavy it stole the breath from his lungs. Last night, all he had seen in the darkness behind his lids was carnage. Blood on the walls and corpses with torn bodies and glassy eyes.

My fault, my fault. His heart burned with remorse. "I never wanted the responsibility of that relic," he murmured.

"If you had told me it was missing, I would have stopped the bloodshed before it began."

"And if we'd given the relic to the merchant in the first place, we could have avoided this situation entirely." Mazen's irritation intensified into an impending headache. He rubbed at his temples. "At least I *tried* to make that decision for myself."

Aisha glowered at him. "What are you implying?"

"That I don't go around doing things only because Omar told me to. All you ever speak about are relics and your obligations to my brother."

"I don't owe it to you to speak about anything else," Aisha snapped as she reached for the doorknob. "My king ordered me to be your bodyguard, not your friend."

Mazen stepped forward as she turned the knob. "Why do you call him that? King." Aisha paused to glance at him over her shoulder. "You speak as if you're his servant, not his comrade."

Aisha smiled at him. A mocking smile. "You think we're *friends*? You're even more foolish than I thought, Prince."

"But you willingly joined Omar—"

"To kill jinn. So long as his orders allow me to do that, I will follow them without question. My *only* goal is to kill jinn. I am more than happy to let my king keep the spoils if there are any to be found."

"But why?"

Aisha scoffed as she opened the door. "My reasons are none of your business."

She had just stepped outside when Mazen called her back. Although he did not want to mention his shadow, he'd decided earlier there was one secret he needed to share with her.

"Wait! Before you go..." He pulled one of Omar's knives out of his belt and, after some hesitation—*It's just a shallow wound*—drew it across his palm. Even though he'd purposely nicked himself with a blade in various places since the incident last night, his heart still fell at the sight of the black blood. He held his hand up to Aisha, who closed the door, face paling.

She strode across the room and took his hand. "When did you discover this?" She swiped at the blood with her finger. It looked like a smudge of dirt on her skin.

"Last night, when the wali cut my shoulder." He recalled the panic pulsing in his chest when he'd washed it, alone and away from prying eyes, at the wali's manor.

Aisha considered the blood for a long moment before tapping the bangle on his wrist. "Take it off," she said.

Mazen blinked. "What?"

"Do it. I want to see something."

Mazen moved away from the window and, after throwing one last surreptitious glance at the door, pulled the bangle from his arm. The familiar and uncomfortable sensation of not belonging in his own skin returned, followed by a nausea that forced him to seek balance against the wall. Trembling, he looked down at his hand. It was no longer calloused, no longer *Omar's*. But most importantly, the blood on his palm was no longer black.

Aisha shook her head. "The black blood looks to be a side effect of the jinn magic."

Mazen pushed his bloodied hand through his hair—*his* hair!—

and nearly cried at the feeling of it beneath his fingers. It had been so long since he'd been himself.

"I didn't realize relics *had* side effects," he said softly.

"Neither did I." Aisha grabbed the bangle from him, squinted at it as she turned it over in her hands. "So long as the blood's not poisonous and has no ill effects, I don't think it matters." She handed it back to him, but when she commanded him to put it back on, he hesitated.

Though Omar's reflexes had helped him survive this far, he missed feeling at home in his own body. "Just for a few minutes, I'd like to take a break from all this treachery."

Aisha scoffed. "Fine." She placed her hands on her hips. "Anything else you want to tell me before I run some errands and find the merchant?"

He blinked at her. "Errands?"

"Have you forgotten that I need to buy another horse?"

Mazen flushed. He *had* forgotten. Aisha's runaway horse had been the last thing on his mind when they fled from the ruins. The merchant had barely been conscious, so Qadir had chosen to seat her in front of him so he could hold her on the way to Dhyme while Aisha rode Loulie's horse.

"Such an impressive memory you have." Aisha snorted. "So? Any other revelations?"

Again, he found his eyes wandering to his shadow, a muted silhouette on the colorless wall. He shook his head. "No, but don't worry about calling the merchant. Let me find her. I know where she is."

He'd seen her storming away from the inn and heading back in the direction of the wali's residence when he returned last night.

To Aisha's skeptical look, he responded, "I have some things I need to discuss with her. Don't worry; you'll have the whole journey to harass her for the relic."

And, though he was nervous to do so, he needed to check in on Ahmed again. No matter his anxiety at seeing the wali—*It's my fault he was possessed; I left the relic in his diwan*—he had a responsibility as the high prince to check on him. He did not think it would absolve the guilt that clung to him like a second skin, but he did not expect it to. He did not deserve that release, not when he had been the whole cause of this disaster.

"Fine." She tilted her head up, chin jutted defiantly. Then she slammed the door behind her, leaving him alone. Mazen sighed.

He wondered, vaguely, if he and Aisha would ever be able to trust one another.

34

AISHA

You speak as if you're his servant, not his comrade.

The words pounded through Aisha's mind, building into a cumbersome headache as she wove her way through Dhyme's central souk. She edged her way past slow-moving morning crowds and sleepy-eyed merchants, all the while ignoring the rumbling of her stomach as she passed carts selling fresh breads and hummus and labneh.

Servant! She was no servant. Nine years ago, when Omar had started rebuilding his father's decimated thief force from the ground up, he'd recruited her off the street first. They were not friends—would never *be* friends—but she was no mindless soldier.

Yes, she was here because of Omar. But she was one of his thieves; she had pledged herself to his service all those years ago, and she never reneged on her promises.

Aisha groaned. Prince Mazen's ability to get under her skin was uncanny. She was tempted to blame it on her sleep deprivation, an embarrassing consequence of her overthinking.

Until last night, the jinn—the *collar*—had been silent since their romp through the dune. Aisha had thought herself immune to the creature's internal mockery. The last thing she'd been expecting when she pried the collar off Ahmed bin Walid's neck was for the jinn to speak to her in memories—reminiscences that were not even hers.

She had gotten so lost in those memories she had forgotten reality. It had not been until she saw the merchant gripping the collar that she realized she'd nearly succumbed to its power.

And as if *that* near failure hadn't been humiliating enough, the bizarre memories had trailed Aisha to bed like mist and encompassed her dreams like fog. Even now, she could remember the vision that had kept her awake: the human man, bleeding crimson into the sand as his tribesmen sawed off his limbs. She remembered blood in her lungs, walls of sand, and the feeling of drowning as her lover's tribesmen cut into her heart—

Aisha bumped headfirst into a young noble wearing a turban stuffed with peacock feathers. She waited for him to apologize. He waited for *her* to apologize. When she simply looked at him expectantly, he scowled and shoved her aside. "Riffraff," he muttered.

Aisha took the opportunity to steal an apology from him in coin— three silver pieces, easily pilfered from his fine, embroidered pockets.

"Fool," she said with a smirk as she slid the silver into her pockets.

The theft improved her mood somewhat as she passed into Dhyme's poorest district, through streets filled with litter and sewage. She had not been lying when she told the prince she needed a new horse, but there was *another*, more important errand she needed to run first.

As she moved deeper into the quarter, she became aware of its pungent scents, of the odors of rotting food and manure that lingered in the air. The smell always took her by surprise, no matter how often she came to this place, and she had to remember to hold her breath as she made her way toward the abandoned neighborhood that was her destination.

She encountered a beggar as she was making her way through the run-down thoroughfares: an old man with empty eyes. Aisha slid a coin from her pocket and tossed it to him.

The beggar gasped as the silver bounced off his knee and rolled into a wall.

"Gods bless you," he called in a raspy voice as she walked away.

A few more turns, and she found herself at the dead end she'd been looking for. There was nothing but a cracked, plastered wall in front of her. Or so it would seem to most people. There was a fissure in the wall where it met the corner, and Aisha squeezed herself through it to get to another alley. She passed through several other hidden passages known only to her and forty others, and then she finally reached the boarded-up house she'd been looking for.

Dust coated the walls and floors, rising to cloud her vision as she made her way through abandoned rooms to a creaking staircase. At the landing was a door, which she knocked on in a particular fashion. She waited one heartbeat, two, and then she entered.

The first thing she saw when she stepped inside was the shelf on the back wall: a resting place for ornaments both bizarre and mundane, shiny and dull. A handful of relics worth a small fortune, hidden in Dhyme's poorest quarter.

Aisha's eyes flickered to the single open window in the abandoned home. A man stood beside it with his arms crossed, watching her. He regarded her with heavy-lidded eyes. "Aisha," he said in his usual monotone.

"Junaid." The name came out a sigh. She had not been certain he would be here. Dhyme was Junaid's hunting ground, but he was rarely in the city. As the thief was the fastest rider in their band, Omar often depended on him to make time-sensitive deliveries.

The scrawny, middle-aged thief settled on the floor, tucked his bony legs beneath him. "I heard of your mission by hawk." His lips lifted in a smile. On his sunken face, it looked like the grin of a dead man. "And I heard about the slaughter in the wali's manor. I assume you're here to tell the story so that I may deliver it to our king?"

Aisha nodded. Omar had not asked for reports, but he expected them.

She stripped the story down to its barest facts—she was not keen on sharing the details of her defeat. The older thief listened intently, reacting only when Aisha mentioned the collar's ability to manipulate the dead.

His eyes gleamed with wonder. "So she is still alive," he murmured.

"The jinn?" Aisha crossed her arms. "It's more alive than any relic *I've* seen."

"Perhaps because it is a jinn king's relic. I imagine those would be more powerful." Junaid looked thoughtful. "There is a tale around these parts about an undead jinn queen, no? Perhaps the collar you found belongs to her."

Aisha frowned. He was referring to the Queen of Dunes, a cautionary tale meant to discourage children from wandering the desert alone. She had not thought to connect the jinn in the ruins to an old campfire story, but Junaid's theory made sense.

"So where is it?" Junaid leaned forward. "Where is this king's relic I am to deliver?"

"With the merchant. The idiot prince gave it to her after the fight. If it disappears, they'll know I stole it."

Junaid blinked at her. "And?"

Aisha scowled. "*And* it's already hard enough to keep their trust. The last thing I need is for them to start becoming suspicious of us. Suspicious of *Prince Mazen*."

When Junaid continued to stare at her placidly, she shook her head and said, "Deliver this promise to our king: tell him I *will* bring him the relic at journey's end. He trusted me to watch the prince. He can trust me to watch a relic."

Never mind that the relic had made her forget herself. That the thing had made her look like a fool *twice*. She would not let it happen again. She was stronger than any jinn—king or not.

Junaid rose with a sigh. His knees cracked as he straightened. "Fine. I am but a humble messenger. I will deliver your words to Omar." He walked past her to the door and picked up a bulky bag she had not noticed. She assumed it was filled with Dhyme-made weapons to be delivered to Omar. She was amazed Junaid's thin body didn't crack beneath its hefty weight.

"You must have the strength of a jinn in that puny body," Aisha said.

Junaid looked up sharply. "That is not a joke to be made in our line of work."

She raised a brow. "And Samar calls *me* touchy." She followed the thief to the door, eyeing the scant display of relics in passing. Weapons, jewelry, clothing—it was mystifying, how many shapes a relic could take.

"You could borrow one." Junaid gestured to the display. "For your next fight."

Aisha thought of the black blood staining the prince's hand. She had never trusted jinn magic; now she trusted it even less.

"No." She rested her hand on the hilt of one of her blades. "I don't need them."

Junaid shrugged his pointy shoulders. "Suit yourself." He pushed open the door. Paused on the threshold. "I'll look forward to toasting your loyalty when you return to Madinne."

Aisha scoffed. "Loyalty isn't loyalty if it's contingent on a reward."

Again, Junaid smiled the dead man's grin. "Wise words, bint Louas. Wise words."

She waited for his footsteps to fade down the hall before she followed him downstairs. The thief doubtless had his own exit—it would be impossible to slip that gigantic bag through such narrow cracks.

Aisha, on the other hand, felt unburdened. Their journey hadn't been a smooth one so far, but they were making progress, and that was the important thing.

Just as Aisha did not mourn the past, she also did not overthink the future. Right now, there was only the present. And in the present, she was one step closer to being done with this hellish journey. But first—she needed a horse.

35

LOULIE

The morning after the fight in the diwan, Loulie woke with a heavy heart. Her dread only worsened when, after blinking sunlight out of her eyes, she found herself lying in one of the wali's guest rooms, no Qadir in sight. At first, she was irritated at him for having disappeared. But then she remembered *she* had been the one to walk away.

She had confronted him. He had apologized. What else was there to do but accept his apology and move on? Qadir had saved her life, had given her the magic to protect herself. Their bond was stronger than this fight. And yet she still felt broken. Still felt hurt.

Loulie sighed as she turned to her preparations for the day. She bathed in one of the wali's private bath chambers, donned her merchant robes and bag, outlined her eyes in kohl, and then set out to meet with Ahmed.

The guards led her into the courtyard, past the diwan, and up to a landscape of ponds and crisscrossing bridges. The wali stood on the longest bridge, a beautiful wooden construct with rails that curved and spiraled like eddies. The bridge hung above a pond: flowered cacti surrounded the water, and golden daisies and marigolds grew between the smooth stones edging their way out of the pond's surface. Sissoo trees loomed above them, speckling the silver water with shards of sunlight.

Ahmed stared at all of this blankly. He turned only when the guards announced her presence. And then, as he always did, he forced a smile onto his face. It was the most halfhearted smile she'd ever seen on him, made even less convincing by the dark circles under his eyes. She noticed he was garbed entirely in white: the color of prayer.

"Ah, if it isn't my favorite guest. How goes the morning, Midnight Merchant?"

"Mundane." She despised the world for continuing on like normal, even though Ahmed's life was falling apart.

Ahmed sighed. "Indeed." He waved a hand at the guards. "You may leave us." The command took the guards as far as the next bridge. Ahmed chuckled without humor at her confusion. "They are wary of me, and for good reason." She realized it was the truth. The guards weren't securing the area; they were securing *Ahmed*. She could feel their eyes from a distance.

Her stomach sank. "But why? What happened last night wasn't your fault."

She had been in his chambers last night when he explained what had happened. He had, without knowing why, been carrying the collar around while preparing for his meeting. He'd been in the jinn-made forest when it started speaking to him. Before he'd known what he was doing, he'd clasped it around his neck and become a prisoner in his own mind.

It was the stuff of nightmares. Loulie knew; she had nearly fallen under the same spell.

Ahmed smiled. A sad, stiff smile. "Unfortunately, it's difficult to blame murder on a very formless, very dead jinn."

Not if that jinn may be the legendary Queen of Dunes.

"Why not? Prince Mazen was possessed. He injured people too." She approached him slowly, fingers trailing the wooden rails.

"Injury is not permanent. Death is." His throat bobbed at the last words, and he paused to stare at their reflections as he composed himself. Loulie yearned to reach out and . . . pat his shoulder? Draw him into her arms? She didn't know. The thought of trying to comfort him terrified her. She was good at fanning flames, not putting them out.

"I'm to visit Madinne in a few days' time," he said, breaking her from her thoughts. "I've already sent a letter to the sultan. I leave my fate in his hands."

Loulie did touch him then—grabbing his sleeve and yanking him toward her so she could glare into his face. "You don't mean that. You aren't a criminal, Ahmed."

Ahmed blinked at her, mouth agape. Loulie wanted to shake him until he murmured, "You said my name." There was wonder in his eyes.

Given the circumstances, there was absolutely no reason for her to be blushing. But damned fool that she was, she was blushing anyway. "Yes, I did. But your *name* was not the point."

Her fingers were still clenched when Ahmed pulled her hand from his sleeve. He loosened her fist and laced his fingers through hers. Loulie stiffened. They had held hands like this before, but Ahmed's grip had never been so tight, his hold on her so desperate.

Normally, this was when she pulled away. Ahmed had always given her space when she became overwhelmed. He had never chased after her. He'd simply smiled and waited for her to return.

But the man holding her hand now was a shattered version of himself. The least she could do was be here for him. No, she *wanted* to be here for him. So this time, she did not pull away.

Ahmed smiled at her—that broken smile that made her heart sink—before turning his gaze to the water. "A criminal is charged by their actions, not their intentions." When he saw Loulie's reflection grimacing at him, he sighed and said, "I will tell the sultan what happened. Nothing more, nothing less. He is a just man; I trust his sentence."

Just. It was the last word she would use to describe the sultan.

Loulie didn't know how long they stood there, watching ripples spread and break on the surface of the water, before Ahmed broke the silence. "I'm sorry. I didn't want to hurt you. But the jinn…" His hand shook in her grip. "I couldn't move. I…"

"I told you already. It wasn't your fault."

"I could have killed you." His voice was whisper soft now. "I *almost* killed you."

"But you didn't."

"Loulie." She startled when he turned toward her. There was an urgency in his eyes that had not been there before. "That relic—you don't truly plan on taking it with you, do you? It will consume you."

"No." She hesitated, and then, because the situation seemed to call for it, she squeezed his hand and said, "I'm the Midnight Merchant. Relics don't possess me; I possess *them*." She had meant for the remark to lighten the mood, but Ahmed's expression only dampened further at her words. "You remember my bodyguard? He has a means of neutralizing the relic; I trust him."

"Your bodyguard..." Ahmed furrowed his brow. "He wasn't there last night, was he?"

"No, he was..." *Tracking rumors of a killer.* She had sent him away because of her own bravado, and probably doomed Ahmed in the process. *No.* She squashed the guilty thought. She had not been the one holding the relic. That had been the prince...

"Wali." Loulie startled at the voice, which came from a guard who had materialized out of nowhere. Behind him, as if summoned by her thoughts, stood the high prince. In true high-prince fashion, he walked past the guard without waiting for his presence to be announced.

"I hope I'm not interrupting." Omar looked pointedly at their joined hands.

Loulie pulled her hand away with as much pride as she could muster. Ahmed seemed to deflate without the contact. He sank to his knees and pressed his forehead to the ground. "Sayyidi," he mumbled. "You have my sincerest apologies for what happened last night. I did not mean—"

"Please, I require no excuses. You are a victim, Ahmed." The prince crossed his arms. "I came to offer my condolences for the loss you suffered and to reassure you that I will personally write to my father and vouch for your innocence. And..." He looked away, brow furrowed. "I came to apologize for my carelessness. I will make sure the sultan knows I was the one to leave the relic in your manor."

Loulie stared, startled by the prince's admission. Even Ahmed looked up abruptly. His cheeks were flushed, though whether with embarrassment or relief, Loulie could not tell. "Please, sayyidi, there is no need for that. You did not submit to the jinn. I did."

The apprehensive wrinkle between Omar's brows became an irritated crease. "Are you disputing the importance of my account, bin Walid?"

Ahmed stiffened. "No, of course not. I am grateful for your honesty, sayyidi."

Omar's lips quirked slightly. "Humility doesn't suit you." The half smirk faded as he turned to Loulie. "You, on the other hand, stole the show, al-Nazari. I'm impressed. I've never seen anyone wield a dagger so well with an injured hand."

Her heart halted, shuddered. *Shit.* She had forgotten about the nonexistent injury. All her focus during the fight had been on keeping her and Ahmed alive.

Why does he have to be so damn observant?

She noticed even Ahmed was looking at her curiously now, his sleep-shadowed eyes flitting to her hand. After a second of hesitation, she raised her bandaged hand and wiggled her fingers. "Jinn blood is always very useful to have on hand." Her heart thundered so loudly in her chest it seemed impossible no one heard it in the silence. "You didn't think I would have given the only blood I have to Rasul al-Jasheen?"

"I would think you had no reason to hide the existence of such blood."

Loulie snorted. She hoped to the gods she wasn't sweating as much as she feared. "Alert you to an invaluable stash of jinn blood so you could steal it from me? I'm no fool."

Except she was a fool. She was so much a fool she wanted to laugh at herself.

Omar looked skeptical of her claim, but he mercifully let her excuse go. Their conversation moved from the courtyard to the diwan and then into the corridors as Ahmed offered them provisions for the rest of their trip. The next—and last—city they would pass through was Ghiban, and it would be at least a week before they reached it.

The talk between the three of them was stilted and awkward, filled with silences and forced niceties. Loulie noted a strange tension between the men. She had the impression they were dancing around each other's words. She didn't think on it for long; it was of no interest to her. She was, however, very interested in the high prince's long pauses. They seemed more thoughtful than usual, as if he were carefully considering his reactions before he made them.

She was suddenly reminded of another thing that had bothered her: his behavior during the battle. The prince had not fought; he had *watched*. It was a perplexing epiphany, and Loulie was resolved to confront him about it.

She never got the opportunity, though.

Prince Omar excused himself before she could demand answers, explaining that he had last-minute preparations to make before they departed that afternoon. After saying his stilted goodbyes to Ahmed, he disappeared, leaving her and the wali alone.

By this time, the ease with which they had conversed had dried up, leaving them bereft of anything to say. So the two of them simply walked—back through the open-air halls and into the courtyard. Loulie noticed Ahmed glance warily at the trees. Most likely, he was remembering the blood that had been spilled beneath them last night. She suspected that even in the future, when those stains were washed off the grass, he would never stop seeing them. What had been an eerie but tranquil place was now a permanent reminder of a once-lived nightmare.

She could not conceive of the breathtaking shame that would warp Ahmed's heart every time he entered his estate and saw these trees. Had Qadir been here, he would have told her the wali deserved to know the fear of his victims. Perhaps he was right. But still, that did not stop Loulie from pitying him.

They were nearing the edge of the copse when Ahmed at last turned toward her. "I am sorry your visit has been so unpleasant, Loulie al-Nazari."

She blinked. "No, I should be the one apologizing. Had the prince and I not brought the relic to Dhyme, none of this would have happened."

Ahmed shook his head. "I have no excuses for my incompetence."

Loulie nearly said *The high prince was every bit as incompetent yesterday!* but held her tongue. It would not do to insult Omar bin Malik in front of one of his subjects.

Ahmed continued, "I have failed in my duties as your host, and I owe you an apology."

Beneath that apology was another one: *I am sorry I could not convince you to accept my proposal.* Every time she came to Dhyme, the wali tried to win her over. Not with tokens or gold or flowers, but with honest conversation. He was the only man she visited for pleasure rather than business. The only man whose company she enjoyed. Whose company she *missed*.

Someday, she would have to face the reality that he could never be her future, but for now, she would keep dreaming that the circumstances of their lives were different.

"No apologies are necessary." She held out a hand. "When I return, I'll tell you about my adventure in full." Because she had faith Ahmed bin Walid would be back. He was a hunter, and hunters were tenacious creatures.

She expected the wali to shake her hand. Instead, he grasped it and kissed her knuckles. "And we shall finally talk, lovely Loulie, of stars and stories."

Loulie was too astonished to say anything.

It was not until she'd left his residence that she noted her clammy palms and racing heart. But then Qadir appeared at her side, and her anxiety vanished into thin air.

They didn't speak. They didn't need to. Qadir was here because it was time to go.

She glanced back only once—and witnessed the disconcerting sight of the wali's shoulders drooping as he walked away. He looked, in that moment, like a defeated general. She suffocated her foreboding and turned away.

36

LOULIE

Their return to the desert was a solemn affair. The prince no longer smirked when she looked at him, Aisha only ever spoke pointedly about the relic belonging to Omar, and Qadir was reticent and grim-faced. It was an abysmal atmosphere, one made drearier by the tension between them.

Their first night out, Loulie barely spoke to anyone, including Qadir. She trailed the jinn on a hunt, pointed out a warbler's nest, and agreed to skin the birds with nothing but silent gestures. The words they did trade were perfunctory, limited to simple questions and one-word assurances as they set up camp and cooked their prey over a fire built by the thieves.

The second day, the tension intensified into a suffocating quiet, one so heavy it pressed on Loulie's shoulders like a physical weight. "Unnatural," Aisha bint Louas murmured, and Loulie realized she was right. Though the desert was normally quiet, this silence was so dense it was oppressive. But for all its strangeness, it was familiar.

"Ghouls," Qadir said, speaking her mind.

The prince sat up straight in his saddle. "Where?"

"Not too far away," Aisha grumbled. "You can tell by the stillness."

Loulie shifted atop her horse to scan the horizon. As far as she could see, there were no undead creatures approaching. But then, ghouls were incredibly slow; she and Qadir had never had problems outrunning them in the open desert before.

"We should alter our course, just to be safe," Qadir said.

Omar sighed. "Better that than waste our time on a needless fight." Perhaps it was a trick of the light, but—Loulie could have sworn his brow furrowed briefly with consternation.

They changed direction, swerving away from the open plains to travel between the dunes. The silence eventually disappeared, only to be replaced by an irritating, howling wind. Not enough to build into a storm, but enough to be a hindrance. They rode faster and harder in the afternoon hours to find more-secure shelter, and by the time stars scattered the sky, they were camping in the shadow of a large boulder. Right before they retired for the night, Loulie overheard Omar say to Aisha, "Never a dull moment with ghouls around, is there?"

Aisha responded with a tired shrug. "Stupid creatures. But at least we can outrun these ones. The quiet in the dune was awful."

Thankfully, they did not run into the ghouls again. Loulie was glad for it. By their third night out, her fortitude had been whittled down to a sliver. Her thighs were sore from hard riding, her shoulders were bunched with nerves she couldn't roll out, and she had accumulated an uncomfortable layer of sand beneath her robes. So when they came upon one of the Bedouin camps on Omar's map, she could not help her sigh of relief.

She leaned forward in her saddle to get a better look at the campsite. Even from this distance she could tell it was small, composed of only four interlocking circles of tents and two corrals—one for sheep and another for camels. The tribesmen were gathered in the center, probably for feasting or stories. It was not long before a messenger detached himself from the group and rode out to meet them. His brown skin bore constellations of freckles—a testament to the many years he'd spent beneath the sun.

Upon noticing the details of Omar's garments, he greeted them with a graceful bow from his horse. "High Prince." His eyes roved over the rest of their group: Loulie wrapped in her unimpressive brown shawl; Qadir, tall and imposing on his horse; and Aisha, her lips pressed into a tight grimace shadowed beneath her hood.

The messenger eyed the thief uncertainly. "Midnight Merchant?"

Loulie bristled. She was glad for her scarf in that moment, because it hid her severe scowl as Omar coughed into his fist and Qadir looked pointedly away.

The grimace remained fixed on Aisha's face as she tilted her chin toward Loulie. The messenger turned, flustered. "My apologies, merchant." He bowed again. "It is an honor to meet you both."

She softened at the greeting. "Likewise. Would we be able to request sanctuary tonight?"

"Of course. We would be honored to host you as long as you need," he said with a respectful nod. Loulie could tell he was a hunter—of animals, if not jinn—from the elaborate bow he wore on his back. She was still admiring it as she and the hunter traded rumors on their way to the campsite.

She and the high prince were, of course, the most highly sought-after gossip. Apparently, the whole desert knew of their journey. After she satiated the tribesman's curiosity and alerted him to the presence of ghouls in the western plains, the man told her of other happenings: the changing weather patterns—scattered rainstorms and troublesome winds; the altered traveling routes; the appearance of hyenas by the cliffs.

"And we've heard rumors of a hunter," he said. They were nearly at the campsite now, and Loulie saw curious children peeking at them through gaps in the wooden gate. "He works alone. Dresses entirely in black and blends into the night, they say."

Loulie nearly fell off her horse. Here it was at last: the rumor she'd been seeking.

"Tell me more about this hunter." Her heart was practically beating in her throat.

The tribesman shook his head. "He's an enigma. They say this area is empty of jinn because he lays traps so effective none have ever escaped them."

"Where does he live?"

"No one knows. He disappears before our hunters can approach." He frowned. "This is just my opinion, but I would stay away from him. No nomad who travels alone is trustworthy."

Loulie had heard that from her own mother many times. Bedouin traveled in tribes. Those who wandered alone had probably been banished, and that was never a good sign.

"Of course. I only want to know more so I can do my best to avoid him." She caught Qadir frowning at her over the tribesman's head. *Liar*, his narrowed eyes said. She ignored him.

Soon they were through the gate and in the camp, where the tribe's sheikh greeted them with overwhelming hospitality. He had their horses led away to be cared for while they seated themselves around a large campfire located at the heart of a cluster of brown tents.

A sheep was slaughtered in their honor, and they were offered a variety of breads, meats, and vegetables. It was the kind of food one daydreamed about: fresh, appetizing, and prepared with familial warmth. It reminded Loulie of home. As a child, she had sat in a circle like this with her mother and father, scarfing down bread and pretending to listen to the adults as they spoke about traveling routes, produce, and politics. She remembered thinking it was all so *mundane* and that maturity sounded like a chore.

But though she had not always been invested in the fireside talks, the meals had been her favorite part of the day. They were the reprieve after a long day of work, a time to exchange not only words, but stories and rumors and confessions. For Loulie, they had also been the best time to play pranks on her long-suffering cousins. Slipping insects into their sleeves, swapping plates, hiding foods— all sleights of hand she practiced in her spare time with her father.

Though she had since outgrown the pranks, her affection for the food was undying. This was especially true for the camel milk, which had a rich and salty taste that filled her with melancholy. She was sipping on that milk now as she took in the animated chatter around her.

The sheikh sat at the head of the circle, listening attentively to the accounts from the tribe's hunters. An elderly woman with silver threaded through her hair reprimanded a group of bickering children who were gambling their food away in an intense guessing game. A flustered-looking tribesman shot bashful looks at a woman working on a loom outside one of the nearby tents. When he wasn't looking, she turned her head to observe him with a secretive smile.

Family. That was the word that came to mind as Loulie took in the domestic scene. It gripped her heart like a vise, made it difficult to breathe. She had become accustomed to—*preferred*—living a solitary life, but it was easier to forget what she had lost in the cities, where the families were scattered and hidden. Sitting around this campfire, she could see the interconnectedness of the lives around her—and she could see herself sitting in the heart of the web, adrift.

She mentally chided herself for her despondency as she tore off a piece of meat, and stoppered her memories before they could overwhelm her. They were well into the second course when she noticed the circle had quieted. She did not realize why until she heard the high prince telling a story. She looked up and saw him waving his hands. Smiling. Not the condescending smirk he usually wore, but an honest-to-gods *smile* that made his eyes sparkle.

"...And though the jinn was trapped, it did not falter. Do you know why?"

"Because it had magic!" cried a young boy.

"Yes, but not just any magic. This jinn was stronger than the others, for its army was made up of immortal shadows. The jinn melted in and out of them as easily as if they were rays of sunshine..."

Loulie recognized the story of the shadow jinn. The longer it went on, the more fictitious it became, until it sounded more like a legend than the truth. She found herself oddly charmed by it. Or perhaps it was not the story that captivated her, but the high prince, who seemed a different, more pleasant person when he told it.

"In the end..." He leaned forward, pausing dramatically. "The shadows dispersed. Because even the mightiest of jinn succumb to a hunter's iron blade."

In the silence that followed, the prince grew stiff, expression shuttering. But then his audience clapped, and his cocky smile returned. Loulie turned away, disgruntled. Had there always been such a discrepancy in his personality?

She was still mulling over this later, when she was bedding down for the night in a guest tent. Normally, she would have vented her frustrations to Qadir, but the jinn had chosen to give her a wide berth that night. As far as she was aware, he was wandering the campsite, watching her from a distance through the fire he'd lit in their lantern. Loulie stared at the lantern-cast shadows until they faded into the darkness behind her eyelids. Thoughts of Omar chased her into slumber.

Always, she saw him out of the corner of her eye, flickering in and out of sight as if he were a mirage. Every time he reappeared, he wore a different face. First, a condescending grin. Then a harsh scowl. Then, disconcertingly, a starry-eyed smile. He lifted a hand to point at her. And laughed.

She realized she was sinking.

The sand sighed as it devoured her. She clawed at the air, but to no avail. She couldn't see. Couldn't breathe. Darkness pressed in on her—

Abruptly, a flame flared into being.

Loulie shot up and out of her blankets. She squinted into the sudden brightness until she could make out Qadir's shadowed figure, and relaxed when she saw the fire cupped between his palms. "Nightmare?" he said softly.

She groaned as she rubbed at her eyes. "I was drowning in the Sandsea."

Qadir's fire shimmered a gentle white. When she squinted, she saw the tattoos on his arms flash the same color. "I could keep this fire alive, if it would help you sleep."

"And attract unwanted attention? No." Her limbs cracked as she stretched. She found she was no longer in the mood for slumber.

Qadir blew on the flame until it was nothing but embers on his palms. His tattoos dimmed as well, until they were just barely visible in the darkness. Loulie had learned long ago that the tattoos appeared only when he used his fire magic. She traced the patterns with her eyes, wondering at some of the less aesthetically pleasing marks.

"So," he said. "I see you're speaking to me again."

She answered with a noncommittal grunt.

His lips quirked. "How convenient. I was just thinking it would be strange to tell you a story and not have to suffer your questions afterward."

She drew her blankets around her like a shield. "Story?"

"You were angry at me for hiding the truth, so I thought I would apologize by giving you a history lesson."

"The subject?"

Qadir raised a brow. "Myself."

"And what will you talk about?" She kept her eyes on his tattoos.

Qadir saw her looking and set a hand on his bicep. "I'll tell you about my markings."

Loulie leaned forward, close enough that she could make out where the patterns connected and diverged. She thought of the way they flared like fire. "Are they made with magic?"

"...Of a kind."

"How did you get them?"

Qadir considered for a few moments before he said, "Some of them I was gifted. Others I received as punishment. In my culture, every mark has a meaning."

"What kind of meaning?"

He shifted so that the inside of his arm was visible to her, and ran his fingers down his veins. The tattoos flared back to life beneath his touch. They glowed red and gold, flickering softly as he traced the curved lines toward his fingers.

She squinted at them. "It's shaped like...a fire?"

Qadir smiled. "Now look at this one." This time, he traced the curve of his elbow. These marks were thin and short and looked less like brushstrokes and more like scars from a knife.

She frowned. "I don't see a shape."

"Because it is a mark of shame."

"It looks like you were scratched up with a blade."

Qadir lowered his arm with a sigh, and the tattoos vanished. "Yes. My shame was carved into me with a knife so that I would not forget it. I deserved it."

Loulie tucked her knees into her chest and waited. She did not expect him to continue, so she was surprised when he kept talking. "I told you once I was no longer welcome in Dhahab. That is because I committed a crime, and criminals are rarely forgiven in my city." He tapped the markings on his skin. "These marks are proof of that."

"What did you do?"

Qadir opened his mouth, closed it. "I would rather not say. It is a long and gruesome story, and I would prefer to tell it without any chance of being overheard." He exhaled softly. "I can tell you one thing, at least. The compass we carry contains the soul of a jinn named Khalilah." His expression softened at her name. "I was resigned to rotting away in a cell, but she saved me. Khalilah led me to your human desert and guided me with her magic."

He reached into the merchant bag and took out the compass. Loulie had always wondered why he looked at it so tenderly. "She can...find things?"

"She is an erafa who was born with the ability to read the future. Even in death, she can locate items and people and foresee a destiny before it passes." Qadir paused, brow furrowed. "We became separated early on, and she was killed by hunters before I could save her. By the time I located her, your father had already found her in the form of the compass. I followed his trail to your campsite."

Layla Najima al-Nazari, it seems saving your life was my destiny. Loulie would never forget those words. They had changed her life. And the compass—her eyes wandered to the dusty object cradled in Qadir's hands—the compass had saved it.

When she again looked at Qadir, his eyes were dark and stormy. "Who was she to you?" she asked softly.

"A friend," Qadir murmured. "My greatest, dearest friend."

The silence that followed was so fragile Loulie could not bring herself to break it. On impulse, she crawled forward and set a hand on Qadir's shoulder. The jinn startled. "What's this? You're trying to comfort me? I expected more questions."

"I'm not obtuse, Qadir. I can see when you're in pain." She was taken aback by his shock. And frankly, a little offended. "What? How heartless do you think I am?"

Miracle of all miracles, the jinn started laughing. It was a genuine sound, one she had been lucky enough to hear only a couple of times in her life. The last time she'd heard it, she had just given Qadir the shamshir. He'd burst out laughing when she suggested he wear it to look intimidating rather than for any practical purpose. The memory still lightened her heart.

"My gods." She grinned. "Who are you, and what have you done with my gloomy partner?"

Qadir was too busy laughing to answer. Loulie wondered, not for the first time, if it was his past that kept him so anchored to melancholy.

When he finally regained his composure, he looked at her and said, "Am I forgiven?"

Loulie sighed. "Yes, on the condition you don't lie to me again."

"Deal." Qadir glanced at their bag. "Does this mean I can carry the bag?"

"What for? *I'm* the merchant." She paused, noticing he'd slipped the collar out from gods knew where in his cloak. She drew back at the sight of it.

"You can relax. It's still sealed. It would be easier to carry in the bag, though."

She ignored the comment and eyed the collar. "What are we going to do with it?" It was one thing to find a home for lost relics—another to give away a dangerous ancient treasure. "Maybe we should bury it somewhere in the desert."

Qadir looked up sharply. "Or we could keep it."

"That's the *worst* idea."

"Trust me." He slipped the relic back into his robes. "I know in your stories she is a malevolent entity, but in ours, the ifrit are morally ambiguous. Let me try speaking to her."

"Speak to a killer?" Loulie scowled. "Do what you want, but I will not forgive her for what she did to Ahmed."

Qadir raised a brow. "You have qualms about a killer murdering other killers?"

"I have qualms about murder, period." *Murder.* The single word made her think back to the killer in black she had been discussing with the tribesman.

It was as if Qadir could read her mind. "Good. If you detest murder so much, then I assume you won't seek vengeance on some killer you may or may not know."

"Of course not." She knew even before gauging Qadir's reaction that she had spoken too fast. She always did when she was lying. She stood abruptly. "I'm going to walk around the campsite before I go back to sleep."

Qadir silently handed her a lantern flashing with his fire.

"You worry worse than my mother did." She grabbed the lantern from him.

Qadir sighed. "You have self-destructive tendencies; I have to worry."

Loulie rolled her eyes and walked away. She was glad Qadir could not see her face, because she was certain the battle waging in her heart would manifest in her expression. Loulie did not know what she would do—but she would do something.

It wasn't in her nature to let bygones be bygones.

37

MAZEN

"Wake up, Prince." Aisha's voice was feather soft, and yet in the extreme silence of the tent, it startled him awake. Mazen slowly sat up, rubbing sleep from his eyes as his foggy mind pieced together where and when he was: the middle of the desert, many miles out from the Bedouin campsite they'd left three days ago, on their way to the city of Ghiban.

He glanced blearily around their tent, which was swathed in the golden shadows of dawn. Their belongings were untouched, their surroundings unchanged. But the silence—that was new.

Aisha was crouched down beside him, a severe dent between her brows. She raised a finger to her lips and mouthed a single word.

Ghouls.

Mazen rose shakily to his feet. He said nothing as Aisha whispered commands, instructing him to pack the tent and secure the supplies.

The unnatural silence was so heavy it made every exhale too loud, every step a too-sharp crunch. The quiet suffocated even the sigh of the wind. It was as if the world itself were holding its breath. Was this the work of the ghouls they had avoided days ago?

It took a great effort to tamp down his fear as he and Aisha collapsed the tent and met the merchant and her bodyguard outside.

They looked miserable, bundled in layers to fight off the frigid morning cold. Loulie had even donned her Midnight Merchant vestments atop her plain attire, though she still shuddered beneath them. Mazen sympathized; his brother's cloak felt inadequate.

Loulie and Qadir acknowledged them with terse nods, then mounted their horses in silence.

It was a tacit rule that no one speak.

Mazen had not realized how loud the desert was until it went completely silent. He had been unnerved the last time they skirted this eerie quiet, but this silence was worse—far worse. Gone was the whisper of the sand and the sigh of the breeze. He had never paid much attention to the noise his horse's hooves made on the ground, but now he could not stop thinking about how loud every crunch was.

Traveling through the desert was an already exhausting endeavor, but to do it while attempting to suffocate all sound made the journey doubly tiring. It suddenly seemed as if every motion was dangerous: the rustling of his equipment as he shifted on his saddle, the click of the stirrups every time he urged his horse in a different direction, and even the hiss of the sand as it gathered and slid off his clothing in undisturbed streams.

Mazen rubbed his hands together in an effort to warm them and tried not to think about how parched his throat was and how he was too nervous to reach for the waterskin tucked deep into his saddlebags. The others seemed to be existing in a similar state of uncertainty. They wore their misery plainly, etched into their faces as frowns and slumped onto their shoulders like an invisible weight. Aisha may as well have been a statue, her gaze trained ahead, her fingers so stiff on the reins it hardly looked like she was gripping them at all.

Hours went by. Mazen spent his time fretting and watching. Mostly, he watched the merchant, who, when she wasn't observing her compass, watched him back. It was incredibly stress inducing. With every look she shot in his direction, Mazen became more convinced she had somehow seen through his disguise. At some point, his combined paranoia and exhaustion became so great it blurred his sight, and the merchant became a vaguely hostile-looking smudge amidst the hills of red-gold sand. He turned away from her, perturbed.

Mazen overthought every motion and look and noise until, miraculously, sound returned to the world. The sun had dipped below the horizon by then, and shadows carved the ripples in the sand into sculpted waves. A distant hawk broke the silence, and then—the wind whistled past them and threw sand in their faces. Qadir let out a long, deep sigh.

Aisha groaned. "The danger's passed." Her voice was hoarse with disuse.

Mazen snapped into action, immediately reaching into his saddlebag for their waterskin. The liquid was tasteless, and yet it seemed the sweetest thing he'd ever had in his life. He had to force himself to take sips and to hand the waterskin over to Aisha afterward.

Loulie glanced warily over her shoulder. "You think those are the same ghouls we evaded before?"

Qadir frowned. "Most likely. Though their tenacity is...unusual."

The merchant groaned. "Is it too much to ask for *one* day of uneventful travel?" She flexed her fingers in Qadir's direction. He handed her their waterskin. Mazen didn't realize he was staring at her until she lowered the waterskin and frowned at him. "Something on my face?"

His thoughts were so formless and scattered that he was at a loss for how to respond. He was just so *glad* to see that her visage had resolved into a definitive shape again.

Thankfully, Aisha filled the awkward silence. "It's a good thing ghouls are slow," she said. "Otherwise, from the sound, we'd have to deal with an army."

Mazen tucked the information away. He had gathered that ghouls deadened noise where they wandered, but it was helpful to know one could estimate the size of a group by the quiet it provoked. Useful and extremely disquieting.

Loulie scowled. "They probably smell the death on the two of you."

Aisha snorted. "Don't act so virtuous, relic seller. If they're tracking any of us, it's you. You have a bag of relics. You're practically walking ghoul bait."

A memory snapped into place at her words; Mazen remembered the story his mother had once told him about the ghouls. One he could still recall the beginning of . . .

"In the desert there exists a group of undead jinn who have one foot in death and another in life. What they lack in strength, they make up for with their sharpened senses. Though they are mostly blind, they can smell magic from miles and miles away."

There was a lull in the narrative as he tried to remember the rest.

"*Sayyidi.*" Aisha's voice was a hiss.

Mazen looked up and saw the merchant staring at him. She looked perplexed.

"Oh." It dawned on him he'd said the words aloud. "Sorry, I was . . . remembering a story."

The merchant looked at him intently, eyes narrowed as if she were trying to read him. Mazen's heart hitched. No, it was as if she were looking *through* him—

He saw a flash out of the corner of his eye.

A hiss of wind in his ear. A thud as something pierced the dirt.

Mazen followed the group's startled gazes to an arrow shaft protruding from the sand. He pressed a hand to his cheek, but there was no cut, no blood. Just a phantom pain chased by a current of fear.

Then: pandemonium.

Another arrow shot past them. One, two—a *volley* of them, coming through a curtain of dirt. One whizzed past the merchant's shoulder. Another grazed Mazen's horse. It rose with a terrified whinny, and Mazen gasped as he dug his heels into its flanks. He was able to remain in the saddle only by holding tight to the reins.

He calmed his horse enough to steady his vision and look beyond the wall of dust. His heart stopped when he saw their assailants: an army of shambling white forms garbed in black, with sunken eye sockets shadowed beneath their hoods. If not for their unnaturally long, wiry limbs and empty eyes, they could have passed as human.

Mazen was torn between wanting to scream and wanting to cry.

"Where did they come from?" The merchant's voice was barely a whisper.

Her bodyguard reached out, set his fingers on her wrist. "Loulie," he said softly. "There are too many; we have to outrun them."

The merchant glanced down at her compass. Even Mazen could tell it was useless, for the arrow was spinning in wild circles. Loulie shoved it into her pocket with a shaky sigh.

And then they fled.

But there was no escaping the ghouls. The air filled with wails and shrieks as the undead creatures fired on them from various directions. Mazen swerved in his saddle to avoid one arrow only to have another tear a hole through his pant leg. He couldn't help the sound of distress that escaped his lips as he flattened himself against his horse. It took all his concentration to maneuver around the creatures stumbling into his way.

Loulie made no such effort. Out of the corner of his eye, he saw her ride right over a ghoul without batting an eye. But the creature retaliated before it fell, sweeping its sword through the air and ripping the bottom of her cloak. Loulie cried out, and the sound caught the attention of her bodyguard. Qadir glanced over his shoulder, eyes wide with alarm. He relaxed only when Loulie waved a hand to reassure him of her safety.

But his eyes—there was something strange about them. They were eerily bright and ... flickering?

Mazen gaped. No, they were *sparking* like fire.

Qadir's gaze cut sharply to him. The bodyguard blinked, and just as abruptly as the strange fire had appeared, it disappeared. He turned away without comment.

Mazen stared at his back, troubled. He wondered if he was losing his mind.

But he did not linger on the strangeness of the sight for long. He couldn't, not with the hordes of black-clad undead closing in on them. The pack had grown denser, the creatures' bodies packed so tightly together they looked like a moving storm cloud. Mazen's heart sank into his stomach when he realized they were surrounded.

"Ambush!" Aisha yelled at the same time Mazen thought, *How will we survive this?*

The thief clenched her hands into fists over her reins. "They're too well organized for a normal horde." She spoke loudly over the chaos. "Someone has to be controlling them."

"Where?" The merchant's voice cracked as she dodged an arrow. "Where is this mastermind you speak of? Because if we can't find them, we're good as dead. We're—"

"Loulie." Qadir's voice was barely audible, but the resignation in it made Mazen wince. He watched as Qadir raised an arm. The bodyguard tapped his wrist, a slight motion that made his skin shimmer oddly beneath the sun.

The merchant stiffened in her saddle. "No." Her response was so immediate, the terror on her face so palpable, that it made the last of Mazen's nerves fray.

"What?" He glanced between them frantically. "What's happening?"

But the bodyguard just looked past him to Loulie. "Trust me," he said softly. Some silent message seemed to pass between them. Eventually, reluctantly, Loulie nodded.

"We keep riding to the center of the mob, then," Qadir said.

Aisha stared at him. "Do you *want* to die?"

When neither Loulie nor Qadir responded, Aisha turned to Mazen. There was a desperation in her eyes he had never seen before. He knew she was waiting for him to object. But...

He had no power here. He never had.

"We're out of ideas." His throat was tight, and he could barely manage his next words. "Whatever this plan is, it's better than nothing."

"It's not a plan," Aisha snapped, but her voice lacked its usual heat. There was despair in every taut line of her body. "It's suicide."

Mazen opened his mouth. Then closed it. He didn't have the

heart to offer reassurances, not when he didn't believe in them himself.

Aisha snapped her reins, pushing her horse harder, faster. "Stay behind me," she called back. "If your gods are kind, maybe they'll spare us."

She turned away and shot after Loulie and Qadir, toward the center of the turmoil.

Mazen muttered a prayer beneath his breath and chased after her.

38

LOULIE

I trust you, Qadir.

The moment Qadir had touched the tattoos on his wrist, Loulie had known what he meant to do. There were far too many ghouls for them to defeat with blades and knives. So Qadir had suggested a different kind of weapon: magic. *His* magic. Fire that would save them, but one that would also condemn him.

He had begged her to trust him. And she would. She had entrusted her life to him many times; the least she could do was trust that he could protect his own. And she—she would protect him too. She wasn't so weak she couldn't watch his back like he watched hers.

"I trust you, Qadir."

Loulie muttered the words on numb lips as the ghouls rushed toward them. As they loosed arrows and her vision blurred with tears. As Qadir fixed his gaze ahead and the tattoos snaking up his arms began to glow.

I trust you. I trust you. I trust you. The words pounded through her mind.

Qadir raised a hand. His fingertips sparked. The markings on his skin burned brighter and brighter, until they were shining so vividly they seemed to set his body on fire, and he became a blinding streak of gold and red.

Loulie had to avert her eyes. She forced herself to breathe. In and out. In and—

She heard something snap beneath her horse's hooves. The sound was followed by an odd but familiar sigh—the hiss of shifting, falling sand.

Loulie looked down just in time to see the landscape beneath her yawn open. Shock muddied her mind as the sand fell away, revealing a trap that had not been there moments ago.

She opened her mouth—to scream, to cry for help—when something shoved her horse away from the chasm. Loulie whirled in her saddle. She saw Qadir riding over the gaping hole, hand outstretched, the light fading from his skin.

There was a moment of stillness. Qadir looked at her urgently. His lips parted.

And then he and his horse plummeted into the abyss.

Loulie was distantly aware of Qadir's name leaving her mouth as a scream. Of sand crunching beneath her feet as she leapt from her panicked horse and sprinted toward the hole.

She could hear the prince and the thief dogging her steps. Yelling her name.

No.

She rushed to the pit.

No.

The chasm was filled with iron. Blades crisscrossed the walls, jutting toward the center like crooked teeth. On the tips of those blades: silver and crimson blood. Qadir's horse, torn and bleeding to death. And at the bottom of the pit, impaled on a graveyard of broken iron, silver blood on his skin—

Qadir.

Loulie began to scream.

39

LOULIE

Once, Loulie had lived a nightmare.

Like a dreamer, she had eventually woken and buried it in her mind. But though she had become very good at forgetting, the memories still haunted her in her sleep. She would see her parents' broken bodies. Would see her campsite going up in flames. She would smell blood and death and forget how to breathe.

And then Qadir would shake her awake. "You were making a face in your sleep. I thought it rude to keep staring."

And just like that, the nightmare would dissipate. Because so long as she avoided belonging anywhere—belonging with *anyone*—she would never have to relive that heartbreak.

But she had been wrong.

Because she was living a nightmare now, and Qadir wasn't waking her up. Now she was yelling *his* name. But no matter how many times she called him, he did not respond.

"Fuck." Loulie vaguely realized Aisha was standing beside her, staring into the pit, face ashen. "Your bodyguard was a *jinn*?"

I have to wake Qadir. The words were roots, drawing her into a safe place untouched by time. When Aisha put her hands on Loulie's shoulders, Loulie pushed her away.

"They're coming." She could barely hear Omar's voice over her pounding heart.

Distantly, she was aware of the smear of silver blood on the blades, of the careful way they had been constructed around the hole. But none of that mattered. She had eyes only for Qadir. She was still willing him to open his eyes and *look* at her, when she heard the sounds of a scuffle behind her.

Frenzied footsteps. The exhale of blades. A loud, inhuman hiss.

By the time she turned with her dagger in hand, it was too late. A group of ghouls grabbed her from behind, and no amount of struggling could break their grip. They clung to her like bloodsucking leeches.

She screamed.

"Shh, none of that." A voice spoke into the chaos, and Loulie froze. It laughed, a soft wheezing sound that seemed to come from lungs filled with sand. "What an honor it is to run into not one, but *two* legends."

She looked up. And stared.

The stranger was garbed entirely in black, more shadow than man. His features were hidden, everything except for his dark eyes, which were barely visible between his layered scarves.

The Hunter in Black. The nameless jinn killer.

She remembered a knife against her skin. Laughter. Blood running down her neck.

Do you desire death or slavery, girl?

A dark fog encapsulated her mind. She moved without thought, lunging forward with a feral cry. The man watched, expressionless, as the ghouls subdued her and made her kneel. His eyes twinkled, and in them Loulie saw her blood-soaked memories.

Ah, a little girl? What a grand prize you will make...

Memories blended with reality as Loulie sagged to the ground. Darkness coated her vision, and in it she saw the slew of nightmares she'd thought buried long ago. She saw her mother waving at a jar, urging her to hide, while killers stormed their camp. She saw the tents go up in flame. Saw her mother's and father's bodies, lying broken on the ground.

And now Qadir . . .

No. Grief splintered her thoughts. *Don't think about it.*

"I did not think you had such sharp claws, Midnight Merchant." The hunter turned away before she could formulate a response, his gaze settling on Omar, who'd been pushed to his knees by ghouls. "I am amused to see you reduced to a mere escort, Prince."

Aisha, who was sitting close enough to the prince to brush his shoulder, hissed between her teeth. "How *dare* you speak to my king like—" The hunter slapped her so fast and hard her head lolled. Loulie was not sure who looked more shocked—Aisha or the prince.

The hunter clicked his tongue. "You never did know when to be quiet, bint Louas." His eyes narrowed. "Hold your tongue, or I will cut it from your mouth."

Aisha blinked, hard and slow. "Wait. *Imad?*"

The hunter did not respond. Not in their language, at least. Strange guttural sounds escaped his throat—more growls than words. The two ghouls holding Aisha pushed her head down until she was prostrated on the ground.

"The very same. I am humbled one of Omar's thieves remembers my name." The hunter's voice dripped with venom. He looked away, back to the prince. Omar looked like he wanted to sink into the sand. Imad looked like he wanted to bury him in it.

"How ironic that our positions are now reversed, Prince. Do you remember our last meeting? When you forced me to grovel and beg forgiveness for *your* crimes?" He stepped forward, feet gliding soundlessly across the sand. Loulie's eyes snagged on his hands, which were bandaged and misshapen.

"Well?" Imad glared at the prince. Omar stared back at him helplessly. There was no recognition in his eyes.

"My king need not waste his breath speaking to a traitor like you," Aisha snapped.

Imad did not even turn to face her. "I will not warn you again, little thief. Seal your lips, or I will make sure you never flap them again."

Aisha's eyes flared with defiance, but the prince sharply said,

"For gods' sake, Aisha, heed the man." He faced Imad with a bravado that quickly wilted beneath his gaze. "What is it you want? If it's gold—"

"Gold? Ha! You could offer me your entire kingdom, and I would not bat a lash. No, I do not care for your gold. I want you." He paused, his gaze straying to Loulie. "And her."

"Go die in a hole." The words escaped Loulie's mouth before she could think them.

Imad reached up and withdrew the scarf from around his mouth to reveal a slanted smile of glimmering, crooked teeth. "Like your pathetic jinn friend?"

Loulie's vision bloomed red. She lurched forward with a scream, knocking one of the ghouls off its feet. She managed only a single step before three ghouls detached from the watching group to restrain her. One knocked a bony fist into her stomach, and she keeled over.

Imad sighed. "Are all women this unruly now?"

Tears rolled down Loulie's cheeks, but they were not from the pain. "Give him back," she whispered.

Imad raised a brow. "You think me a god? I am flattered, merchant. But while it is in my profession to take lives, I'm afraid I am not in the business of giving them back."

The last vestiges of Loulie's rage burned away, leaving behind nothing but a damp sorrow. The tidal wave of grief washed over her suddenly, taking with it the last of her strength. She collapsed to her knees with a sob.

"I hadn't expected the mighty King of the Forty Thieves to travel with a jinn." Imad's voice was quiet beneath her screaming grief. "I didn't believe my ghouls when they said they'd smelled one. But then I thought, what's the harm in setting up a trap? I'm glad I did. I don't want to think about the chaos your jinn would have wreaked with its magic."

Imad snapped his fingers and said something in the strange foreign language made up of garbles and grunts. A command, Loulie realized as the ghouls poked and prodded her. They stole Qadir's dagger and peeled the rings off her fingers. One of them grabbed the bag of infinite space from her saddle.

She watched blankly as they stole Aisha's blades and Omar's belt of black daggers. The prince shuddered as they reached for the bangle on his arm. He mumbled something—a prayer—beneath his breath. The ghoul unclasped the armlet.

One moment Loulie saw the high prince. The next, Omar was gone, replaced by a man with bright golden eyes. She stared, uncomprehending, at Prince Mazen.

Imad's smile faded abruptly. "What trickery is this?"

The man in front of her was undeniably the bumbling, curious prince she'd rescued in the souk. The sheltered storyteller yearning for adventure. The only royal whose company Loulie had found tolerable.

No matter how many times she blinked, Prince Mazen remained. The stories, the softness around the edges—it hadn't made sense to her. Until now.

This whole time, she'd been traveling with the wrong prince.

The prince did not answer, only eyed Imad warily.

"But how?" Imad reached forward, as if to touch him.

Many things happened then.

Aisha bint Louas, who'd been keeled over on the ground, suddenly lunged toward one of the ghouls. She stole one of her blades back and lopped off its head. There was a blur of movement as she swung her shamshir at Imad. And then—

A scream. Splatters of crimson on the sand. Imad's bandaged hands, red with blood.

"You bitch!"

His eyes sparkled with murder as he grabbed a knife and struck at Aisha. The first blow bounced off her shamshir. The second knocked the blade from her hands. The third struck her face and drew a scream from her lips. The fourth ripped a gash into her shoulder.

Imad struck again and again, until the sand beneath Aisha was stained with her blood.

Imad flipped the dagger, raised it into the air, and—

"Stop!" The prince slid in front of Aisha, arms held out. "Please." His voice cracked.

Imad halted. He glared so hard at the prince, Loulie feared he would kill him. But then slowly, he sheathed his dagger and barked an order at the ghouls.

The last thing Loulie saw was Prince Mazen crouched over Aisha's limp body, desperate tears in his eyes. Then Loulie was struck in the head. She experienced a pain so terrible it knocked the breath from her lungs. And then finally, blissfully, darkness.

40

MAZEN

Mazen woke in what looked like the ruins of a prison cell. Moonlight filtered into the chamber through holes in the ceiling, illuminating the dust on the floor and turning it an ominous bone white. The cell was barren, surrounded by three walls of stone and one made of thick iron bars. Behind them stood Imad and beside him, a ghoul.

"Sabah al-khair, Prince."

"What...?" Mazen sat up slowly. He'd expected to be bound and gagged, but there were no shackles on his arms or legs.

"Sleep well?" Imad raised a brow.

Mazen blinked. He opened his mouth—and froze when his memories came rushing back. He remembered Qadir, dead. Loulie, screaming his name. Aisha, bleeding out on the sand. He approached the bars, heart beating in his throat. "What have you done with Aisha?"

The last thing he remembered was shaking her, begging her to hold on, *hold on*—she was one of Omar's forty thieves, and how could she be killed by some random murderer? And then: pain and darkness.

"Bint Louas is in one piece," Imad said. "Injured, but alive. She is lucky. I ought to have punished her more severely." He reached out and curled his fingers around one of the bars, and Mazen saw the bloody wounds Aisha had ripped into his bandages.

He took a cautious step back. "What do you want from us?"

Imad's lips quirked. "Truly? I never wanted anything from you. But now that you are here, it seems I must change my plans." He leaned closer to the bars, close enough for Mazen to make out the details of his face in the moonlight. He was at least as old as the sultan, with harsh wrinkles etched into his sun-scorched skin, and gray-white hair dusting his cheeks and chin.

Do not underestimate a man based on his appearance. It was the advice his father offered when they were dealing with scheming court politicians.

Imad was an old blade but not a dull one.

Mazen paused, recalling their earlier conversation. "You were looking for my brother?"

"That is correct. The moment I heard Omar bin Malik was leading the Midnight Merchant in this direction, I decided to investigate. And yet..." He raised a pointed brow. "It is not the high prince I see before me, but his younger brother. How did this come to be?"

Idiot that I am, I allowed myself to be blackmailed. Mazen swallowed a laugh. He truly was a fool. To have thought this tromp through the desert was preferable to suffering the consequences for escaping the palace. To have thought it would be an *adventure*.

"It was advantageous for my brother and me to switch places."

"Is that so? It hardly seems so now, does it?"

Mazen couldn't decide if he wanted to punch himself or Imad more. "No," he said softly. "It doesn't." He looked long and hard at the man, then said, "Why chase rumors of my brother in the first place? What do you want with him?"

Imad's expression hardened. "You mean to tell me you do not know who I am?"

"I don't think we'd be having this conversation if I did."

Imad hissed. At first, Mazen thought it was a response meant for him, but then he noticed the ghoul behind Imad shift. It handed him a key ring.

"How are you...?" Mazen looked between Imad and the ghoul. "How are you controlling them?" In his mother's stories, the ghouls were free-roaming terrors, not obedient soldiers.

Imad raised a brow. "I shall let you ponder. It will give you something to think about while we wait for your brother."

The reality of his situation began to sink in. Mazen combed desperately through his memories, trying to recall Imad's words. If he knew both Omar *and* Aisha...

"Are you a thief?"

"I am not *just* a thief, boy. I am one of the legendary forty thieves." Imad stepped forward, black eyes narrowed to slits. "Once, I even worked with the sultan."

Mazen balked. So Imad was not one of Omar's thieves—he was one of his father's. But how? His father had proclaimed his thieves had died in some tragic incident long ago, when Omar first took over as King of the Forty Thieves.

"If you were one of my father's thieves, why are you holding a grudge against Omar?"

Imad smiled thinly. "That is between us and does not concern you. Your only job, Prince, is to sit here and wait while I send the ransom note." He crossed his arms and leaned against the wall. "However. Though you are my prisoner, you need not be treated like one. Tell me one thing, and I shall make you comfortable until his arrival."

Mazen eyed him warily. "What?"

Imad reached into his pocket. Mazen expected him to withdraw a weapon—instead, he pulled out the bangle. He clasped it to his wrist, and a heartbeat later, he wore Omar's skin. Mazen gaped at him as he flexed his fingers, which were no longer malformed. "Truly remarkable." He looked at Mazen. "I am familiar with your family's story and already know this is a jinn king's relic. But I want to know: Does your brother possess other kings' relics?"

Mazen hesitated.

Why does it matter? he wanted to ask, but he knew Imad would not answer. When he remained mute, the thief sighed and said, "I don't know who you think you're protecting, but know this: you may idolize your brother"—Mazen nearly laughed aloud—"but he is not a good man. Whatever he did to convince you to take his place, he did it because he has ulterior motives."

Mazen frowned. There was a connection between the kings' relics and Omar's "ulterior motives," he was sure, but he refused to dig deep enough to find it. Omar was insufferable, but he was still his brother. He would have to be insane to trust a killer over him.

"Ask my brother your question," Mazen said. "This is none of *my* business, after all."

He didn't know where he dredged up the courage to say the words, but he was evidently more surprised than Imad, who simply stepped away with a shrug. "You are lucky I need you alive, Prince. But remember, any discomfort you"—his eyes flashed—"or your companions experience is your fault."

All that came out of Mazen's mouth was a weak sound of protest. Imad ignored him. He spoke a word of command to the ghoul, who obediently stepped in front of Mazen's cell door, a sword in its hand.

"Try not to irritate the guard." Imad turned and walked away.

"Wait!" Mazen grasped the bars. "Don't hurt Aisha or the merchant. Please."

But Imad never even looked back. Mazen called his name again, but the only response he received was his own voice, echoing back at him from the dreary infiniteness of the corridor.

Belatedly, he realized the ghoul was staring at him. He took one look at its ghastly, torn-up face and doubled back until he was pressed against the wall. *Breathe*, he commanded himself, and he did. Slowly. In. And out. He suppressed the wild urge to scream at the walls.

He could not stay here. That much was apparent. Also apparent: the impossibility of escaping. He had no weapon, no plan. His eyes drifted across his cell. The holes in the ceiling were too high for him to reach. As for the ghoul—even if he could somehow coax it into his cell, he had no weapon to face it. And even with one, he was useless. His only talents included sneaking, running, hiding...

He stopped. And stared at his shadow on the floor.

Oh.

He scraped at the silhouette. Relief crashed through his veins when it curled beneath his fingers. *Imad may be able to take my knives, but he could never steal my shadow.*

The ghoul whirled, sniffing at the air. Too late, Mazen remembered it could smell magic. When the ghoul faced him, Mazen had the shadow—now very much a magical relic—clenched in his fingers.

The ghoul stared. Mazen stared back. He thought of Aisha's crimson blood on the sand, and Qadir's silver blood on the swords. And he came to a decision.

His relief sharpened into determination. *If no one is coming to help me, I have no choice but to save myself.*

"Ah!" He held the shadow up with a dramatic gasp. "What manner of magic is this!"

The ghoul shoved a key into the door and stepped into the prison with unbalanced, frantic footsteps. It snarled and reached out a bony hand. Mazen gathered his courage and kicked it as it kneeled before him. The creature stumbled back, but not before swiping the blade across his arm, drawing blood.

Mazen tried to steal the ghoul's blade. He grabbed for the hilt. The ghoul drove an elbow into his chest and knocked the air from his lungs. Mazen retaliated by shoving his full weight into the ghoul's side. Or at least, he tried to. But he lost his footing and fell on the creature instead. They collapsed to the ground in a heap.

There was a moment of panic as Mazen rushed to untangle his limbs from the ghoul's. He choked back tears as the pungent smell of its rotting body invaded his senses, and just barely managed to gather himself before the ghoul struck at him again. The blade nicked his arm. But this time, he managed to grasp the hilt.

He and the ghoul wrestled the blade back and forth.

Finally, Mazen pried the weapon from its cold hands.

Panic gave him the courage to swing the blade and the strength to drive it into the creature's chest over and over and over again until it was a sinewy mess of gore and muscle. Mazen nudged the remains with a foot. When the corpse didn't move, he smiled, laughed, and then promptly vomited his guts out in a corner of the room.

He was trembling as he swiped a hand across his mouth. His every instinct screamed at him to escape, but he shoved the urge aside. Loulie and Aisha had saved his life—he refused to leave without them.

It didn't matter that he was a coward. Cowards knew how to flee and hide, and that was good enough. Mazen threw his shadow over his head and snuck out of his prison.

41

LOULIE

Loulie balanced on the edge of a hell divided into two prisons: sorrow and hatred. But the moment she woke and beheld her captor, rage triumphed over both. *Murderer.* She recognized his robes. She would never forget the sight of them drenched in the blood of her tribespeople.

She forced herself to sit up and, in doing so, noticed her wrists and ankles were shackled to a stone floor splattered with silver. Jinn blood, she realized. When she looked closely, she could make out what appeared to be torn roots peeking through cracks in the stone. The rest of the cell was completely bare, a prison with four walls and a single iron door.

She focused on Imad, who sat in front of her on a stool, arms draped over his knees. She took in the sight of his abyss-like eyes and graying brows. The faded freckles that ran across his nose like blood. She thought about how she wanted to gouge out his eyes and feed them to a fire.

Fire. The word triggered a memory, a person. She shoved her grief away before it settled.

"I realized something while you were sleeping," Imad said. "Your robes—you were from the Najima tribe, weren't you?"

She managed a stilted breath. "You would know, wouldn't you? Murderer."

Imad's only response was an exasperated sigh. He shifted on his stool. Loulie's heart leapt and sank when she saw the bag of infinite space behind him. All her provisions and relics were in that bag. Everything except for the Queen of Dunes' collar.

And Qadir's shamshir.

Again, the sorrow speared through her chest. Again, she pushed it away and forced her attention back to Imad. "How did you find us?"

She'd spent all these years thinking her past was behind her— and then this man had appeared before her.

Imad regarded her thoughtfully. "No doubt you've faced ghouls before. So you must know of their ability to track magic." He shook his head. "I don't know if my ghouls sensed your jinn or your bag of relics, but it doesn't matter. Neither can help you anymore."

That wasn't the whole story. It couldn't be. She and Qadir had traveled the desert many times without being attacked by ghouls. However Imad controlled his ghouls, he'd been using them to find something. Her mind strayed to the memory of Prince Mazen kneeling in the sand. She was still too shocked to feel cheated.

"You were looking for Prince Omar," she said.

"Yes, I was looking for the high prince." He considered her with his unreadable expression. "Imagine my surprise when I found you and Prince Mazen instead."

Loulie said nothing. Prince Mazen, Imad, Aisha—there were too many unknown variables for her to come up with a plan. And even if she could, she was trapped.

"Where are we?" She glanced around the empty cell.

"Someplace no one will ever find you." Cryptic words. But it didn't matter whether they were a lie or the truth. Somehow, she would escape. "How about a trade, Midnight Merchant?" He leaned forward. "You give me the information I seek, and I answer your questions. You have nothing to lose."

She clenched her hands into fists. "And why would I want to talk to *you*?"

Imad's lips curled into a sly, terrible smile. "Don't you want to know who hired my companions and me all those years ago?"

The words plunged through her like a sword, effortlessly piercing the armor she had built up over so many years. *He could be lying*, she thought. But even if he was, the bastard was right. She had nothing to lose.

"What do you want to know?" Her voice cracked. She was too desperate to be ashamed.

"Smart woman." Imad reached into a pocket and withdrew the golden bangle the ghouls had stolen off the prince's wrist, the one he'd been wearing this entire journey. "Let us speak of magic," he said. "Tell me, do you know where this relic came from?"

She scowled. "How am I supposed to know where the prince gets his trinkets?"

She wanted to slap herself for using that word. Not trinkets, *souls*. And of course the prince had been using one—the sultan probably had a relic for every occasion.

"I thought that if anyone knew, it would be you, famed collector of magics." Imad stared at the bangle for a long moment before clasping it onto his arm. Between one blink and the next, he disappeared. In his place stood the high prince, with Imad's smirk fixed to his face. Loulie shut her mouth when she realized she was gawking.

"Tell me, merchant. Was it your jinn who guided you to the relics you possess?" The voice that came from his lips was, disconcertingly, Prince Omar's.

Loulie bristled. "That's none of your business."

"You are stupidly secretive for someone whose life is in my hands." He clasped his hands and inclined his head. Loulie wondered if he was actually in Omar's body or if it was an illusion. "This jinn of yours, is he the one that burned my companions years ago?"

"The very same. How the hell did *you* survive?"

"The gods saw fit to make me their messenger," Imad said quietly. "I was on the outskirts of the camp when your jinn's inferno raged. I was the only one to make it out alive. The Najima tribe died, my comrades died, and yet . . . my job was unaccomplished."

Loulie shuddered at the emptiness in his eyes. "Your job?"

"I am a thief first, a killer second. I only destroy those who stand in the way of my goal."

Thief. The desert was home to many thieves, but—a band of them skilled enough to slaughter a tribe? And if Imad knew Omar and Aisha...

Is he one of the prince's thieves?

Imad was still talking, his voice an undercurrent to her confusion. "There was treasure at your camp, merchant. A relic so valuable we were ordered to kill any in the vicinity so they would never reveal its existence. It was a jinn king's relic."

Loulie's mind clouded over with memories. *There are many mysterious things in the desert, Sweet Fire,* her father had once said. *If ever you find such items, you must take great care of them, for they may be relics enchanted by jinn.*

She remembered her skepticism. *Is this compass filled with magic, then?*

His laughter. *It does not work for me, but perhaps it will guide your way.*

And then: a jinn kneeling before her, pointing to that same compass after everyone she loved had perished. *Layla Najima al-Nazari, it seems saving your life was my destiny.*

A relic that could locate other relics. That could foresee a future yet to pass. A relic so powerful it could belong only to a jinn king. An *ifrit.* Loulie forgot how to breathe.

Imad's eyes twinkled with mirth. "Ah, so you remember. Will you tell me what it looks like?" He patted her bag. "I'd rather save myself the trouble of testing all your supplies."

Loulie was at a loss. What should she do? He would take the damned bag with him either way, and she was helpless to stop him. She tried pulling on her shackles, but the metal was unyielding, cutting into her wrists without mercy.

"No?" Imad sighed. "I'm afraid our conversation is over, then." He hefted the bag over his shoulder and walked toward the cell door.

"Wait." She surged upright. "Wait! You promised me answers!"

Imad paused just long enough to say, "I promised you answers for answers. But since you have given me nothing, I will try my luck elsewhere."

How dare he! She was no one's prisoner. She was the Midnight Merchant, Loulie Najima al-Nazari, and she would get revenge on this man who had killed her family and . . .

Qadir.

The weight of his death descended on her in full then, until she was bowed beneath its weight, body racked with sobs. Qadir wasn't coming for her. No one was. She was stuck in this godsforsaken place in the middle of nowhere, and she had no magic and no blade, and gods, had she always been so weak? So *useless*?

The last sound she heard before she was trapped in silence was the thief's footsteps echoing through distant, empty halls.

42

MAZEN

Mazen traversed decrepit corridors that were fortunately empty and unfortunately dark. He tripped over rocks, lost his footing in sunken patches of sand, and stumbled into ghouls moments after learning of their existence. The creatures could not see him beneath his shadow cloak, but they could *smell* the magic on him when he was nearby, and Mazen was beginning to realize they had very good noses.

And yet for as useless as his shadow was, he could not bring himself to shed it. While it did not offer the same security as Omar's body, it was an invigorating illusion all the same. He had always felt most confident in disguise—no matter if that camouflage was a name, a body, or a magic shadow.

Thankfully, the skirmishes were quiet, and the prison he wandered was empty of humans. Still, he was extremely suspicious of how easy it was for him to stay alive. So much so that by the time he reached the doors marked *Makhraj*, he was certain it was a trap.

Please don't let there be ghouls on the other side of this door, he thought.

Unsurprisingly, there were ghouls on the other side of the door.

Mazen sprang forward before they could react, shoving one to the ground and plunging his blade through the second's throat. It toppled, but before Mazen could pull out his sword, the other ghoul recovered and swung its blade at him. Mazen ducked with a yelp. He landed on his knees, scrambled backward toward the second corpse, and yanked his sword out with a gag. When the first ghoul came at him again, he attacked its legs and tackled it to the ground. He ran the blade through its chest. Once, twice. A third time, just to be sure.

By the time he silenced the two guards, his body was shaking with adrenaline.

He took a deep breath, steadied his trembling hands, and forced himself down a corridor thankfully brighter than the one he'd come from. As he walked, he became aware of the wind whistling through cracks in the ceiling. Eventually, those cracks widened into holes large enough for him to make out the sky, the moon. And then the ceilings vanished altogether, revealing an endless expanse of star-speckled black.

Mazen glanced at the walls: the only stretch of color in the ruin's otherwise plain interior. There was one wall so spectacularly detailed it forced him to a stop. This mosaic depicted the seven jinn kings he'd seen in the Queen of Dunes' ruin. There was the shapeshifting jinn in the form of a flaming bird, and beneath it was the jinn with the dara'a cut into two halves. He spotted the fish jinn with the luminescent scales, the jinn made of wood and flowers, the jinn crafted from mist, and—there, a jinn leading an army of ghouls. The Queen of Dunes. He glanced at the last figure, who in the dune had been a shadow with gleaming eyes.

He had assumed this last king was the shadow jinn, but the figure in this much clearer depiction made it evident he'd been mistaken. Here, the jinn king was a cloaked figure with a jeweled turban who stood stoically amidst the chaos, hand raised toward the fiery sky. The color reminded Mazen of the color Qadir's eyes had flashed during the ghoul attack.

At least now he knew he wasn't crazy. The man's—jinn's—eyes really *had* been on fire. The thought sobered him. If he wasn't careful, Imad would kill him too. Mazen did not think the thief would make the mistake of underestimating him twice.

He resumed walking, following the corridor around a bend and into a dead end. No...an open end? Sure enough, he found himself at a hole in the wall, one large enough to climb through. He carefully slid through and abruptly found himself on the threshold of the desert. He inhaled sharply as sand crunched beneath his boots. It was real. He was *outside*.

But his joy was short lived, for he realized he had not truly escaped. He had been in only one of many ruins; the crumbling landscape stretched on for miles, a labyrinth of broken walls and winding stone roads that led to a barely standing palace. Farther out, Mazen spotted the telltale shapes of ghouls, and beyond that...

Oh gods.

The dunes surrounding the ruins were shifting. No, not so much shifting as *falling*. There was no base—the sand simply spiraled into an endlessly churning void that surrounded the ruins like a river of quicksand.

Somehow, these ruins stood in the center of the Sandsea. Not the Western Sandsea, where they were headed, but an unplotted segment of the sea Mazen didn't remember seeing on Hakim's map.

Mazen took many panicked, stilted breaths. And then, in an effort to calm himself, he took a few slightly less panicked deep breaths. *Imad can leave this place. There must be an exit.*

Cautiously, he wove his way through the ruins. He was on the lookout only for creatures of the damned, so when he snuck up to the ruined heart of the palace and saw a man—a *human* man—standing outside, he nearly had a heart attack.

The man was tall and barrel-chested, with arms and legs that were corded with muscle. His face looked as if it had been chiseled by an incompetent sculptor; jagged hook-shaped marks marred his cheeks, and his nose was so crooked it looked broken. Mazen was not sure what scared him more: the fact that the man was human or that he was not Imad.

The dread was still sinking in when he heard a voice, distinctly human, yell, "Yalla! The meeting's going to start without you if you don't get your ass in here."

The barrel-chested man grumbled, then turned and walked through the entrance. Mazen waited a heartbeat. Two. Three. Then he chased him inside.

It immediately became apparent that this ruin was better maintained than the other structures, with most of its walls still holding. The corridor they passed through had a high ceiling and was lined with iron doors. Lantern-bearing ghouls stood sentinel between them, their empty eyes staring blankly ahead.

That was, until one of them turned in his direction. It sniffed at the air, took a step forward, and—

"Ss!" the man hissed. "No wandering, spawn." The ghoul instantly retreated.

Mazen held back a sigh of relief. Whatever language Imad was using to order around the ghouls, it seemed it was unnecessary for basic commands. He was grateful for the hierarchy of human authority here, puzzling as it was.

They came to a large archway guarded by two ghouls, who froze at a word from the man. The chamber inside was massive. Save for a few torn tapestries hanging from the walls and some dusty rugs scattered across the floor, the space was mostly empty. It looked as if it had been gutted by thieves. Candelabras illuminated the room with an eerie, weak light. Beneath them, Mazen saw bare pedestals that had probably once displayed treasures.

Perhaps in the past, the room had been glorious, but now it looked like a storage room. And standing in the middle of it were men of varying shapes and bulk. Some were old, others young, and *all* of them wore weapons.

Mazen had just stepped inside when the chatter quieted. He heard footsteps and turned to see Imad enter the chamber. He was followed by a slow-moving man. "Where do you want her, Imad?" Imad's companion called.

Mazen backed into the shadows as Imad brushed past him.

"Here." Imad stopped in the center and pointed. The armed men stepped back, giving him a wider berth. "Set her at my feet," Imad said.

The man shoved his prisoner—a woman—forward. Mazen balked at the hatred on her face. At the anger shining in her single eye, for the other was sealed shut with blood. And then he realized who she was, and he had to stop himself from running to her.

Because though he could see her, Aisha bint Louas could not see him.

She looked as if she'd been through hell and back. Her clothes were soiled, cloaked in layers of grime. Blood stained her skin, and her hair was a mess of tangled waves. Mazen had never been more terrified for her.

And terrified *of* her.

"So, bint Louas, are you ready to talk?" Imad raised a brow.

Aisha spat at his feet. "I have nothing to say to you, snake."

"Mm." Imad shifted. Mazen saw the glimmer of the bangle moments before Imad clasped it to his wrist and became Omar. "What about now? Will you speak to your prince?" His voice was soft, mocking.

Aisha trembled in her bindings but said nothing.

"You think Omar will appreciate your martyrdom? You are easily replaceable."

"This, coming from the man who was thrown away." Aisha's eye swept across the room, taking in the sight of the stoic-faced ruffians who surrounded them. "I see you've replaced your comrades with thugs. How the mighty have fallen."

A heavy silence followed her words. Aisha heedlessly spoke into it. "What are you but an old man who refuses to retire? An old man who was unable to steal a single relic for your prince? I owe you nothing. My king—"

Imad struck her across the face. "Your *prince* is a monster," he snapped.

"You only curse his name because you were too weak to honor it. You murdered an entire tribe, and for what? You returned relic-less, with only blood on your hands!"

"Your prince never found the relic either." Imad reached into his pocket. "But I have accomplished what he has not." He pulled out an object. A small disc made of wood and glass.

A memory snapped into place. Mazen remembered Qadir sitting by the campfire in al-Waha al-Khadhra'a, a compass on his knee. It was the same compass. The one Loulie had used to lead them through the desert. He was sure of it.

Aisha laughed. "A compass? You've gone senile."

Imad smiled. "Lead me to Jassem," he said. Mazen could barely make out the arrow shuddering beneath the glass before Imad tossed the compass to the barrel-chested man Mazen had followed inside.

"Holy hell," Jassem said. The other men began to mutter.

Aisha's eye narrowed. "You stole that insignificant thing from the merchant's bag thinking it was a king's relic?" She scoffed. "What's it going to do? Lead you to treasure?"

"Treasure? No, I plan on using it to locate other, more important targets. More important *people*." Imad flexed his fingers, and Jassem tossed the compass back to him. He tucked the compass back into his pocket and traded it for a knife hidden in his sleeve. "Now, tell me." He held the weapon to Aisha's cheek. "How many other kings' relics does the prince possess? Answer me, bint Louas, and I might spare your other eye."

Mazen saw Aisha's throat bob beneath the silver edge. She said nothing.

The men began to jeer. Imad just smiled as he pressed the blade into her skin and blood rose to the surface.

Mazen stepped forward—and stopped when a pair of ghouls burst into the room. Imad pulled the knife away with a hiss. *"What?"* A brief one-sided exchange ensued in which the ghouls screamed and gestured frantically down the corridor.

"What do you mean there's no relic?" Imad was on his feet in seconds, rushing past a quivering Aisha. "Watch the thief," he said, and then he left the chamber.

A fragile silence reigned for all of a few seconds before one man scoffed. " 'Watch the thief,' he says. Like we're his dogs!"

Another laughed. "You'd rather not be in on all this? Think of what we have to gain if Imad actually slays the legendary Stardust Thief." A murmur of assent went up at that, but Mazen blurred out the words and focused on Aisha. This was his chance to save her, if he could find some way to get her out without dying.

"Which relic do you think's gone missing?" one of the men was saying.

"Perhaps a relic from the merchant's bag?"

There was more muttering. Mazen silently stalked forward. Aisha had walked here; her legs were not bound. He just had to create an opening for her to escape. But how? How...

His eyes snagged on a flimsy tapestry featuring an intricately woven face filled with so much anguish it made him shudder. It reminded him of a shabah. Of those vengeful spirits he'd been so terrified of as a child. How could he not have been wary of them when his father had murdered so many of his brides in the palace courtyard? When he'd been young, the realization had filled him with so much terror he'd imagined the executed brides stalking him through the corridors and peering at him through windows in the dead of night.

But that horror had since dampened to an overwhelming sorrow. Though it was his father's hands that were coated in blood, Mazen was still a part of that gruesome legacy. The sultan's victims may not have haunted the corridors as shabah, but...

Mazen paused, inhaled. He had an idea.

He glanced around the room. His eyes fell on a cracked pot displayed on one of the pedestals. He made his way over to it. Picked it up.

And threw it across the room.

No one noticed it sailing through the air. They did not notice it, in fact, until it was a shattered mess on the floor. The brutes all paused to stare at the shards.

Mazen plunged into his memories. He recalled the way the wind had murmured in his ears when he was hiding from the spirits beneath his blankets. The way the hairs on his arms had risen and his throat had gone dry as his room grew cold. He fashioned the memory into a feeling and then into a sound. A soft, eerie mumbling.

The men became restless, muttering to each other as Mazen slid silently across the room, hissing and cackling. He suppressed a grin as he brushed against banners and drummed his fingers against walls, ruffling the fabric in his wake and creating an ominous tapping sound that made his spectators shrink back in fear.

Mazen found, oddly, that he was *enjoying* himself.

When a man approached, Mazen slid around to his blind side and nicked him with his sword. The villain turned and slashed at the air. "Shabah!" he yelled, and the men immediately grasped their weapons and scattered.

Only Jassem remained by Aisha. "There's no such thing, fools," he snapped.

Mazen approached, gripping his sword tight enough to make his knuckles numb. He honed his fear into conviction. *I survived the Queen of Dunes. I survived the shadow jinn. This is nothing.*

He sidestepped Jassem and knelt behind Aisha, who stiffened when he sawed at her bindings. She whipped her head around as they fell, and Mazen pushed his sword into her hands. "Run," he whispered. And though Aisha trembled at the sound of his voice, she did not hesitate. Even bloodied and weak, she rose quickly. Jassem turned, mouth hanging open. "What—"

It was the only word he managed before Aisha slashed at him with the blade, drawing a line of crimson across his chest. The big man recovered quickly, but Mazen tackled him before he could give chase. The criminal fell back with a cry that was more startled than pained.

Mazen used the opening to throw a punch—only to have Jassem catch his wrist midstrike. The shadow parted between Mazen's fingers like a curtain.

Jassem stared. Mazen imagined what he was seeing: reality parted in front of him, and a sliver of Mazen's face peeking through. Jassem was too shocked to move. Mazen was not.

He kneed Jassem in the groin. The man released his hand with a roar of pain.

Mazen turned and fled.

43

LOULIE

Loulie knew immediately when Imad returned to her cell that something was wrong.

There were *human* men with him. Mercenaries or cutthroats, if the weapons at their belts were any sign of their occupation. The men were the first indication that something had changed. The second was Imad's stormy expression. Before, he had been the picture of calm. Now his eyes—Omar's eyes—flashed with a dangerous light.

Before Loulie could speak, Imad lurched across the cell and grabbed her by the collar of her robe. "What trickery, merchant?" His words flecked spittle onto her face.

Trickery? Her mind spun even as she glared at him.

He shook her hard enough to make her teeth rattle. "No games!"

Loulie looked him right in the eye and spat in his face. Imad slapped her. Stars burst before her eyes as her head lolled.

"Don't play dumb with me. You knew about the prince's relic."

She gritted her teeth against the pain. Tasted metal in her mouth, realizing she'd accidentally bitten her tongue. "I already told you I know nothing about the damned bangle."

"Not the bangle." He pressed her to the wall. "The *shadow*."

She stared at him. *Has he gone mad?*

When she said nothing, Imad shoved her back and stepped away. He looked between the men flanking him. "You're sure of what you saw?"

They shared a glance over his head. "Yes, it happened shortly after you left. We thought there was a shabah in the room at first," said the younger. "But then we saw the prince's face—"

"And he and bint Louas got away?"

The men said nothing, only looked at him helplessly. Imad fixed his scowl on Loulie. Her stomach twisted as he stepped closer. "You knew," he murmured.

No. She didn't say the word aloud. Imad wouldn't believe it. Hell, she didn't believe it. Any of it. The thief and the prince, escaped? A shadow relic? What did that even *mean*?

"I do not care if I have to slice the boy's shadow from his body; I will have it." The mask of calm had returned to his face. "And you will help me steal it."

No. She tried to speak, but her throat had gone dry. The more Imad's glare bored into her, the more difficult it became to breathe. She remembered the edge of a knife against her throat.

Do you desire death or slavery, girl?

She gritted her teeth. *No.* She was Loulie al-Nazari, and she was not the helpless girl she'd been when her tribe was murdered.

She lunged at Imad. Desperation fueled her as she tore at his robes and gouged gashes into his arms. Imad pushed her away with the same effort one would use to swat away a fly. Loulie came at him again, heedless of reason.

There was only that void of loss and anger inside her. *Not again, not again.*

Imad's men grabbed her by the arms. "You want to be difficult, al-Nazari?" His gaze was deadly in its blankness. "Then we will do this the hard way." He reached into his pocket and withdrew something silver. *A shackle*, she realized when she saw the chain jutting from its side.

Imad barked a command. The older man withdrew a swath of silk and stuffed it into her mouth. The other held her nose. *No, no, no…*

Her world went dark.

—ɱ—

Loulie awoke in an ancient, extravagant chamber. The ceiling portrayed a war between jinn cloaked in fire and humans wielding iron weapons. The colors were faded, the faces a blur, but the red and silver blood splatters were perfectly rendered. Loulie glanced away from the ghastly depiction as she sat up and looked around her. She saw mountains of gold and sparkling marble columns. Long, beautifully detailed carpets and elaborate tapestries that looked like they belonged in the sultan's treasury, not this dusty ruin. And then she saw the human men—a little fewer than a dozen, watching her from every corner of the room.

"Welcome, merchant, to our treasure chamber." The high prince came into view. Loulie startled, then remembered the bangle he was wearing. Not Omar.

Imad smirked. "I confess it is amusing to watch you balk at my appearance."

Loulie clamped her mouth shut against a retort. She eyed the men stationed around the chamber. "Who are they?"

The moment she spoke, she felt a shocking chill at her neck—a cold so sharp it numbed all other sensation but pain. She keeled over with a soundless gasp.

Imad chuckled. "Sorry. You spoke before I could explain." He crouched beside her and lifted her chin so he could look her in the eyes. "I thought it would be better if I did most of the talking. And to that end, I have given you a little gift." Loulie felt his fingernails against her skin. "This relic punishes you for speaking by shooting a needle into your neck."

She pulled away from him, breathing hard. Imad stood, eyes shining as he gestured at the men watching the spectacle with hungry eyes. "To answer your question: my companions are fellow outlaws. They are the ones who brought me news of your travels." He angled his head. "These ruins are our sanctuary."

Loulie knew she should focus. Plan. Escape. No one was coming to save her. The prince wouldn't put himself in danger for her, and neither would the thief. To them, she was an easily dispensable pawn. The only one who had ever cared was Qadir. And he was...

Dead. The sorrow washed over her anew. *He's dead.*

Distantly, she heard Imad talking. He was pacing as he spoke of his plan to capture the prince. She was to be the bait, yes, and he had ghouls—he gestured to them all, hidden in shadowed corners—who would sniff the prince out when he arrived and...

He stopped suddenly. "Let us speak of something more interesting, mm?" He reached into his pocket and withdrew a knife. Loulie balked at the sight of it. *Danger*, her sluggish mind screamed, and she pushed herself back, away. But then Imad lowered it, and she saw the gold qaf on the hilt. The first letter of Qadir's name.

"When your jinn companion died, I had my ghouls return to the trap to search for a relic. They found nothing. Only a dead horse and flowers and ivy twisting around the blades. I did not realize why, at first, until I remembered the strange blade you were carrying." He flipped the dagger back and forth. It shimmered a soft blue beneath the wall sconces.

Qadir's voice, nothing but a memory, echoed in her mind. *We jinn live on in the items most precious to us. It is how we guide the living, even after death.*

Loulie did not know what had happened to the collar and the shamshir, but she knew the knife Qadir had given her all those years ago was important to him. Other than the compass, it was the only belonging he'd brought with him from the jinn realm.

Imad smiled at the horror on her face. "Ah, so I was right. You *do* have his relic." He pocketed the knife.

Loulie swallowed. She needed that knife, even if it was just a piece of Qadir.

"I must apologize, al-Nazari." Imad jerked his hand to the side. She realized only when her head was yanked in the same direction that he was pulling the shackle's chain. "I don't mean to hate you," he said. "You are as much a victim in all of this as I, and yet you have prospered as I suffered. While I faded into obscurity, you became a legend."

For a few moments, the chamber was quiet, the only sounds the crunch of gold beneath the men's boots. Loulie focused on the sand spiderwebbed between the tiles. It was the only way to keep her panic at bay.

Imad stepped closer. He yanked her up by her hair, forced her gaze up. And that was when she saw his knife. Not Qadir's blade, but a nondescript weapon she didn't recognize. Imad pressed it to her throat.

"Such a blissful quiet this is. I wonder what it would take for you to break it. You ought to scream, merchant. The prince will never find you otherwise."

She wasn't weak. She would not scream. She wouldn't—

The pain was sudden and fierce, lancing through her veins with an intensity that made her world flare white. An anguished groan left her lips.

"Have you ever stopped to think what you would be had we not killed your tribe, al-Nazari?" She could feel blood running down her collarbone, seeping into her scarves. "You would have been nothing. Just a woman, married to some Bedouin man."

She could feel her heartbeat. In her head, her ears, her fingertips.

"Be grateful you lived a fulfilling life. That you were not like me, banished." He loosened his grip on her hair. She collapsed to the ground, gasping.

Tears pricked her eyes. *Don't cry.* Ran down her cheeks. *Don't cry.*

"Even quiet, you're as stubborn as a mule." He tilted his head at her, gaze thoughtful. And then he said, "Hold her down."

His companions grabbed her. Loulie managed to punch one man in the arm and bite the other on the wrist before they shoved her to the ground. "Turn her over and hold her legs."

She writhed beneath her captors, but they were too strong. She felt the kiss of the knife against her ankles.

"Please." She felt the needle pin her throat. Felt the pain shudder through her body. And she didn't care. *"Please."* Her voice climbed an octave.

"You ought to have begged for mercy earlier. Perhaps I would have taken pity on you."

Imad stabbed the knife into her ankles.

44

AISHA

Nine years ago, when Aisha had become a thief, she'd made a promise to her king.

I will not run.

As a child, she had fled from danger. She had run through burning fields as her family was slaughtered and her village was destroyed. Then the jinn had found her, and they had carved a mark into her skin for every family member who died trying to save her.

So Aisha had promised never to run again. She had vowed to become powerful enough to face her adversaries head-on, so that they no longer had the ability to drag her back, screaming.

Nine years later, she had broken her promise.

The halls were a blur as she ran through the ruins, the world tilted and off-kilter as she struggled to see through one eye. She sprinted clumsily through the halls, the prince's sword in her hands, and she thought, *I do not want to die.*

Imad had said she was replaceable. She'd always thought herself above such fears. But he was right; though she had been chosen by him, Omar would never risk his life for her.

She collapsed against a wall when she was sure her assailants' footsteps had faded, using the moment of reprieve to gather herself and catch her breath. She needed to find the prince.

The prince who had, with some strange magic, *saved* her.

Aisha lowered herself into a crouch and glanced around the corner. She tried to ignore the throbbing pain behind her eye. It was useless now; she only hoped it wasn't infected.

She heard the soft thud of footsteps behind her and whirled, heart beating in her throat as she searched the periphery for Imad's men.

"Aisha," a voice whispered from the ether. And then Prince Mazen appeared out of thin air. Or rather, his *face* did. Aisha stared, flabbergasted, at his floating head.

"It's me," the prince said. He sounded out of breath, as if he'd just sprinted through the corridor. "Mazen."

She remembered the magic Imad had used to appear in Omar's body. She raised her sword. "Prove it. In Dhyme, I said you were confusing two professions. What were they?"

For a few moments the prince just stared at her. Then he inhaled sharply and said, "I remember. You told me you were meant to be my bodyguard, not my nursemaid."

Aisha suppressed a sigh of relief as she rose slowly from her crouch and approached him. She studied the magic he was wearing. It seemed to be a cloak—when she looked closely, she could make out the fuzzy outline of his body. "So that's how you snuck into the chamber. What kind of twisted magic is this?"

"The useful kind." He laughed weakly. "At least, it's useful when you're not being chased by magic-smelling ghouls." He cast a nervous look over his shoulder. Seemingly satisfied that he was no longer being pursued by undead creatures, he peeled the magic off him, revealing both his previously invisible body and the cloak that had made it so. He dropped the fabric to the floor. Aisha watched in awe as it stretched into his shadow. "I think it's from the shadow jinn."

A realization snapped into place. Omar had confided in her that he hadn't been able to find the shadow jinn's relic after defeating it in the sultan's diwan. Now Aisha knew why.

She snorted. "It's a magic that suits you."

The prince frowned. "Because I'm a coward?"

She paused, remembering she'd called him that in the Wanderer's Sanctuary. That he would bring up such a flippant barb now, when they were in such peril, made her laugh. "That's one way of putting it. It's—"

Footsteps. Two pairs. Coming from around the corner.

Aisha moved on instinct, pressing herself against the wall and drawing her sword. Her grip on the foreign blade was awkward, but it would suffice. She was not sentimental about her weapons. All that mattered—all that had *ever* mattered—was that they could cut. She pressed a finger to her lips as the prince hurriedly threw his shadow over his head and vanished.

Soon the footsteps were right beside her. Aisha lunged. The men reacted too slowly. She looped her arms around one's neck, pressed the edge of her blade into his throat, and glared over his shoulder at his companion. "One more step and I'll cut his throat."

The second man was undeterred. He rushed her with his blade.

But the assault never came.

One moment he was running toward her. The next, he was struggling in place with his sword arm bent awkwardly behind him. Aisha couldn't see the prince, but she could hear his quavering voice coming from behind the captured man. "Tell us where the merchant is."

The assailant beneath Aisha's blade shuddered. "In our treasure chamber."

Aisha hesitated. *A trap?*

The prince's prisoner shifted. And then—he broke free, wrenching away Mazen's invisible hand and throwing himself against the wall. The prince gasped.

The man Aisha had captured threw her off in the same moment, nearly knocking the blade from her hand. Aisha staggered. She just barely managed to duck an incoming strike from her assailant as she rushed the other man. The prince's shadow had fallen from his shoulders, and Aisha saw him crushed against the wall, hands uselessly outstretched to shield himself from his attacker, who was raising his blade.

Aisha stabbed him in the lungs before he could bring it down.

Prince Mazen made a choked sound of distress as the dying man collapsed in front of him.

The still-living man came at them with a roar. Aisha reached for her sword, but it was stuck fast in her victim's shoulder. Thankfully, the prince was faster. He grabbed the corpse's sword off the ground and swept it through the air. The motion was clumsy, panicked, but it still landed. The sword lodged itself into the villain's shoulder.

The man screamed. Prince Mazen screamed.

Aisha experienced a moment of startling clarity. She slid behind the prince as the killer pulled the sword out of his shoulder with a grunt. Mazen stumbled back, gripping the now-bloody blade with shaking hands.

Aisha was ready for him.

No sooner had he fallen into her than she wrapped her arms around him from behind and grasped his hands over the sword hilt. The prince stiffened. Aisha marveled at the softness of his hands in her calloused ones. She could feel his frenzied, fragile heartbeat beneath her fingers.

She pushed the observations away and focused on guiding his blade. Their opponent was still staggering from the first wound, so when she and Mazen plunged the sword into his chest, he did not retaliate.

He groaned, bled. And slowly, he died.

Mazen's hands were shaking so badly Aisha could barely keep hold of them. The moment she peeled herself away, he keeled over like a puppet with cut strings.

"Prince?" She stepped forward.

He abruptly straightened. He looked unbalanced, like a passenger on a ship trying to acclimate themselves to the turbulent sway of the ocean. "I'm okay."

Aisha frowned. "You've killed ghouls before, haven't you?"

The prince breathed in deeply. "Yes," he said through clenched teeth.

She looked at him for a long moment before she handed back

the sword. "Then come on. Let's find this treasure chamber." She reached down to pluck the sword off the fresh corpse, then strode on ahead. The prince followed.

They passed through more ruined corridors, saw more dusty wall paintings. Aisha was unaccustomed to filling silences, but she tried to comfort the clearly unhinged prince by musing aloud her opinion that the ruins had once belonged to jinn. She hoped the speculation would distract him, maybe even coax him into telling one of the stories he was so obsessed with, but Prince Mazen didn't respond. He was staring at his hands. At the red smeared on them.

"Prince?"

Mazen didn't respond. His eyes were foggy, unfocused.

Aisha thought again of his frantic heartbeat. His uncalloused hands. The man before her was not a warrior. He was a pacifist. And in protecting him, she had potentially broken him.

She set a hand on his shoulder. The prince startled and looked up.

"You lied to me." She frowned. "You're not okay."

"No," the prince said. "No, I'm not. I just—" He took a deep, shaking breath. "I just killed a man."

Looking at his crumpled, teary expression, it occurred to Aisha she had stopped mourning her victims long ago. A small, muted pang ran through her chest. "If it makes you feel any better, I was the one who swung the sword."

Mazen laughed softly, dejectedly. "Right. Because I'm an incompetent coward."

Coward. There was that word again, the one she had hurled at him in the tavern. Evidently, it had done more damage than she had anticipated. She had not realized it was possible for the son of a politician to be so sensitive.

But then, long ago, she had lived her life without armor too.

"We all start as cowards."

Mazen's expression fell. Aisha set a hand on his cheek before he could turn away, guiding his gaze back to hers. "We're all afraid, Prince. The only difference between a hero and a coward is that one forgets their fear and fights, while the other succumbs to it and flees." Something released in her at the words, though she couldn't say what it was. "Your fear of death does not make you weak. Only human."

The prince, for once, was completely quiet. He stared at her with wide eyes.

Aisha released his shoulder with a sigh. He was the one on the verge of tears, so why did *she* suddenly feel so vulnerable? "I should not have made that word into a weapon," she mumbled. "I was wrong about you. If you were truly a coward, you'd have left me and fled."

The prince swallowed. His eyes were glassy.

"You can cry all you like after this is over. But right now, I need you."

The prince managed a weak nod. Aisha turned and continued down the corridor. She was relieved to be able to turn away from this conversation, except—there was still one thing she needed to say. A word that had been on the tip of her tongue since he rescued her.

"Prince?"

"Yes?"

"Shukran." It was only a single word, but it eased her heart.

She angled her head slightly, enough to catch the prince's returning smile. "Afwan."

It was barely a conversation at all, and yet it somehow felt like the first time they'd spoken. Not as a thief and a prince, but as Aisha and Mazen.

Perhaps that was why their conversation flowed easier afterward and why, when they returned to their wandering and the prince asked her about Imad's grudge against Omar, she answered him truthfully. She confirmed that Imad had been one of the sultan's forty thieves and that, after Shafia had died and the title of king was bequeathed to Omar, Imad had worked for the prince. But their camaraderie had been brief.

"Omar's first and last order for the sultan's thieves was to capture a priceless relic." She hesitated, knowing Mazen would not appreciate this next truth. "They tracked it down to a Bedouin campsite and cut through the entire tribe to get to it."

The prince stared at her in horror. "But why?"

"The jinn-king relics are a secret. Omar did not want rumors to spread." Aisha flinched. It sounded like a flimsy excuse even to her own ears. "Their efforts were for nothing, in the end. They died at the hands of a mysterious jinn, and only Imad survived to tell the tale. He returned to Madinne and blamed Omar for his comrades' deaths. Then, because he's a haughty fool, he challenged your brother to a duel and lost."

Mazen frowned. "So his hands…"

"An injury from the duel." She paused at a bend in the corridor. When she ascertained that what lay on the other side was just another empty hall, she beckoned Mazen to follow. "The sultan punished Imad for his insult by banishing him," she continued. "And Omar had no choice but to start again."

This part of the story she knew well, for it was when she had entered the narrative. "He chose forty of us by his own hand, and we have served him since." She paused, her gaze falling on a series of intricate diamond patterns that unspooled across the wall's cracked surface like golden thread. "I was there when Omar and Imad fought," she said. "Your brother and I ran into each other on Madinne's streets; he recruited me before Imad returned."

"How did you two meet?"

"I tried to pick his pockets." When he simply stared at her, she shrugged and said, "He saw potential in me. Anyway, that's why I witnessed Imad's defeat. That is why he hates me."

"I think he hates everyone," Mazen murmured.

Aisha remembered Imad storming toward Omar in the courtyard nine years ago. She remembered the way he had glared at her. *You've replaced us with a woman? A* girl? *You have tied your own noose!*

Aisha shook the memory from her head with a scowl. "Yes, he is a miserable creature."

There was a momentary silence. And then: "So Imad has a jinn king's relic now?"

Aisha frowned. She'd expected Imad to possess the cursed collar. Instead, he'd taken out the merchant's much less impressive compass. She assumed he meant to use it to track down Omar—a rather underwhelming use for a so-called powerful relic. "I doubt it. I thought he was going to pull out that relic from the dune, but either he doesn't know of its power or the merchant lost it somewhere."

They had just turned a corner when she heard it: a scream so shrill it pierced her eardrums. For a few moments, Aisha was too shaken to reach for her blade. The prince stepped forward during her moment of hesitation. He started walking. Faster and faster, until he was running.

"Prince!" She chased after him. "What are you doing!"

But the prince had apparently lost all sense of reason and was darting mindlessly toward the chamber where the scream had come from. The treasure chamber, no doubt.

It was a trap; it had to be. And the stupid prince was heading right into it.

Aisha gave chase. The world swam before her eye as she ran, but she ignored her exhaustion. Prince Mazen had saved her life, and she was hell-bent on repaying the favor.

Aisha did not mourn the past, and she did not overthink the future. But the present—that was something she could shape for the better with her blade.

And she would not run from it.

45

MAZEN

Mazen turned the corner and blanched at the sight before him. At the end of the hall was a doorway that led into a room filled with mountains of gold. The treasure chamber. And coming from that chamber: the scream. Mazen had never heard an agony so loud, so bare.

The Midnight Merchant. Panic gripped his heart.

The scream came again, a sob-riddled wail that sent shivers up his spine.

He pulled his shadow around him and paused at the open doors. The chamber was whole: no gaps, no natural light. There was only the firelight from the sconces. Imad and the merchant were barely illuminated by the hazy glow.

Loulie lay unmoving on the floor, the stars on her robes lost beneath a constellation of blood splatters. Imad circled her like a vulture in Omar's body, twirling a knife in his fingers.

Mazen surged forward. He had no plan. He had no *time*.

He didn't see the ghouls until it was too late. Until they were shrieking and rushing toward him. He kept running, even as the human men shifted and Imad searched the emptiness for him. Mazen crashed into him before he could attack the merchant, slapping the knife out of his hand. It was all he managed before he was jumped from behind. He tumbled, and the shadow cloak collapsed to the floor.

One man reached for it while another pinned him to the ground. "Won't come off," he said to Imad.

"Search the perimeter for bint Louas." When he looked at Mazen, his gaze—Omar's gaze—was terrifyingly blank. "So we meet again, Prince. You've made quite a mess of things."

The fire behind Imad flickered and dimmed. The blood on the merchant's clothing looked garish beneath its light. Mazen quivered. "What have you done to her?"

"Anyone with eyes can see." Imad reached out and grabbed him by his shirt. Mazen saw a dagger in his hand. It was a different weapon than the one he'd knocked away: a dagger with a gold letter embedded into the hilt. "I made the mistake of underestimating you once, Prince, but not again. If I must drag your brother here to avenge your corpse, so be it."

He raised the knife. It flashed through the air faster than Mazen could scream. He felt the coldness of it against his skin and—

Nothing.

Slowly, he eased his eyes open.

The blade had been straight before, but now it was inexplicably crescent shaped, its point curved away from his throat. Mazen was still staring when Imad stabbed him again, and he saw the moment the blade hit his chest and *bent*.

Imad's face paled. "What?"

The fire behind them wavered again. It turned a deep and ominous green.

Imad spun, clutching at something hidden beneath his cloak. Mazen saw a chain hanging from his neck, a glimmer of gold between his fingers. An amulet.

"Attend me," Imad whispered as he grasped the amulet. His nervous gaze swept across the room. When he next spoke, the guttural syllables of the ghoul language came from his mouth. But the ghouls surrounding the perimeter did not respond. They were frozen, their heads tilted eerily, as if they were listening for something.

There was movement. Not from the fire, which danced wildly on the sconces as if possessed, but from the knife still in Imad's hand. Mazen saw a pair of blazing eyes blink at him from the surface of the blade.

Behind them, the entrance doors slammed shut, and the fire in the room dimmed, sighed, and died, plunging them into darkness. The chamber went eerily silent.

And then an invisible force swept through the room like a whirlwind, pressing the air from Mazen's lungs. Chaos unfurled in every direction. Mazen heard the slap of hurried footsteps, the hiss of murmured curses. He heard Imad, speaking into the discord with Omar's voice. "What sorcery is this? Who—" The thief gasped. "No. *No!*"

Somewhere nearby, there came an inhuman howl. Mazen heard the chattering of ghouls in the darkness. Shuffling. Tearing. And then a scream.

Imad was mumbling what sounded like a fervent prayer beneath his breath. Mazen heard the thief stumble, and—something metal clattered to the floor.

Imad's blade?

Mazen reached for it. In his grip it was no longer crescent shaped but, there—a pair of red eyes blinked at him from the faintly glowing surface. *Well?* said a voice in his mind. *Are you just going to sit there?* Mazen recognized the voice. The eyes. It was impossible and yet...

Not impossible. Jinn do not die like humans.

He squinted into the dark. "Al-Nazari? Lou—"

Fingers wrapped around his wrist from behind. Mazen whirled in a panic. He relaxed only when, in the dim light coming from the blade, he saw Loulie staring at him with glassy eyes. The moment she saw the knife, she clawed it out of his hands.

Mazen took in the blood on her scarves, her robe. She had never looked so small. So exhausted.

"We need to get out of here," he said gently. "Can you move?"

A muscle feathered in her jaw. She shook her head.

Mazen glanced at her feet, but he was unable to see anything beneath the bloodied hem of her robe. He took a deep, shuddering breath. "I'm going to pick you up, okay?"

The merchant said nothing as he curved an arm under her legs and set a hand on her back; she only pressed a palm to his chest as he rose. He wasn't sure if he or she was trembling more as he turned and stumbled through the dark. The blade, as if to conceal them, had stopped emitting light, making it impossible to see anything—including the exit.

The darkness was impenetrable. Mazen barely managed a few steps before he froze, overwhelmed by the invisible chaos. He heard ghouls wailing, men yelling, swords screeching—

The merchant nudged him, then pressed something round into his hands. Mazen ran his fingers over glass, wood—a compass? He remembered the instrument in Imad's hands. How in the world had Loulie taken it from him? Before he could ask, a strange thing happened.

The wood beneath his fingers began to warm, and a familiar song pounded through his head. *The stars, they burn the night and guide the sheikh's way…*

The world faded. He was drowning. Chained to a boulder, falling beneath the water—

The memory abruptly dissipated.

My apologies. He stopped breathing when he heard the voice in his head. *I thought you were someone else*, said the Queen of Dunes. *I confess, all human men look the same to me.*

His mind spun. The voice definitely belonged to the Queen of Dunes, but—how? Had Imad stolen the collar from the merchant's bag and brought it with him? The question was replaced with a more perplexing realization: for some reason, he suddenly knew how to navigate his way through the dark room. It was as if there were an arrow in his mind, pointing him toward the exit.

By the time he stumbled into the doors, the magic was making his blood hum. He was dizzy as the merchant took the compass back from him and reached for the door—and then drew away with a soundless gasp as the blade in her hand brightened, revealing one of Imad's men, standing guard.

He blinked, discombobulated, in the hazy light. "You think you can get past me, Prince?" The man raised his weapon. It was at that exact moment the doors behind him burst open. The killer was knocked off his feet and stabbed in the back. Aisha stood behind him, clutching the sword driven through his chest.

Her wide-eyed gaze met Mazen's. "What are you doing? Run!"

Loulie's grip on him tightened as he ducked out of the room and rushed after Aisha, back into the halls blessedly lit by torches. He turned back only once, to witness Imad's companions giving chase. The moment he and Aisha turned the corner, she stopped him and said, "You're not moving fast enough. Give me your shadow."

Mazen frowned. "I can't just *give* you my shadow—"

"You can peel it off the wall, can't you?" She gestured impatiently. "Hand it over."

Mazen reached for the shadow. He pried it from the wall and, shoving aside his hesitation, threw it at Aisha. He was shocked when she actually disappeared. She seemed just as surprised, though her reaction was short lived, fading as she shifted the shadow cloak onto her shoulder. She held out a hand to the merchant. "I'll take your dagger as well." Loulie's glare turned murderous. She shook her head.

"If I'm going to buy you time, I need a weapon. *Give me* the dagger." Aisha reached for the weapon. Mazen yelped when it burst into flame in Loulie's hand.

Aisha pulled her hand away. *"Shit."*

Loulie stared at the fire, blinking rapidly. For a few moments she was still, her gaze unfocused as she looked at the blade. But then she seemed to come back to herself. She shoved the dagger at Aisha without comment. The thief gasped when she wrapped her fingers around the hilt. "It has a *voice*?" She paused, face paling. "Wait, is this—"

"Yes." Mazen backed up a step. "It's Qadir. Don't lose him."

Aisha nodded, pulled the shadow over her head, and disappeared.

Mazen heard the soft patter of her footsteps and then the surprised yells of men falling to an invisible wraith.

He resumed fleeing. For the first time since escaping the chamber, he glanced at the compass. The mental arrow in his mind had disappeared when Loulie put the compass on her lap, but he could still read the compass in her cupped hands. The twitching arrow guided them down a flight of stairs, pointing decisively ahead. He remembered what Imad had said about its power.

"This—is this a king's relic?" He glanced down at the merchant.

Loulie shrugged. Mazen paused, realizing she had yet to speak. He glanced at her throat. At the shackle and the chain hanging from it.

His heart clenched at the sight. "The reason you can't speak..."

She touched a finger to the band.

"And can't walk..."

She pressed her lips together and said nothing.

Imad. Mazen swallowed his anger. He focused on following the compass, on moving through the ruined corridors, pushing in flimsy wooden doors with his foot, and—

Why was the relic leading him deeper into the ruins?

He stopped, noticing for the first time the way the walls pressed in on them. The gaps and holes he'd become so accustomed to were absent. They had reached a dead end.

"Al-Nazari," he said softly. His voice was barely a croak. "Where are we?"

But the merchant looked just as confused. She shook her head, face pale.

"I should have gone out the way I came in. But the Sandsea..." He fell back against the wall, despair and exhaustion washing over him. The merchant tugged on his sleeve, a silent question in her eyes. He realized she didn't know that they were surrounded by the Sandsea. That if there was an escape, he didn't know where it was.

He looked frantically around them, but there were no doors, no passages. No escape.

His gaze fell to the floor. And snagged on his shadow. Mazen blinked. If his shadow had returned, then Aisha...

"End of the line, Prince."

Mazen whirled to see Imad standing behind him, still in Omar's body and flanked by human men. One had Aisha pinned to his chest and held a knife to her throat. Though she struggled against him, his grip was unshakable. The blade at her neck was beaded with red. Mazen stared in horror. He glanced between the men, searching for an opening, for...

He paused, realizing who—what—was missing. "Where are your ghouls?" he said weakly.

Imad stepped forward and pulled open his cloak. Mazen flinched back, but the underside of the cloak was empty. The amulet he had been wearing was gone. "Running amok." The thief's voice took on a shrill edge. "Your jinn rendered my relic useless. She took control of *my* ghouls and clouded my mind with her terrible song."

A memory flashed through Mazen's mind of the Queen of Dunes' song. He recalled the fissure that had opened in his mind to let in memories that were not his. Where had she come from? *How* was she here?

Imad took another step forward. Mazen saw silver glint between his fingers. Throwing knives. "Now, because of your jinn, I must resort to torture the old-fashioned way." He raised a hand, snapped his fingers. "Kill her."

Mazen was too busy gripping Loulie, too busy fearing for *her* life, to notice the killer behind Aisha shift. He did not notice the gleam of his knife until it was too late.

Until it tore a gash into Aisha's throat.

There was no scream. No cry.

Just Aisha's single-eyed gaze, boring into him desperately. And then nothing. The spark of panic faded, and Aisha bint Louas collapsed.

The world tilted.

Mazen was aware of his heartbeat. Of breathing in and in and in. Of a scream, beating wildly in his chest. Of the merchant, biting her fist so hard blood trickled down her knuckles.

"Your brother took everything from me." Imad was close enough to stab him, close enough to kill him. "Now I shall take everything from him."

Mazen couldn't stop looking at Aisha. At her impossibly still body.

Get up, he thought desperately. *Get up!*

But Aisha didn't move.

She had been so confident, so powerful. An unfaltering force of nature. If she could not survive, how could he?

"I'm sorry," he whispered. To Aisha. To the merchant.

Again, the world shook. Mazen stumbled on his feet as the walls shuddered. He no longer had enough strength to hold the merchant, to stand—not even enough to *see* right. He blinked.

The world righted itself.

Then, again, it shook. Tilted.

And cracked.

There was a sound—Mazen recognized it as the sigh of cascading sand.

Imad turned. Mazen followed his gaze to the web of cracks breaking across the surface of the ancient walls. They spread and stretched like veins, pulsing, thrumming, until the walls burst and a torrent of sand crashed through the room in the form of a gigantic wave.

Mazen stumbled back as Imad was swallowed.

The world disappeared, replaced by a hazy veil of black.

And then there was sand in his eyes and nose and throat, and the merchant was no longer in his arms, and *Gods, I can't breathe, I can't breathe, help...*

He was sinking, sinking, sinking. Until—

The sand beneath him gave way, and Mazen fell into nothingness.

46

LOULIE

Layla could not stop staring at the stretch of sparkling, flowing sand. This was her first time seeing the Sandsea up close. It took her breath away.

"Majestic, isn't it?" She whirled to see her mother riding beside her on one of the tribe's camels.

Layla glanced back at the shifting gold-red tides. "It looks like the ocean." Some people said the sea was infinite, that it had no bottom. Was the Sandsea the same way?

"The jinn live there," her mother said. "So far down only the strongest can climb out."

Layla tilted her head. "Does that mean if we dove deep enough, we could visit the jinn's world like they visit ours?"

Her mother smiled wryly. "The jinn have magic, dearest one. Magic to help them break through a tide of endless sand. We do not have that same power; we would stop breathing before we reached the bottom." Layla startled when her mother set a hand on her shoulder. "We are wanderers, but even we must never venture into the Sandsea. It is too dangerous." She raised a brow. "You hear me, Sweet Fire? Do not ever walk into the Sandsea."

Layla turned away to hide her flush. It wasn't that she'd actually been considering it. Just that she was . . . curious. She cleared her throat. "You told me once the Sandsea was made from jinn fire?"

Her mother's gaze turned wistful. "The Sandsea is a rip in the world, made from a fire so fierce it has never stopped burning. That kind of magic—you must stay away from it. Do you understand, Sweet Fire?"

—⁂—

Loulie did not understand.

She did not understand why the Sandsea had suddenly swallowed the ruins and why it had not yet killed her. Everywhere she looked, there was sand. And yet that sand was more a tunnel than an ocean, a churning eddy of red and gold that spun around her like a tornado.

She fell, and it was like falling into the sun.

Is this what the Sandsea has been all along? A tunnel to the center of the world?

But then, finally, the end came.

She hit the ground hard enough to have the breath knocked from her lungs. Slowly, she forced herself to sit up. She spotted the prince first. He was on his knees a few feet away from her, digging the compass out of the sand. She had recovered it in the darkened treasure chamber when Imad threw it away during the scare—she was glad it had made it down here with them.

She glanced around, noticing they were surrounded on all sides by walls of falling sand. Then she turned her gaze upward. And beheld the gigantic hole above them. Sand fell from its edges, dusting her lashes. She could just barely make out the crumbling ruins, which meant that they were...beneath them now? How was that possible?

"Midnight Merchant?" The prince was batting sand from his eyes.

She waved him over. The prince rose, glanced up. His mouth fell open. "Oh," he said weakly. And then his eyes went wide and he whirled toward her. "Aisha?" The name was a plea.

She swallowed, shook her head. She'd seen Aisha die, just as she'd seen Qadir die.

Qadir. She froze. *The knife!* She looked around for it desperately.

But there was only sand. The ground was sand, the walls were sand, and there was nothing else, no one else. *No, no, no!* She was a damned *fool.* She had given Aisha the knife, and now it was gone. But no—she had lost Qadir once; she refused to lose him again.

Distantly, she heard the prince yelling her name. His voice was laced with panic. She did not understand why until she followed his horrified gaze to the hole. That was when she saw the nameless terror—a shadowy being coated in blue fire—falling through the opening. The thing rushed toward them so suddenly. Loulie had no time to react. One moment the world was warm and golden. The next, it was hot and red and *burning.* If falling into the Sandsea had been like falling into the sun, then this was like walking headfirst into an inferno.

The sliver of metal at her throat grew unbearably hot. When she touched the metal, she felt fire. Fire caressing her skin and warming her palms.

Fire she recognized.

Invisible fingers pressed down on her own. There was a final flare of heat and then—freedom. The shackle crumbled to ash and fell from her neck. Loulie gasped, looked up, and beheld a wall of flames.

The fire faded from blue to gold to red to black and then into the shape of a man. A man so faded he was nearly nonexistent. The whorls on his skin ran together like water, and his ruby-red eyes were so bright they were devoid of irises.

Familiar yet unfamiliar. Loulie was in too much shock to say his name.

The phantom reached down to pick her up. Being held by him was like being held by smoke. There was a soft pressure at her head, a gentle heat soaking her skin. But mostly, there was relief. A relief that coursed through her veins and screamed *safe.*

"You." The prince stepped back, clutching the compass. *"How?"*

The fiery apparition ignored him and flicked a wrist at one of the walls of sand. It parted like a curtain, burning away into crackling embers and opening up into a tunnel. The phantom glanced down at her, pressed a blade into her hands. Qadir's knife. His red eyes blinked at her from the surface.

"Qadir." She gripped the blade.

He was back; he was *back*.

"Compass," Qadir rasped in a parchment-thin voice. He pointed to the tunnel and looked at Mazen expectantly.

The prince stepped back. "How are you here? How are *we* here? What kind of magic..."

The walls of sand shuddered. Loulie looked up just in time to see sand come crashing through the hole above them. It was nearly upon them when Qadir lifted his hand and conjured a shield of flame. The sand dissipated into sparks upon impact, but it was coming hard and fast, and the pressure was breaking the shield. *"Go!"* he roared.

The prince bolted toward the tunnel. Qadir followed. He was smoke and wind and moved so fast Loulie felt as if she were flying. He kept one hand outstretched toward the sand, parting it with heat as they ran. Loulie heard the hiss of sand as it crashed behind them, filling the tunnel.

She pressed her tearstained face into his shoulder. "I'm here," he said softly. If she concentrated hard enough, she could almost pretend he was not smoke, that he was flesh and blood and that he was here. Truly *here*.

"What a pathetic way to die," she said.

"You're not going to die."

"The arrow won't stop changing direction!" Mazen called up ahead.

"We're almost there," Qadir called back, his voice so soft Loulie barely heard it over the tumultuous roar of the sand behind them. She turned her head, and blinked as light assaulted her senses, as the sand sloped upward toward a hole glowing with sunlight. A hole that led *outside*.

"You see? Almost there." His voice was faint. *He* was faint. She could barely feel his hands anymore.

"Don't leave me." She clung to him fiercely. "You're not allowed to leave me."

She could feel the light pressing into her eyes now, could feel the kiss of the wind against her skin as they wove their way through sinking ruins and ran up a hill of falling sand, climbing higher and higher until—

A scream tore through the air. Loulie looked up and saw the prince, nothing but a shadow haloed in blinding light. She saw him collapse to his knees and slide down the slope, gripping his arm. She became aware of the second shadow only when a knife whistled past her ear and cut through Qadir's smoky form. The jinn's arms gave way, and she was suddenly falling, coughing sand as she tumbled down the slope.

"*You*. It was you we were looking for." She recognized Omar's voice. And when she looked up and saw him pointing uphill at Qadir's misty body with madness in his eyes, she recognized that too. She remembered the chains. The collar. The knife against her throat.

Not Omar.

The laugh that left Imad's throat was a broken thing. "You *lied* to me, merchant." He hobbled toward her, dragging a clearly broken leg behind him. His skin was marred with odd black splatters that shone like blood. "Your compass is not the relic we were ordered to find. The king's relic we searched for—it didn't exist. And your jinn…" His breathing was a wet rasp. "Is more than just a jinn, isn't he?"

Loulie, look at me.

Loulie stared at the thief, uncomprehending.

LOULIE. The dagger in her hands grew hot with fire. She looked down and saw Qadir's narrowed eyes. *Do you still want your vengeance?* His voice echoed in her mind even as his mute, shadowy form slid down the hill toward her.

Imad's laughter was so loud and wild it made his body shake. "It's no wonder he lives! Do you know what he is, girl?"

He killed your family, Qadir said.

"Everything that's happened—it's his fault!" cried Imad.

He destroyed your tribe.

The fire glowed with such an intensity it burned dark spots into her vision. And in those patches of darkness, she saw the nightmare. Her campsite on fire. Her family, dead.

"Midnight Merchant!" The title startled her from the memories. She looked up, past Imad and Qadir, and saw the prince. He sat atop the dune, holding his bloodied arm and yelling her name. *Loulie. Midnight Merchant.*

She gripped the dagger. She was not Layla. She was not weak. Not anymore.

It didn't matter that she couldn't walk. She could crawl. And so she did, clawing her way through the sand until she could slash at Imad's legs. He retaliated by kicking dust into her face. Loulie blinked back tears and aimed for his bad leg. She plunged her dagger into his foot.

The fire coating the blade was a living thing. It spread up Imad's leg, coated his clothing. And then it began to burn through his skin. Imad stumbled away with a scream, wildly tearing at his attire. Loulie reached for his ankle. The fire curved away from her fingers just long enough for her to pull Imad down. For her to pin him to the ground. When he tried to defend himself, she deflected his strike and buried her knife in his chest.

Not enough. She stabbed him again.

His skin burned. *Not enough.* Crumbled to charcoal. *Not enough.* She slashed and stabbed and screamed and sobbed, and it was strange, so *strange* that no matter how many times she cut him, there was no blood. Just that strange ink that kept seeping out of him, and *Why won't he bleed? He deserves to bleed; he deserves to HURT.*

She was sobbing so hard by the end of it that she dropped the dagger. She felt warmth at her back, arms around her shoulders. "Don't look," Qadir whispered as he picked her and the fallen blade up. And she didn't. Not until they mounted the dune and Imad was nothing but a distant blot of ash.

Then: sunlight. She had to blink back tears to see. And when she could, she saw Qadir's fading face above her. His red eyes had lightened to their shade of human brown, but they were barely an impression.

Loulie grabbed at his chest. "Qadir," she said, willing him to solidify with the name.

He smiled at her weakly. "You did it. You avenged your family."

His smile faded first, followed by the rest of his body. He lowered her to the ground as he vanished, as he went from man to smoke to dust.

The prince grabbed her before she collapsed, and carefully lowered her to the ground. The two of them sat side by side, watching the ruins sink into the Sandsea. The prince grasped his injured arm and prayed. Loulie stared resolutely ahead, trying not to cry and failing.

She had her vengeance, but it was an empty triumph.

47

AISHA

Aisha was dying.

Or maybe she was already dead. It was hard to tell.

The pain was a current of agony, coursing through her veins and making the world go black. She was too busy focusing on it to feel anything else. Thus, she did not realize the world had shattered beneath her until her body slammed into the ground.

She didn't scream. She couldn't. Her throat was torn, and the last of her words had spilled onto the sand with her blood.

To live is a matter of belief, Omar had once told her. *The wicked live longer simply because they believe themselves to be invincible.*

Her king had lied to her. All this time, she had believed. That she was the best. That she could not possibly die.

And yet here she lay. Broken.

Aisha opened her eye. It burned like hell, but she refused to die in darkness. At the very least, she would die staring daggers into her murderer.

But Imad was gone, and the prince and the merchant were nowhere to be seen. There were only endless hills of sand. When had she escaped the ruins? Maybe she *was* dead.

But then she saw it—a shadow standing amidst the dunes. A silhouette of smoke with gleaming red eyes, wearing a band of gold around its throat. *Jinn*. Aisha's vision went foggy. Her body convulsed without her permission. Pain—pain so terrible it forced a soundless scream from her throat—racked her body.

When she could focus again, the jinn was standing before her.

Was it...the Midnight Merchant's bodyguard?

The silhouette blinked at her. It said nothing. Did nothing. She was becoming convinced it was a hallucination, when it reached up and pulled the collar from its throat. The jinn grasped her hand—she could barely feel it, certainly couldn't *move* it—and set the collar in it before walking away.

Aisha's vision clouded. She blinked rapidly to clear it. A futile effort. When her sight stabilized, she was still hallucinating. This time, she saw a wraithlike woman who was all angles and bones. Her eyes were like wells of ink, and her plaited hair swung like a pendulum.

Aisha wondered if this was the god of death.

But then the woman's lips broke into a disarmingly mischievous grin, and Aisha knew she was not some benevolent god. "Salaam," said the woman. "Would you like to die?"

Aisha startled at the voice. It belonged to the undead queen who had mocked her in the desert. The same jinn who had possessed the wali of Dhyme. It was the voice that had whispered *Find me, jinn killer* in her mind. It seemed that in the end, the jinn had found her first.

The jinn king—queen—crouched down. She tilted her head. Her braid continued swinging on a phantom breeze. "Or perhaps you would like to make a deal?"

No deal. Aisha had not avoided falling prey to a jinn in life only to succumb to one in death. Jinn were monsters. Jinn were the *reason* she had made herself into a weapon.

The queen raised a brow. "Are you certain?" She leaned down and, before Aisha could pull away, laced their fingers together. Ice and fire and death and light and *life* crackled through Aisha's veins, crashing through her with the potency of poison.

"I can fix you."

Aisha shuddered. She could feel her body. She could *breathe.*

"Don't you have things you still need to do?"

Aisha thought of Omar. Omar, turning to her in the darkness of her bedroom with a smile on his face. *I can trust you to see this through to the end?*

Of course.

You promise not to die?

She had scoffed. *A thief steals lives. They do not have their life stolen from them.*

"I will fill in the pieces of you that are broken," the queen said. "But those pieces will belong to me as well. Do you understand? I will take one of your eyes. And…" She tapped Aisha's chest. Her heart stuttered. "I will take your heart and share your body."

Aisha shuddered. *You took everything from the wali of Dhyme.*

The queen narrowed her eyes. "That was possession. This is a deal."

Why offer me a deal when I am one of the jinn killers you despise? When I despise you?

"Because it is beneficial to us both. The only way I can truly exist in your world is with a vessel. A mind. And for that, I require a deal."

Aisha's gaze locked on the landscape behind the jinn. It was nothing but a band of twinkling darkness. It reminded her of the night sky.

As a child, she had always wondered if the sky was endless. She knew that the one she was looking at now *was* endless. That there would be no coming back from it.

An image hung suspended before her: a dream encroaching on reality.

She was falling. Prince Omar watched her from a distance, eyes dark with disappointment. She was too ashamed to reach for him, so she let herself drop, let herself fade…

"I'm sorry." The voice made her pause. It was not Omar's.

When she looked up, Mazen stood before her, shame etched onto his face. Irritation bubbled in her chest. It was insulting. That he should apologize to her when he'd saved her.

She wanted to strangle him. She wanted to hug him.

But—she clung desperately to the part of her mind that insisted neither prince was worth this. She had not refused to use jinn vessels for so long only to become one herself. This magic had torn her life apart.

"Magic is not just destruction. It is also salvation." The jinn held out a hand. "Are you truly so stubborn in your beliefs that you would run from this last opportunity?"

Aisha thought of the words she'd spoken to Mazen: *The only difference between a hero and a coward is that one forgets their fear and fights, while the other succumbs to it and flees.*

Aisha wasn't conceited enough to call herself a hero, but she was no coward.

She would not give up. She would not *die*.

Her eyes found the jinn queen's. *If this is a deal, then you must agree to honor* my *terms as well.* She expected an objection from the jinn and was surprised when the queen smiled instead, her teeth glowing an eerie white in the dark.

"Smart human," she said.

You have to promise you will never use me as a puppet.

"I told you that this was a deal, not possession." The queen dipped her head. "But if my word is so important, you shall have it, hunter. I promise I will never force you to do anything against your own volition. Your will is your own."

Aisha should not have been able to move her hand. But somehow, she managed to grasp the queen's outstretched fingers. *Deal.*

The jinn smiled a fox-like smile. "A jinn hunter and a jinn. What a great duo we will make." She squeezed her hand. Aisha's heart began to beat. Louder and louder and louder until she could feel it pulsing behind her eyes and pounding in her veins.

Slowly, painstakingly, she returned to life.

48

MAZEN

Once, when Hakim had first become a prisoner, he told Mazen freedom was a right only appreciated by those who lost it. *That is the way of all lost things. One does not truly understand a thing's value until it is gone.* Mazen had never felt that as profoundly as he did now, sitting in a cave with nothing but his brother's ill-fitting clothes on his back.

The Sandsea was a distant ever-shifting ocean, the surface disturbed occasionally by a sinking building. It was hard to believe he had been in those ruins hours ago. Even harder to believe there had been four of them before they entered.

Mazen gripped his newly bound arm—he had ripped off a sleeve to stanch the bleeding—and cast a surreptitious look over his shoulder at the merchant. Loulie al-Nazari was still facing a wall, ignoring him. Her slashed ankles were hidden beneath her robe.

Neither of them had talked about what came next.

But then, he wasn't ready to continue their quest as if nothing had happened. To keep pushing toward Ghiban when the memory of so much death hung in the air. Not when Aisha—

When he blinked, he saw her slumped on the ground in a pool of blood. Aisha bint Louas, one of the forty thieves, dead before he could scream her name.

He hugged his knees to his chest and breathed out slowly. He wouldn't cry. He'd done enough of that earlier, when he brought the merchant to this cave at the edge of the Sandsea. She had just stared blankly as he collapsed against the wall and sobbed, her grief either already dried up or screaming silently inside her.

Perhaps the merchant found solace in silence. Mazen did not. To him, the quiet had always been a void to fill. But he did not know how to fill this silence. There were too many questions between them, and too much guilt. The merchant had not yet asked about his disguise or his purpose, and he did not want to bring it up. He was too ashamed.

Some motion in the desert caught his attention. He looked up—and froze.

"Al-Nazari." The merchant didn't turn. He called her again, and she whirled with a glare that twisted into a pained grimace as she shifted her ankles. Mazen pointed outside at an approaching smudge. "Someone's coming."

He had watched the merchant burn Imad and the bangle—*Gods, it was an ancient family artifact!*—to ashes. He had watched Qadir fade to smoke and Aisha die. He had no idea who was coming for them, but whoever it was, they were making a straight line for their cave.

Unthinkingly, he reached for Omar's belt of daggers and felt nothing. His brother's blades were gone. The only weapon they had was Qadir's knife, and he was certain Loulie would let them be mauled to death before she relinquished it to him.

But still, he had to try. He had to...

He blinked. Narrowed his eyes. "What...?"

"*What?*" the merchant snapped.

"Aisha," he said softly.

It was a grief-induced mirage. A hallucination. Jinn magic. It had to be.

And yet he found himself stumbling out into the desert, rushing toward Aisha—*Not a mirage, not a mirage*—until he was close enough to see the blood on her. It was everywhere: caked onto her like a second skin. Only, the lacerations were gone. And where the gash at her throat had been, there was now a band of skulls that glimmered beneath the varnish of blood.

The Queen of Dunes' relic.

He remembered the wali of Dhyme, speaking in that uncharacteristically soft voice, laughing as he stabbed his companions and painted the floor with their blood.

Before he could run, Aisha bint Louas stepped forward and gripped him by the shoulder. "Aren't you going to welcome me back?" She grinned, and it made her eyes shine with a mischief he'd never seen before. Then, abruptly, the grin faded. "We need to talk," she said, voice suddenly gruff, and then she unceremoniously dragged him behind her toward the cave.

As if nothing had happened.

As if she had not somehow, impossibly, been revived from the dead.

—⁂—

Aisha told them the story of her resurrection in front of the campfire. Mazen noticed the way her hands darted through the air and the way her lips sometimes slanted into a lopsided smirk. Subtle changes. But there were other, more obvious differences as well—her scars, for instance. They'd become an unnatural gray, one that reminded him of dead things. And her right eye—the one that had been sealed with blood—was now more black than brown. It shone like obsidian in the firelight.

It was an unsettling sight, one that evidently put Loulie on edge too. Mazen did not miss the way her grip tightened on her blade every time Aisha looked at her. Paranoia had dug roots into Mazen as well. More than once, he found himself reaching for knives he no longer had. It was impossible to look at Aisha without remembering the Queen of Dunes had tried to kill them—twice.

Wariness clung to him like a shroud when Aisha finished her tale. Before he could speak, the merchant leaned forward and said, "So who are you? Aisha bint Louas? Or the Queen of Dunes?"

Aisha opened her mouth, paused, then closed it. Mazen could tell by the tightness of her jaw that she was gritting her teeth. But then, slowly, the tension disappeared from her body. "Don't waste your breath on stupid questions. I could never be anyone but myself."

She and Loulie silently stared at each other. Mazen inched away. Sitting between them was like being battered on either side by a frigid wind.

The merchant shook her head. "I don't believe you."

Aisha scowled. "I would never succumb to a jinn."

"Then what do you call this?" The merchant gestured sharply. "Coexistence?"

"You think I wanted this? I already told you: we struck a deal because this is the only way she…" Aisha paused, breathed out slowly. "The only way *we* can exist in this world. If the jinn had wanted to kill you, she could have used my corpse to do it without striking a bargain."

Mazen felt himself fidgeting. He stilled his hands. "So to be clear, she no longer wants to murder us?"

"I do not." Aisha uttered the claim so quickly even she seemed surprised. She straightened. Again, there was that flicker of irritation across her features. "The jinn wrongly thought you were murderers because of the relics you carried. But *I* am the jinn hunter. If she wanted vengeance on anyone, it would be me." A sardonic smile flitted across her face. "But instead, we made a deal. You can see her priorities have changed."

There was a beat of silence as they stared at each other. Though Mazen felt slightly more at ease, Loulie regarded Aisha with stony skepticism. "Then tell us the rest of the story. What happened to the jinn that gave you the collar?" *Qadir.* Mazen heard his name, even unspoken.

Aisha raised her brows, inclined her head. "What is he to you, merchant?"

Loulie frowned. "I see no reason to answer your question if you will not answer mine."

Aisha crossed her arms. "He left. Disappeared. But he would

have come back for me." She scowled. "For the *collar*. He and"—
she clenched her hands—"the queen know each other. He used her
power to control the ghouls in the treasure chamber."

The memory unfurled in Mazen's mind. He was back in Imad's
pitch-black treasure chamber as some invisible force brushed past
him. Only, in this recollection, he saw the force was Qadir and that
he was walking through the dark with the collar around his neck,
humming a soundless song. The Queen of Dunes' song. Mazen
wondered how long it had taken for the cutthroats to realize the
ghouls had turned on them.

"I should have realized something was amiss when Imad didn't
mention finding the collar," Loulie mumbled. "But I never thought
Qadir would be..." She trailed off, gaze blank.

Aisha eyed the dagger in Loulie's hands. "So your bodyguard
was a jinn."

Was. Mazen did not miss the way the merchant's eyes flashed at
the word. But she said nothing, only glared silently, knife gripped
between trembling fingers.

"It sounds as if you knew Qadir even before we recovered your
relic from the ruins." Mazen found his gaze straying to Aisha's darker
eye when he spoke. If there was any piece of her that belonged to the
jinn, it was that eye.

Aisha's lips quirked. It was nothing but a twitch, there one
moment and gone the next, but Mazen experienced the disconcerting feeling of being judged by not one, but two women. "Yes," she
said. "But I cannot tell that story without his permission." She stood
and stretched, then began to walk away.

"Wait!" Mazen stood and followed her. "Where are you going?
You can't just—"

She turned to face him. "When was the last time you ate?"

The question took him by surprise. His stomach, which had
been tight with nerves, suddenly churned with hunger. How long
had it been?

"Exactly. We can continue this discussion after I hunt." Mazen
eyed her blood-drenched clothing. As far as he could see, she had

no weapons. She must have read the question on his face. "Humans use falcons to hunt." She gestured outside with a thumb. "I have ghouls."

Mazen edged his way to the entrance. The moment he saw the six ghouls standing sentinel outside, he fell back with a cry.

Aisha sighed. "How do you think I got out of the ruins? Ghouls are very good at digging." When he simply stared at her, she added, "Imad forced them to do his bidding with a relic he *stole*"—her voice dripped with disgust—"but I can summon and dismiss them with my magic, so long as they are nearby."

"But—" He had so many *but*s, he didn't even know where to begin. He glanced helplessly at Loulie, but she was not looking at him. Her attention was fixed on the dagger. He realized, with some shock, that there were tears on her cheeks.

Aisha slapped a hand on his shoulder. "Join me, Prince."

"But," he said again. He was not keen on being alone with a deadly jinn.

Caution battled with guilt. In the ruins, Aisha had saved him. He wanted to trust her. Wanted to believe that if she was strong enough to circumvent death, she was strong enough to keep her mind intact. He cast another nervous look over his shoulder at Loulie.

"The ghouls will be standing outside," Aisha said. *She'll be fine* was the unspoken claim, but Mazen was still worried.

Aisha gave him no chance to reconsider; she pulled him out of the cave before he could protest again.

49

LOULIE

Once she was alone, Loulie raised the dagger and murmured, "Qadir?"

There was no response.

In the ruins, he had returned for her. He had been smoke and fire and shadow, but he'd been *alive*. Now even his reflection was gone.

"You sank ruins to save me." She rubbed furiously at her cheeks, despising her tears but unable to stop them from falling. "And now, what, you're just going to fade away? I thought you were stronger than that." The tears came quicker, shaking her body and making her vision blur.

You are the weak one, said a small voice inside her head.

And it was that confession, that truth, that finally broke her. All these years she'd been trying to distance herself from her past failures. *Layla* had been too young and helpless to save everyone she loved. So as Loulie, she'd vowed to become stronger, wiser. Someone who, unbeholden to anyone, would be able to rescue herself without worrying about losing others.

But she had failed—to save both herself and Qadir.

She did not know how long she sat there crying, only that by the time her tears had dried, the prince and the thief had not returned. She didn't care.

The emptiness was a chasm inside her, and it grew deeper and deeper until it swallowed her whole, pulling her into a dismal, fragmented sleep. When the nightmares continued to wake her, she gave up on slumber and decided to search for the missing prince and thief. She moved to stand—and cried out when excruciating pain shot through her ankles.

Her legs. She had forgotten.

She looked up at the sound of footsteps. They were soft, so faint she could barely hear them. She saw a hazy shape. A man-shaped shadow.

She squinted. "Prince?"

The man stepped forward, and in the flickering firelight she saw it was not Prince Mazen. No, this man was badly burned and wounded, and barely standing upright.

Her heartbeat tripped. "No, but—you're dead." She scrambled back, only to find herself up against the cave wall, legs quivering with pain.

The man she had burned, the man she had *killed*, drew closer, knife raised. "If I must die," Imad rasped, "I shall take you with me." He lunged.

Loulie screamed as a hand came down on her shoulder. She gasped and tried to wiggle away. "No!" The word was a plea, a prayer. "No, no—"

"Loulie, you're dreaming." The voice was so soft it was barely audible, and yet it washed over her like a soothing wave, smoothing the edges of her panic. She eased her eyes open.

A red-eyed shadow sat before her. Another blink, and the shadow became a solid man with umber skin and faded tattoos. She focused on his eyes: soft and brown and human.

"You were making a face in your sleep," Qadir said. "I thought it rude to keep staring."

Loulie threw herself at him with a choked sob. Pain lanced through her ankles, but in that moment, the injury did not matter. She waited for Qadir to dissipate into smoke. Instead, he wrapped his arms around her and pulled her to him. He didn't say anything, just sat there quietly as she cried into his shoulder. For a time, they stayed like that, the silence broken only by her hiccups and, when she had quieted, the crackle of the campfire.

There was silence. Soft and comfortable.

Eventually, Loulie pulled away to look at his face. He looked perfectly human. She reached out to touch his cheek. Perfectly *solid*.

His expression softened. "You were dreaming, so I woke you."

Loulie stared at him, daring the planes of his face to crumble to dust. But he remained. "You died," she said at last, voice hoarse.

She did not realize she had pulled away until Qadir reached out to set his hand atop hers. "Never dead. Incapacitated, but not dead. I am sorry it took me so long to find you."

"But the trap—"

"Enough to wound me. Slow me down."

"You were smoke…"

"It is no simple thing, re-forming a body so badly damaged."

Loulie swallowed. "But the swords were made of *iron*."

Qadir scoffed. "Who do you think I am?"

Imad's words wafted through her mind like poisonous smoke. *It's no wonder he lives! Do you know what he is, girl?*

"I don't know." She could barely say the words over the knot in her throat.

A tangled web of memories unfurled in her mind: Qadir, confessing he could not return home. Imad, speaking of a relic so valuable any who saw it were ordered dead—a jinn king's relic. She remembered the hunger in his eyes as the ruins collapsed. The way his voice had trembled as he approached her and Qadir. *You. It was you we were looking for.*

Her mother had told her stories about the seven jinn kings, who had power enough to sink their world. *Ifrit*, Qadir called them. But that was a word for terrible, fearsome jinn. For the creature that had revived Aisha with twisted dark magic. For the legendary jinn in the lamp.

Not Qadir.

She pulled her hand away. Qadir's eyes dimmed. "Loulie…" He

looked as if he were about to reach for her again when he turned, eyes narrowed.

Aisha bint Louas leaned against the cave entrance, arms folded over her chest, one ankle crossed over the other as she surveyed them with a catlike smile Loulie knew was not her own. The look made her heart thud nervously. She had barely trusted the thief when she was just herself. Now that she was hosting a deadly jinn, she trusted her even less.

But Qadir seemed unconcerned. "I see you made your deal."

Aisha clicked her tongue. "*You* is not my name. Can you say 'Aisha'?"

"My gods." These words were spoken by Prince Mazen, who stepped into the cave, holding a bloody hare by its feet. He stared between them, bug-eyed. "How are you alive?"

Qadir frowned. "Who's asking? Prince Mazen, or is this another disguise?"

The prince at least had the decency to blush. Loulie wanted to punch his embarrassed face. For so long, her anger at him had been muted by her grief. But now it was back, sparking inside her like an unruly flame. The first time he had lied about his identity, she had sympathized with his plight. Evidently, that meant nothing to him.

Aisha scoffed. "How delightful that we've *all* been keeping secrets." She grabbed the hare from Mazen, strode over to the fire, and began to skin it with some shard she'd apparently acquired in the desert. "Perhaps we should have a heart-to-heart?"

No one spoke into the silence that followed. Loulie knew she should try to take charge. She was the Midnight Merchant, after all. She was—*useless*. The realization hit again, so hard it made her shudder. It was true. What was she without her relics? Without *Qadir*?

It was Qadir who at last broke the silence. Not with a word, but with a sigh that made the fire in front of them waver. "Fine." He gestured, and the campfire rose, twisting and stretching until it morphed into a marvelous landscape of shining minarets and domed buildings. "Let us speak of lies and truths, and of the story hidden between them."

And so he told them the tale of the seven jinn kings, but his version was different from the human tale. In Qadir's story, the jinn kings were not a nameless group of villains; they were a collective of jinn so powerful they were given their own name. *Ifrit*: beings of fire whose magic so defied the natural order, it was feared even amongst jinn.

He swept his fingers through the fiery mirage of the city, and it re-formed beneath his fingers, separating into seven figures. "The ifrit were different from normal jinn in that they could learn multiple magics, not just the one they were born with. They were named, however, for the affinity they specialized in."

He reached for the nearest fiery silhouette and altered its shape, morphing it into a large, flaming bird with many tails. "The Shapeshifter," Qadir said.

He touched the second figure, which hopped and spun through the air. "The Dancer."

The third figure perched itself on a flying rug and held up a skull. "The Resurrectionist."

Loulie glanced at Aisha, who caught her gaze and looked away, brow furrowed.

"So you *are* the Queen of Dunes," the prince mumbled.

"Stop calling me that," Aisha said sharply. "The jinn may speak through me, but only when I grant her permission. I am still myself."

Qadir pointedly cleared his throat as he reached for the fourth figure, which swam through the air with angled limbs. "The Tide Bringer," he said.

The fifth figure clasped its hands in prayer. "The Mystic."

The sixth figure pressed its hands to the ground. Flaming trees shot up in a circle around its hunched form. "The Wanderer."

Then Qadir drew his fingers through the last form. He crafted a turban made of smoke for its head and a cloak of blue fire for its back. The figure strode around their campfire like a sentinel, its blue cape billowing soundlessly on a nonexistent wind. "The Inferno," he said softly.

The prince made a sound of awe. Loulie said nothing. She felt

Qadir's gaze on her. She knew what the look on his face would convey even without seeing it: *I'm sorry I never told you.*

A storm of emotions rose inside of her, a thicket so thorny she could barely discern one virulent feeling from another. Every time she tried to focus, her concentration fractured and she remembered the pain in her legs. She had never felt so broken before. So bone-deep tired.

When she said nothing, Qadir returned his gaze to the fire. He shaped it once more—this time into eight forms. He set one on a throne and had the others kneel before it.

"The ifrit served a king who ruled from his throne in Dhahab. They were both his warriors and his advisors and were sworn to protect their country. For hundreds of years, there was peace." He stared for a long time at the flickering image of the bowed jinn. Then he sighed, and the fire lost its shape. Loulie was startled to see beads of ash on his face. His chest rattled every time he breathed. *It is no simple thing, re-forming a body so badly damaged.*

"In the legends..." The prince paused, color coming into his cheeks, as if he were aware of how strange it was to refer to history as myth. "In the legends, the seven kings brought the wrath of the gods down on them. They buried the jinn world beneath the Sandsea."

Aisha laughed, a soft chuckle that seemed misplaced coming from her slanted lips. "Gods? There were no gods—only you humans."

Even Loulie looked up at this, but Aisha—or the Resurrectionist, whoever the hell she was in the moment—only stared forlornly into the fire. "One day, humans came to our lands. We thought them harmless creatures. An incompetent, magicless people. Our king was curious, so he welcomed them into our city."

"It was ill advised," Qadir murmured. He spoke lightly, as if he'd lost the strength to project his voice. "When they found out our blood could heal and that our relics could be wielded as weapons, they came after us with iron swords and spears."

"They were relentless," Aisha said. "We could not destroy all of them, so..."

Qadir turned away. "We ran from them. We disobeyed our king and buried our country deep beneath the sand so that no human could ever reach us."

The weight of those words settled slowly. To sink a landscape of ruins was one thing. To make an entire country disappear was another. Loulie crossed her arms and swallowed. She imagined falling forever, imagined her home and her loved ones suffocating beneath the sand.

"They made us suffer for our betrayal," Qadir murmured.

Loulie glanced at the faded scars running up his arms. *My shame was carved into me with a knife so that I would not forget it. I deserved it.*

"Those of us who didn't want to suffer fled to the human world," Aisha said. She held up the hairless rabbit and, after a significant pause, threw it into the fire. The prince made a sound of protest that quickly collapsed into a gasp, for the fire did not burn the hare; it cooked it. "Of course, all of us suffered in the end."

A sullen but short-lived quiet permeated the cave before the prince cleared his throat and said, "In our legends, they call you the Queen of Dunes. They say—"

"Enough." Aisha's voice was sharp, cold. "I tire of these jinn stories."

The prince blinked, looking thoroughly perplexed. He turned that look on Qadir, who shook his head. "My past is my past. I buried it long ago, and I intend to keep it that way." He glanced up and caught Loulie's eyes. *Forgive me.*

There was nothing to forgive him for. This was not Qadir's fault. And yet—she could not stop reliving the moment Imad had apprehended them in the ruins. *You. It was you we were looking for,* he'd said. Not the compass, not a relic. The thieves had unknowingly been searching for an ifrit—a creature that had stumbled into her tribe's burning campsite that night, looking for his compass, and who had found it in the hands of a tortured girl. It had been the thieves who killed her family. Qadir had *saved* her from them. And yet if Qadir had not been wandering by their campsite in the first place, if the thieves had not tracked him to that area...

They would still be alive.

The realization opened a gaping hole in her heart. It didn't matter that it was irrational. Her memories were a stronger force, pushing away everything until there was nothing but a deep anguish, one that ought to have been extinguished with Imad. But the flame had not gone out; it smoldered somewhere inside her, screaming, *What if, what if?*

"Loulie," Qadir said softly.

"I've heard enough for the night." She felt hollow. Drained. "We'll speak more tomorrow." Her words had the finality of an executioner's ax. The quiet persisted into their halfhearted meal. Later, the prince and Aisha took their conversation outside, leaving her alone with Qadir.

Neither of them spoke. Not until Loulie was ready to sleep and Qadir reached out and touched her shoulder as she was limping away. "I apologize," he said. "It was selfish of me to only ever want to be Qadir in your eyes." Gently, he squeezed her shoulder. "Thank you for fighting so hard to reclaim my dagger in the ruins."

He exhaled softly, then slid his hand off her shoulder. "I managed to save this as well." He tapped something at his hip: a familiar scuffed-up scabbard. Loulie's heart jumped into her throat at the sight of it. Imad had not mentioned the blade when his ghouls investigated the hole.

As he always did, Qadir read the question in her expression. "I hid the blade in the desert before I infiltrated the ruins." He shook his head. "You have taken care of my dagger all these years; it is only natural I would protect a gift from you in the same way."

Loulie had no words. Even if she had, she would not have been able to speak, tight as her throat was. So she said nothing when Qadir offered her a feeble smile and said, "Tomorrow, when I have regained more of my power, let me heal your injuries?"

All she managed was a nod before she turned away, eyes burning with unshed tears.

When she did finally sleep, her rest was plagued by nightmares.

50

MAZEN

Mazen rose with the sun. After hours of trying and failing to fall asleep in the freezing cave without any blankets, he moved to the mouth of the cave to watch the sunrise. The sky was beautiful, clear of clouds and painted in hues of blue and gold. He imagined those colors stretched across the desert sky like a tapestry, pictured his father, hands clasped behind his back, a soft smile on his face, watching this same sunrise from his palace balcony.

The sultan had always been most amiable before sunrise; Mazen liked to think it was because he had yet to don the mask he presented in court. Sometimes, when his father had been in a particularly good mood, he'd told Mazen stories. Stories about Amir, the first sultan, and his brother, Ghazi, the first qaid.

Mazen slumped against the cave wall. He missed that version of his father.

"Sabah al-khair." He startled as Aisha stepped into the sunlight, looking amazingly well rested for someone who had been dead and resurrected the day before. "Since you're up early, do you want to go hunting with me?"

Mazen cringed. Yesterday he had watched ghouls maul a hare to death. It had not been "hunting" so much as a distraction. He hadn't realized until later that Aisha had wanted to draw him away from Qadir, whom she'd sensed coming. Maybe she had wanted to give the jinn and the merchant time to work out whatever rift had grown between them.

Mazen darted a glance over his shoulder. Loulie and Qadir lay on opposite sides of the cave, backs turned to each other. It seemed Aisha's plan had failed.

"Come." Aisha grabbed his wrist and pulled him outside.

Mazen groaned as he rubbed at his eyes. "I thought I had a choice?"

"No. I just thought I'd give you the option before I forced you into it."

And so they "hunted" once more, taking two ghouls with them and venturing into the desert to look for prey. Mazen wrapped his arms around himself in a useless effort to fight the chill. It was warmer outside beneath the light of the rising sun, but only marginally so. He was envious of Aisha, who didn't seem to feel the cold at all in her tattered cloak.

The two of them followed the ghouls until a familiar, unnatural silence fell upon the desert. Mazen halted in place. This same thing had happened last night when the ghouls spotted an animal. At first, he had been convinced he and Aisha were their target, that whatever strange magic Aisha had gained from the ifrit had finally turned against her. But then the ghouls had brought back a hare, and Mazen had nearly sobbed with relief.

He and Aisha watched the ghouls climb a distant rock formation until they disappeared. They stood together in tense silence, waiting. Yesterday, Mazen had feared a possessed Aisha would bring him out into the desert and murder him. But thus far the Queen of Dunes had responded to him with exasperation, not violence. Mazen hoped it stayed that way.

Unbidden, he found his eyes wandering to the scars on Aisha's arms, nothing but a flash of gray beneath her cloak. She caught his gaze and raised a finger. "My face is up here, Prince."

Mazen flushed. "Sorry, I was just looking at—"

"My scars, I know. You are always too curious for your own good."

She crossed her arms and shifted her gaze to the Sandsea. Mazen took one look at the ocean of ever-shifting sand and turned away, perturbed by its calmness. So much had happened in those sinking ruins—events he knew would be branded into his memory for the rest of his life.

He could not forget, so he did the next best thing: he attempted to distract himself by asking a question. "How does it work? This deal between you and the Queen of Dunes?"

Aisha's eyes snapped back to him. "That's *Resurrectionist*—" She cut herself off to glare at her feet, jaw clenched. Gradually, the tension eased from her body. "We're still working it out. The deal was that I offer her my body in exchange for my life."

"So she occasionally controls your movements?"

"No. But her thoughts—those are more difficult to untangle from my own."

There was another beat of silence. Mazen did not bring up the sharp smiles he had seen slip onto her face, or the uncharacteristic gestures he had noticed yesterday. Instead he said, "And what have you gained from this deal? Besides, ah, your life?"

"Other than an inner voice that never shuts up? The ability to command a bunch of undead brutes, apparently." Every word was sharp, bitter.

Mazen wasn't sure whether to offer an apology or a consolation. He mused quietly on his response until Aisha looked up, and—perhaps it was a trick of the light, but her expression seemed to soften. "I chose this fate for myself, Prince; I do not need your pity."

His heart sank. *Sympathy is not pity*, he wanted to say.

Not for the first time, he wondered at the thief's jaded infallibility. *We all start as cowards*, she had told him in the ruins. But it was hard to imagine she had ever been craven. The only time he had seen her falter, when she had been desperate for help—

It took a great deal of effort to shove aside the memory of the knife cutting through her throat and to quiet his reeling mind. Thankfully, the return of sound to the desert scattered his thoughts. He looked up as the ghouls returned, carrying...another hare.

His stomach grumbled dejectedly.

Aisha raised a brow. "What, were you expecting a jackal? A wolf?"

"No expectations." He sighed. "But I was hopeful."

About an hour after they'd left, they made their way back to the cave. The sun had fully risen by the time they turned back, casting the landscape in a hazy, dusty light that blurred the distant dunes. Gentle winds brushed against their ankles, disturbing scrubby grasses and rippling the sand. It wasn't the worst weather to travel in, but Mazen found it difficult to be relieved when he was so exhausted.

When they returned to the cave, they found the merchant standing outside, waiting for them. Aisha chuckled—the soft, breathy sound he'd heard yesterday. "Ah, the miracle of jinn blood. So you can walk now?"

"Well enough," Loulie said stiffly. Mazen eyed her stance. From the way she was leaning against the wall, it was evident she was trying to keep the weight off her ankles. Mazen remembered his own injury. How, even healed, it had pained him for days. And he'd been able to *rest*.

Aisha brushed past Loulie with the hare slung over her shoulder. "Such a prideful creature you are. I recommend staying off your feet at least until I finish preparing the food." She disappeared into the cave. Loulie remained leaning stubbornly against the cave wall.

A thought occurred to Mazen as Qadir joined them outside.

"We have no horses." They stared at him. He cleared his throat and said, "How are we going to get to Ghiban without horses?"

Qadir was clearly unimpressed. "You have two legs, don't you?"

Mazen blinked. *These people are insane. We can't cover that distance on foot!*

As it turned out, they could and they did. Mazen just hated every moment of it.

With provisions, the two-day journey would not have been so awful. But trudging through the desert in his own body, wearing nothing but his brother's ill-fitting clothing, was a harrowing experience. The first day, none of them spoke. Talking only made Mazen more aware of how much the cold air dried his lungs, so he walked in silence, trying all the while to ignore the exhaustion weighing down his limbs.

The compass, at least, was a blessing. When it wasn't guiding them down the most painless path to Ghiban, it abruptly changed direction to alert them to the presence of game and water. The former, Aisha "hunted" with her ghouls. The water, they found mostly in cacti and plants, which Loulie chopped into with her knife and drained with a cloth. They had no waterskins to store the liquid in, so they drank as much as they could before moving on.

Even when the sun set and the moon rose, they pushed forward. Without any shelter to protect them from the frigid winds, they had to keep moving to conserve warmth. It was only in the morning, when the sun rose, that they drowsed.

The second day, Mazen woke to find Aisha roasting lizards over the fire while Qadir shared news that he'd found a creek nearby. After their sad meal, they followed Qadir to the water source and used it to refresh themselves and sate their thirst. Everyone was in a better mood when they returned to the journey. Aisha was even humming—that awful song the Resurrectionist had sung in Ahmed's diwan.

Loulie turned in her saddle. "That song," she snapped. "What is it?"

Aisha paused. "An old lullaby from Dhahab. When I am lost in the world of the dead, it brings me back to the present." She glanced at Qadir. "He knows it as well."

"I was not lying about the song being from Dhahab," Qadir said softly.

Loulie looked down at the sand and said nothing.

Gradually, the dunes disappeared, replaced with looming cliffs that glowed like fire beneath the sun. A rocky pathway revealed itself, and the sand became littered with red stones. Mazen, who had never seen such a landscape before, was in awe.

"Your mouth is hanging open." He turned to see the merchant

walking beside him. Her face was pale, and sweat dampened her brow. He wanted to ask if she was all right, but it was a foolish question.

"I've never been to this part of the desert before," he said.

"No? Is that why you're here, taking your brother's place?" She frowned. "To sightsee?"

Mazen grimaced. He'd been mentally preparing himself for this conversation since they set out, but now he was at a loss for words. "It's complicated," he finally mumbled.

The merchant narrowed her eyes. "Then we'll stop. We need to talk."

So on the merchant's command, they made one last stop, settling into a cave hollowed into one of the cliffs. Mazen unwound the scarves from around his face, spat sand out of his mouth, and talked. He settled on the truth, bareboned as it was. He had been blackmailed because of his own cowardice. He was going on this journey because his brother had important security-related business in Madinne, and the sultan did not know, because, of course, he would never have allowed it.

He expected the merchant to scream at him when it was over. To grab him by his tunic and shake him until his teeth rattled. Instead, she shook her head and said, "You're a fool."

Mazen blinked. "I'll admit I was lacking in foresight, maybe, but—"

"You think your brother would send you on this quest so he could stay behind and implement *security* measures?" She scoffed.

Mazen felt something inside of him fray. "What do you know about my brother?"

"I know he's a murderer."

"And? You don't seem to mind the blood on Ahmed bin Walid's hands."

The merchant froze, eyes wide, body trembling. When she next spoke, her voice was a lethal whisper. "How dare you compare your brother to the wali of Dhyme. Ahmed did not give the order to kill a tribe of humans for a godsdamned *relic*."

Mazen recoiled. Aisha had told him about this in the ruins; how had he forgotten? *Because Omar is family*, he thought. *And with family, we always try to forget.*

But how did Loulie know? Why would Imad tell her that story unless...? He stared at her. She was breathing fast in that way a person did when they were holding back tears.

...Unless that had been her tribe.

He swallowed. "Loulie, I'm—"

"Sorry? Your apologies are meaningless to me, Prince. I have no reason to trust your sincerity when you have been lying to me this entire time." She turned her glare on Aisha. "And *you*. I trust you even less, whoever the hell you are. A thief, the Resurrectionist—either way, you're a cold-blooded killer."

She rose and limped out of the cave.

"Leave her be," Qadir said sharply when Mazen began to rise. "Or do you plan to tail her like a hound even now?" Something flickered in his eyes—something that may have been fire.

Mazen deflated. What else did he have to offer besides apologies, empty as they were to her? He could not even give her answers. He looked at Aisha, who shrugged beneath his gaze. "Don't look at me. I don't know Omar's mind. But..." She raised a brow. "Your father sent us on a similarly perilous quest. Sometimes power requires sacrifice."

Mazen glared at her. "It's not worth it if that power requires *others* to be sacrificed."

Aisha's lips quirked into a sardonic smile. "You truly do not know how to think like a prince, do you?" She laughed, and her voice took on the softness he'd come to associate with the Queen of Dunes. "Our world isn't built on morals. Humans, jinn—we're all selfish creatures. Your brother sought power, so he put others' necks on the line for it. It's the way of the world."

Mazen bristled. "And possessing an innocent man and killing his friends—that's the way of the world too?"

Aisha scowled. "If by 'innocent man and friends' you mean murderers who slaughter jinn for no reason, then yes." She never broke eye contact as she stood. "I would even go so far as to say that killing them is justice," she said coldly, and then she walked away.

Qadir tilted his head. "You are very adept at digging yourself into holes, Prince." He rose with a sigh. "I still do not trust you, but I trust your brother less. I do not know what he is plotting, but know this." His eyes darkened with smoke. "If your family tries to harm Loulie, I will sink your city. And if you breathe a single word of my history to them..." He smiled. An unfeeling smile that sent a shudder down Mazen's spine. "I will personally make you regret it."

The deadly promise hung in the air, thick as the smoke clouding the ifrit's eyes as he exited the cave. Mazen had to force himself to follow. *He* had chosen this, and he had no choice but to see this hellish journey through.

After that, it did not take them long to reach the road to Ghiban. Aisha banished the ghouls with a command as they stepped onto the dirt path, disintegrating them into sand with a snap of her fingers. Mazen was unsure whether he ought to be relieved or nervous that Aisha could so easily control the queen's magic.

His anxiety dampened somewhat as they joined other journeyers on the main road. After days of isolated travel, it was a relief to see other people. Mazen felt more at ease amongst the crowds. The merchant, on the other hand, was forced to doff her starry layers. She looked smaller without them, reduced to a plain tunic, a pair of trousers, and shoes that were so dusty they looked more brown than gold.

They meandered through cliffs and up rocky inclines until they came to the city. Spires and domes made of stone stretched across a rocky plateau lush with vibrant gardens and crystal blue lakes. The city sat in the center of a small valley, surrounded on three sides by waterfalls that emptied into the settlement's surrounding silver rivers, which glowed beneath the moonlight.

Mazen managed a soft, awed exhale.

Finally, they had arrived at Ghiban.

The final city before the lamp.

51

LOULIE

Unlike in Madinne or Dhyme, where nature was reserved for the elite, Ghiban was chock-full of natural delights. Even the steep decline into the city was filled with green; sunflowers peeked out between cliffs, yellow grasses sprouted between cracks in the ground, and wooden lanterns woven through with flowers hung above them, illuminating the pathway. This high, one could see all the city districts: plots of land divided by streams and connected by bridges.

It was beautiful. So beautiful it made Loulie's heart ache. For this natural beauty, like the rest, had been born of jinn blood. Stories were told of the battle that had waged on these cliffs between the humans and the marid, the fabled wish-granting jinn said to have remained in the human world after their cities sank into the Sandsea.

Loulie's mother had told her the story once: after many years of being taken advantage of, the marid revolted against the humans, positioning themselves at the tops of the cliffs so they could call down waterfalls to crush the human army in the valley. But the humans were ruthless; they employed thousands of men as a distraction, sacrificing them to the marid's magic to buy the rest of them time to scale the cliffs from the other side.

Legend had it that after slaughtering the marid, the humans hung their corpses from the tops of the cliffs, and there had been so much silver blood running down the rocks, it had transformed into a cascading stream of water. Sometimes, when Loulie stared hard at the streams winding around the city, she thought they glittered like stardust.

It was beautiful, and it was horrible.

The path led down into Ghiban's main souk, a space made up of small brick and stone shops with outdoor displays and stalls. Loulie turned toward the crowds littering the square. She normally detested packs of people, but now she slipped gratefully into the hordes, wanting to put as much distance between herself and the others as she could. Mostly, she sought to escape from Qadir, who was constantly watching her with that beseeching gaze. She would not, *could* not, talk to him. Because the moment she did, she would remember the past. She would remember her own uselessness. And she would unravel.

She bit down on her lip as a surge of self-pity gripped her. These damned emotions would be the end of her. The world descended into a palimpsest of blotchy colors without her permission, pressing in as she elbowed her way through throngs of people.

"Layla!"

Merchants shoved jewelry in her face; marketgoers smiled at her beneath the shadows of their hoods. She bumped into a man. A pickpocket. He apologized even as he snuck a hand into her pocket.

"Layla!"

She slapped his hand away, tried to pretend she was angry. But the realization was there, unavoidable: *There's nothing for him to steal.* Her heart sank.

"Layla!" She felt a hand on her shoulder and swatted it away on instinct. She realized belatedly that it belonged to the prince. She opened her mouth to yell at him—and stopped.

He'd remembered to use her name. The one she donned when she entered the souk as a customer. It was meant to be a shield, so why did his saying it aloud make her want to cry?

"Should I call you something else?" He eyed her warily as he rubbed his hand.

"No." She inhaled sharply, hating how small her voice was. "What do you want?"

"Mostly, I want to know where we're going."

"An inn." Saying it aloud gave her a goal to keep her focused. But the calm was short lived, for when they finally made it to one, she realized they had no gold. The panic had just returned when Aisha slammed a fistful of coins on the table.

"You forget I'm a thief," she said by way of explanation. She set a hand on the prince's shoulder and steered him away, through the inn's tavern and into the single corridor where the guest rooms were located. The prince glanced over his shoulder. Loulie flinched at the pity on his face. She hated him, this lying prince who pretended to have a heart of gold. But mostly, she hated herself for inspiring that sympathy in him.

"I'm going to the hammam," she said to Qadir, and left before he could stop her.

The nearest communal hammam was a spacious place, a collection of smaller chambers filled with medium-sized baths carved directly into the stone floors. The last time Loulie had been here, it had been packed with women meeting for some weekly gathering. She was relieved to see that crowd was absent today; she wouldn't have been able to carry on a conversation even if she'd tried.

She stored her clothes at the vestibule, passed the first bathing chamber—she was keen on avoiding the laughing women inside—and made her way to the middle archway, wherein lay the chamber with the most amiable temperature, neither too cold nor too hot. The room smelled of jasmine and was dimly lit with lanterns placed at every corner of the bath. Some of the tension eased from Loulie's limbs as she slid into the water and closed her eyes.

For a time, her mind was blissfully blank.

She did not know how long she sat there before she opened her eyes and noticed the ceiling vents had been opened to let in air. Gazing up at the starry sky, she was reminded of how long the day—the journey—had been. And it was at that point the memories she had been trying to suppress surfaced. Tentatively, she began to sift through them.

Nine years ago, Qadir had lost a compass in the desert. A compass that had been found by her father. A group of thieves had tracked down the jinn searching for that compass and had killed her tribe to protect the secret of that quest. The jinn—*ifrit*—had killed them and taken her under his wing. For redemption, he'd told her, but how was she to know that was the full truth, when he'd kept so many things from her?

But what was most painful to her was not the lies. It was the truth.

That her tribe had been nothing but collateral damage. That all these years, the person who had ordered her parents dead had been hiding behind gilded doors. And now she was traveling with his brother and working for his father.

She was trapped, and there wasn't a godsdamned thing she could do about it.

She did not realize there were tears rolling down her cheeks until ripples spread on the surface of the bathwater. She let herself cry without reservation. Because she was alone, and there was no one there to see her shatter.

It was a testament to the extremity of her grief, she thought, that her mind wandered to Ahmed bin Walid. What she wouldn't give to be in his company now. Dancing in his diwan, conversing in his courtyard—it didn't matter. When she was with Ahmed, she was able to forget her reputation and insecurities. At least, for a time.

That was the problem with respites; they were temporary. Flimsy dreams at best.

And yet Loulie still found herself yearning for the quiet comfort that washed over her when she sat with Ahmed in his diwan. She wished, in that moment, that she lived a simpler life. One where she was not so scared of losing other people.

It was unfortunate that wishes, like dreams, were imaginary.

Later, when Loulie dried her tears and returned to the inn, her and Qadir's room was empty. Save for the few relics she had on her, along with Qadir's shamshir, which was leaning against the wall by the bed, they had no belongings left. There was, however, a lone lantern sitting atop the desk, flickering with a soft blue light.

Loulie fell onto her bed without acknowledging it. The fire was unoffended. It never wavered, never burned out, and never stopped watching over her.

52

MAZEN

Mazen was blinking sleep out of his eyes when Aisha threw a bundle of garments at him. "You look like you've been rolling in the dirt," she said by way of greeting.

"Sabah al-khair to you too," he mumbled as he looked at the clothing: a pair of cheap trousers and a shirt. There was even cloth for him to fashion into a ghutra. He looked up at Aisha, who had already washed and changed. He was surprised to see she had not covered her arms; both her scars and the faded henna overlaying them were visible. A scarf was wrapped loosely around her head, draping her features in shadow. Mazen could barely tell her eyes were different colors.

"Let me guess." He held up the tunic. "Thieving?"

She shrugged. "The merchants won't miss them. Now yalla, go wash up. We don't have all day."

Mazen stared at her. "We're not leaving already, are we? We just got here."

"What, you think we can continue our journey without horses and equipment?" She snorted. "I'll be sure to tell your brother it was your own stupidity that killed you."

"Is it necessary to always throw my words back at me?"

She leaned against the wall, crossed her arms. "It is when you say foolish things."

She didn't tail him when he left in search of the men's hammam. Mazen found it not far from the inn, in a simple building tucked into a corner of the cliffs. Bathing there was... strange.

This was mostly because, having his own personal bathing chamber in the palace, he'd never bathed in the company of other men. It was a profoundly peculiar experience, one that made him acutely aware of how unmuscular he was. And yet it was a relief not being in his brother's body. Being *himself.* It was only as he was dressing that he remembered what that meant.

He had lost the bangle. An ancient, priceless artifact enchanted by an ifrit.

A sudden, terrible weight crashed down on him, making him stumble in place. He had felt the loss of it before but had not realized how monumental it was until now, standing there half naked in his own body. Omar's body had been armor. Even though he was certain he didn't have to worry about being recognized in Ghiban, he still felt vulnerable.

But maybe I do not need *to be myself.* Without her merchant robes, Loulie was Layla. And without his royal ornaments, he'd been Yousef.

Yousef. The name tasted like harmless escapades and lofty dreams. This identity, at least, was a character he felt comfortable playing. He decided he would use it here. He returned to the inn, found Aisha in the tavern, and told her this.

She snorted. "Amazing how even now you have your head in the clouds." She stood and walked toward the door. "Come, let's find a chai shop."

He followed after her. "What about the merchant?"

As if he'd summoned her, Loulie al-Nazari stepped out from the crowds, dressed in simple attire. She had draped a shawl loosely over her unruly curls, which were a fuzzy halo around her face.

"I'm coming with you." Her voice, hard like steel, brooked no argument. She strode ahead of them, Qadir nowhere to be seen.

They followed her past tiered wooden houses and quaint shops, through patches of flower-strewn greenery populated by citizens enjoying the cool, crisp weather. Mazen was envious of their non-chalance, of their bright smiles and carefree laughter.

He glanced at the burbling streams running past them and thought of silver blood. Of Qadir, run through with a dozen knives. Of Aisha, bleeding to death in ancient ruins. Dead, both of them. Or so he'd thought. But here they both stood, revived with magic he didn't understand. What would his father say if he knew he was traveling with ifrit?

He would have tried to kill them long ago.

Mazen suppressed a sigh as they reached the souk outskirts, where early-rising workers huddled in groups, venting about their mundane problems beneath shaded canopies and inside small shops. Mazen noted the shops' impressive outdoor displays: tables show-casing everything from vibrant fabrics to glazed plates to rows of spice-filled tins. Because it was still early in the day and many of the displays were yet unsupervised, the city guard was out patrolling the square, on the lookout for overeager customers with slippery fingers.

The three of them passed by the still-quiet shops and made their way toward a chai shop with an outdoor patio. There, they settled at a table and ordered pita, hummus, and a platter of olives with their remaining pilfered gold.

"I want to be clear about something," the merchant said after their server delivered the plates. She ripped off a piece of steaming bread and tossed it into her mouth with a grimace. "I may be obligated to go on this journey, but I refuse to finish it blindly." Her bright eyes, so much like shards of fire, darted between them. "I want answers." It was an effort not to balk beneath her gaze. "I'll start with you, Prince. Tell me what happened nine years ago with Imad."

She was glaring at him, and yet—surely this was a step toward forgiveness, if she trusted him to provide truthful answers? Though there was not much to tell, Mazen eagerly shared what he knew. Nine years ago, he'd been only thirteen, and he could not remem-ber Omar's orders. Nor could he remember the supposed sparring match between Imad and Omar. But he knew what Aisha had told him and what his father had said.

"My father always claimed his thieves died in a freak accident," Mazen said. "That they fought a terrible jinn and did not survive. I never knew about Imad. And..." He hesitated. "I never knew there had been so many casualties. Not until Aisha told me."

They both glanced at Aisha, who shrugged. "All I know about the incident is that Omar was desperate to get his hands on a jinn king's relic, and he was willing to do whatever it took to obtain it. As you can see, the thieves he sent to kill the ifrit failed. He has not gone to such extremes again." She raised a brow. "I doubt he knows you survived, al-Nazari."

If he did, you would not be here were the unspoken words.

Something occurred to Mazen then. Something he hadn't thought of before. "How did Omar locate the relic—or, ah, Qadir— in the first place? How did he know where to send his thieves?"

Aisha opened her mouth—and closed it, a quizzical look passing over her features. *She doesn't know*, he thought with amazement.

The merchant scoffed. "Yet another question I intend to ask him when we return to Madinne." She stared hard between the two of them. "I hope you didn't plan on using me to find the lamp only to throw me into the Sandsea. Because I refuse to die by your hands."

Mazen balked. "Of course not!"

But the moment he said the words, he realized he had no way of knowing. Clearly, his father had not cared for her safety. He'd hired her for her tracking skills. Her compass.

The merchant looked unconvinced, but she did not linger on the subject. Instead, she turned the conversation back to Imad. "When I cut Imad in the ruins, there was..." She faltered. "Ink under his skin. Or black blood?" She eyed them suspiciously. "Why?"

Mazen sighed. He had not been able to watch Loulie al-Nazari hack the thief to pieces, but he'd seen the black blood. The bangle's side effects, revealed. When he told the merchant this, she crossed her arms and said, "I've never heard of such a thing." She paused, glanced at Mazen's shadow. "But I guess there's still a lot I don't understand about jinn magic."

She asked about his shadow last. It was a gratefully straightforward story. Afterward, the merchant sighed and said, "It was wise of the jinn to make your shadow her relic; it kept her magic out of your brother's hands."

Mazen paused. He had not thought of it that way before. But now he remembered that his father and Omar *had* been looking for something in the diwan. A relic they never found.

Silence hung between them after that, broken only by the crunch of bread and the aggressive clatter of the women's chai cups every time they set them down on plates. As was his habit, Mazen filled the silence the only way he knew how: with conversation.

"I'd like to start again, on a new scroll." He put a hand to his chest and flashed what he hoped was a sincere smile. It had been so long since he'd worn his *own* smile that he half worried it had become permanently crooked, like Omar's. "I'd like to reintroduce myself. My name is Mazen, and I am—"

"A liar." Loulie scowled.

Aisha glanced at his shadow. "The Prince of Darkness?"

Mazen paled. "What? Why?"

"You have a magic shadow and often lurk in dark corridors."

"But Prince of Darkness makes me sound like a villain!"

Aisha smirked, and the merchant—it was only for a few seconds, but she smiled. Not a smirk, not a sneer, but a genuine twitch of her lips.

"I thought you were going by Yousef?" Aisha said.

Mazen's smile turned sheepish. "I am. I think it's a good idea in the cities, at least."

The merchant's expression softened enough that the dent between her brows relaxed and faded. It seemed ages since he'd introduced himself to her as Yousef.

"Well then, *Yousef* Merchant." Aisha set down her empty cup and stood. "I'm going to see if I can 'acquire' some more equipment. The least you can do is gather enough coin to purchase horses."

It was a task much easier in theory than in practice. Mazen had never done a day of honest work in his life, and Loulie was accustomed to selling merchandise, not skills. It was unsurprising that they didn't find jobs that suited either of them.

Mazen's mood only dampened when, while searching for employment, they stumbled upon information from Madinne. Loulie was visibly relieved when they learned Ahmed bin Walid had been declared innocent of his crimes and was staying in the palace as a guest. Mazen could not help but be anxious. Ahmed had noticed him wearing the relic in Dhyme; would he be able to pick apart Omar's disguise when he saw that same bangle?

He was still brooding over the possibility when day faded to night. They were wandering through the heart of the souk when his rumination gave way to inspiration; he spotted a storyteller—marked as such by his ornate cane, which depicted carvings of various mythical beasts—sitting under the shade of a cloth canopy and telling stories to a fascinated crowd.

Mazen stopped to watch him, to admire the flutter of his hands through the air and the fluidity of his shifting expression. When the story was over, the old storyteller bowed, and his audience leaned forward to drop coins into a tin can.

Loulie nudged him. "Prince?"

He smiled. "I have an idea."

It was a small, humble idea that, less than an hour later, became a small and humble reality. Mazen charmed a stall owner into letting him borrow a dusty rug while the merchant "borrowed" one of the lanterns hanging from the date trees around the souk.

She set the lantern down in front of him as he seated himself on the rug. "A lantern for ambiance?" He flashed a smile at her. "What a great idea."

"It was Qadir's idea. He wants to help you."

Mazen turned, half expecting the bodyguard to be standing behind him, but the sullen ifrit was nowhere to be seen. He looked quizzically at the merchant, who pointed at the lantern. He followed her gaze to its base.

A small black lizard with gleaming red eyes blinked up at him.

"Qadir can shapeshift," she said. When Mazen continued staring, she sighed and said, "He rides on my shoulder sometimes. It's less conspicuous."

Without warning, the ifrit lizard scrambled up Mazen's leg and arm until he was sitting on his shoulder. "I'm doing this for Loulie," he said in a voice so soft it sounded as if it were coming from inside Mazen's head. But the gruffness—Mazen startled at the memory of it. He remembered this voice. It had spoken to him during his first encounter with the shadow jinn, had pulled him out of his trance.

So Qadir had been with her then.

"I thought I was crazy," Mazen mumbled.

"Because you are. A sane man wouldn't have gone on this journey," Qadir said.

He frowned. "That's not—"

The merchant hissed between her teeth. "Stop. You look like you're talking to yourself." She reached down to wrap the tail end of his ghutra around his shoulders and mouth. The ifrit immediately tucked himself away into the folds. "There. Now you at least look mysterious." She stepped back, arms crossed. "But mysterious doesn't sell. How are you going to make coin without a reputation? No one's heard of Yousef the Storyteller."

"*Yet.* But they will." He grinned at the surprise that flickered across her expression. He may have been a man of few talents, but storytelling was in his blood.

"Can you manipulate the fire?" Mazen whispered to the ifrit.

A flame burst to life inside the lantern, glowing red and blue and green and yellow. Mazen considered it. And then he smiled. "Here's what I want you to do..."

It began with a clap. With a bright smile he flashed at passersby.

He clapped again, and the fire in the lantern flickered.

A third time, and it flashed white.

A fourth time, and the flame darkened to the murky blue of the deep ocean. Some of the citizens paused to inspect the mysterious fire.

On the fifth clap, the flame dimmed to a green that cast the area in deep shadows. Quite the crowd had gathered by then. A young boy pushed his way through it and pointed at the lantern, mouth hanging open. "How are you making it do that?"

"What, this?" Mazen lifted the lantern, looked at it for a long moment, then blew onto the glass. The audience stared in awe as the fire inside disappeared—and then roared back to life. They cheered, as if he'd performed some magic trick.

He lifted the lantern with a flourish. "Behold! This is no ordinary fire." The blaze dimmed further, so that his audience was cloaked in darkness. "This is an immortal flame, crafted by none other than the Jinn King of Fire."

Qadir scoffed in his ear. "Such pretty lies you spin."

But Mazen did not think it was a lie at all. To him, stories were truths painted over in gold.

He set the lantern down. "Neither here nor there, but long ago..."

The first story he told was of the so-called King of Fire, who was so fearsome he could burn anything, even the sand on which they stood. But the King of Fire was not without a heart, and he fell in love with a human, a girl who dressed in stars. The king loved her dearly. So dearly that upon his death, he ordered the girl to bottle his flame so he could watch over her always. The girl honored him by gifting his fire to her descendants and having them tend it forever.

"And it is that same fire you see before you."

When the story was over, the audience clapped and cheered. Mazen grew drunk on their adulation. He forgot about the gold. He forgot about everything but the tales, which he told well into the night. He told them stories about the Hemarat al-Gayla, the fearful donkey creature that devoured children who strayed too far from home in the heat of the day; of Bu Darya, a fish-man who drew his prey into the ocean by pretending to be a drowning human; and of the firebird, the majestic bird that trailed streaks of flame through the sky.

Loulie al-Nazari spoke in between the stories, holding out a pouch of silk and proclaiming, "The storyteller Yousef has traveled far and wide to share these stories with you! They are rare and precious, like relics. But every treasure has a value measurable in coin..."

They were a good team, he and Loulie. She knew how to pull in the crowds, and he knew how to keep them. Their audience remained enthralled even as the souk darkened and merchants began to pack their goods. By that time, those who remained were drowsy but expectant, lingering to see if he would tell another story.

Loulie caught his eye. *One more?* she mouthed.

Mazen considered. If this was to be the last one, he needed to make it impactful. The late-night tales were always the stories that lingered longest in a listener's memory.

An idea snapped into place so suddenly it was as if it had always been there. Mazen had traveled with legends and watched stories come to life on this journey, but he had done it all while living a lie in Omar's skin. Now, though, he was no longer his brother, and he was free to tell his own truths. Free to breathe life into his *own* history.

Most of his family's stories were secrets. But there was one tale everyone knew, one whose details had been ingrained in Mazen's heart since he was a child: a part of his family history, compressed into a fiction and made legend. One he knew better than anyone else.

"If there is to be only one more tale tonight, let it be the one about the storyteller who changed her fate with her fables. Let it be a story about stories and the power they have to sway mortal hearts." Mazen smiled. He clasped his hands and began to tell them his last story.

His mother's story.

The Tale of Shafia

Neither here nor there, but not so long ago...

There lived a Bedouin storyteller named Shafia, who was known for her near-perfect memory and evocative performances. Beautiful, bright-eyed, and wise beyond her years, she was said to have the perfect anecdote for any situation. Her reputation was so widespread that even those in the cities knew of her talent. This was how word of her came to reach the sultan's wazir, who traveled for seven days and seven nights to meet with her. When he came to her tribe's land, he prostrated himself before the sheikh and pleaded for an audience.

Shafia met with the wazir in her guest tent and bade him to tell her his woes. He shared with her a disturbing tale: his once-benevolent sultan was afflicted with a grief so profound it clouded his judgment. He had lost his first wife to childbirth and his second to betrayal, and ever since killing her in punishment, he suspected every woman plotted to shame him.

"Every week since the second wife's murder, he calls for a new woman to be brought to him," the wazir said. "And at the end of every week, he accuses her of some slight and kills her." He pressed his forehead to the ground and spoke humbly: "They say you have mended broken hearts and charmed beasts with your stories, wise storyteller. So I beseech you: tell me how to calm His Majesty's unnatural rage."

Shafia considered. Then she said, "There is a truth to every story, and I have not yet discerned this one. I will meet with your sultan and speak with him myself."

The wazir frantically shook his head. "The only way to meet with the sultan now is to consent to be his wife. You will not survive the week!"

Shafia simply smiled at him. "Loyal wazir, one cannot know the outcome of a journey if one is not brave enough to take it." And so saying, she went to prepare for her departure.

Her family despaired at her decision. They tried to convince her to stay, claiming she had little to gain and much to lose. But Shafia was resolute, so there was nothing to do but honor her courage and pray for her safety as she rode out with the wazir. Seven days and seven nights passed before they came to Madinne's gates, and then the wazir guided her into the city and to the palace, where the sultan sat upon his throne.

"I have brought a legend before you, Your Majesty," said the wazir. "A storyteller named Shafia, who has a request of you."

Shafia bowed. "I would ask the honor of being your wife, Your Majesty."

The sultan's surprise was second to his suspicion, but he none-theless agreed to the storyteller's request. He warily welcomed Shafia into his palace and had sad-eyed servants dress her in the richest robes and purest golds. They attended to her every need until the end of the week, at which point the sultan called her to his chambers. No woman had survived this encounter with him, but Shafia was unafraid as she entered his room.

"I have a question for you," he said when she arrived. "Will you answer it truthfully?"

"You have my word, Your Majesty."

"Then tell me: Why did you offer yourself to me?"

Shafia thought for a few moments, and then she said, "Have you heard the story of the haughty merchant who woke to become king for three days? Much like he believed himself to be hallucinating, I too thought I was dreaming when the wazir sought me out. How could I not be compelled to follow him to your palace and seek out the truth when given the opportunity?"

The sultan hissed in anger. "You told me you would answer my question, but instead you speak in riddles! Continue like this and you will pay for your deceit with your life."

It was just as the wazir had said. The sultan had found some bizarre fault with her and intended to kill her for it. But Shafia did not wilt against the unexpected threat. "My apologies, Your Majesty. As a storyteller, I draw most of my truths from allegory." She looked out the window to the sinking sun. "If you find it permissible, I would tell you the full tale before you take my life." The sultan hesitated but, in the end, bade Shafia to continue.

So it was that the storyteller told him the tale of the proud merchant and the shrewd king. In the story, a king overheard a merchant ridiculing his decrees and decided to play a trick on him. He commanded his servants to bring the merchant to his palace in the dead of night and to address him as king when he woke. At first the merchant believed he was living a dream, but he soon realized how difficult it was to rule. Eventually, the true king revealed himself to the merchant, and though he had originally meant to punish him for his gall, he instead decided to reward him for his mettle by making him his advisor.

"The merchant did not understand the king's true burden until he was given the opportunity to walk in his shoes," Shafia explained. "That is why I came when called—so that I might know the full story. But I must confess: I am nowhere near as wise as the merchant, who advised the king on various issues. There was, for instance, the matter of the conniving jinn who infiltrated the king's army..."

Shafia was clever, weaving one story into the next until the sun rose, at which point she paused. The sultan demanded she continue, for he wanted to know how the king would handle the jinn. But Shafia feigned fatigue and humbly asked if he would delay his judgment by one night so that she could refresh herself before concluding the tale. The great ruler thought to himself, *What is one more night?* and he agreed to her request. He had soldiers watch her the whole day until she returned that night. Again, she wove one story into another. In the next adventure, the king agreed to pardon the jinn for its scheming if it traveled with the merchant to find a relic—a wish-granting ring said to belong to a jinn king.

"And how did they unearth this ring from beneath the Sandsea?" the sultan asked.

Shafia gazed wistfully out the window. "Might I have one more night to finish the story, Your Majesty?"

And so it went. Every night the storyteller answered one question, provoked another, and asked for more time. Days passed into weeks and weeks into months, until the stories became conversations. The sultan asked Shafia for advice about policies and jinn, and she shared her wisdom in the form of fables. Soon everyone in the desert kingdom knew she had avoided death. It was only then, upon hearing the rumors, that the sultan realized he had fallen into the storyteller's trap. Worse, he realized he had fallen in love with her. Fearing he had doomed himself to another betrayal, he told himself he would gauge Shafia's loyalty by allowing her to speak on his behalf during his audiences.

But Shafia was as humble as she was wise. When bickering merchants, sobbing mothers, and aggrieved soldiers came asking for advice, she would say, "I am but a storyteller who draws my truths from allegory, whereas the sultan speaks from experience. I would never be so presumptuous as to offer counsel in his distinguished presence."

The deflection was as effective as it was flattering, for the sultan still deferred to Shafia's judgment when it came time to offer his verdicts. A year passed, and everyone rejoiced at the miracle of Shafia's stories. Everyone except for the sultan, who still harbored the lingering suspicion he had been played for a fool. He devised one final plan to save his heart. One night, as Shafia was about to drift off to sleep in his arms, he stole a knife off his bedside table and held it to her throat. "I have a question for you," he said. "Will you answer it truthfully?"

Shafia looked at him without flinching. "You have my word."

"Then tell me: Do you have a final wish before you face death?"

And Shafia responded, with tears in her eyes, "Do you remember the story about the merchant who woke to become king for three days? Once, I likened my situation to his. But I knew we were not the same. You see, I knew this was a dream all along, and that someday it would have to end." She set her hands atop his trembling ones and said, "Though I could never understand your burden, I beg you to remember my advice. I came to you because I wanted what is best for this kingdom. And I believe you do too. May you prosper, Your Majesty."

The sultan flung his dagger away with a cry. "I asked you for a wish but instead you wish *me* fortune! You foolish creature." He pressed his forehead to hers and said, "But I am the most foolish, for shielding myself with violence for so long. Forgive me, my love."

The two of them lay in each other's arms, mourning everything that had been lost. But on the morrow of the next day, there was hope. The sultan was a changed man, one who swore to redeem himself at the side of the storyteller who had saved his kingdom. For a time, the two of them ruled with compassion. But death, that great divider of love, comes for everyone. In the end, even our beloved storyteller met an untimely end.

But we must take heart! Though only the gods know how long we may live, we humans are the ones who decide when legacies die. Though Shafia is gone, her memory lives on through the lives she touched.

That, gentle friends, is the power a story has.

53

MAZEN

There was a fine line between being set free by the truth and being shackled by it. Having lived in a world of forced niceties and calculated sincerities his whole life, Mazen knew the dangers of honesty. And yet as he finished his story, he felt weightless in a way he never had before. There was a freedom to sharing the truth when others did not know it was his.

His heart lifted at the astonishment on his listeners' faces. His mother's story had always been a whispered tale threaded together by rumors. But now he had breathed life into it.

There was no applause this time. Instead, Mazen took his audience's overwhelming gratitude in the form of coin. When they asked him how he knew the tale, he told them a half truth: he had visited Madinne and spoken to the sultan himself. They believed him. Or at least, they were enchanted enough to *want* to believe him.

Triumph welled in his chest as his listeners walked off, but the feeling dissipated when he noticed Loulie squinting at him. "You didn't mention yourself in the story," she said.

He blinked at her, startled. "No, because that history is... mine."

His memories of his mother were not fodder for tales told in dark souks. They were precious, fragile, and he preferred to keep them hidden away like gems in a treasury.

Loulie shook her head. "That's not what I mean. You said that Shafia's memory lives on in the lives she touched, but you are the one who told that story. You ought to give yourself"—she raised a pointed brow—"Prince *Mazen* some credit for carrying on her legacy."

The acknowledgment made a soft warmth unfurl in Mazen's chest. He couldn't help the smile that curved his lips. "Next time, then."

The merchant turned away and reached for the silk pouch. She set it between them, then paused, her eyes flicking up to meet his. "I'm curious: How much of that story was true?"

His smile wavered. The truth was that his father had never explained why he'd killed so many women in cold blood. The *truth* was that his mother had never understood either.

It was as if he was possessed, she had once told him. He remembered the faraway look in her eyes when she'd spoken, the way she had tucked her hands into her sleeves as if fighting a chill. *But he was different when I told him the stories. Not suspicious, but thoughtful. Not angry, but regretful. He was himself when he was with me.*

His mother's account was the closest Mazen had ever come to the truth, but it was still only a small piece of it. Which was exactly what he told Loulie.

"This is just a facet of the history," he said. "A polished diamond shard. Only my father knows the full truth, and—I do not think the story would be quite so uplifting if he told it."

It pained him to say that, but it was an easy confession. The sultan was not a good man, but he was softer around the edges with Mazen. Perhaps that was why, even though Mazen had always feared his father, he loved him in spite of that terror.

"No, it would be a different story entirely." Loulie tilted her head, thoughtful. "And it wouldn't be nearly as lucrative as this version, I think."

Mazen smiled despite himself. "No, I suppose it wouldn't."

He shifted closer to help count the coins in their bag. Qadir, who had remained quiet on his shoulder this whole time, peeked his head out of Mazen's ghutra to eye the gold as they totaled it. Mazen was amazed at the final count. Though it was not enough to buy horses, they had earned it themselves, and it made him proud to count it.

"You make a good manager, Layla," he said.

He was surprised to see a triumphant smile on her face. Bright and honest and lovely. And then she *laughed*, and the sound made his stomach flop. "And you're a good storyteller," she said. "Though I do question the accuracy of that first tale you shared, about the King of Fire and the starry-eyed human."

Mazen flushed. "I had to think of something on the spot. Qadir seemed to like it."

"Hmph," Qadir said.

Loulie's smile vanished at the mention of the ifrit. Mazen immediately regretted bringing him up, but there was nothing he could do to bring back her smile. Though he tried to engage her in conversation many times as they were walking back to the inn, she no longer seemed in the mood for idle chatter.

He was able to ask her only one last thing before she and Qadir retired for the night: whether she would come and tell stories with him tomorrow.

The merchant considered. "You have more poignant family stories up your sleeve?"

Mazen's heart lifted. "No, but I'd like to think I know a few more lucrative ones."

She smiled vaguely. "Tomorrow, then."

Mazen smiled at her back as she turned away. "Tomorrow," he echoed.

—⁂—

But when tomorrow arrived, there was only Aisha, shaking him awake and insisting they grab iftar. After a meal of bread and za'atar, Mazen asked her where the merchant had gone. "Off with Qadir," she said with a shrug. "Apparently, there are rumors of treasure up on the cliffs. The merchant went to see if it was sellable."

Evidently, he couldn't hide his disappointment, because Aisha said, "The merchant told me about your storytelling adventures. Never fear. I will be your manager today."

"Don't you have things to steal?"

"Of course. But I can make time to watch you work." Her eyes sparkled with something like amusement. "I didn't even know you were capable of it."

As it turned out, "working" was a far cry from what Mazen did. Mostly, he sat there staring sullenly out into the souk, wondering how he was going to bring people to his space without a magic fire. It was harder to convince an audience to listen to stories in the heat of the day, harder to keep them interested when they had work and the surrounding merchants spoke so loudly they all but drowned out his thoughts. What he had to offer was hardly as enticing— or *material*—as the appetizing foods and eye-catching accessories being peddled around the souk.

Aisha looked severely unimpressed by him. Mazen did his best to ignore her until she sat down in front of him and said, "Tell me the story of the Queen of Dunes." Her lips were curved in that telltale way that told him it was not just Aisha sitting before him.

He hesitated. "The human version?"

"No, tell me *your* version. The one with the dune and the army of ghouls."

Mazen startled. Yesterday, he had shared a part of his family's history, but he had never thought to tell *his* stories. They hadn't been the most heroic adventures, but he supposed he'd lived through them, hadn't he?

And so, in a grandiose voice that carried across the alleys, he told her the story of Yousef the Adventurer, who had stumbled into the lair of the Queen of Dunes, the terrifying jinn king who commanded armies of ghouls.

"And so Yousef found himself in a glorious corridor! One that shone from floor to ceiling with beautiful mosaics. It seemed like something out of a dream. But alas! It was a place of nightmares..."

He did not remember when the crowd gathered, only that he

started hearing gasps and murmurs, and when he looked up, there was a group of marketgoers. His story became more exuberant in the presence of an audience.

"And he ran!" cried Mazen. "He ran and ran and ran as the sand crashed down around him and the ruins collapsed. *Yalla!* screamed his inner voice. *Yalla, yalla!*"

And the children began to chant with him, clapping their hands and crying, "Yalla, Yousef! Yalla, yalla!"

"And then—" Mazen held out his hands, and the children quieted. He leaned forward and, in a much softer voice, said, "Yousef escaped. And do you know what he held in his hand?"

"The queen's crown?" Aisha looked like she was trying not to laugh.

Mazen released a grievous sigh. "Nothing!" He splayed his fingers, revealing his empty palm. His audience was distraught. The story ended on a note of uncertainty, with the promise that the Queen of Dunes was still out there.

He told more stories based off his own adventures after that, stories he proudly dubbed "The Tales of Yousef." And, just as Loulie had, Aisha asked for donations. She was not as adept at playing the crowd, but with a deceptively gentle smile she gathered enough coin for a few meals.

For an hour or so, things went smoothly. They had secured a captive audience, and Mazen had no shortage of stories to offer them.

But then there was a charge in the air, and a sudden chaos overtook the souk, enveloping the space so quickly there was no time to understand it. One moment all was calm, and the next, there was shouting from flustered, panicked marketgoers as a young boy sprinted down the thoroughfare, screaming at the top of his lungs.

He was nothing but a blur, a flash of color that darted in and out of Mazen's vision. Some of the audience members surged forward to investigate while others drew back with anxious mutters. Aisha brushed past them all to the front of the crowd. Mazen rose and followed, breath trapped in his lungs as he stared at the quickly emptying square.

"Please!" the running boy shouted. He glanced around desperately at the nervous onlookers. "Please, help me! I—"

Something flashed through the air and hit the boy in the back. His words collapsed into a gasp as he crumpled to the ground. Mazen stared, uncomprehending, at the arrow protruding from the child's back. His confusion only deepened when he saw silver blood pooling on the ground. *A jinn.* He stared numbly. *A jinn child?*

The souk was so quiet Mazen didn't dare breathe. When he tried to inch closer to the road, Aisha grabbed the hem of his tunic and pulled him back. There was a warning in her eyes. Mazen looked again at the boy, then at the witnesses hiding in alleys and peering out windows. The crowd was frozen in shock or fear. No one approached the boy.

That was, until a lone man strolled down the thoroughfare. He walked until he reached the dying jinn, then plucked the arrow from his back as easily as if he were plucking a rose from a garden. He sliced the boy's throat before he could scream.

"Nothing to worry about!" the killer called in a singsong voice. "The monster is dead."

He slung the body over his shoulder and turned to walk back. The souk came alive at his proclamation, suddenly filled with a cacophony of voices as marketgoers piled onto the streets to watch the murderer stride off with the boy. Mazen felt the inexplicable urge to hide as the killer passed—then stopped to look at them. He had bright, shiny teeth and eyes dark as buttons. "Aisha! Beautiful, poisonous Aisha! I knew I saw a familiar face. How have you been? It's been months since we spoke."

"Tawil." Aisha's voice was stiff, cold.

Tawil laughed, an infuriatingly loud sound that made Mazen's blood boil. "Only you would give a fellow thief such a cold reception, bint Louas." His smile faded when he saw Mazen. "It seems we have much to discuss. Wait for me, eh? I have a corpse to bleed."

The smile returned as he walked away, as the marketgoers thanked him for ridding Ghiban of a filthy jinn. *Blessed thief,* they called him. *Savior. Hero.*

"Killer," Aisha murmured. Her eyes—both brown and black—shimmered with rage.

54

LOULIE

The compass led them to a rocky incline a two-hour hike from Ghiban. Loulie climbed up steep pathways littered with gravel and red dust, meandered along crooked trails, and inched past drops running with rushing water.

It was not the most perilous journey she'd ever made, but it was easily the most difficult on account of the pain that shot through her injured ankles with every step. By the time they were near the top, her legs trembled and sweat coated her forehead and neck.

Truly, she should not have taken this journey. But she had to. To prove to herself she was capable. That she did not need to rely on Qadir.

And yet here they were. Both of them. Qadir had refused to let her go alone and was trailing her from a distance, watching silently as she struggled. He did not try to help her, and because it was clear she was in no mood for conversation, he did not speak to her. Even yesterday in the souk, he had been quiet, content to accompany her just to make sure neither she nor the prince "did anything stupid," as he put it.

Loulie was so trapped in her thoughts, she did not notice the dip in the cliff ledge. She stepped too hard and would have slipped off the edge had Qadir not grabbed her from behind. She realized only belatedly that she had reached for him at the same moment.

The two of them stood there, trembling, staring at each other.

And then Loulie pulled away, curled her fingers into a fist, and kept walking.

She was still shaken when they reached the top of the cliff, a plateau so high she could see the entirety of Ghiban: the winding streams, the patches of green, and the vibrant souk in the center, filled with crowds of people and charming displays. She glanced at the water crashing down the cliff, then looked at its source: a large lake only steps away.

"The water is infinite," Qadir said when he saw the confusion on her face. "Created by jinn blood, no doubt."

Like that damn forever-refilling hourglass. Once, she'd thought it worthless. Now that she knew the true nature of relics, she realized it was anything but.

She pulled out the compass—the last magic she had left besides Qadir's knife—and squinted at the arrow. It was pointing at the lake. Of *course* the relic was underwater.

"Ideas?" Qadir stood behind her, glaring at the lake. He'd never liked water.

Loulie sighed as she began pulling off layers. When she was down to her most basic garments, she slid out of her shoes, set down the compass and knife, and edged toward the water.

"Be careful," Qadir called.

Wet sand gathered between her toes as she stepped into the lake. She saw rocks, moss, and then, there—a glimmer of silver. From this distance, she could not tell what it was, only that it was buried beneath silt. She stepped forward. Once, twice, and then the sand shifted beneath her feet and she slid. By the time she caught herself, the water had risen to her chest.

She cursed beneath her breath.

"Loulie?" Qadir called from the bank.

"I'm fine," she mumbled, and continued walking. Soon the water was up to her chin, but the relic was close. She could see now that it was a ring.

She paused to count down in her head—*Thalathah, ithnan,*

wahid—and dove. She plunged into a darkness that grabbed at her with cold, invisible hands. She shoved down her fear as she swam deeper, clawing through the sand in her blind search for the ring. Pressure built in her ears. It had a sound: a moan that penetrated deep into her bones.

Come on, come on...

She felt something cold and hard beneath her fingers and grasped at it desperately. Relief flooded her body as she caught hold of it.

And then the thing moved. It wasn't a ring. It was too large, too slippery. Too *sharp*.

She jerked away, but too late. The thing grabbed her wrist and pulled her down. Her eyes shot open. She stared into the darkness, and the darkness stared back. Milky-white eyes with dilated pupils blinked at her from the gloom. And beneath those eyes: a crescent-shaped mouth filled with rows of sharp teeth.

No. She dug her nails into its scaled flesh. It only tightened its grip.

No! The sharpened teeth parted beneath her feet and the glazed white eyes blinked, inches from her own. Loulie scraped at them, desperate, and the beast roared, making the entire lake shudder. Cracks of silver speared through the darkness. Fins, she realized. Large, razor-sharp fins shimmering with dull scales. And one of those oddly shaped fins was just beginning to loosen around her wrist.

Loulie clenched her teeth and kicked. The silver-tipped darkness thrashed against her, but she was persistent. Another kick, and she managed to pull free. Her lungs were starved of air and her ankles were on fire, but she pushed herself up toward the surface. Or at least, she tried to. But her body was suddenly heavy, and the water was pulling her down, down, down...

When the thing grabbed her again, she was too weak to fight back.

But no, wait—it was pulling her...up?

She crashed through the surface of the water with a gasp, even as someone—*Qadir?*—pulled her to shore. He set her down at the water's edge and ordered her to breathe until the pressure in her lungs eased and she stopped coughing up water.

When he spoke, his voice was jagged at the edges. "Loulie?"

He sat shuddering beside her, rivulets of water trickling down his muscled back and chest. Though he'd avoided soaking his shirt, she had the impression he had drenched more than just his skin, for his eyes were a pale, feeble yellow. The color of a dying flame.

"So you *do* know how to swim." Her words were barely a rasp, and for some reason, that made her laugh. It made her laugh so hard she started crying.

Qadir pulled her to him. "I'm sorry," he said softly. "I did not realize there was anything in the water."

"What?" was all she managed between her hiccups.

"A dendan," Qadir said. "You remember the stories Old Rhuba used to tell?"

Loulie *did* remember. Old Rhuba had always described the dendan as a monster fish, a creature big enough to eat ships whole. But in his stories, the creature died after devouring human flesh or hearing a human voice. This monster did not seem so feeble to her.

"Jinn blood changes living things," Qadir said, as if sensing her thoughts. He cast a forlorn look over his shoulder at the still water. "Like ghouls, all kinds of creatures are drawn to our magic. This is what happens when such a monster has been drenched in jinn blood."

Loulie thought of the massacre between the marid and the humans. How the mythical dendan had found its way here into fresh water, she did not know, but if it was sensitive to the lamentations of the dead, then she could see why it had developed a taste for human flesh. It was no wonder this relic had been here for so long.

The relic! She pushed herself away from Qadir and glanced at the water, heart sinking. She had failed. She had failed in this *one* simple thing...

"Looking for this?" Qadir held out a glimmering object: a ring inlaid with a cerulean-blue jewel. Loulie grabbed it from him, eyes wide.

"How did you get this?" She slid the ring onto her finger. Nothing happened.

"The dendan had eyes only for you." He leaned over her shoulder to tap the gem at the center. "It allows you to breathe underwater. I slid it onto my finger when I was under the surface. The magic did not last long. Maybe seven or eight heartbeats, at most."

It was, like the hourglass, a humble magic. And yet she was relieved. "It will sell, then."

"You know magic always sells."

She nodded quietly. Now that the danger had passed, she realized with greater clarity where she was. Who she was with. She had come here to prove to herself she was not useless. And yet, again, she had needed Qadir's help.

Her shoulders slumped as she looked away. "Thank you for saving me."

"You look disappointed."

Not disappointed, just ashamed.

"Loulie." He slid closer, until their shoulders were touching. "Talk to me."

Loulie pulled her knees to her chest and stared resolutely at the water. "There's nothing to say." The words caught in her throat as she said them. The truth was that she missed talking to Qadir. She missed *him*.

"Fine. Then I will speak, and you can listen." Out of the corner of her eye, Loulie saw him drape an arm over his knee. He was dry, not a single bead of water left on him. But that was hardly surprising, given he could combust into flames. "Do you remember what I told you in Dhyme? That the compass led me to relics so I could find a place for them to exist after death?"

His sigh was heavy enough to make his eyes cloud over with smoke. "It was the truth. I could not seek redemption in my country after what I had done, so I sought it here, in the human world. My greatest fear was that Khalilah would lead me to my fellow ifrit." He smiled, a self-deprecating twitch of his lips that was barely discernible. "I told you before I was a coward; that is also true. It is the reason I did not tell you I was an ifrit. The reason I have not sought out my old companions." His smile slipped. "The reason I sank a country."

There was silence. And then a few breaths later, Qadir spoke again: "I thought I might be able to run forever. But then that fool of a human sultan asked you to track down an ifrit's relic, and I realized I had to make a choice. I could run, or I could face my past." Loulie felt his gaze shift to her. "I had planned to tell you the truth when we found the lamp. But then you recovered the Resurrectionist's relic and witnessed her magic. I saw your rage and fear, and I withheld the entire truth, thinking you would shun me if I told you I had the same power."

Loulie stifled a nervous laugh. He had to be pulling her leg. How could he not see that she depended on him? That she always had?

"Why stay with me at all?" she said. "You don't need some weak human girl to help you face your past." The words escaped before she could stop them. Panic echoed through the hollow chambers of her heart, building until she could barely breathe.

Qadir stared at her, wide-eyed. When she tried to slide away, he grabbed her by the shoulder and turned her around. "Weak?" His eyes shimmered with a fierce blue light. "Is that what all this is about? Why you've been sulking?"

Loulie was rendered speechless by the intensity of his gaze. She'd been expecting exasperation, not this anger shining in his eyes. "It's the truth, isn't it?" She hated how bitter the words were. How small and self-pitying. But the moment she said them, a dam broke inside of her, and the rest of the confession came out as a torrent of words. "I couldn't do anything. Not when my tribe was killed and not now. I can *never* do anything without your help. If I hadn't had your knife in the ruins..." She blinked back tears. "If you hadn't been there..."

"It is not weakness to rely on others for help," Qadir said. Loulie did not know when, but at some point, she had reached for his hand. Now she was holding on to it as if it were some lifeline. *Weak*, said the voice in her mind. *Weak, weak, weak.*

"Loulie." Gently, so gently it made her tremble, Qadir set a hand on her cheek and turned her face so that she was looking at him. "You rely on me, but I also rely on *you*. We are a team, you and I."

"But I don't—"

"You are the most courageous person I know, Loulie al-Nazari. Without you, I would still be aimlessly wandering the desert, lost in my grief. You are *not* weak. That is why I follow where you walk: because I trust you." His expression softened. "What happened to your family—I truly am sorry. Loulie..."

She did not realize she had started crying again until Qadir ran a thumb over her cheek, wiping away a stray tear. "I would never have followed your family's trail if I'd known someone was tracking me. I was only walking where the compass bade me to go. I was..."

"Lost?" Loulie rubbed at her eyes. "Yes, I know." She forced herself to look him in the eyes. To hold his gaze. "It's not your fault."

Something inside of her released with the words, leaving her feeling—not empty, but deflated. Not weak, but vulnerable. She could have turned away then. Could have heeded the voice in her mind that said, *You should let him go*, but she realized she did not want to. She wanted to stay with Qadir. And Qadir—he could have left many times. But he was still here.

"You're not going to disappear on me again, are you?"

Qadir never broke her gaze. "No."

"Even if the compass leads you somewhere else?"

"I told you before, didn't I? We are connected. The compass led me to you, and it is with you I shall stay until destiny demands we part ways."

"You make it sound like it's not your choice to stay or go."

"Some things *are* out of our control. You know that just as well as I. All we can do is make choices based on the cards fate deals us. But so long as fate allows me to stay with you, I will not leave you, Loulie. That is a promise."

It was the most Qadir-like answer, and it made her laugh despite herself. It was more a choking sound than a chuckle, but it was enough to make her smile. "I will kick your ass if you lie to me again, Qadir."

Qadir shrugged. "Fair enough." He stood and held out his hand.

In response, Loulie grabbed his tunic up off the ground and threw it at him. "Put your shirt on. You're indecent." She gathered her own layers as she glanced down at the city, which, after everything that had happened, suddenly seemed more energetic. More inviting.

"Loulie. Something for your troubles." Qadir was holding something out to her. Her heart lifted at the sight of the two-faced coin.

"I didn't realize you had more than one," she said as she took it from him.

Qadir pulled his tunic over his head with a shrug. "You never asked. But this is the last one, so do not lose it."

Loulie looked at the gold. *Is Qadir telling the truth about wanting to stay with me?*

She flipped the coin. It came down on the human side. She stifled a sigh of relief. "Fine. Let's go. We've wasted enough time."

Qadir raised a brow. "Time to make some gold?"

Loulie grinned through her tears. "Yes. Let's go sell a relic."

55

AISHA

Aisha had never liked Tawil. No, dislike was insufficient. *Hate* was more accurate. She'd hated Tawil ever since Omar had made him a thief. He was an insufferably cocky bastard who killed jinn for glory rather than justice. A show-off who made every murder a spectacle.

This kill was, like the others, a performance. Tawil took the jinn boy into the souk, bled him out in front of an audience, and afterward, had the audacity to bow. Worse, people clapped for him. Before, Aisha would have found this reception annoying. Now it made a deep, dark rage boil in her blood. She blamed the Resurrectionist, whose hatred fueled her own.

What a despicable human, she hissed in Aisha's mind. *We ought to kill him.*

"Don't tempt me," Aisha murmured beneath the applause of the crowd.

Afterward, Tawil returned to speak with them. When he asked Aisha why their plan—Omar and Mazen's switch—had gone awry, Aisha simply said, "There have been some unexpected circumstances." Tawil barely acknowledged the prince. In fact, he insisted that he and Aisha finish their conversation somewhere more private.

"Thieves' business" was the excuse he gave Mazen.

The prince's aggravation was apparent in the dip of his lips.

Aisha was almost disappointed when he didn't object. She'd become convinced he was growing a backbone, but perhaps not.

After promising to find the prince later, Aisha followed Tawil through the souk and across a bridge to another sector of Ghiban. It was easy to keep track of him in the crowds; the city's separate, capacious isles were easier to navigate than Madinne's clustered tiers and Dhyme's winding streets. Though the central souk was the most thriving, each district contained shops and a residential area, making it easier for travelers to stock up on equipment and find accommodations.

Tawil led her across four bridges and through four districts until they came to the fish souk, where local seafood was on display. Aisha stole a bowl of finger shrimp and eyed piles of dead-eyed trout and river fish as they strode through.

Eventually, they came to a shack by the docks. Tawil entered through the back door, strode down a cobweb-filled corridor, and opened a hidden trapdoor in the kitchen. Aisha hesitated at the entrance. She was not sure why, exactly. She had been in this place before. Had, in fact, stayed here while passing through Ghiban on hunts. It was a thief hideout, after all.

And yet she was nervous.

Tawil's laugh echoed from the darkness. "Worried I'll murder you in the dark?"

Aisha bristled. *He should be worried I'll murder* him *in the dark.* She slid down the ladder and realized only after shutting the trapdoor behind her that she didn't know whose thoughts those were. Hers—or the ifrit's?

Does it matter? We are one and the same.

Aisha gritted her teeth in annoyance. *We are not.* She tamped down her irritation as she entered the underground chamber: a thief storage space filled with tapestries, furniture, weapons, scrolls—and relics, resting on slanted cabinet shelves. Though this place belonged to all the thieves, this was Tawil's stronghold; Ghiban was *his* hunting ground.

Tawil spun toward her as she entered, that irritating smile on his lips. Aisha wasted no time chiding him. "What the hell was that in the souk?"

He blinked at her, wide-eyed. "Sometimes the city folk forget we exist; I thought to remind them. But that's unimportant. Look here." He reached into the satchel at his hip and withdrew a glass orb, which he tossed to Aisha. "This seems like a relic our king would like, eh? It shows you your memories."

She had no way of testing Tawil's claim, for when she touched the orb, it was not *her* memories she saw. These memories belonged to the owner of the orb: a young jinn boy named Anas. Aisha was able to discern from his hazy memories that he'd carried this orb with him because it was a memento from his mother. That it was the only thing he'd managed to bring with him to the human world.

Anas's final plea echoed in her mind. *Please! Please, help me!*

Aisha tossed the orb back to Tawil and shoved her hands in her pockets to hide their shaking. She had known the true nature of relics ever since Omar recruited her. It had never bothered her that they contained souls. But how could she ignore the fact now, when one of the damned things was talking to her?

You said before that the dead do not speak. The Resurrectionist's voice brushed gently against her mind. *But how would you know, when you did not have the ability to listen?*

Tawil must have mistaken her unease for irritation. He laughed. "No need to be jealous."

Aisha cleared her throat. "Can we talk about what's actually important? How is Omar?"

"From what I've heard, he's been spending most of his days in the company of an annoyingly attentive wali. The man is like a leech; he refuses to go back to his city and asks too many questions. Omar has someone from the guard watching him."

Irritatingly observant politicians aside, if Omar was commanding people in the guard now, it at least meant his plan to incorporate thieves into the qaid's force had gone smoothly.

Tawil raised a brow. "Clearly, he's faring better than *your* prince. Care to explain why Prince Mazen is no longer in disguise?" He crossed his arms. "And perhaps you'll tell me about the so-called legendary relic you found in a dune? Junaid sounded very impressed in his letter."

Aisha bit back a scowl. She didn't *care* to tell the thief anything, but she had no choice if Junaid had already filled him in. She relayed the short version of what had transpired, the most important recollection being the ordeal with Imad. She did not tell him she had nearly died or that the collar had saved her from death, and yet—his eyes wandered to the silk around her neck.

He lunged toward her without preamble.

Aisha grabbed his wrist before he touched her. Searing hot pain shot through her veins at the contact. Tawil pulled his hand away the moment she did. They both stared at each other.

Tawil laughed weakly. "What was that?"

Aisha stepped away with a growl. That heat—where had it come from? Did Tawil have some kind of relic on him? "Speak for yourself, you ass."

"The queen's collar—you have it around your neck. I can see it."

She drew the silk closer to her chin. "And?"

"Aren't you going to give it to Omar? You know he's looking for kings' relics." He tilted his head, eyes widening. "Or don't tell me you're actually *keeping* it, bint Louas? This wasn't part of the plan, you know."

None of this is part of the plan! she wanted to scream, but she could not bring herself to say the words. The memory of that strange heat still lay beneath her skin, and it made her wary.

"Give it to me." He held out a hand. "I'll deliver it to him."

She was grateful Tawil was shorter than her, so she could look down her nose at him. "I don't take commands from haughty children."

Tawil's bright façade cracked. He glared at her with a vehemence that made her skin prickle. "You're a bitch, bint Louas, you know that?"

"And you're a bastard. Now, do you want to keep throwing names at each other, or shall we talk business like adults?" She was just about to return to their discussion when she heard a sound and paused. She and Tawil glanced at a pile of collector's coins in the corner. Even as they watched, a few trickled to the floor.

Tawil shrugged it off, but she knew immediately that something was off. There was a buzzing in her ears. She focused until it became a voice: *I am here*, it said. And then Aisha did not just hear it; she saw it: the shadow relic, visible through the eye the ifrit had gifted her.

And beneath it: Mazen bin Malik, spying on them.

He had followed them. *That* was why he hadn't objected to being left behind.

Aisha was torn between anger and pride. The latter won out. She had not yet revealed things the prince couldn't know; she was safe. *Omar* was safe. But now that he was here—well, she couldn't give him information, but there were other ways to reward him for his bravery.

"Let us continue this discussion aboveground. I'm famished." She walked to the ladder before Tawil could protest, and turned back only once to glance pointedly at the cabinet. "You have quite the collection, Tawil. I can only imagine how much gold you could get from all this."

Tawil was a prideful creature. Even if he *did* realize some of his relics had gone missing, he would not tell Omar.

She saw the understanding in the prince's eyes. And then—he was nothing but a shadow on the wall. She hid a smirk as she made her way outside.

56

LOULIE

Mazen bin Malik was waiting in the inn's tavern when they returned. The moment he saw them, he rushed past the occupied tables with disconcerting purpose and handed them a burlap sack. Loulie peeked into the bag. And stared.

"Relics," Qadir said, confirming her suspicions.

They both looked at the prince, who raised his hands and said, "I can explain."

And so as Loulie donned her merchant robes, he told them. About the young jinn murdered in the souk and of the thief who killed him. Loulie presumed even Aisha bint Louas must have despised the man if she'd encouraged Mazen to steal from him.

There was only one thing that bothered her about the situation. Namely, that the compass had not led *them* to Tawil's stash. Qadir smiled faintly when she brought it up. "Khalilah knows the future," he said. "She led us to where *we* needed to be."

Loulie was in too good a mood to bring up her dislike of destiny. She was glad, at least, that the relics had ended up in their hands so she could sell them to people who *weren't* members of the murderous forty thieves.

She was about to follow the prince out of the room when she paused and, out of habit, turned back to search for the bag of infinite space. Her stomach sank when she remembered it had been lost in the ruins. *But at least we recovered our most important belongings. And...*

Her eyes wandered to the shamshir sheathed at Qadir's hip.

He raised an eyebrow at her. "Have you not noticed I have been wearing it this whole time? Why would I leave it in a place any simple thief could break into?"

"You had it displayed on the wall of our room for *years*."

"Dahlia would be insulted if she knew you were so skeptical of her security."

"You know that's not my point." She followed Qadir down the corridor and toward the entrance, where the prince was waiting for them.

"I told you I would keep this blade safe. Here, that means carrying it on my person."

"You think you'll ever use it? I know it's hardly an enchanted knife, but—"

"An object's worth isn't determined by whether or not it is enchanted." His lips curled into one of his familiar not-quite smiles. "Besides, I have no doubt this blade *will* serve me. I just hope the day I must rely on it is far in the future."

Loulie hoped so too. On the cliffs, Qadir had told her they were a team. And as his comrade, she would do her best to make sure he did not have to use the shamshir. She would rather he carry the blade around as an accessory forever than feel pressed into using it as a last resort. But if he *did* ever have to use it... she hoped it was as efficient as it was elegant.

When they met the prince at the door, he insisted on accompanying them to the souk. "You saw me work," he said cheerfully. "It's only fair I get to see *you* deal with customers."

They set up shop in the foreigners' souk, a small market on an outlying isle where travelers sold goods from all over the world. Because the souk was filled with visiting merchants rather than established ones, there were more stalls than buildings here. Merchants packed and left at a moment's notice, so the souk was always in flux. As a result, there were always stalls available. It was at one of these unembellished stalls that Loulie began to set up.

She settled into the comfortable routine of eavesdropping while she displayed her relics. Normally, she would have kept her ears out for potential customer leads. Now she found herself listening for news about Ahmed. She wished he were here to see her work; gods knew the last time she'd tried to sell relics in his presence, it had ended in bloodshed. And yet even after the suffering of that night, he had still smiled at her when she left. Had still been able to make her heart flutter with nothing but a flowery promise and a hand kiss.

Tentatively, Loulie probed at a possibility she always tried to dismiss: a future in which she accepted Ahmed's marriage proposal. She pictured them wandering the desert together, living the adventures they were only ever able to share as stories. She imagined them sleeping together beneath the stars and bantering beneath the sun.

And then she thought of Qadir, and the dream dissipated.

Shame heated her cheeks as she returned her attention to the stall. What was she thinking? It didn't matter that Ahmed was kind to her. He was still a jinn hunter and a devout believer who would kill Qadir if ever he realized the truth about him.

She suppressed a sigh as she returned to her work. Out of the corner of her eye she noticed Prince Mazen wandering the souk, staring in awe at imported goods: intricately patterned glass lanterns from the west, topaz-centric jewelry from the south, eye-shaped charms that warded off evil from an island to the east. His wide-eyed amazement drew her back into the present. He thought those shops were impressive? Wait until he saw *hers*.

He hadn't made it far when she announced the opening of her business. A crowd formed immediately, staring at the merchandise with hungry eyes. Loulie felt a profound peace wash over her as she charmed, bartered, and batted her lashes at potential customers. By the time the stall was emptied, she was nearly drunk with euphoria. When the prince approached from the outskirts where he'd been observing, she grabbed him by the shoulders and shook him.

"We're rich!" she cried.

It was true; they had gone from being dirt poor to having enough coins to bathe in. Normally, it would have been a satisfactory amount. Today, it was a small fortune.

The prince shook his head, looking dazed. "Truly?"

Qadir looked up and said, "We're going to need a bigger bag."

Loulie grew mournful as she remembered the bag of infinite space, but then brightened at the prospect of having so much of her weight be in gold. They ended up splitting the coin to carry it, and because Loulie was in the mood to celebrate before they set off tomorrow, they purchased entry to one of the entertainment ships winding through the city canals.

It was, in essence, a luxurious floating tavern where patrons drank with abandon and poets and musicians took to the stage to tell scandalous tales and sing lewd tunes. The ship cabin was large but cozy. Tables lay scattered beneath a sea of shisha smoke, occupied by grinning guests who whispered and laughed over expensive drinks. Above the crowds hung dimly lit lanterns that bobbed like sleepy fireflies in the darkness, dappling the walls with warm firelight.

For the first time in months, Loulie forgot herself in that dreamy space. She drank and laughed and savored the fuzzy, pleasant feeling brought on by the alcohol. She marveled at the intricately designed swaying lanterns hanging from the ship's ceiling and grinned up at the smoking storyteller onstage, who looked as if he were floating on colorful clouds.

"So now you know!" the storyteller cried. His cheeks were flushed, his eyes glassy. "If you cut down a tree without knocking on the roots, you invite a jinn into the world!"

Loulie snorted as the storyteller stumbled from the stage to uproarious applause. He was replaced by a small band of men playing uplifting music. Loulie bobbed her head and reached for her wine, only to find it gone.

"Your lips are stained," Qadir said. He twirled the glass in his fingers, brows raised.

She grinned. "And yours aren't stained at all. Give me my wine, dry man."

When she reached for it, Qadir leaned back and drained the glass. Loulie shoved his shoulder, but she was laughing. The wine made everything so *pleasant*.

"Dry no longer," Qadir said as he set down the glass.

Loulie wiggled her brows at him. "I dare you to get absolutely drunk."

"I dare you to not." Qadir sighed. "I would rather not have to carry you to the inn."

"I can walk just fine." She stood. And swayed. When Qadir reached forward to steady her, she grabbed his hand and leaned forward with a conspiratorial smile. "Dance with me?"

"I'll pass."

"You're a grumpy old man." She pried her hand from his and twirled away, into the crowds. At first, she could hear Qadir calling her name, but then his voice was just a thrum beneath the drums.

A current of ululation rippled through the room. Loulie saw women flipping their hair, men clapping their hands. There were a few people at the center, performing a debka line routine. She recognized one of the men. Prince Mazen. He was smiling—he'd been smiling for *hours*—and twirling across the ship with surprising grace. Midspin, he caught her gaze.

His smile grew brighter as he held out a hand. Loulie did not realize she'd rushed forward to take it until their fingers were pressed together and they were circling each other.

The prince pulled her toward him. "Are we still rich?"

Loulie grinned. "Criminally."

He laughed, and it was the raw, unchecked laughter of a child. Loulie was awed by him, by this strange man who smiled even when his world was falling apart. He looked at ease here, every bit the handsome, bright-eyed storyteller who'd opened up to her in the souk.

Handsome, ha! It's a good thing Dahlia isn't here to suggest marriage.

She gripped his palm. "Please tell me you know how to dance."

The prince grinned. "Of course. What kind of decadent would I be if I didn't?" He shifted his hand so that their palms were pressed together. Then he raised their joined hands in the air, and they danced. More than once, Loulie nearly tripped on his feet.

"Are you sure *you* know how to dance, al-Nazari?" The prince's grin was a slash of mischief on his face. Loulie had not known he could smile like that, with a challenge in his eyes.

His words sparked something in her: a fire usually only Qadir could call forth. When they next spun, she purposely overstepped and stomped her foot down close to his instep. The prince stumbled back, mouth open in a comical O. She batted her lashes and said, "I think you should watch your own feet, Prince."

He quickly recovered his composure. The next time they spun, it was he who jutted his foot out, trying to catch her off guard. It continued like that, their movements less a dance and more an intimate obstacle course in which they both tried to avoid each other's feet. Loulie stopped swaying and started dodging, making the world tilt with every step.

By the last pluck of the oud string, she was too exhausted to anticipate the prince's last movement: a sweep that, to everyone else, looked like a bow. Instead, he swept her off her feet.

Loulie fell against him. She felt the rise and fall of his chest as he laughed, the warmth of his hands at her hips as he steadied her and said, "I think this means I win?"

She stood there, fingers bunched in his shirt as she struggled to hold herself upright. As she became aware of the prince's heartbeat and of the contours of his body against her own, she wondered, suddenly, what it would be like—to be able to lean on someone without feeling vulnerable. To trust someone implicitly, not just with her heart, but with her body.

For the second time that day, her fuzzy mind conjured an image of Ahmed. She imagined him sitting beneath the stars, smiling softly as he raised a glass in her honor. *Tonight, let me serve you.* She wondered what it would be like to rest her head on his lap, what his lips would feel like on her neck...

She shoved herself away from the prince, heat staining her cheeks.

He blinked. "Al-Nazari?" She turned and walked away before he could grab her.

She pushed into the crowd, which was devolving into a blur of vivid colors, crooked smiles, and too-loud laughter. She tried to focus, but her mind was still on the damn wali. Smiling, charming Ahmed bin Walid, whom she turned down every time because he was a murderer. Because he killed jinn like Qadir.

And because, deep down, she was terrified of commitment. Of *trusting* someone.

Abruptly, she hit a wall. She stepped back and looked up, only to realize it was not a wall at all, but Qadir. There was concern in the hard tug of his mouth. "Ready to leave?"

Loulie squeezed her eyes shut. "Not yet." She eyed the effervescent bottles lining the bar shelves. "I need another drink."

She needed to stop thinking. She needed to stop feeling.

Otherwise, she'd be in for a rough night.

57

MAZEN

They returned to the desert with horses and equipment the next day. Mazen felt like he'd woken from a dream. For some reason unbeknownst to him, the merchant refused to speak about last night. He'd thought she was beginning to enjoy his company the same way he relished hers, but now he wondered if he'd inadvertently done something to reopen the rift between them.

At least she'd made up with her bodyguard; his presence softened her anger into a calmer irritation. Mazen was envious of their relationship. What must it be like, he wondered, to be so close to someone you could demand all their secrets? He had Hakim, but Hakim was his brother. *And the only honest member of the family*, he thought grimly.

His father's past was a mystery, and who knew how many secrets Omar was keeping?

Mazen pushed his unease away, resolved to focus on the journey. Though they had lost their map—he cringed every time he thought about his brother's beautiful work buried in the Sandsea—they were not directionless. They had the merchant's magic compass, after all.

The arrow guided them down crooked pathways between cliffs and through quiet valleys cut through with the occasional brook or stream. Though the weather was more hospitable here than in the open desert, the terrain was not. The pathways were bumpier, and it was not long before Mazen discovered new aches in his back and thighs. But those pains were a small grievance, trifling in comparison to the tenacious ghouls and deadly killer they'd faced.

In the daylight hours, Mazen trailed Aisha on hunts, helped Qadir build traps, and joined Loulie on trips to refill the waterskins. He was not especially good at the first two tasks—he scared off prey and possessed the uncanny ability to sabotage incomplete traps— but at least he could fail without worry of giving away his identity. And the water gathering was a respite, a time for him to take in his surroundings without worrying about the road ahead.

It was unfortunate that his good mood was fleeting, dissipating when, a few days later, they arrived at their first outpost after leaving the cliffs. When he went to gather supplies, he overheard gossip that sent his mind spinning. He heard talk of chaos in Madinne: of more frequent jinn attacks, more death in the souk. The news unnerved him. Hadn't Omar stayed in the city to improve its security? If so, why were there *more* jinn coming to Madinne?

But the most perplexing rumors were the ones about himself— there were reports he'd been sneaking out of the palace in his royal garments, alone. He was nonplussed, unable to understand why Omar would betray his trust so explicitly.

I never should have left. Mazen trapped the regretful words between his teeth.

Soon this would all be over. He would bring the lamp back and…what? Some ifrit would "save" them all, and his father would lock him away in his room forever for disobeying orders? It seemed a terrifyingly plausible nightmare.

Later, when they set off into the desert once more, Mazen shared the news with the others. Aisha shrugged off his accusations, insisting she was not privy to Omar's thoughts. Mazen knew that was not the truth; he had overheard her and Tawil speaking in their hideout, after all. He just didn't know how to decipher their conversation.

When he had no success gleaning answers from her, he turned

the conversation to the lamp they were seeking. He asked Qadir about the being trapped inside.

"You told me you didn't know anything about the lamp," Loulie said to Qadir, voice laced with accusation.

Qadir, who sat atop his horse with the usual nonchalant expression upon his face, only raised a brow in response. "Because I do not. I wasn't in the human world when one of my companions was trapped in the lamp. But..."

Aisha shrugged. "It has to be Rijah."

Qadir sighed. "Yes."

Mazen stared between the two of them. "Rijah?"

"The Shapeshifter," Aisha said. "Your stories speak of a jinn king with a bloated ego. If there is even an inkling of truth to them, then they are referring to Rijah."

Mazen thought of the story that had been passed down through his family. He'd originally believed that human stories about the jinn were fables, but maybe they were just one version of the truth, complicated over time.

"Gods, they're going to be livid," Aisha said. "Stuck in the Sandsea for hundreds of years? What a nightmare."

Mazen blinked. "They?"

Qadir shrugged. "Rijah is whatever Rijah wants to be. Man, woman, child, beast, they are all of those things and more."

It was a novel concept of identity, and Mazen was thoughtful as they lapsed into peaceful silence. The quiet remained as they traveled through gorges and into flat desert plains, where the sun finally made its reappearance. Mazen would have lain down in the sand and basked in its warmth if the others hadn't been so set on making good time to their destination. He wished he shared their eagerness, but no, all he had to look forward to was some unknowable punishment.

He sat back in his saddle and tried to ingrain the details of this moment into his mind: the clear and endless sky, the shadows of distant tents on the hazy horizon, the hiss and sigh of the ground beneath his horse's hooves. He even relished the weight of the sand on his clothing and in his boots, knowing it was a testament to his travels.

This is not a story, he told himself. *This is reality, and I am living it right now.*

Even if his future was dismal, he was determined to make this final reprieve last as long as he could. And so he focused on his surroundings and the awe they inspired in him. He watched as the landscape became awash in the red-gold shades of sunset, and when the sky darkened, he marveled at the shadows, which spread across the desert like ink stains.

There were stars glimmering in the sky by the time they came to an oasis. The merchant and her bodyguard sped ahead, bantering as they raced toward their destination. Mazen held back a sigh as he watched them go. He wished *he* had that easygoing repartee with Loulie.

"Your jealousy is showing, sayyidi." Aisha pulled up beside him. She took a swig from her waterskin before handing it to him. He drank to avoid answering.

Afterward, he swiped a hand across his mouth and said, "What do you make of the news from Madinne? Weren't you all supposed to *stop* jinn from breaking into the city?"

"That was the plan. Obviously, something's gone amiss."

There was another short silence before Mazen said, "I know you and Tawil were discussing something you didn't want me to overhear. You were talking about a plan—"

"A plan to lead *you* through the desert in one piece."

"That's not what it sounded like. It sounded like Omar was searching for ifrit relics."

Aisha sighed. "And? Collecting relics for him is one of my responsibilities."

"Not *ifrit* relics." Mazen frowned. "You're hiding something from me. There has to be a reason my brother is so wary of Ahmed bin Walid. A reason he's sneaking out as me."

Aisha mirrored his frown. "It doesn't matter what you think. I'm not obligated to tell you anything." She looked down her nose at him, unimpressed, before riding ahead.

Later, after they set up camp, Mazen sat at the edge of the oasis, beneath the shadow of a date tree, and stared at the stars reflected on the water. He thought about how the first time he'd come to such a place, he'd been his brother. Now he'd regressed into Mazen-sometimes-Yousef, a prince so spineless he couldn't even demand secrets from his own subjects.

"Can't sleep, Prince?"

He was startled out of his reverie by the merchant, who suddenly stood beside him, gaze trained on the star-speckled water. She didn't look at him as she said, "Does this remind you of home? Of the lakes in your palace courtyard made from jinn blood?"

"That's not fair," he said quietly. "*I* haven't killed any jinn. Why do you assume I share my brother's morals?"

"Why *shouldn't* I assume? You're both liars who share the same father."

The accusation made his heart sink. He had been hopeful Loulie was beginning to see him as himself, without any masks. But though it was dispiriting, he supposed it was natural that her animosity toward his family colored her opinion of him.

But Loulie surprised him by continuing, "At least, that's what I would have said before I heard you in the souk." Her eyes finally settled on him. "My parents used to say a story could reveal the heart of the teller. I see that truth in you. When you shared your mother's history, I heard her optimism reflected in your words. You are not like Omar."

Mazen swallowed. Why did it suddenly feel like his heart was in his throat? "I hope not." His gaze sank to the water. "In any case, I have more in common with Hakim than Omar, and we don't share any blood at all."

"Have the two of you always been close?"

"Always. Ever since he came to the palace." Mazen deflated with his sigh. It had been a long time since he remembered the moments he spent with his whole family. He remembered the meals they'd shared in the courtyard, the nightly stories his mother had told. He remembered the way his father had smiled, with unbridled joy in his eyes. The way Hakim had wandered the gardens, bright-eyed and free, pointing at different flowers and describing them to Mazen.

"When my mother was alive, the palace was a sanctuary for us, not a prison." His voice cracked, and he had to pause to take a deep breath. "My father was a different person then too. He was kinder, more patient. My mother taught him to trust again after...well, you know."

"The wife killings," the merchant murmured. "He really never explained why he did it?"

Mazen shook his head, mute. The rumors always said it was Hakim's mother who had inspired his distrust, but that had never seemed like the full truth. The sultan himself never spoke of those murders. Mazen suspected he never would.

"Well, Shafia was a marvel for being able to change him," Loulie said.

"She was." He pulled his knees to his chest, rested his chin on them. "Back then, my father was too. He didn't care about jinn and relics. He talked about redemption."

Once, I wanted to be like him.

He could see the merchant watching him out of the corner of his eye. She surprised him by saying, "Well, if there's anyone who can show him the meaning of redemption, it's you."

Mazen looked up at her. "Me?"

The merchant shrugged. "The way I see it, you could have left me behind in the ruins, but you came back. And when I asked you about Imad, you answered me honestly." Her lips quirked. "I can tell; you're easy to read."

"You saved me before too. Twice." He sighed. "My father was the one to send you on this quest. The least I can do is try to see you safely through it."

The merchant turned away with a snort. "Your honesty is a foible, Prince." She paused. "But also a treasure. Don't underestimate your ability to influence others."

She left him alone to puzzle over the words.

58

AISHA

Some nights, when Aisha was alone, the desert spoke to her of death. She heard the distant cry of souls buried beneath the sand and the murmurs of relics lost to time. And some nights, when she let her mind wander, she heard a voice from memories that did not belong to her. It was soft and lilted and full of laughter.

When she closed her eyes, she could see its owner: a tall, handsome man with a bright smile. And though she did not know him, her heart would nonetheless soar. *My queen.* He grasped her hand and kissed her knuckles. *I love you, habibti. Forever and always.*

But then that memory would collapse, replaced with an image of her beloved bleeding crimson into the sand and screaming as his tribesmen tortured him. *Traitor*, they said. *Infidel.* And then he was dead, her precious Munaqid, lying broken in a pool of his own blood as they came for her, and she couldn't breathe; there was only rage, and a sorrow so deep it was endless.

"Stop," Aisha gasped. Her breathing was ragged, her eyesight hazy with tears. *"Stop."*

She came out of the memory with a cry, body trembling as she fought to put a lid on emotions that were not her own. She scowled, hating that even now, a vision of the ifrit's human lover was trapped behind her eyelids. She recognized that name—*Munaqid*. It was the name of the human who had saved the world from the Queen of Dunes in the legend.

The ifrit scoffed in her mind. *The only one Munaqid saved was me.* She paused. *But our time together could only last so long. His tribe killed us in the end.*

The first time the queen had shown Aisha this vision, in Dhyme, she hadn't been able to decipher it. Now that the answers were before her, she wanted nothing more than to forget them.

"I don't care," Aisha said, but her voice was thick with tears. She cursed as she stood and paced. She glanced over her shoulder at the tents they had set up for the night. She knew that Qadir was awake. She'd felt his eyes on her when she left the encampment.

The ifrit chuckled in her mind. *Did you know that back then, I was known as Naji? I made a deal with that human girl, same as I made a deal with you. We were one, Naji and I.*

Aisha shuddered. It was hard to dismiss the reality of the ifrit sinking into her *own* mind when, so often, she was unable to distinguish between their thoughts. True to her word, the Resurrectionist had not forced her to do anything against her will—but what did that matter if her presence continued to erode Aisha's autonomy regardless?

"That's not what the stories say. They say you tricked her and stole her body."

And? Your human stories are born of fear. Easier to believe a jinn would possess a human rather than work with her. That a human would kill her, not fall in love with her.

Aisha said nothing. She glared into the dark, quiet night and thought about how full of shit the ifrit was. Jinn did not help humans, and humans did not help jinn. Her deal with the Resurrectionist had been made purely out of necessity.

But the memories—those were real. Aisha could feel it. Even the memories that sometimes surfaced of Qadir screamed of truth. They were rare, those memories, but they edged into her mind when she let her guard down. In them, Qadir wore brilliant robes and a less than brilliant frown. His eyes were clouded over with smoke, filled with a sadness so profound it shattered her heart.

"Enough." She pressed a fist to her forehead and breathed slowly in and out until her mind was clear and she could focus on *her* problems. She grasped at the memory of her conversation with Tawil. The more she remembered, the more her skin prickled. She did not realize she was breathing so hard until the ifrit spoke gently in her mind: *You are distressed.*

"No shit." Aisha resumed her pacing. It kept her centered.

But every time she remembered that conversation, she faltered. Tawil had told her that Omar's plan would soon reach its conclusion. The suspicious wali was taken care of, and even the mistrustful qaid had not come close to uncovering his plot.

Aisha didn't care. She had never truly cared about Omar's plans when they were secondary to her own goals. But that was not the case with Mazen. *I envy you, Aisha,* Tawil had said. *You have an easy job! All you have to do is lead a sheep to slaughter.*

Aisha groaned into her hands. Gods, she was going to be sick.

Always, she had done what Omar commanded. She owed him that. He'd seen potential in her when no one else had. Back when she'd been an unmoored thief in Madinne—parentless, villageless— he had put himself in her path, and when she tried to steal a locket from his pocket, he'd grabbed her wrist and said, *How would you like to be a king's thief?*

Omar had given her the power to enact revenge on the jinn who had stolen her life.

She had never questioned him. But now...

Prince Mazen saved your life, the Resurrectionist said softly.

Aisha's legs were so weak she had to sit on a nearby boulder.

I would think deeply about—

"Leave me alone!" Her voice was so shrill it made her flinch. She cast a look over her shoulder, searching for movement at the campsite, but there was nothing. Qadir, probably, could hear her. She would have to warn Omar about him. They would need to alter their plan to account for his magic. Perhaps Tawil, cocky bastard, would have some ideas.

She paused, remembering the heat that had burned her fingers when he touched her. She shook the memory from her mind. It wasn't important.

The ifrit scoffed. *Willful ignorance will get you nowhere.*

For the first time, Aisha wondered if maybe it would have been easier to die. But dying was akin to failure, and she had never failed, had *refused* to fail since losing her family.

She had not come this far just to break for some softhearted prince.

So Aisha took a deep breath, pieced together her faltering resolve, and returned to her and the prince's shared tent. Prince Mazen lay in his bedroll, curled on his side with an arm draped across his forehead. In the beginning, she remembered he had tried to comb the dust out of his hair before he retired every night. Now he lay unperturbed in a very dusty bedroll, lightly snoring. Even though he *still* only knew how to make a fire and didn't know a single thing about wielding a sword, he had become more competent, she thought. Braver.

Aisha turned away with a grimace. She wrung the dust from her cloak, wrapped it around herself like a second skin, then stretched out on her bedroll. She squeezed her eyes shut and attempted to stop thinking. But though the ifrit had mercifully gone quiet in her head, the desert still whispered. It took all she had to quiet its voice and keep her mind blank. *The dead do not speak*, she thought desperately.

The desert wind's responding cackle sounded like laughter.

59

MAZEN

The future weighed on Mazen's arms and legs like shackles. His body was heavy as they crested the dune overlooking the last out-post. Beyond the oasis, the Western Sandsea was a glittering ocean of sparkling, shifting sand. According to the map they had lost, there were pathways—both above- and underground—that would allow them to navigate it.

If the paths existed, they were well hidden. From their vantage point, the Sandsea seemed impenetrable, infinite. And yet this was their final destination. Mazen ought to have been relieved. Instead, he was filled with dread.

He tried to settle his nerves by speaking into the silence. He addressed Aisha, who rode beside him. She seemed especially sullen today, too distracted to even roll her eyes at him.

"So about the ifrit in your mind..."

Her gaze snapped to him. Mazen smiled nervously. "I've been wondering if you had a name. 'The Resurrectionist' is a bit of a mouthful."

Aisha raised a brow. "You already know who I am. I am Aisha bint Louas." When Mazen simply stared at her, the thief sighed and said, "I need a body to act in this world, Prince. And while I can force my mind on others through possession, that is not how a *deal* works. No, your thief and I are one and the same." She paused, a wry smile on her lips. "Even if she has yet to accept this."

"Her name used to be Amina," Qadir said, casting a glance at her over his shoulder.

Aisha scowled. "*Used* to be."

Loulie, who was riding beside Qadir, snorted. "You jinn are all so melodramatic."

Aisha's cheeks colored at this, but she said nothing until they arrived at the outpost, at which point she excused herself to search for supplies. After promising to meet them by the tents, she rode off, leaving Mazen to follow Qadir and Loulie.

He was shocked by the number of travelers. Whereas the rest of the oases had been small and quiet, this one was teeming with people. Mazen saw immediately that there were two areas: a miniature souk made up of small clay buildings and scattered stalls, and a larger camping area by the water that had a corral for horses and camels. In the market, travelers dressed in foreign garb bartered and gossiped and exchanged goods and currencies from all over the continent. Mazen saw artists and mapmakers, poets and storytellers, soldiers and smiths.

He did not realize until they'd reached the tent area that it was because this place was a tourist destination, a way for travelers to see the Sandsea up close. He was bewildered. But while the merchant and her bodyguard were obviously disgruntled by the crowds, Mazen was relieved. Crowds had always made him feel safe.

That was why, after helping Loulie tie their horses down in the corral, he returned to the souk. Mazen breathed in the smells of spices and food and musk and smiled. Quite unintentionally, he flashed that smile at a young tribeswoman who was out shopping with her mother. She smiled back before turning away with a blush. Her stern-looking mother saw him and frowned. There was some intense scrutiny in her gaze he didn't understand.

Surely I don't look that *suspicious?* He could not help but be offended.

Of course, it *had* been a few days since he'd bathed, and his hair and clothes were matted with dust, so maybe he did look like some sand creature. He stepped back into the crowds, away from the glaring mother. Conversations slid past him like smoke.

"Blasphemous! No man could pull that off..."

"...He was imprisoned by his father for years! Isn't that enough of a reason?"

"...in Madinne! An absolute tragedy. Gods bless the innocents who died in that struggle."

Mazen stopped so abruptly a merchant nearly knocked him over. He cursed at Mazen as he rushed past. Mazen barely heard him. He turned and spotted the gossiper wandering into an alley with his conversation partner.

He followed, pausing just long enough to drape his shadow over his head before he chased after them. He ran to the other side of the souk, but by the time he arrived, the men had disappeared into the crowds.

Weak-kneed, Mazen fell against a nearby wall to catch his breath. It was okay; he could ask around for news from Madinne. Surely there were others who could enlighten him.

As he stood, a flicker of color caught his eye. An illustration tacked onto the wall. Curious, he stepped back to view it in full detail.

His own face, illustrated in remarkably vivid detail, frowned back at him. There were words printed beneath the image: *Mazen bin Malik, exiled prince of Madinne. Traitor to the throne. Wanted for murder of the sultan.*

Mazen stared.

Murder.

He tried to breathe and failed. His heart leapt into his throat and then down into the pit of his stomach. He experienced the peculiar sensation of drowning in himself.

Wanted for murder of the sultan.

There were numbers beneath his name, but he couldn't read them. The world swam before his eyes. He stumbled in place. Pressed a palm to the wall, breathing hard.

Murder of the sultan.

Mazen was vaguely aware of the feel of parchment beneath his fingers. Of the heavy tread of his feet as he made his way back through the souk. Air trapped in his lungs. Stomach churning. *Can't breathe, can't breathe.* His heart beating so fast it felt like it would burst from his chest.

He did not know how he made it to the tent, only that when he did, his lungs were starved of air. The shadow slid from his shoulders as he stumbled inside, where Loulie was waiting for him.

"What...?" She paused when she saw his face.

His breathing hitched, and a small broken sound left his mouth.

"What...what's wrong with you?" Loulie stepped forward and frowned at the parchment in his hands. He had stolen it off the wall without realizing. He held it out to her. *Breathe*, he commanded himself, but every breath was a hiccup that made his heart seize.

The moment Loulie grabbed the parchment from him, he collapsed. Qadir was there to ease him to the ground as she unrolled the parchment and stared, wide-eyed, at the wanted poster.

"Oh." Her voice caught. "Oh *fuck*."

60

LOULIE

"Where is Aisha?"

Panic had, rather than clouding Loulie's mind, made it sharper. She pushed past the fallen prince and ducked outside. Aisha's horse was still absent from the corral. "Shit," she murmured as she stepped back inside.

The prince was sobbing now, a miserable keening sound that made her heart hitch. Qadir was crouched beside him, gripping his shoulder. He looked up at Loulie and frowned. "Gone?"

"Gone." Loulie ran a hand through her curls. *Off to get supplies. What a lie.*

She wanted to scream. This whole time, she'd been fearing the wrong person. Mazen bin Malik had never been a danger to her. And the sultan—he was dead now. Murdered by his own son. Omar had thought this through; even had Mazen still been in disguise, the damage was done. *He* was a wanted man now.

Loulie tore the wanted poster to pieces and threw it at Qadir, who burned it to cinders before it hit the ground. "How far do you think she's gotten?"

Qadir shook his head. "With more than half an hour's start and a horse? Far."

"You think the Resurrectionist will stop her?"

"She knew Aisha's mind the moment she saved her from death. If she did not stop her then, she will not now." He glanced at the prince. "Can you speak?"

The prince was trembling like a newborn camel calf, but he managed to nod.

"Did Aisha say anything to you, anything at *all* that might explain what has happened?"

The prince opened his mouth to speak. Some sound left his throat, but it was not a word. He pressed his lips together and hung his head as tears gathered in his eyes. When he finally spoke, his voice was small. "It's my fault."

Loulie stepped toward him. "What do you mean?"

"It's my fault. I left. I shouldn't have left."

Before she could ask him to clarify, Qadir fixed her with a stern look. *Don't push him.*

Pity settled over her as she stared at the heartbroken prince. She knew the sorrow of losing family. She remembered how the loss had gnawed at her bones and dug itself into her heart. She remembered not being able to speak or think. She remembered having a gaping hole inside of her, an emptiness that consumed everything.

Without Qadir, she would have lost herself in that emptiness.

The prince had no one. And worse, the world had been turned against him. Words failed her. What did you say to a man who had lost his family and also been betrayed by them?

Qadir stepped away and grabbed their lantern. The moment his fingers touched the metal, a bright blue flame burst to life inside the glass. He handed it to Loulie. "I will go gather information. Call me through the fire if anything happens." He squeezed her shoulder, picked up his shamshir, and left the tent.

Loulie turned to the prince, who had thankfully stopped crying but was now staring blankly at the ground with glassy eyes. A tremor racked his body even as she watched.

Loulie hesitated. *What now?*

She was good at talking, but only when it was *at* people. She knew how to use words as a weapon and a shield, but she'd never been good at using them to comfort others. Even when she was a child, her parents had bemoaned her lack of empathy and her inability to listen.

The prince did not acknowledge her as she stepped closer. Did not so much as shift as she awkwardly seated herself beside him and set a hand on his shoulder.

They both flinched at the contact.

Then, slowly, the tension eased from his body, and he sat there, mute and trembling. This close, Loulie could see the smile wrinkles at the corners of his eyes, the flush of his tanned skin. He was a soft man, ill suited to the harsh realities of the world.

And here he was, facing them alone.

The prince took a deep, shuddering breath. "If I hadn't been so selfish..." He trembled. "If I hadn't *left*..."

"If you hadn't left, you'd be dead."

The prince stared at her. Loulie winced. The words had come out unbidden. They were a fact, she realized, and though she was not adept at navigating her own emotions, she knew she could trust facts.

"You were a scapegoat, Prince. A man hell-bent on patricide..." She faltered when more tears gathered in his eyes, but pressed on. "Clearly, Omar had the commitment to see this through. Had you been there, you would have been an obstacle. Don't blame yourself for a crime you didn't commit."

Tears streamed down his face. "I *lied* to my father."

"Your lies did not kill the sultan. Your brother did."

The prince pressed a fist to his forehead and turned away, shoulders trembling. Loulie inwardly cursed. And she'd been doing so well too...

The tent flap opened. Loulie sighed. "Finally. It took you long enough."

But when she looked up, it was not Qadir standing at the entrance, but an older woman garbed in layers of silk. A man wearing a sword at his hip stood beside her. The woman pointed at Mazen and said, "That's him. Look at his face and tell me that *isn't* him."

The man with the sword—a mercenary charged to keep the

peace, by the looks of it—glanced at Mazen. He seemed on the verge of apologizing when the prince looked up. The mercenary's eyes widened. The prince stared at him in silence.

Loulie picked up the lantern. "Qadir?"

The fire cackled softly, and then nothing. She had no time to think about what that meant. The mercenary had yelled for backup and was now approaching them. Loulie slammed the lantern into his knee and gripped the prince's wrist at the same time. The mercenary doubled back as she surged forward, dragging Mazen out with her.

Outside, visitors stared at them unabashedly, first with curiosity and then with fear as mercenaries entered the space, yelling Prince Mazen's name. Loulie grabbed the prince and ran toward the corral. But there were already mercenaries there, ready for them.

"Let them have me," the prince said. "What use am I to you, anyway?"

Loulie dug her nails into his wrist. He cried out. "Shut up and listen." They were close to the corral now. "When I give the signal, run for the horses. I'm counting on you to free them."

"W-what's the signal?"

But there was no time to explain. The mercenaries were approaching, telling her to move away from the prince.

Qadir had said she was the bravest person he knew. Now she would prove it to herself.

When the mercenaries were close enough to touch, Loulie reached into her pocket and withdrew Qadir's dagger. She slashed one mercenary in the arm and threw herself at the other, sending them both tumbling to the dirt. The moment she let go of the prince's hand, he paused, stumbling and staring at her with wide eyes before he ran for the corral.

Loulie rose to her feet, but too slowly. One mercenary grabbed her by her hair and yanked her backward. She tried to elbow him, but to no avail; he was standing far enough away that she could not reach him.

He said something, but it was lost beneath the shrill sound of a scream.

Her captor paused, gasped. "What in nine hells?"

Loulie craned her neck to see what he was looking at. There was smoke—smoke and *fire*—coming from the souk. Before the mercenary could recover from his shock, Loulie angled her knife and slashed it through her curls, cutting both her hair and his grip.

It was perfect timing: the corral doors burst open, and the prince came charging toward her on his horse. He reached out a hand. Loulie grabbed it, throwing herself across the saddle and holding on for dear life as the burning souk blurred in her vision.

61

LOULIE

That night, neither of them slept. Loulie was too jittery, nervous that the mercenaries would give chase. She had commanded the compass to lead them to a hiding place, and it had brought them to a plateau overlooking the Sandsea. It was there that they waited for Qadir.

All the while, Loulie cursed herself for forgetting their supplies at the oasis. The loss of her merchant apparel made her inwardly and physically shudder. The desert was freezing, so cold she burrowed herself into the prince's side without even thinking to ask for his permission. The prince didn't seem to mind; he was either too numb or too cold to care. They sat there like that until the sun rose and Qadir appeared on the horizon—a lone figure walking toward them. It was a relief to see their bag of supplies slung over his shoulder.

Loulie wrapped her arms around herself and stood to meet him. "What happened?" She had to clench her teeth to keep them from chattering.

"The rumors say a magical fire burned through the souk." Qadir paused before her. Even at a distance, he exuded a warmth that thawed the chill in her bones. "Apparently, though it looked real, it was nothing but a mirage."

"Imagine that."

Qadir reached out to touch her frayed curls. "Your work, I assume?"

She managed a weak smile. "What, you think a mercenary would cut it for me?"

"I suspect even a mercenary would make a cleaner cut." His gaze softened as he turned to look at the prince, who had not moved. Qadir snapped his fingers, and a fire burst to life in front of him. The prince sidled closer to it.

Once Loulie had donned her warmer merchant layers and they were all seated in front of the fire, Qadir told them what he'd learned. Shortly after being spotted in Madinne by commoners, "Prince Mazen" had been locked in his chambers indefinitely by his father. The act had garnered sympathy—or perhaps understanding—for what the prince had done next. He'd turned some of the royal soldiers, staged a coup, and stuck a knife through his father's heart.

Prince Mazen looked like he could barely sit upright. "Those are no royal soldiers." He shuddered. "They're my brother's thieves. I overheard Aisha talking about them." He looked up, glassy eyes locked on them in desperation. "My brother," he said weakly. "What of Hakim?"

Qadir grimaced. "There was no news of Prince Hakim. He seems to have vanished in all the chaos." He turned to look at Loulie. "Since the coup was mostly contained to the palace grounds, I trust Dahlia is safe."

Loulie managed a weak nod. Dahlia was a woman of the black market. If she needed to escape, she would use the underground tunnels. But there was still another person whose fate Loulie did not know. When she tried to lock gazes with Qadir, he turned away, hesitation embedded in the furrow of his brow. Loulie's heart hammered in her chest.

There was nothing she could do to prepare herself for his next words.

"Ahmed bin Walid is dead," he said.

The words hit like a hammer. Loulie swayed. It felt as if the world had been pulled out from beneath her feet. She had to place a hand on the ground to balance herself.

"His body was found by the palace gates," Qadir continued. "The rumors vary; some say the wali led the prince's uprising. Others say he was helping palace staff escape when he was ambushed by soldiers. He died with a blade in his hand. A warrior to the very end."

Loulie stared at him numbly. *No.*

She did not realize she was digging her nails into her palms until Qadir reached forward and gently uncurled her fingers. He clasped her shaking hands in his. The normally comforting heat of his skin barely warmed her. Loulie couldn't stop shivering.

The prince fidgeted. "I think Ahmed knew something was off the moment he saw me in Dhyme." He hung his head. "I believe he suspected Omar of scheming and tried to stop him."

If the words were meant to comfort her, they failed.

She could not stop reliving her departure from Dhyme. Could not stop seeing the melancholy smile on Ahmed's lips. She remembered the way he'd kissed her hand, and the words he's said to her: *And we shall finally talk, lovely Loulie, of stars and stories.*

A stray tear slid down her cheek. One, two, and then she was sobbing, her body shaking with the force of her tears as Qadir wrapped an arm around her. He pulled her toward him.

She felt empty, as if some piece of her heart had been smashed. She had taken Ahmed bin Walid for granted. He had seemed immortal—a charismatic, well-liked hunter. A hero, to some.

How could such a man be gone? Without ceremony? Without so much as a goodbye?

Grief shattered the rest of her thoughts, and Loulie buried her face in Qadir's shoulder as she cried. She wept until her throat was hoarse and her tears had run dry.

And then she let rage consume her sorrow.

Wallowing in grief would accomplish nothing. But fury would help her burn a path forward. And at the end of that road, if she was persistent, there would be vengeance.

For her family. For Ahmed. For *her.*

She peeled herself away from Qadir and glanced at the prince.

She saw her emptiness reflected back at her in his eyes. He was a victim now, same as her.

And just like her, he could prove he'd been underestimated.

She turned to Qadir. "What happened after the takeover?"

Qadir's mouth twisted into a grimace. "The prince fled. Rumors say that the sultan's council has assumed control of the city until Omar returns. If what Prince Mazen says is true, then the current army is probably being led by Omar's thieves."

Loulie frowned. "If Omar hasn't gone back, then..."

"He's searching for ifrit magic," the prince said.

Qadir sighed. "Then he will be looking for the lamp. I doubt Aisha bint Louas came all this way just to keep you from returning to the city."

The prince flinched at that but said nothing.

Loulie crossed her arms. "Well. At least we know why your brother sent you on this journey, Prince."

"He deserves to die," the prince said quietly. There was an unnatural stoniness to his expression as he said the words, a deadly calm that was so unlike him it made her cringe. He looked up at her with bloodshot eyes and said, "There's no need to call me Prince anymore." He wrapped his arms around his knees and stared blankly into the fire.

Loulie frowned. "Do you mean that? About your brother? Because I don't want you to object when I stick a blade through his throat."

"I'd kill him myself. But I..." He shook his head, swallowed. "Why should I stay? You're no longer obligated to drag me along. You don't even need to look for the lamp."

She bristled at the morose look on his face. At the defeated slump of his shoulders.

"Loulie and I were trapped the moment your father forced us into this quest, bin Malik," Qadir said, voice gentle. "We do not have the luxury of running, even now. Your brother will eventually find his way to the lamp, and I do not intend to let him take one of my old comrades."

"You could join us," Loulie said. "We're probably the only ones in the desert who won't turn you in for the reward."

Mazen eyed her warily. "How will you find the lamp? You don't even know where it is."

Loulie scoffed. "You're forgetting we have Qadir, who can burn holes in the sand."

Qadir held up the compass. "And a compass that can locate anything."

The compass and Qadir. She had never thought it would be so simple. Once, Qadir had told her the sultan underestimated them. She could still remember her response: *He'll regret threatening us.*

Now she made another promise. "We'll make your brother regret this. I swear it."

Their enemy had changed, but their goal was the same: find the lamp, outwit a corrupt noble. Loulie was going to make Prince Omar suffer. She had lost everything because of him. Now she would take everything from *him*. She would destroy him so thoroughly not even ashes remained.

She stood and held out a hand.

And after a few long moments, Mazen took it.

"Come." Qadir faced the desert with a grim smile. "The lamp awaits."

62

AISHA

Aisha had been a killer for many years, but only now did she feel like a criminal, waiting for Omar at the rendezvous point Tawil had specified. She sat in a cave at the outskirts of the Sandsea, staring into the sunset. The sky looked like it was on fire, the clouds wisps of smoke.

"Why haven't you stopped me yet?" she whispered to the air.

The ifrit shifted somewhere in her mind. *Because I made a deal with you.*

Aisha scoffed. "A terrible deal. A jinn killer and a jinn cannot coexist."

Silence. But then a soft chuckle. *I never make bad deals.*

Aisha opened her mouth to protest but then decided it wasn't worth it. She'd grown accustomed to the ifrit's nonanswers. She dug her heels into the sand with a sigh as she watched the horizon, waiting for the familiar shadow of her king. She wondered what form he would take.

When the undead voices started murmuring into the quiet, Aisha spoke again, asking a question that had been on her mind for a long time. "You can revive people from the dead. So why did you not 'become one' with Munaqid?"

Because he, unlike you, had already passed on. Had I brought him back, he would have been mindless as a ghoul. Aisha took a deep, shuddering breath. *That is why I let his tribesmen dismember my body. Because without Munaqid, I was lost.*

"And now?" Aisha said.

I have found you, and we are lost together.

Aisha did not know how to respond, so she said nothing. She had felt the ifrit's loss in her memories. She could not deny they had both suffered at the hands of murderers—jinn *and* human alike. She tried not to ponder that blurred line too deeply. If she started thinking about crimes caused by humans—senseless crimes like the slaughter of Loulie al-Nazari's tribe—she would start questioning everything about her sense of justice.

And she could not afford to question things, not now.

She squinted at a blur of motion on the horizon and blinked a few times to make sure she was not seeing things. But no, there was the shadow. As it drew closer, Aisha saw it was Tawil riding toward her. A falcon rested on his shoulder, but the moment he stopped at the cave, the bird flitted to the ground. It plucked at the bangle hanging from its leg, and then it transformed into a man. A man Aisha respected. A man she feared.

Instinctually, she got down on one knee and dipped her head.

"What's this? You know better than to bow to me, Aisha. Rise." When she looked up, Prince Omar was smiling at her. He hardly looked like royalty in his simple tunic and pants. But he *did* look the part of a thief with the belt of daggers around his waist.

"Are you not the sultan now? I ought to show you the proper respect."

Omar laughed. "How can I be sultan when I am journeying with the Midnight Merchant?" His eyes glittered with mirth. "No, it will be weeks before the honor passes to me."

Aisha rose to her feet. Normally, she could look Omar in the eye without batting a lash. Now she found it difficult to hold his gaze. "I...lost the bangle," she murmured.

Omar held up his relic. "A small sacrifice. I have its twin. Besides." He stepped forward, that easygoing smile on his face as he reached toward her. "Junaid and Tawil told me you have something far more valuable." He pushed away her scarf. Aisha was aware of the coolness of the collar around her throat.

Omar touched a finger to the relic.

Aisha became inexplicably, violently sick. The world blurred. She closed her eyes with a hiss. *No*, the Resurrectionist said. *Look.*

Aisha forced her eyes open.

And saw a phantom. A beautiful woman with soft brown eyes stood behind Omar, watching Aisha over his shoulder. Aisha did not know her, and yet she *recognized* her.

Once, they had been friends. While they both dealt in memories, Aisha—the Resurrectionist—had been death, and this woman's magic had been life. *I love humans*, she'd once said. *They are the gods' creatures, same as us, so why should we harm them?*

Because they seek to destroy us, the Resurrectionist had replied.

But her friend, ever the pacifist, had refused to believe this. *They only fear us because we are more powerful. If we show them we are equals, they will not harm us.*

And they had tried. Their king had tried. But the humans had abused his kindness. They had slaughtered jinn and stolen relics, and still Aisha's friend had said, *I do not believe they are irredeemable.* Those had been the last words she spoke to her before their world sank and she disappeared forever. Later, the Resurrectionist felt her friend's death from a distance. But she had never known where or what her relic was.

Aisha stared. The ifrit—the Mystic, she had once been called—smiled at her sadly.

And then she was gone, dissipated into thin air as Omar drew his hand away. "Have you heard a single thing I've said, Aisha?"

She swallowed. "Yes. I was just...distracted by the voices."

Omar raised a brow. "Voices?"

"The dead," Aisha clarified. "The relic lets me hear their voices."

Omar stared at her. She knew that look; it was the stoic façade he wore to stop others from gauging his reaction. Aisha forced herself to hold his gaze.

Why was an ifrit following him? He had promised he would tell them when he found a king's relic. And she knew Omar; he would never allow anyone to tail him, not even a ghost.

"In my personal opinion, sayyidi…" Tawil smirked. "I don't think bint Louas can handle the relic. Even in Ghiban, she was a little foggy-eyed."

Aisha scowled. "Me, foggy-eyed? *You're* the one who had their treasure stolen."

She could still remember his face when he'd apprehended her the morning after the merchant's sale. He'd been panicked, stuttering over his words as he cursed her. Now his face contorted again as he glared at her.

"That's because *you*—"

"Enough." Omar's voice was soft but dangerous, and Tawil stopped talking. "We have no time to bicker. I've called for reinforcements, and I do not want to be late for our rendezvous." He frowned. "You know how long I have searched for this lamp. I will wait no longer."

She *did* know. Omar had scavenged this area for years, looking for the relic. But it had not been until just recently, when the sultan commanded Prince Hakim to chart the location based on Amir's writings, that Omar had finally pinpointed its location. Aisha wondered if he'd held off killing the sultan for those coordinates. If he'd waited patiently for an opportunity to frame his brother for his murder.

She shoved thoughts of the prince away before they could sink in. She had always known that Prince Mazen was a scapegoat. But that did not lessen the weight of her guilt any. She *owed* him for saving her life. Besides that, she had come to find his company tolerable. Enjoyable, even. And now she had betrayed him, and he would never forgive her for it.

You can still turn away from this, the Resurrectionist murmured in her mind.

Aisha clenched her fists. No, she couldn't. She wouldn't.

You cheated death; cheating a king would be easy.

"Enough," Aisha snapped. She didn't realize she'd spoken aloud until she noticed Omar and Tawil frowning at her.

"Voices again?" Tawil said with a sneer.

I would like to murder him, the ifrit murmured. That, at least, was one thing they could agree on. But Aisha pushed down the Resurrectionist's annoyance and forced herself to nod.

She breathed in deeply as Omar walked past. Tawil followed him with a huff. The moment his elbow connected with her shoulder, Aisha reached out and gripped his arm. Heat—sudden and bright and *angry*—pulsed through her fingers.

Tawil pried his arm from her grip with a scowl, but she saw a muscle twitch in his jaw as he clenched his teeth. "Let me be clear," he said. "My king may trust you, but I do not."

Aisha watched his back until it disappeared. She heard the echo of footsteps as Omar and Tawil descended a pathway that led beneath the Sandsea. How the pathway existed beneath the sinking sand, Aisha did not know, but she was suddenly terrified to follow.

I don't trust you either, she thought.

It did not occur to her until later that the words were not just meant for Tawil.

63

LOULIE

They traveled through the Sandsea for many days, using the compass to guide them across the arduous landscape. Because the pathways running through the sinking sand were so narrow, they opted to leave the horse behind where someone from the outpost could find it. It was already a perilous enough journey without it. And yet Loulie was glad the crossing took all her concentration, because when she wasn't preoccupied with surviving, she lapsed into mourning for Ahmed bin Walid. By the end of every day, she was physically and emotionally drained.

And yet sleep evaded her. When she closed her eyes, she saw Ahmed.

Ahmed, dancing her around the diwan. Ahmed, eyes bright with wonder as she told him about her latest adventure. She remembered his buoyant laugh, his shining smile. And she remembered the word tattooed on his wrist: *Mukhlis*. Loyal. To her.

The memories carved a hole in her heart. But though she felt hollow, she knew it was nothing in comparison to Mazen's sorrow. Try as he did to stifle his cries, she could hear him sobbing. It was only on the last night of their journey that his tears dried and his expression hardened. He was putting on armor, she realized. Steeling himself for what was to come.

That last night, they set up camp on a patch of stable land in the middle of the Sandsea. Qadir sparked a fire, took the last of their food provisions from their bag, and said, "We reach the lamp tomorrow."

"Finally," Loulie mumbled.

"The ifrit inside, this Rijah…" Mazen shifted. In the firelight, his golden eyes were brighter, fiercer. "What happens when we free them?"

Qadir shrugged. "I haven't seen Rijah in hundreds of years. It is hard to say what captivity has done to their mind. But of all the ifrit, Rijah is the most likely to pursue revenge." Silence hung in the air as Qadir roasted strips of dried meat over the fire. After a few moments, he added, "If given the choice, I think they would kill your brother over you."

"That's not very reassuring," Mazen said.

Loulie groaned. "*None* of this is reassuring."

Calm as she was on the outside, she was internally panicking. The present was not a problem; she could throw herself into a fight so long as she didn't have to consider the consequences. But she could not stop worrying about the what-ifs.

What if Omar found the lamp first? What if he captured them? What if she *was* able to kill him? Murdering a forgotten thief to avenge her family was one thing. But murdering a prince set to take his father's place? She would never be able to show her face in this country again.

Qadir sighed. "Don't think too hard on it. What will be will be."

The words sparked a memory: a calmer moment aboard a ship. Loulie smiled. "Sage advice, oh mighty jinn."

Qadir smiled back at her.

Mazen looked bewildered. "Are you two always this calm before jumping into peril?"

"The trick is to fake it until you make yourself believe it," Loulie said. It was Qadir's advice, and she had never clung to it as fiercely as she did now.

The next day, Loulie strode ahead with the compass, slowly

turning bends and stepping down crooked paths until she stopped. The compass's arrow was jittering so wildly it looked possessed.

"We've arrived," Qadir said.

Loulie eyed their surroundings skeptically. As far as she could see, this stretch of the Sandsea looked the same as any other. She looked questioningly at Qadir, who shrugged and walked straight into it. The sand around him burned away, revealing a sloped tunnel that led into the Sandsea. When Qadir turned to face them, the markings on his skin blazed gold and red, and his eyes danced with fire. He sighed, and wisps of smoke curled out from his lips like shisha from a smoker's mouth.

Loulie rolled her eyes. "Show-off."

Mazen simply stared, slack-jawed.

"Don't fall behind," Qadir said, and then he turned and walked deeper into the Sandsea, burning a hole through the world as he did so. For a few moments, Loulie stared quietly into the darkness. Fear, sudden and primal, froze her in place.

Mazen stepped forward so that the two of them stood before the Sandsea together. He flashed her a weak smile. "Fake it until you make yourself believe it, right?"

Loulie glanced one last time at the outside world—at the sun hanging in the crystal blue sky and the smoky clouds in the distance. Determination sparked in her. *I'll be back*, she thought.

They stepped into the darkness of the Sandsea.

64

MAZEN

A long time ago, when Mazen had been a boy and his father had first told him the story of the lamp, he'd asked why, in all the years the lamp had existed, the royal family had never retrieved it.

Tell me, Mazen, do you know of a way to enter the Sandsea?

Mazen had suggested a ship that dove into the sinking sand. His father had laughed—one of those rare, honest laughs that shook his whole body—and said, *What you suggest is magic, my son. You would need magic.*

Now, as Mazen wandered into the Sandsea, he felt that magic gather on his skin like invisible dew. It hung like mist in the damp air and made the darkness before them shimmer. He would have been in awe if he hadn't been so anxious. Because he had no idea what he was doing.

But then, his life had been out of his hands the moment he'd gone on this journey. Now his future had been burned to cinders, and his memories lay in the depths of a cavernous hole. Every time he stood at the edge of that pit, every time he thought of his father, of Hakim—it took all that he had to resist falling in and succumbing to his misery.

So he did not ruminate. He followed blindly, all the while thinking, *This is all I have left.*

Eventually, the dark tunnels widened into cavernous chambers filled with hills of blue-white sand. Rivers of sand cascaded down the walls from the darkness above them. The chamber was only the first of many impossible wonders. As they continued, the landscape grew increasingly more spectacular. Soon there were trees growing from the sand. And then entire forests, entire *buildings*.

They passed through golden gates couched between deity statues Mazen did not recognize and stepped into what appeared to be an abandoned souk. To Mazen's left: pots of spices and nuts; a cart stacked high with fabrics that changed color and pattern; and iridescently glowing ceramics. To his right: glass lanterns filled with multicolored smoke; shattered mirrors that reflected his face with multiple expressions; and delicately decorated boxes of lokum. He shifted his gaze upward and gaped at the stall canopies, which shifted color before his eyes. Some were trimmed with intricate, shimmering gold patterns that moved fluidly, like water.

"Qadir." The merchant's voice was faint. "What is all this?"

Qadir did not respond. He headed toward a copse of glittering fruit trees in the center of the souk. Mazen followed. His initial opinion of the apples was that they were oddly shaped: less round and more...sharp? He reached for one of the lower-hanging fruits and gasped aloud when his fingers brushed the surface.

The fruit was made of glass.

Qadir plucked an apple off the tree and bit into it without hesitation. Mazen could hear the sharp crunch of glass as the ifrit chewed, but Qadir seemed unconcerned. He was smiling.

"I grew up with these trees," he said. Though he was looking at Loulie, his gaze was far away. "They only grew in the capital, and the fruit they bore was five times more expensive because it came from magic seeds."

Mazen cautiously took a bite of the apple. He experienced the strange sensation of glass breaking between his teeth and melting into sugar on his tongue. He immediately took another bite. *Delicious* was a woefully inadequate description.

Qadir wandered away, moving deeper into the empty souk.

Loulie immediately gave chase. Mazen followed after stuffing the rest of the apple into his mouth.

"How is any of this down here?" Loulie called. "Qadir!"

But Qadir was walking so quickly now that they had to run to keep up with him. He led them down twisted alleys and into thoroughfares taken up by extravagant buildings with stunning stained-glass windows and shining gilded doors. And then eventually, he stopped at a bridge made of solid gold. Mazen gasped for breath as he stopped beside him and looked up—up, up, up. For on the other side of the bridge was a palace with such tall minarets they faded into the infinite darkness above them. The building was oddly blurry, its details undefined.

A mirage?

"Qadir!" Loulie grabbed Qadir's arm, but the ifrit just dragged her along as he stomped onto the bridge. She cast a desperate look over her shoulder, and Mazen rushed forward to grab his other arm. The ifrit shoved them off with enough force to send them tumbling to the bridge.

Living, breathing fire shone in his eyes as he whirled on them. *"Do not touch me,"* he snapped, and his voice was so loud and deep it made the bridge rumble.

The ifrit turned and walked away, leaving them to stare at his back. "Something's wrong," Loulie muttered. She rose and dusted off her robes. "We need to follow him."

They crossed the shining bridge and burst through the entrance. By the time they saw Qadir again, he'd reached the end of a dark corridor. Mazen continued to give chase until the merchant suddenly stopped and he had to skid to a halt to avoid crashing into her.

He glanced over her shoulder. "What is it?"

The merchant had slid the compass out of her pocket and was staring at it. The arrow was quivering, pointing to an archway farther down the corridor.

Loulie frowned. "The lamp?"

The arrow shuddered in response. She bit her lip. "I can't lose Qadir. But the lamp . . ."

"I'll find it." Mazen tried to smile but was too nervous to lift the corners of his lips.

Loulie's expression lightened as she led him down the corridor to the archway designated by the compass. Mazen was overwhelmed by the sight inside.

It was a treasure chamber. The fullest, most impressive treasure chamber he'd ever laid eyes on. The floor was impossible to see beneath mountains of gold so tall the tops were lost to darkness. Glittering jewels and lavish artifacts lay scattered atop the piles as if they were mere trinkets. It was a staggering sight, like something out of one of his mother's stories.

Loulie breathed out softly. "Damn."

"What *is* this place?" Mazen mumbled. "Is all of this...real?"

"That's what I intend to ask Qadir." Loulie hesitated, then shoved the compass into his hands. "I'll be back. But if I don't return soon, use the compass to find us." She turned and bolted through the corridor they had just come from.

Mazen faced the mounds of treasure. He followed the compass to a corner of the room drenched in sunlight that, as far as he could tell, came from the emptiness above him. He tucked the relic away and began sifting through the mound, which certainly *felt* real beneath his hands. Treasure slid through his fingers as he searched. But then eventually, he found what he was looking for: a simple copper oil lamp.

He plucked it from the pile with trembling hands. Was this small, unspectacular thing truly what they'd been looking for all this time? It didn't *feel* like a relic. He tilted it one way and then the other. When nothing happened, he opened the lid and peered inside. It was empty.

He rubbed at the body, thinking that perhaps instructions had been inscribed onto the surface beneath all the dirt.

But there was nothing.

The lamp was just that—a lamp.

65

LOULIE

Trying to stop Qadir was like trying to move a boulder: it was impossible. Loulie tried to break him out of his trance by yelling his name, but Qadir never seemed to see her. She followed him down dark corridors and through chambers filled with ancient furniture. They passed chests made of solid gold, beautifully colored tile-top tables, mounted weapons with hilts of precious jade and silver, glass cabinets filled with tiny *moving* porcelain creatures—and Qadir never so much as blinked or questioned where they were.

She slid the two-faced coin out of her pocket.

Is Qadir possessed? She flipped the coin. The jinn side came up. *No.*

Is he being influenced by magic? The sultan's face frowned up at her. *Yes.*

When she looked up, they were in a chamber similar to the one they'd first entered, only it was not so much a room as an endless stalagmite-filled *landscape* with no apparent end. Blue-white sand trickled down the spires, pooling on the ground like water. A flicker of motion caught her eye, and she looked down to see her own reflection gaping at her from the ground.

"What in nine hells is this place?" She tucked the coin away and pulled out Qadir's dagger, eyeing the space cautiously as they advanced. She did not like this place with the strange, reflective sand that mirrored her fear at her from various angles. Even more alarming: when she glanced over her shoulder, she saw that the entrance—and exit—to the room had vanished.

Panic hummed through her veins. *What kind of magic is this?*

Qadir stopped. Loulie nearly ran into his back. She paused, heart thundering in her chest as she moved to stand in front of him. "Qadir?"

"Khalilah." His voice broke on the name. She blinked, followed his gaze to a hill of sand about a mile away. At first, she saw nothing out of the ordinary. Just endlessly falling sand and their own reflections staring at them from a distance. But then she realized one of the reflections was a solid person: a brown-skinned woman with a nest of braids trailing down her back. *Khalilah.* Loulie recognized the name. It was the name of the jinn in the compass.

Qadir brushed past her, eyes trained on the jinn with a desperation that made panic bubble in her chest. This was an illusion—it had to be.

Or a distraction. But from what?

That was when she heard the whistle and saw a flash of red in the air.

And then pain in her cheek. Blood dribbling down her chin.

"Qadir!" She shoved him out of the way as another arrow whizzed past his face. Qadir stumbled, turned, and blinked. His gaze sharpened.

The invisible archer gave them no time to think. Another arrow came, and then another and another, until the air was full of them. Qadir moved sluggishly, raising his hand and conjuring a wall of fire to burn the incoming projectiles.

Only—the arrows burst through the flames, undeterred. One caught Loulie's sleeve; another grazed her leg. Qadir caught one arrow in the shoulder, another in the stomach, and the last in his chest. Loulie cried out as he collapsed to his knees, ash dripping down his face. She crouched beside him as his fire burned low and disappeared, and stared in horror at the silver blood running from his wounds.

The arrows were crafted from iron.

She heard laughter, slow and mocking. "Well, *that* was disappointing." She turned to see a man with a wide, shiny smile approaching. He walked with his bow strung, arrow nocked and pointed at Qadir. "Don't move, merchant."

The archer paused feet away and made a sweeping gesture with his hand. Another figure approached. A heartbeat later, Aisha bint Louas stood behind Qadir, her sword at his neck. "Immortal you may be, ifrit, but even you need time to heal."

Rage, dark and twisting, burned through Loulie's heart. Aisha's expression was utterly impassive. She raised her brows. "Salaam, al-Nazari."

"Traitor," Loulie spat.

The man laughed. "*Traitor?* Who did you think she was working for? We are the forty thieves; we serve one man, and one man alone."

Loulie stared at the stranger, the thief with the iron arrows clearly meant to disable jinn, and then she glanced at Aisha, who stood patiently behind Qadir.

Waiting. They were both waiting.

Omar, she thought, heart sinking. *Omar bin Malik is here.*

66

MAZEN

Mazen threw the lamp to the ground and pressed his palms to his eyes. *We came all this way for nothing.* The realization pulled him back down into his despair. No matter what happened, he would still come out of this a criminal. There was nothing waiting for him outside. His father was dead, his home overtaken, his brother vanished, his title gone.

He sat there shaking for a long time, lungs tight, body tense. Though the minutes were immeasurable, he had the impression that a significant amount of time passed before he finally raised his head. It occurred to him Loulie had not returned.

After some hesitation, he picked up the useless oil lamp, rose to his feet, and headed for the entrance. He'd made it only a few steps when he noticed the man sitting on a nearby heap of sand, silently watching him.

Omar.

Mazen forgot how to breathe.

One of Omar's brows inched up far enough to wrinkle his forehead. "Salaam, Mazen." He rose and dusted off his clothing. "You're as pale as a wraith."

Run, said a voice in his head. But another voice, one that did not speak in words, urged him to stay. This voice was black and fuzzy, and so loud it blocked out reason.

"How was your adventure?" Omar said.

The static spilled into Mazen's vision. He saw Hakim fleeing from rioting soldiers. His father lying on bloody bedsheets. Omar wearing his face, drenched in the sultan's blood.

"How droll. You're normally more talkative." Omar paused feet away, hands clasped behind his back, shoulders lifted high like a general's. Like a sultan's.

"Let me tell you what happens next, Mazen. First, you will hand over the lamp. Second, we will return to Madinne, where you will be tried for your crimes. If you do not obey, I will kill the merchant." He smiled after delivering the instructions—the same charismatic smile he wore in court. It made Mazen see red.

"How dare you." The words came through the dark static buzzing in his mind.

Omar blinked at him, smiled. "You'll have to be more specific."

And it was that smile, that godsdamned grin, that broke Mazen. Reason fell away. There was only that black, humming voice and the urge to destroy. He moved without thinking, lunging toward Omar with a scream. The world collapsed into darkness. Rage. Desperation. And a sorrow so deep it painted everything a soulless gray.

And then: sharp pain in his gut. He registered Omar had punched him in the stomach. He staggered backward, wheezing.

"All this time, and you still don't know how to fight, akhi?" Omar punched him again, this time in the face. Mazen tasted blood in his mouth as he fell.

When Omar reached for him again, Mazen grabbed his arm and dug his nails into his skin. "You lying *snake*." He dug deep enough to draw blood.

He relented only when Omar twisted his arm, when something *cracked*. Pain shot through his shoulder, so terrible it made him scream. There were tears in Mazen's eyes when Omar stepped away, holding the stolen lamp in one hand and concealing his injury with the other.

"You killed our father. And for what? You gained nothing!"

"Do you truly think that, Mazen?" Omar laughed. A soft,

hollow sound. "Unlike you, I have never done anything without reason. I have simply taken what was rightfully mine." He leveled his blank gaze on Mazen. "The old fool was going to name you sultan."

Mazen's heart plummeted to the soles of his feet. The static cleared, replaced with a memory of his father seated before him in the diwan. *Who has ever heard of a prince who doesn't know how to use a blade? You hold the weight of a kingdom on your shoulders, Mazen. You cannot protect it with just good intentions.*

"No," he said weakly.

"Yes." Omar scoffed. "As always, you are too blind to see what is right in front of you. You do not deserve Madinne."

"And you do? You're a coward." Something flashed in Omar's eyes, but Mazen pressed on: "You killed our father and blamed it on *me*."

Omar did not respond. He approached slowly, with all the foreboding of an encroaching storm. He pulled his hand away from his wound, revealing the smear of blood on his arm.

It was black.

Mazen's breathing hitched. He'd forgotten about the black blood, the same blood that had run through his veins when he was in Omar's body. That had run through Imad's. Aisha had called it a side effect of the bangle. He'd believed her.

"You have it all wrong, Mazen. It is because *you* are a coward that I could pin this crime on you." Mazen was barely listening. He was still staring at the blood.

Human blood was red. Jinn blood was silver. Black blood...

Omar's arm shot out. Mazen felt cold fingers on his wrist, an icy heat in his veins. Something shimmered unnaturally on Omar's ear. His... earring?

Mazen gasped as the world faded into a canvas of muted colors. Beneath it, Omar's voice was a barely discernible whisper. "If only you knew, Mazen, how terrible our father was." The colors reshaped themselves into a crystal clear image of the sultan, who loomed above him.

"Look at your hands," he commanded, and he had no choice but to obey.

His hands were covered in black blood. His blood.

"You have the blood of a sinner in you," the sultan said. "You are a blight on this world." Each word was like the lash of a whip. *"There is only one way to remedy this."* He crouched down and grabbed his chin, forcing him to look into his eyes. *They had the same eyes—he'd always hated that they had the same eyes.*

"Show me you are not like her," the sultan said. "The jinn are monsters; kill them."

"And me?" His voice—Omar's voice—was soft, weak. "Am I a monster?"

The sultan shoved a black dagger into his hands. He recognized it; it was the dagger the sultan had forced him to soak in his blood. Jinn blood can heal things, *he had said.* Let us see if your tainted blood can destroy them.

"That has yet to be determined." The sultan pointed at the knife. "If you are not a monster, you will do as I command and slay the jinn. Do you understand?"

He swallowed. "I understand."

The memory dissipated, and Omar stood before him again, smiling. Only, this smile was not coy or twisted. It was despondent. Pained.

"If you would blame anyone for this, Mazen, blame our father. He told me once that the only way to rightfully gain something was to steal it. This is nothing personal." Omar hauled him to his feet and out of the chamber.

Phantom colors still danced before Mazen's eyes, an afterimage of the vision he'd seen. It had to be magic, but he didn't understand where it had come from.

He glanced at the black knives on his brother's belt—the ones Mazen had used to decimate ghouls with only a strike—and at the smudge of black blood on Omar's arm. *You have the blood of a sinner in you.*

The words hung over his head, an ax waiting to fall.

67

AISHA

Aisha saw Omar's reflection first. He was smiling—the smirk he wore when he was flaunting a victory. It had never bothered Aisha before, but seeing it plastered on his face now, as he dragged Prince Mazen behind him, made her bristle.

Omar walked past without sparing her a glance. Mazen, however, lifted his gaze. The sultan's youngest son looked as if he'd been in a fight; there was a smear of blood on his swollen jaw, and he was holding his arm at an awkward angle, as if he were in pain.

Aisha forced herself to look stoically back at him even as his expression crumpled and her heart fell. She turned her attention to the lamp Omar was holding in his other hand.

The object didn't speak to her like relics did, and yet she had the distinct impression it was alive. Alive and unhappy.

Omar stopped before the merchant. "Midnight Merchant," he said.

Loulie glared. "I see you've added patricide to your list of accomplishments."

"You never were good at greetings, were you?" He gestured toward Tawil, who lowered his bow and went to stand behind Mazen. Then he glanced up at Aisha and made a flicking motion toward the merchant.

He commands you like a dog, the Resurrectionist observed.

Aisha wordlessly stepped away from Qadir and grabbed the merchant. The jinn looked up in alarm as she dragged Loulie away. Aisha managed to pull her back a couple of feet before the merchant broke free of her grasp, whipping around and grazing her with her knife.

Aisha stepped back. She glimpsed the red beading on her skin and exhaled shakily.

It didn't matter that she had been brought back by an ifrit. She was still human. Still *herself*, and she would not let a conniving ifrit manipulate her.

The Resurrectionist sighed. *The only one you are fooling is yourself, human.*

Aisha scowled at the pity in the ifrit's voice. She forced herself to focus on Omar, who was lowering himself into a crouch before the merchant. "I hope you were just as pleasant with Imad," he said conversationally. "Which, speaking of, I must thank you for dealing with him. By the time I realized he was a threat, you'd made him into a corpse."

Had the merchant been a jinn, Aisha suspected her glower would have set Omar on fire. "Is that what you do to thieves who get caught? You kill them to destroy evidence of the murders *you* had them commit?"

Omar's smile fell. "Ah. I'm afraid in that regard, I take after my dearly departed father." He stepped away from them. " 'Where jinn are involved, there are always casualties,' he used to say. The kings' relics are a closely guarded royal secret; it would not do to leave behind survivors."

Aisha clasped her hands behind her back, breathed out softly. This story had never bothered her before. So why did it unsettle her now?

Because you realize the dead do *speak*, the Resurrectionist said. *That even when they are gone, they speak through the loved ones they leave behind.*

Aisha stared at the merchant. At the mournful slouch of her

shoulders and the anger burning in her eyes. "So you killed my tribe because it was inconvenient to let them live?"

A shadow passed over Omar's face as he looked at her. "Not all of us are lucky enough to die martyrs. For most, death is only ever happenstance. You think you are special, al-Nazari? That your tribe was special? You are all only human. Weak, fallible, and mortal." His eyes flashed. "Ahmed believed himself to be invincible too. That conviction was his downfall."

The merchant stiffened, her face going dangerously blank. "What did you do to Ahmed?"

"The wali was too curious for his own good. He thought to sneak around *my* palace and unravel my plans. He came close." He sighed. "But even hunters can be cut down."

Aisha, trapped in her own mind, did not see the merchant shift until it was too late.

Loulie lunged toward Omar, her dagger burning bright with fire as she thrust it forward—

And stabbed the prince in the shoulder.

Aisha was too shocked to move. Fire licked at her king's clothes and face as he stared at the blade impaled in his shoulder. And then he smiled.

And disappeared.

A relic? Aisha thought at the same time the queen said, *His earring. It is ifrit magic.*

The merchant fell, still clutching the dagger she had driven into Omar's shoulder. Aisha whirled at the sound of Omar's voice, which was coming from her right. "Tell me, bodyguard. Are you the jinn king I sent my thieves to find all those years ago?" The prince stood in front of Qadir, completely unharmed. Aisha stared, uncomprehending.

Qadir did not respond with words. His eyes flashed red as he cut a hand through the air.

And set the prince on fire.

This time, Aisha saw Omar *ripple* like water before he disappeared. She startled when he appeared right beside her. "No matter."

He smiled. "My thieves may have failed me then, but I will have your relic now." In a single motion, he pulled a dagger from his sleeve and ran it across his palm, drawing... black blood?

A memory sparked in her mind of black blood oozing from Prince Mazen's wound. He had been in Omar's body then. Aisha had assumed it was a side effect of the relic, but there was no bangle on Omar's arm when he pressed his bloodied hand to the lamp.

There was a beat of silence, followed by a rush of intense heat. Aisha braced her feet as a dense smoke burst from the lamp and swept across the area. She could barely see, could barely *breathe*. But she could hear Omar's voice beneath the crackling storm. "Jinn king!" he yelled. "You are bound to me and you will *serve* me."

All at once the smoke withdrew. Aisha gasped air in through her lungs as she looked up.

The creature standing beside Omar was a silhouette of smoke, features undefined except for its eyes, which were a turquoise blue that glittered like diamonds. Its body was made up of undulating storm clouds, and the fire pulsing beneath its skin flashed like lightning.

Aisha dared a glance at the others. The merchant and the prince both looked spellbound, staring at the ifrit with their mouths hanging open.

Tawil was in a similar state of shock. "The Shapeshifter," he murmured.

The title made Aisha's skin prickle; she recognized it.

Omar turned to Qadir, who had risen to his feet and was pulling Tawil's arrows from his skin. Silver blood gushed from his wounds as they began to heal. "Rijah," he said softly.

Rijah. The Resurrectionist's voice was a sad echo, her grief a hole in Aisha's heart.

The mass of smoke shuddered at the name.

"Jinn of the lamp," Omar said. "I command you to kill the jinn king before me."

Without preamble, the creature of smoke pounced, transforming into a panther that knocked Qadir to the ground. Qadir grabbed the panther's jaws as it lunged for his throat, but his hands were quivering, his face blanched with terror.

The merchant stumbled to her feet and rushed toward him. Unthinkingly, Aisha gave chase. It was easier to act than to think. Easier to follow the plan than to question it.

The Resurrectionist's voice brushed through her empty mind. *And here I thought you had returned to life to carve your own path.*

"My path, not *yours*," Aisha snapped. She gained on the merchant until she was close enough to tackle her from behind. She pressed a sword to her throat. Loulie struggled, but to no avail. Together, they watched Qadir battle the ifrit. When he conjured a wall of flame, the ifrit pushed past it in the form of a great, flaming bird and rushed at his face with its talons, shrieking as Qadir held out a hand and threw a gust of wind at it.

"Give it up, merchant." She heard Tawil's voice behind her. "Sit back and enjoy the show. The Shapeshifter is sure to give us a good one."

Shapeshifter. There was that title again. It had been in Qadir's story about the seven ifrit.

The jinn version.

She shuddered as Tawil approached. She remembered his nervous laughter when she'd touched his burning skin. The way he had shrunk away from her when she gripped his arm.

Finally, the Resurrectionist said. *You see clearly.*

Tawil approached. He stepped closer, dragging Mazen behind him. Closer. Closer.

Aisha's surprise flared into indignation. She whirled, pulling her sword away from the merchant's throat and slashing it at Tawil. Tawil gasped and grabbed at the wound on his arm, but not quickly enough to conceal the silver blood oozing through his fingers.

Aisha gripped the hilt of her sword. "I knew it."

Tawil paled. "I can explain—"

But she didn't need an explanation, not when the realization had already dawned on her. Without flinching, she grabbed a knife from her belt and stabbed Tawil in the throat. Silver gushed from his lips as he crumpled to the ground.

He deserved that. The ifrit's pleasure was an undercurrent to Aisha's own anger.

Mazen sidestepped the thief's body, face ashen. The merchant's wide eyes flicked between her and the corpse. There was a tense pause as they watched Tawil bleed out. Then they all faced Omar, who had not moved. Aisha glared at him.

"I was going to tell you after this was all over," he said, voice eerily calm.

After he had finished using you, the Resurrectionist said.

Aisha glanced at the silver blood pooling on the ground. She thought of the recollection in Junaid's eyes when she had brought up the collar's existence to him. The strange injury on Samar's arm, healed far too soon.

"How many of us are jinn?"

Omar regarded her stoically. "More than half."

She was baffled. She'd become one of the forty thieves to *kill* jinn. How was it that so many of her comrades were jinn? That they were killing *other* jinn?

Omar approached. "The jinn who flee into the human lands are criminals in their world. Is it so strange I would work with jinn who want to exterminate them? Our goals align." He paused, dared a smile. "You are different, Aisha. I did not make a deal with you. I *chose* you."

I chose you. How long had she clung to those words, believing them to be the truth? She had always believed the reason Omar recruited her was because he'd seen a kindred spirit in her. She had never considered him a friend, but she had trusted him.

And he'd used that trust against her. He had used *her*, even knowing her hatred of jinn.

Omar ventured a step closer. Aisha responded by throwing a dagger at his face. She was irritated when it went right through him.

"An illusion?" Mazen murmured.

"Ifrit magic," Aisha said. She had always thought Omar's stealth was unnatural but had never questioned it. But now she could not stop looking at the earring—at the *relic* on his ear that made that stealth possible. How many other illusions had he crafted with that magic? In all the years they'd hunted together, Aisha had never seen him bleed black blood. Had even that been a trick? An elaborate deception created by his mother's earring?

The last piece of the puzzle slid into place.

Let us show them the truth, the Resurrectionist said.

Aisha set her hands on Mazen's and Loulie's shoulders. "Look," she said, and the cursed magic running through her veins enveloped all their senses, allowing them to see the phantom behind Omar. The similarities between them were striking; they had the same-shaped face. The same thin nose.

The merchant inhaled sharply. "An ifrit?"

The Resurrectionist spoke through Aisha: "Here, you know her as the sultan's first wife. But in our world, she is a powerful illusionist. In our world, she is an ifrit: Aliyah the Mystic."

Once, Aliyah might have been Aisha's target. But Aisha did not seek out the dead.

She had never believed in chasing the past, but the present—there lay a vengeance she could claim with her blade.

The ifrit's voice brushed through her mind. *And with my magic, if you choose to wield it.*

Aisha could feel that magic beating in sync with her heart. So far, it had remained an extra, unwanted sense—a way for her to hear and speak to the dead. But now it was being proffered to her as a weapon.

She hesitated. Magic had destroyed her life. But perhaps when sharpened into a weapon of her making, magic could help her reclaim control of it. Aisha nodded mutely.

Together, then. She could hear the triumphant grin in the ifrit's words as her power scorched through Aisha's veins. The heat of it was exhilarating. Overwhelming.

Aisha breathed in deeply to relax her thudding heart and trembling limbs. She thought of Samar, who had promised to sing her praises when she returned to Madinne, and Junaid, who had proposed a toast to her loyalty. What a shame that she would have to disappoint them both.

Aisha looked at Omar and made a new vow.

I promise I will kill you, she thought.

She always kept her promises.

68

MAZEN

Aliyah the Forgotten. That was what the citizens of Madinne called the sultan's first wife behind closed doors. To Mazen, she had always been a specter, a story his father never told. She was from a time before the wife killings, a memory inaccessible to all of them, even Omar. At least, that had been his belief.

But now, all the disparate pieces clicked together. Aliyah, an ifrit. The sultan, a jinn killer. Finally, Mazen understood why Omar's blood was black. Why he hated the sultan. But—

"Why? Why would you kill jinn if your mother is one?"

Omar sighed. "As always, you ask the wrong questions, Mazen." He slid a knife from his sleeve and angled it toward them. Mazen tensed, poised to flee—and then he heard Omar's voice coming from behind. When he turned, his brother was close enough to stab him. The merchant shot forward with her knife, but the strike only broke Omar's body into smoke.

The first Omar—*Real or an illusion?*—rushed at them with his blade. There was a shriek of metal as Aisha held up her sword just in time to catch the attack. "I'll be relieving you of the king's relic now, Aisha." Omar slid the dagger off her sword, aimed it at her heart.

Aisha retaliated with a slash, but Omar disappeared before it landed.

He reappeared behind her. Aisha turned.

And Omar buried the knife in her chest.

No! Mazen pushed his brother away. He had let Aisha die once. How could he—

Aisha grinned, baring crimson-coated teeth. Both of her eyes were black as midnight. "You'll have to try harder than that, jinn killer."

She snapped her fingers, and the corpse that had been Tawil reached out and gripped Omar's ankle. For the first time in his life, Mazen saw fear on Omar's face. Then the corpse *pulled* and Omar fell, the lamp tumbling from his hands and to the ground. A heartbeat later it was in Loulie's hands. She turned and ran toward Qadir.

Mazen chased after her.

Qadir and Rijah fought in a raging storm, the winds around them as much a barrier as a cage. Loulie stood helplessly at the edge, starry robes billowing in the gust. Before she could protest, Mazen stole her knife and sliced his palm.

Understanding lit her eyes. She handed him the lamp.

The moment he pressed his bloodied palm to the surface, he felt it: power, thrumming beneath his skin. Hundreds of years ago, his ancestor had tricked an ifrit into enchanting this object for him. His father had warned Loulie that the relic worked only for ones who shared his blood. That was why Omar had been able to use the lamp, and why the sultan had never feared Loulie using it against him.

"Rijah!" Mazen yelled into the storm. "You are bound to me and you will serve me!" He held up the lamp. *"Stop!"*

The winds ceased. The moment the storm cleared, Loulie rushed toward Qadir and threw her arms around his neck. For a few moments, Rijah simply stood, watching them. Then they stepped forward and, midstride, transformed from a shadow into a woman with sharp, angular features and a crown of braids atop their head. When Mazen approached, they stomped toward him.

"Human." Their turquoise eyes sparkled. "I'm going to rip out your throat." Mazen found himself stupidly holding the lamp up

like a shield. "You think I, the mightiest of jinn, will abide your abuse? You think I—"

"Rijah." The ifrit stopped at the sound of Qadir's voice. "He is a friend, not an enemy."

Rijah glared at Mazen with a vehemence so intense Mazen half feared they would set him on fire. Instead, they turned and said, "Who, then? Introduce me so that I may kill them."

"There," Qadir said. He raised an arm and pointed at Omar, who was fighting Aisha and her reanimated corpse. Then he pointed to a human-shaped smudge approaching from the east. "And there..." Mazen followed his gaze to the west, to another shadow. There were figures approaching from all directions.

Mazen failed to comprehend where they were coming from—the strange room was so massive he could perceive no walls nor doorways.

"Reinforcements?" Loulie's face was pale.

From here, all Mazen could make out was their black attire and the glint of hidden weapons. If what Omar had said was true, then it was possible they were jinn. Or thieves. Or both. "They can't just be my brother's thieves," Mazen murmured. "There's too many of them."

Loulie grimaced. "But *how*? Has your brother been hiding this force all along? How did they get here?"

When she looked at him expectantly, Mazen just shook his head helplessly. The sultan had said there were multiple paths beneath the Sandsea, but Mazen did not know which Omar had used. His brother's business had always been a secret; Mazen had no idea where to even begin unraveling his plans.

The jinn of the lamp strode past him, cracking their knuckles. "It does not matter if there is one or one thousand. I will burn them all to the ground." They cast a look over their shoulder. Mazen shrank back at the violence in their eyes. "You may be able to command me, idiot human, but if you get in my way, I will murder you."

Mazen blinked. He stared down at the lamp. An ifrit—his to command? It was a dizzying thought. One that had not quite sunk in.

The merchant reached out and stole her dagger back, startling him from his reverie. She looked at her bodyguard. "Qadir, fire?"

The blade obediently burst into flame, but Qadir looked wary. "What are you doing?"

Loulie scoffed. "Killing a sultan killer." The words brought Mazen back to the present. He breathed in as Loulie rushed past him, Qadir limping after her. Rijah rushed to offer a hand, turning their back on Mazen and making it clear they would not wait for orders.

"How can I help?" he heard Rijah say.

"I do not deserve your help," came Qadir's weak response.

Loulie sighed. "But we *could* use it. If you're the mightiest of jinn, prove it."

She and the ifrit kept throwing heated words at each other until Qadir made them concede to watch each other's backs. And then they headed into the battle, leaving him behind.

Mazen wanted to follow after them, but his body refused his commands. "I..." He felt eyes on him and looked up to see Omar. Omar, who had escaped his battle with Aisha by leaving her to deal with his reinforcements. Omar, who stared at him blankly from a distance, fingers brushing his ear.

Again, Mazen saw that strange, muted glow coming from Omar's earring.

And then the world seemed to shudder. And break. The pale sand faded, the thieves disappeared, and everything fell into a darkness so complete Mazen had the distinct feeling he'd been plucked from the world like a thread torn from a tapestry. When his mind finally caught up to reality, he was no longer standing in darkness.

Mazen was in his mother's chambers. At first, he was confused. *Why am I here?* But then he remembered: he was delivering a message from his father. "Uma?"

His mother lay on her bed, unmoving. He called her again, softly. When she did not answer, he drew close enough to peer at her face. Her eyes were open.

He drew back, heart beating in his throat. That was when the dread began to set in, when he realized her eyes were unseeing. He saw the blood staining her skin and the knife protruding from her chest, where a crimson stain was spreading.

He stumbled away from the bed, the body. He realized he was screaming. He heard footsteps, cries from the soldiers outside, but their voices were distant, unimportant. Mazen fell against the doorway, heaving, eyesight blurring, and—

He entered his mother's chambers.

Again? He blinked.

His mother lay on her bed, unmoving. He hesitated. "Uma?" He took one step into the room before freezing, caught off guard when someone stepped past him. Omar.

"Omar!" he hissed. "Can you not see she is sleeping?"

But Omar was not listening. He paused in front of the bed, a vacant expression on his face. And then: a flicker of motion. A glimmer of silver up his sleeve. Mazen's mother shifted, eyes twitching beneath the weight of sleep. Mazen reached out toward her. *No.* Omar's knife came down. *No!*

Her eyes shot open with her pained gasp. A shudder racked her body as she looked at Omar. Her lips moved, forming soundless words. Omar leaned close enough for his lips to brush her ear and said, "The sultan stole my mother from me. Now I shall steal *you* from him."

He stepped away and tore at the blankets, replicating a struggle. He sparked a match and singed the curtains, creating evidence of a nonexistent jinn fire. Then he escaped out the window without looking back. The sultan had claimed Mazen's mother was killed by a jinn.

He had died without knowing the truth.

The vision shifted so that Mazen was in front of his father's bed. His father, pale and sickly, looked at him with wide, glassy eyes. Mazen had seen his father angry before, heartbroken, even. But never fearful.

"You warned me never to trust anyone, yuba," he said. The words were Omar's, but the voice—he was horrified to realize he was in his own body, and that there was a black knife in his hands. "You ought to have heeded your own advice." He cut a ribbon of blood into the sultan's neck with his knife. *No! Yuba. This isn't me. This isn't me!* He wanted to reach out and shake him. *Yuba, please. Please wake—*

"Up!"

The vision shuddered.

"Get *up*, Prince." Mazen felt a hand on his cheek. And then—a slap. The world slanted. One moment he was in his father's chambers; the next, he was collapsed on his knees in the sand, breathing hard and clutching the lamp. Someone tilted his face up.

Even though the world was hazy, he could make out every scar on Aisha bint Louas's arms. Her black eyes were opaque as coal, and the collar at her neck was so bright it was nearly blinding. Mazen squinted, blinked. There were tears in his eyes.

"My father—"

"Dead. But you are still alive. Unless you plan on succumbing to ifrit magic?"

Mazen could still feel that magic pressing on his mind, digging into his senses. Every time he blinked, the memories threatened to pull him under. Perhaps a nightmare was better than this. In a nightmare, he could lose himself in self-loathing. He could...run.

The word sharpened his mind. *We all start as cowards*, Aisha had once told him. *The only difference between a hero and a coward is that one forgets their fear and fights, while the other succumbs to it and flees.*

He slapped himself. The world came into horrifying clarity. He saw fire and smoke, swords and blood. The mysterious reinforcements were here in full force.

"The most powerful illusions are crafted from memories." Aisha stood. Mazen saw that she had two swords now. No doubt she had pilfered the second from a corpse. There looked to be many now. While Mazen had been trapped in the past, the world had gone to hell.

"Is this whole place a mirage, then?" His throat was dry. "We were in a souk before, and then a palace, and now...?"

"Aliyah can paint the world in shades of memory, including her own. I assume she threaded these illusions together to confuse you."

Mazen thought of Qadir's forlorn smile in the souk. His sudden anger on the golden bridge. Perhaps Aliyah meant to ensnare as much as confuse them.

"And the lamp? Why was it in a room that looked like a treasury?"

Aisha sighed. "Perhaps it was coincidence it ended up in that particular illusion. Perhaps Aliyah's magic reacted to Rijah's. How would I know? Our magics are similar, but not the same." She shook her head. "Aliyah is strong—some of her illusions are so real, one can touch and taste them. But they are just that: elaborate, mind-altering illusions."

She began to walk away, back to the fighting, when Mazen called after her. "You betrayed my brother. Why?"

"Because I am not a *tool*," Aisha snapped. She rushed off without another word. Mazen eyed the battle from a distance. He saw a creature of fire darting in and out of the battle—Rijah—and what might have been the merchant weaving through the smoke. It was pure chaos. Mazen knew he would be easily defeated. The moment they saw him...

He eyed his shadow on the ground, forgotten in all this chaos.

Then I just won't let them see me.

He stuffed the lamp into his satchel, threw his shadow over his head, and went searching for his brother.

69

LOULIE

At first, she and Qadir fought back-to-back. But it soon became apparent that though Tawil had been easy to dispatch, the rest of the thieves were not so easily defeated. They had fire in their eyes and magic in their blood. Loulie was out of her element, and she was out of ideas.

And worse, Qadir was almost out of energy. Though his wounds had healed, there were bruises where the arrows had punctured his skin, and ash beaded his skin.

She had to find Omar. She had to kill him. She turned to tell Qadir her plan and faltered when she saw he wasn't there. He was at the bottom of the dune, pushing two thieves back with torrents of wind—a magic affinity she had never seen before today. One of the jinn managed to plant his feet against the gust. The sand rippled oddly beneath his feet. Then, with a gesture, he caused the sand to rear up in a wave beneath Qadir's feet.

Qadir fell back, the wind died, and the jinn sprinted forward with his blade. Qadir sidestepped, stumbled. And then he did a shocking thing. Perhaps it was because he had lost his concentration. Perhaps it was a desperate reflex. In one swift motion, he slid the shamshir out of its scabbard and stabbed it through his attacker's chest. There was a moment of stillness. And then Qadir pulled the weapon from the jinn's body. Shock briefly rippled across his features, then hardened into resolve.

The jinn growled—not in pain so much as annoyance—as he dissipated into smoke and re-formed feet away. Loulie was running toward the solidifying jinn with her knife when Qadir held out a hand. *"Stop."* The authority in his voice made her freeze.

The ground groaned and shuddered. She nearly lost her footing as Qadir burned sand inches from her feet. The landscape collapsed, opening up into a massive hole. The second jinn shapeshifted into a bird and flew away before he fell. The one that had faced Qadir with a sword and ground-shifting magic was not so lucky; his scream faded as he tumbled into darkness.

"Qadir!" She sent him a severe look across the hole. *Don't die.*

His brow furrowed. *You too.* He turned to the next battle, shamshir in hand.

Loulie returned her attention to the fighting hordes. Most of the jinn were battling each other—Aisha bint Louas was reanimating every corpse and forcing it to face its once comrades. Loulie could see Rijah as well, tearing and smashing their way through bodies as if they were walls to be destroyed. She used that chaos to her advantage, skirting the edges of the battle and ducking beneath blades in her search for Omar.

She'd just spotted him fighting a corpse when she crashed into someone. She stepped back, flaming knife raised, and saw—nothing.

But then the air in front of her shimmered and *parted*, and Loulie inexplicably saw golden eyes peering at her through some tear in the world.

"Mazen?" She stared at him.

He opened his mouth to respond, but the words pitched into a scream. "Behind you!" She turned to see a bloodied thief holding a sword inches from her face. He was too close to parry. Too close to block. She squeezed her eyes shut.

And eased them open when the strike did not come. She saw the thief on the ground, struggling against an invisible force.

Mazen. He was invisible, but she could hear him praying beneath his breath.

She lunged toward the fallen thief with her dagger. Its fire was useless against the jinn, but the blade still cut. Right into the jinn's chest. The jinn retaliated by lashing out at her with his knife. Loulie caught the strike in her arm. Pain blossomed beneath her skin.

Then, abruptly, she and the jinn were both whisked off the ground. A heartbeat later, she collapsed back to the dirt, Qadir's knife beside her. She looked up and saw the thief. And she saw the gigantic bird clutching him in its talons. "*AFWAN*," Rijah said in a loud, booming voice that dripped with disdain. Loulie looked away as they tore the jinn to shreds.

"Shukran," Mazen called up weakly as the Shapeshifter flew away. The prince turned and approached her, half his face unveiled. It was an eerie sight.

She spoke before pride clogged her throat. "Shukran." *For saving me.*

Mazen blinked, nodded. "My brother—you promised me revenge."

She hesitated. It was strange to see her own vengeance reflected back at her in the eyes of a softhearted storyteller. *Violence does not suit him*, she thought, but she shoved the thought away. It did not suit anyone.

"Stay behind me." She made her way back into the fight. When she glanced over her shoulder, the prince had disappeared, but he was close enough she could hear his breathing.

Omar was everywhere and nowhere. Sometimes he grinned at her mockingly from a distance. Other times he was in the thick of battle, disappearing moments before his opponents struck him. An illusion, Loulie realized.

She cast a look over her shoulder at the crumbling landscape. Qadir stood in the center of the chaos, tendrils of smoke unrolling from his body as he faced his opponents with his blade. Though he was still burning holes into the sand, the reinforcements were never-ending, and it was clear his strength was waning. Who *were* these jinn the prince was working with? How had he found them in the first place?

"You look lost, al-Nazari." Loulie whirled to see Omar standing behind her, a patronizing grin on his lips. "Why not use that compass of yours to find me?" He chuckled at the surprise on her face. "Oh yes, Aisha told me all about your magic."

Loulie flinched. In all this chaos, she had forgotten about the compass. That she'd left it with Mazen. She nearly cast a look over her shoulder but stopped herself. If Omar was suggesting it, it had to be a trap.

"No? Then try your luck." The prince raised his hands.

Loulie ran toward him, brandishing the flaming dagger. Just as it had before, Qadir's blade went right through him. Omar chuckled as she pitched forward. She fell, and when she looked up, there were three of him standing around her in a circle, each with his black knife angled at her.

"Goodbye, merchant," they said in a voice that echoed three times over. Loulie fell to her knees just fast enough to avoid the arc of their blades. Her eyes slid to the sandy ground.

To the single reflection of Omar looming above her.

The epiphany hit like lightning as Mazen, invisible but yelling, ran forward and shoved into the illusions. All three were shocked.

Loulie felt an invisible hand on her shoulder.

"Akhi!" Omar's eyes were bright, his smile stretched so wide it was almost manic. All three princes wore the same expression. "Aisha told me you had stolen the shadow jinn's relic. What a perfect magic for you!"

Loulie's mind whirred. The reflection—the reflection was the key. The ifrit's relic could conjure Omar's likeness, but it could not replicate a reflection. Her eyes darted between the phantoms and the reflection, until she saw the real Omar: the one approaching from their left. He would put up a fight, but Loulie could best him. She could...

No. She dug her fingers into the sand. How many times had she leapt into danger to prove that she was invincible, only to have to be rescued?

It is not weakness to rely on others for help, Qadir had said.

"The reflection," she murmured. "The real one has a reflection." She shuddered. And then she spoke words she had never spoken before: "Help me."

The prince squeezed her shoulder, and then his hand was gone.

"I know why you killed the sultan." Mazen's disembodied voice came from somewhere to her right. One of the princes, not the real one, turned to face him. The others continued to stare pointedly at her, eyes narrowed. As if they were suspicious of her.

"I knew you would see in time," said the Omar that had turned to him.

"He killed your mother?" Mazen was circling the area. Another illusion shifted, searching for him.

"He did," Omar said lightly. "He told everyone she died in childbirth, but the truth is that he saw her bleeding silver and murdered her." He laughed. "Do you know why the sultan killed so many of his wives, Mazen? It is because, after his second wife's betrayal, he was convinced my mother was *possessing* them out of vengeance."

Somewhere nearby, Mazen inhaled sharply. "How would you know?"

One of the princes scoffed. "Because he told me. You know how the sultan liked to boast about his kills. He told me she was a monster and that if I wanted to prove we were not the same, I had to kill for him."

"And did he tell you to kill my mother?"

All three princes smiled. Loulie's panic faded to shock.

"Did you show me that memory out of spite, Omar? To break me?"

One of the princes chuckled. "Nothing so convoluted as that. I just enjoy seeing you angry."

Another illusion lunged forward but struck air. Mazen's voice came from somewhere nearby: "Maybe our father was a monster, but you're a monster too." The second Omar struck. This time Loulie heard a yelp, scrambled footsteps. "You told everyone you were going to save Madinne from jinn, but you *led* them to the city, didn't you? The shadow jinn—you provoked her. You *brought* her to our home. All so you could convince the sultan to put your thieves into his army. All so you could trick him."

The shadow jinn had warned Loulie of killers in black. Now she realized the jinn had not been referring to the thieves that had murdered her tribe, but to Omar's own forty thieves.

The prince inhaled sharply. "And Hakim, he never did anything to you. And yet you—"

The third Omar hissed. "That *bastard* escaped. Ahmed bin Walid doomed himself when he stepped in to protect him. He died for your pathetic, inconsequential brother."

Loulie dug her hands into the sand. Tears burned behind her eyes, but she would not cry. The wali of Dhyme had always been loyal to the crown. All Loulie could do was hope he had found some peace in sacrificing himself for one of the princes.

And she—she would make his sacrifice worth it. Somehow.

Loulie couldn't see Mazen, but she could hear the shaky relief in his voice when he responded, "Ahmed bin Walid was a loyal man. But you... Father would never endanger Madinne. You're worse than he was."

"Sometimes," Omar said quietly, "you must burn and remake a city to save it." He moved then, and his shadows moved with him, all of them stabbing the same space.

Mazen screamed.

Loulie rushed forward. She threw herself on the real prince.

Omar had just enough time to look startled before she dug the knife into his throat—or tried to. The prince shoved her off, and the knife went into his shoulder instead. But it was enough to unbalance him. Enough of an opening for Mazen to grab him from behind as the shadow fell from his shoulders.

"I don't care how many injustices you've suffered." He looped his arms around Omar's throat. "You stole everything from me!" He pulled.

Loulie pounced again on Omar. She'd just barely managed to pull the knife from his shoulder when he kicked her, hard, in the stomach. She gasped as pain flared through her body. The shock of it drove the air from her lungs, and she crumpled to her knees. There were tears in her eyes when she looked up and watched Omar throw Mazen off him with a roar of rage. Mazen clung to his legs and pulled him to the ground.

The illusions had disappeared, but there were other, physical reinforcements approaching. Loulie put them out of her mind as she crawled toward Omar.

Mazen was still clinging to him, trying to grasp Omar's ear. "You stole my mother. But you still have yours, don't you? In this damned relic!"

Loulie saw the glint of silver in Omar's ear. His crescent earring. *The ifrit's relic.* The godsdamned magic behind all these illusions.

Loulie braced herself. She gritted her teeth against the pain and sprang at the prince. Reached for his ear. Omar elbowed her in the gut. Loulie hissed and hung on until, until, until—

She tore the earring out of his ear.

Omar screamed.

Loulie staggered away, the bloody earring clenched in her fist. One of the reinforcements grabbed her from behind.

Blood trickled down the side of the prince's face as he approached. "I'm going to kill you." His voice was soft, calm. Behind him, Mazen was on his knees, hand pressed to an injury on his arm. He looked at Loulie in silent desperation.

But Loulie couldn't make the relic work. It was cold and dead in her hands. Despair washed over her as their enemies closed in. A few reinforcements were heading toward Mazen with drawn bows, while another group approached Omar.

Omar stepped closer. He was ten feet away. Eight. Seven. And then he suddenly stopped. His eyes grew wide with confusion. He looked down and saw that he was sinking.

Understanding dawned moments before her captor's grip disappeared. Loulie shrank away as they collapsed beside her, their back so shredded she could see their spine. Above her loomed Rijah, transformed into a majestic bird with quills twelve paces long.

A legendary rukh.

And yet here it was, lowering itself to the ground beside her. She startled as Rijah extended a wing speckled with silver blood. She was even more surprised when Qadir slid down that wing. Before she could say anything, he grabbed her hands in his alarmingly transparent ones. "I have an idea," he said in a parchment-thin voice that made her heart sink. "Do you trust me?"

Omar's laughter sounded behind them. "Whatever plan you speak of, it will fail!" Loulie turned to see reinforcements helping him out of the sinking sand.

Qadir cut a glance at Rijah. On some silent cue, the bloodied bird rose into the air and flew toward Mazen. The archers beside the prince snapped into action, loosing their arrows as the ifrit soared overhead. Rijah swept the projectiles away with a beat of their wing, but the archers were relentless. They pummeled the great bird with arrows, providing cover for Omar and making it difficult for Rijah to land.

"Don't you understand?" Omar's voice was soft, mocking. "There is no escape. You are an enemy of the people now, merchant. If I do not find you, someone else will." He grinned, eyes flashing. "You are doomed."

The future—it was the concern Loulie had refused to consider. She no longer had the luxury of ignorance. Not with so many enemies pressing in, with Qadir reduced to smoke.

"Loulie." Qadir pressed a palm to her cheek. "Do you trust me?"

"He's right." She could no longer hide the quaver in her voice. "There is no future for us."

Qadir blinked his ruby-red eyes at her. "There is no future *here*."

Loulie stared at him, not understanding.

"If you cannot hide in this world, then hide in another."

His words washed over her in a great, icy wave. Suddenly, she couldn't breathe.

"No," she said softly. "The jinn world—"

"An escape."

She stared at him. "This was your plan all along."

Qadir gripped her hands. "Trust me."

It was the reason he'd been so calm. Because he'd been concocting a backup plan. And he had not told her.

"I'll find you again. But I need to make sure no one gives chase. I need to keep you safe."

"I told you I would kick your ass if you kept something from me again."

"You need to be alive to do that." He glanced over her shoulder. Omar was recovering his balance on solid land. His reinforcements stood around him, weapons drawn, awaiting orders. Somewhere in the distance, fires raged. Aisha bint Louas was a blur of color, hiding behind an undead army. "Please," Qadir said, voice breaking.

The harried rukh landed beside them again, Mazen on its back. It shuddered with exhaustion as it lowered a wing.

"I trust you," Loulie said softly. "Promise not to die."

Qadir leaned forward and pressed his forehead to hers. One last time, she felt his warmth envelop her. "I promise," he murmured. And then he drew away. "Take care of them, Rijah. And...I'm sorry."

The great bird bowed its head. *"IT SHALL BE DONE."* Their bright eyes glinted with impatience as Loulie stepped onto their wing and settled on their back. She fixed her eyes on Omar as the bird rose into the air. Held the earring up for him to see, then tucked it into her pocket. She wasn't running. She was simply retreating to live another day.

"Wait." Mazen shifted. Loulie followed his gaze and saw Aisha bint Louas standing a short distance away from her undead army, looking at them. "We can't just *leave* her here," he whispered. "We have to save her."

Aisha bint Louas stared at them a moment longer.

Then she turned and walked back toward her army.

Loulie blinked. "I don't think she *wants* to be saved."

Arrows cut through the air before the prince could protest again. Rijah swerved to avoid them, and she and Mazen both barely managed to stay on their back.

"*HOLD ON,*" the gigantic bird screeched.

Loulie had just enough time to grasp the rukh's quills before it plummeted down one of the holes. The last thing she saw before the world disappeared was Qadir, facing the gathering army with his blade. And then there was darkness, and a terrible heat was chasing them down the void. Mazen clasped his hands over hers. Loulie gripped them back.

They fell and fell, the sand following them down, blocking the light and their way back. They fell for a long time. So long Loulie feared there was no end. But then—sand. Blessed, blessed sand. Ground beneath their feet. An end.

Or, perhaps, a beginning.

70

LOULIE

At the bottom of the hole lay a cave so cold it immediately leeched the heat from Loulie's body. She was shuddering as she slid off the rukh, the tears that had been running down her cheeks freezing as soon as she fell to the ground. Mazen followed, his face smeared with blood.

He stared past Loulie at the hole, gaze blank.

"ARE YOU STUPID?" the great bird bellowed. *"MOVE."*

On cue, there came a low groaning sound, and then the sand that had been chasing them down the hole rushed toward them in a torrent. Rijah swept them out of the way with a flap of their wing. Loulie fell against the cave wall and watched as the sand piled, the mound growing higher and higher until it was a column that went to and through the ceiling.

The bird loosed a sigh. *"HUMAN FOOLS."* They began to shrink, their quills softening into skin, their body collapsing until it was human shaped. All of this happened in moments. Loulie was amazed when the ifrit cracked their now very human neck and groaned. They had shifted into the form of a man with high cheekbones, fierce eyebrows, and long brown hair. The injuries hidden beneath their feathers were now gory badges somewhat concealed by plain garments. Rijah saw her looking at the wounds and scowled.

"What? You look like shit too," they said.

"I didn't say anything," she snapped back. But the fight had left her body. When she thought about Qadir fighting a horde of jinn...

"Are you coming, humans?" Rijah had walked on ahead and paused only to glance back at them. A blue flame slithered between their fingers like a snake. The jinn raised a brow. "I was commanded by my king to watch over you, but I do not intend to baby you."

Loulie was preparing another retort when the weight of Rijah's words sank in. "What do you mean, *king*?" The word was a whisper on her lips. "You're all jinn kings. You're all ifrit."

Rijah looked at her like she was stupid. "What, did he not tell you?"

Secrets, secrets. So many secrets. She had thought Qadir had revealed everything to her when he confessed that he was an ifrit. But now she remembered the tale he'd told about the seven jinn kings. He had fooled her into thinking there were seven ifrit, with an eighth king to rule them. But the human story had always been about *seven* jinn.

Loulie did not realize her knees were wobbling until Mazen came to stand beside her. He set a hand on her shoulder to balance her. "He called himself the Inferno," he said.

"A fitting name for a king whose magic is as old as the flame of creation, no?"

Stupid. She bit back a self-mocking laugh. *Of course he would never say anything.*

Qadir had told her before that he ran from his problems. That he had been fearful of her reaction to his confession of being an ifrit. This—what was this but an added layer? Another secret. She was already numb to them.

Loulie stared blankly after Rijah. Slowly, Mazen grabbed her hand. "Come on," he said gently. "Let's go see where we are." Despite his bloodied face, he looked, well, not broken. Though the light in his eyes was faded, there was a glimmer of curiosity in them.

He had changed, she thought. But then, maybe she had too.

She allowed him to lead her through the cold cave after Rijah.

After Mazen had given his condolences to the ifrit for what was at least a hundred-year-old grudge, he said, "My name is Mazen, by the way. I'm of royal blood but no longer have any claim to the throne."

Rijah turned, tilted their head. "Your brother ousted you?"

"Yes," Mazen said. "I'm pretty sure he was going to use you to . . ." He faltered, glanced at Loulie. She looked away with a sigh. Why was he looking at *her*?

"To destroy the jinn? The world?" Loulie couldn't see Rijah's scowl, but she could hear it in their words. "What else would a power-hungry fool want but destruction?"

That was the question none of them could answer. Omar bin Malik was working with jinn to steal ifrit magic. But *why*? And to what end?

Memories flooded her mind: Dahlia, laughing with her in the tavern as she smoked her shisha pipe. Ahmed bin Walid, smiling as he twirled her across the diwan. Qadir, pressing his forehead to hers. *Trust me.*

How many more people would she lose before the gods were satisfied?

Mazen seemed just as uncertain. "I wonder if Aisha knows." His expression fell. "I hope she's okay."

"Even though she betrayed you?"

Mazen nodded. He said nothing after that, only squeezed her hand as they neared the entrance. Loulie felt the change before she saw it. The air grew warmer, and a soft wind began to push at her robes. Then: sunlight.

Rijah paused at the cave entrance. Loulie and Mazen froze beside them.

"Gods," Mazen whispered in awe.

Where the sky would normally be, there was an ocean. Schools of fish swam through the water like colorful clouds, and water crashed down in the form of waterfalls. Gigantic birds patrolled the air while down below, gorgeous cities of gleaming silver and gold dotted the vibrant landscape.

"Welcome," Rijah said, "to the world of jinn."

Loulie clutched the dagger. *I'm here, Qadir*, she thought. *And I'm waiting for you.*

ACKNOWLEDGMENTS

For five years, *The Stardust Thief* has been a personal sanctuary, a world I carried with me through various upheavals and moves. What a surreal feeling to know that it will now sit on shelves in other places and that it will grow roots beyond me. There are so many people I need to thank for helping me shape this small and humble idea into the book it is now.

First and foremost to Jennifer Azantian, my agent: Thank you for being such a stalwart champion and for helping me strengthen the story's narrative. Your enthusiasm and love for these characters (especially Aisha!) means so much. Thanks as well to Ben Baxter for helping me sharpen the little details.

Working with the Orbit team has been a dream. To my US and UK editors, Brit Hvide and Emily Byron: I am so grateful for your keen editorial insight. Thank you for encouraging me to push the boundaries of this world, and for reassuring me that it was okay to give these characters more time to breathe. Brit, huge thanks for the ghoul and interlude talks and for your sage wisdom about hats— you know the ones!

Thanks to Tim Holman, Anna Jackson, and Alex Lencicki for welcoming this book into the Orbit family; Nadia Saward, Angeline Rodriguez, and Joanna Kramer for your editorial perspective; Ellen Wright, Angela Man, Nazia Khatun, Madeleine Hall, and Casey Davoren for getting the word out there; Rachel Hairston and everyone in sales for finding this story a place on shelves; Lauren Panepinto, Lisa Marie Pompilio, Stephanie Hess, and Alexia Mazis for making it a piece of art; Tim Paul for the beautiful map; and Bryn

A. McDonald, Rachel Goldstein, and Tom Webster for wrapping it up into a fantastic book-shaped package.

To my very first reader, Jasmine Peake: Thank you for cheering me on as I wrestled with that behemoth first draft. I will forever be grateful to you for handling my work with such care and for loving Loulie and Mazen from the get-go. You are the best partner in critique.

Emily Rives, you bring my characters to life on a canvas like no one else. Thank you for those early sketches of Loulie and Mazen, which have inspired so much.

Gates Palissery and Elizabeth Anderson, your critique helped me solidify the foundation of this story so I could build it up stronger. Thank you for being so thoughtful and thorough.

Monica Bee and Morgan Paine, thank you for keeping me afloat through this process with your kind words and incredible feedback. Also, thanks for reminding me about the horses!

Alanna Miles, thank you for welcoming me into your home and celebrating every creative success with me, big and small.

Angeline Morris, thanks for always being there to listen to my brainstorm-rambles and for sending me all those incredible "MAZEN, WHY?" texts as you read.

Arianna Emery, thank you for assuring me multiple times that, yes, I could cut all those words, and yes, the story would be better for it. (It is!)

Sarah Mughal, thank you for being such a wonderful cheerleader. I'm so grateful for our uplifting and enlightening conversations.

George Jreije, thank you for being the best hype man. You are one of the kindest, most supportive people I know, and I'm so glad to share a debut year with you.

Kamilah Cole and Jennifer Elrod: Thanks for the laughs, memes, and joy. I'm so grateful for your enthusiasm.

A huge shout-out to all the amazing beta readers who provided feedback on a full draft: Mallika, Sravani, Ani, Devon, Leta, SJ, Rebecca, Jessica, JJ, Yasmine, Mallory, Kit—thank you for your helpful commentary!

My biggest, most heartfelt gratitude goes to my family. To my sister, Neesa: You were my first and best audience. Thanks for letting me ramble and for laughing at all my character voices. Dad, the heart of this book was inspired by the tales you shared with us, so thank you—for the stories, for the history lessons, and for inspiring me to delve into the oral story tradition. Mom, thank you for surrounding me with library books and for being my biggest and most optimistic advocate. Your belief in my work has always meant the world to me.

To Nama: Some of my earliest memories are of the towers of books you had in your room and the stories you told with that mischievous sparkle in your eye. I wish I could have given you a copy of this book for one of your towers, but I will forever carry the memory of your excitement for its impending release. Thank you for everything.

Lastly, thank *you*, reader. A storyteller breathes life into words, but it's the readers who keep the story alive. Thank you for taking this book on a new adventure.